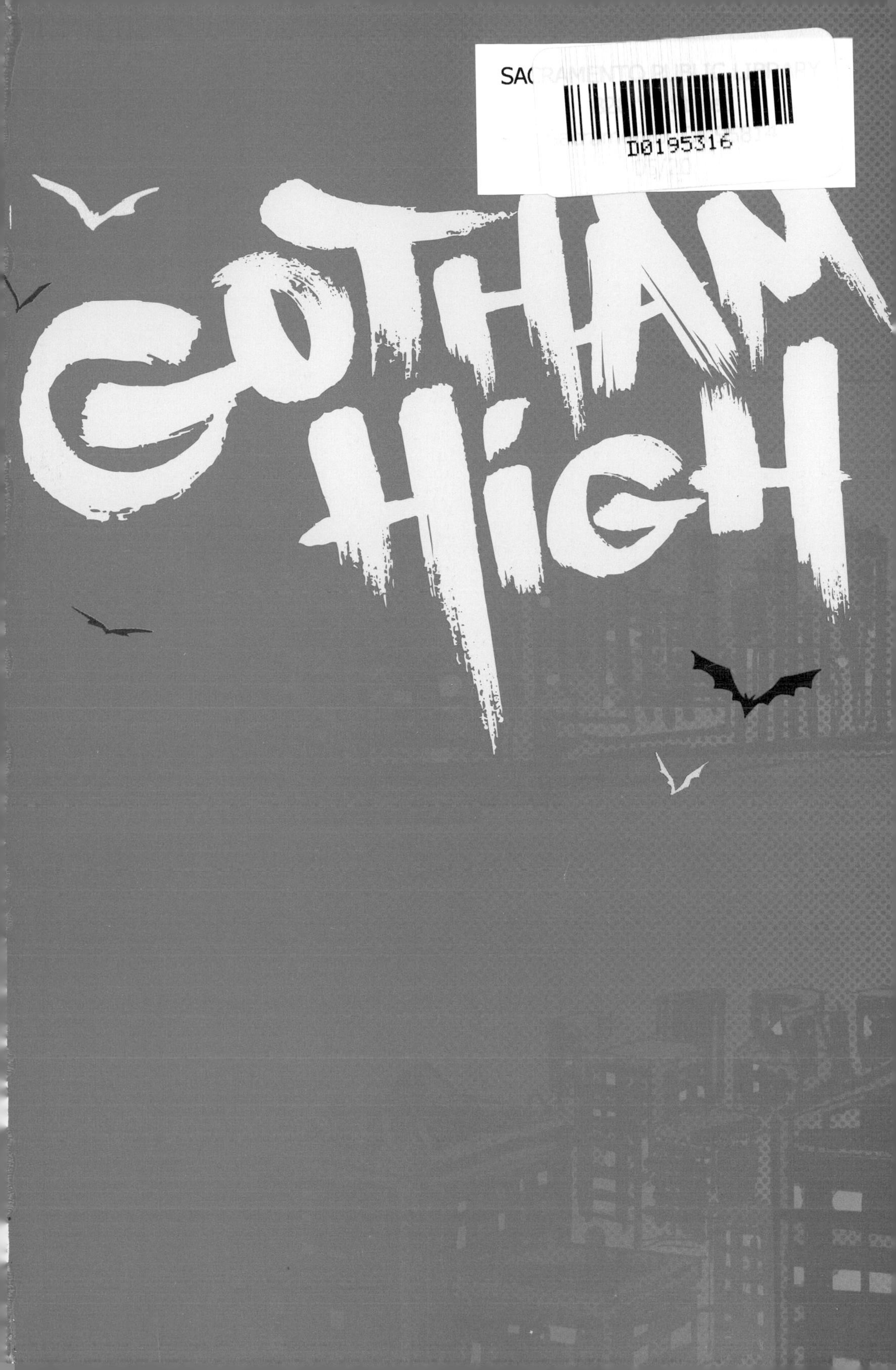
GOTHAM HIGH

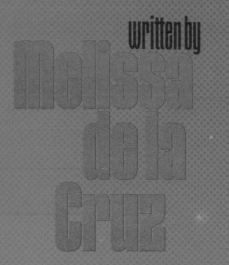

written by
Melissa de la Cruz

illustrated by
Thomas Pitilli

colored by
Miquel Muerto

lettered by
Troy Peteri

BATMAN created by **BOB KANE** with **BILL FINGER**

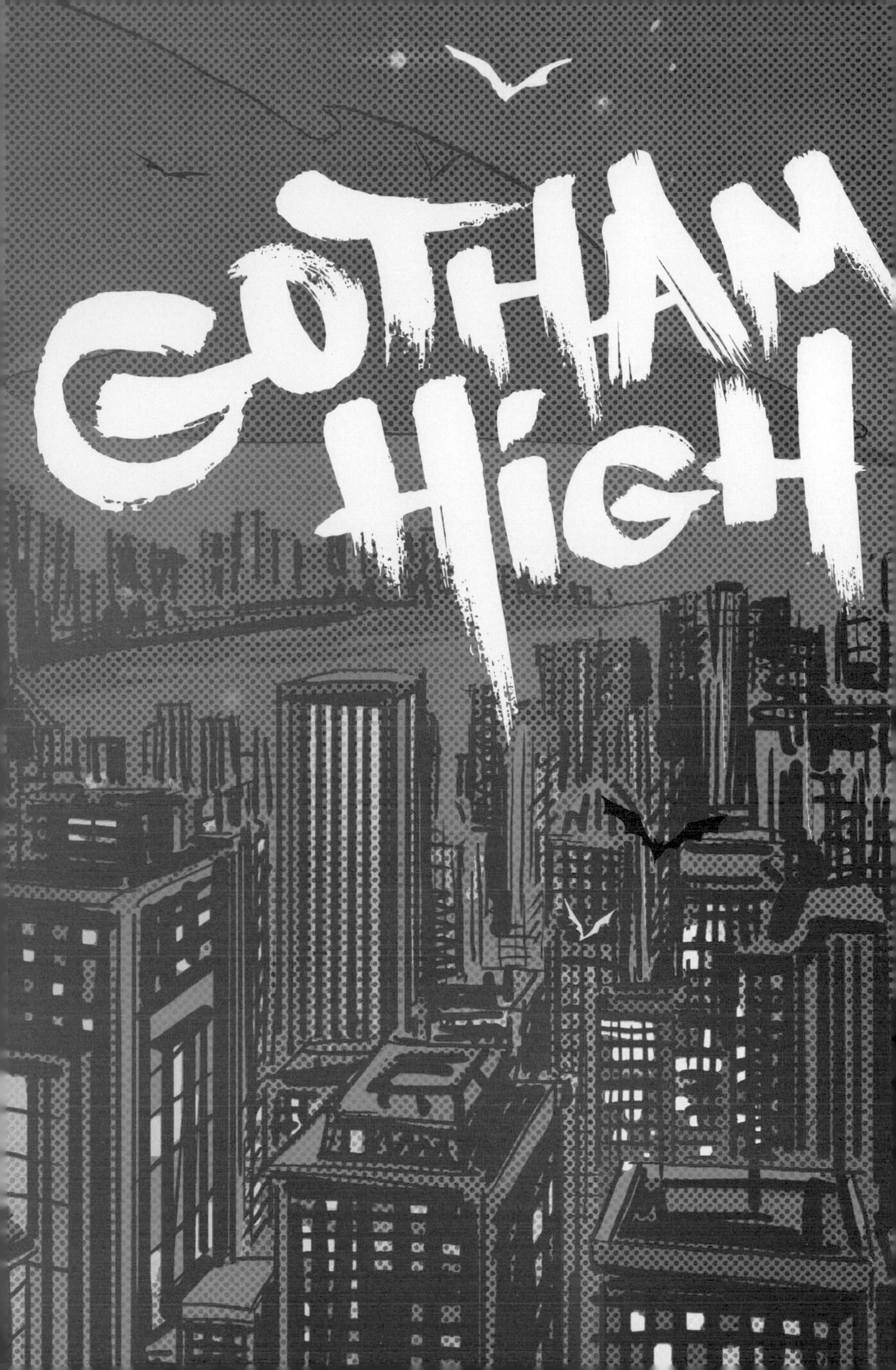
GOTHAM
HIGH

SARA MILLER Editor
LIZ ERICKSON Assistant Editor
STEVE COOK Design Director - Books
AMIE BROCKWAY-METCALF Publication Design

BOB HARRAS Senior VP - Editor-in-Chief, DC Comics
MICHELE R. WELLS VP & Executive Editor, Young Reader

DAN DiDIO Publisher
JIM LEE Publisher & Chief Creative Officer
BOBBIE CHASE VP - New Publishing Initiatives & Talent Development
DON FALLETTI VP - Manufacturing Operations & Workflow Management
LAWRENCE GANEM VP - Talent Services
ALISON GILL Senior VP - Manufacturing & Operations
HANK KANALZ Senior VP - Publishing Strategy & Support Services
DAN MIRON VP - Publishing Operations
NICK J. NAPOLITANO VP - Manufacturing Administration & Design
NANCY SPEARS VP - Sales

GOTHAM HIGH

DC – a WarnerMedia Company.

DC Comics, 2900 West Alameda Ave., Burbank, CA 91505
Printed by LSC Communications, Crawfordsville, IN, USA. 2/28/20.
First Printing.
ISBN: 978-1-4012-8624-8

PEFC Certified
This product is from sustainably managed forests and controlled sources
PEFC/29-31-337
www.pefc.org

Library of Congress Cataloging-in-Publication Data

Names: De la Cruz, Melissa, 1971- author. | Pitilli, Thomas, 1985- artist.
Title: Gotham High / Melissa de la Cruz, author ; Thomas Pitilli, artist.
Description: Burbank, CA : DC Comics, [2020] | Audience: Grades 10-12 | Summary: After being kicked out of his boarding school, 17-year-old Bruce Wayne returns to Gotham City to find that nothing is as he left it, and when a kidnapping rattles the school, Bruce seeks answers as the dark and troubled knight.
Identifiers: LCCN 2019059199 | ISBN 9781401286248 (paperback)
Subjects: LCSH: Batman (Fictitious character)--Juvenile fiction. | Graphic novels. | CYAC: Graphic novels. | Batman (Fictitious character)--Fiction. | High schools--Fiction. | Schools--Fiction. | Kidnapping--Fiction.
Classification: LCC PZ7.7.D436 Go 2020 | DDC 741.5/973--dc23

For Dr. Anthony Wang, my brain
surgeon and a real superhero,
thank you so much.
　　　　　　—Melissa de la Cruz

Dedicated to my parents, for
always supporting my love of
art and comic books and forever
encouraging me to follow my
passion.
　　　　　　—Thomas Pitilli

PART ONE

Remembrance of Things Past

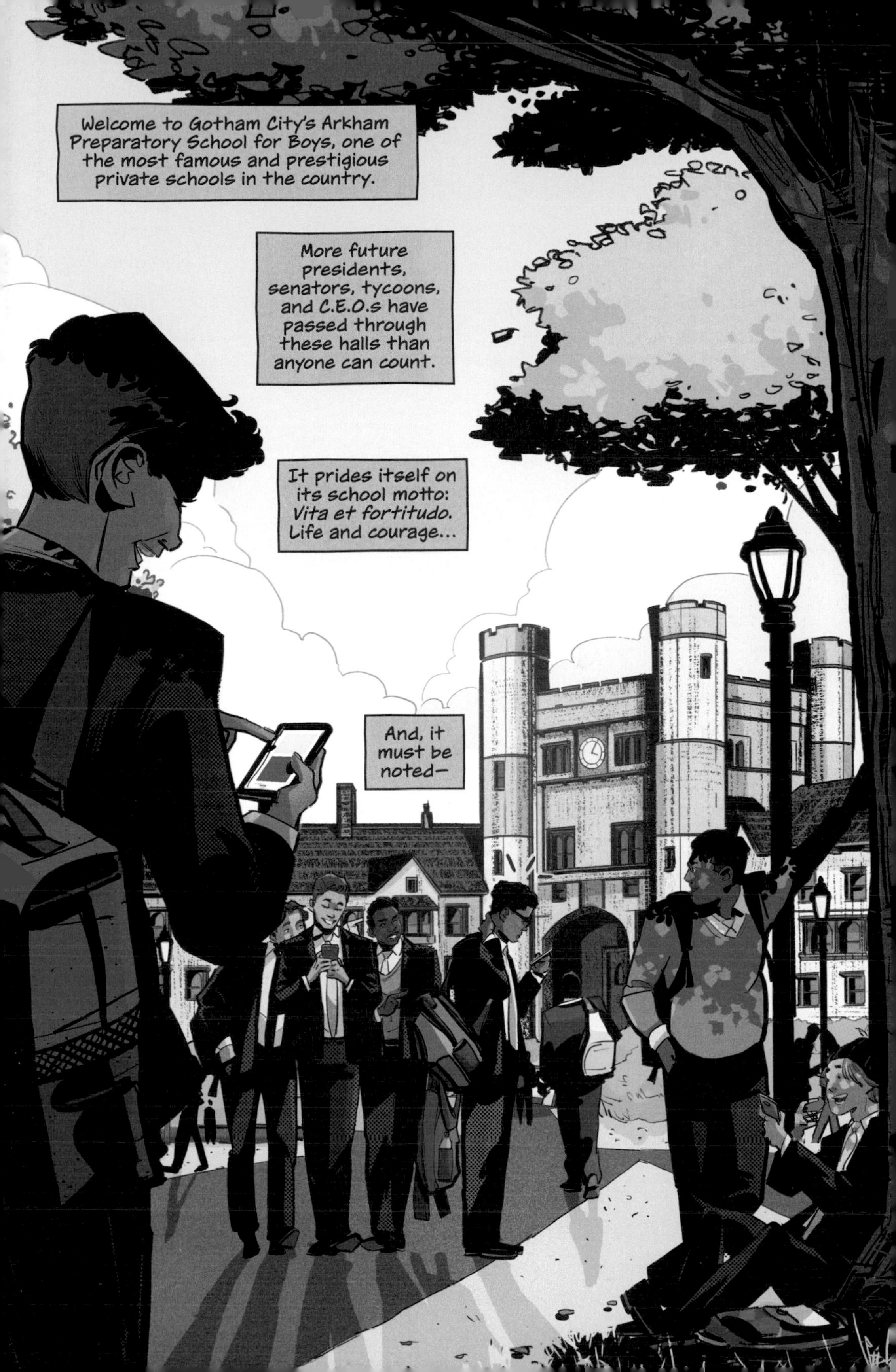

Welcome to Gotham City's Arkham Preparatory School for Boys, one of the most famous and prestigious private schools in the country.
More future presidents, senators, tycoons, and C.E.O.s have passed through these halls than anyone can count.
It prides itself on its school motto: *Vita et fortitudo.* Life and courage...
And, it must be noted—

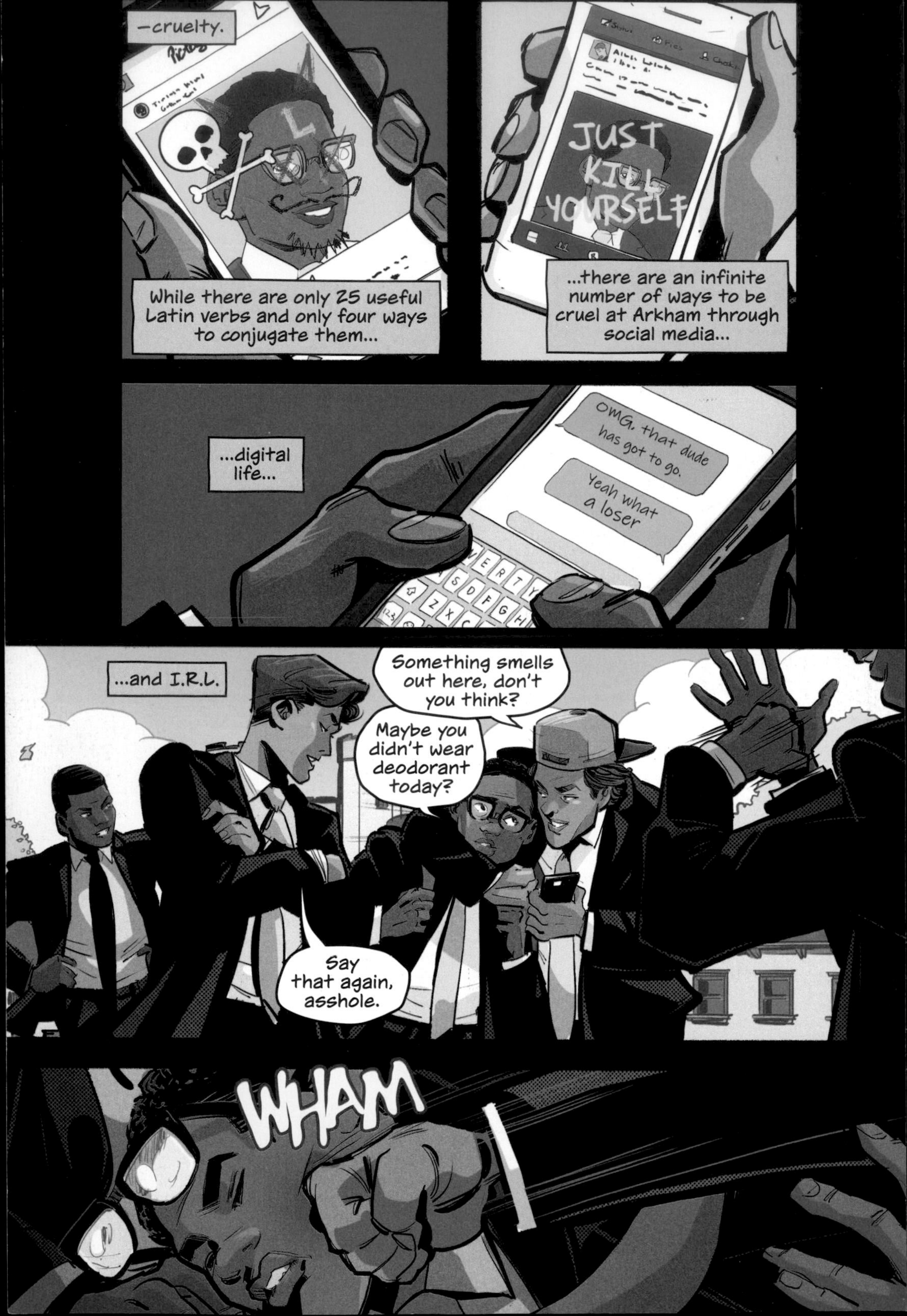
—cruelty.
JUST KILL YOURSELF
While there are only 25 useful Latin verbs and only four ways to conjugate them...
...there are an infinite number of ways to be cruel at Arkham through social media...
...digital life...
OMG, that dude has got to go.
Yeah what a loser
...and I.R.L.
Something smells out here, don't you think?
Maybe you didn't wear deodorant today?
Say that again, asshole.
WHAM

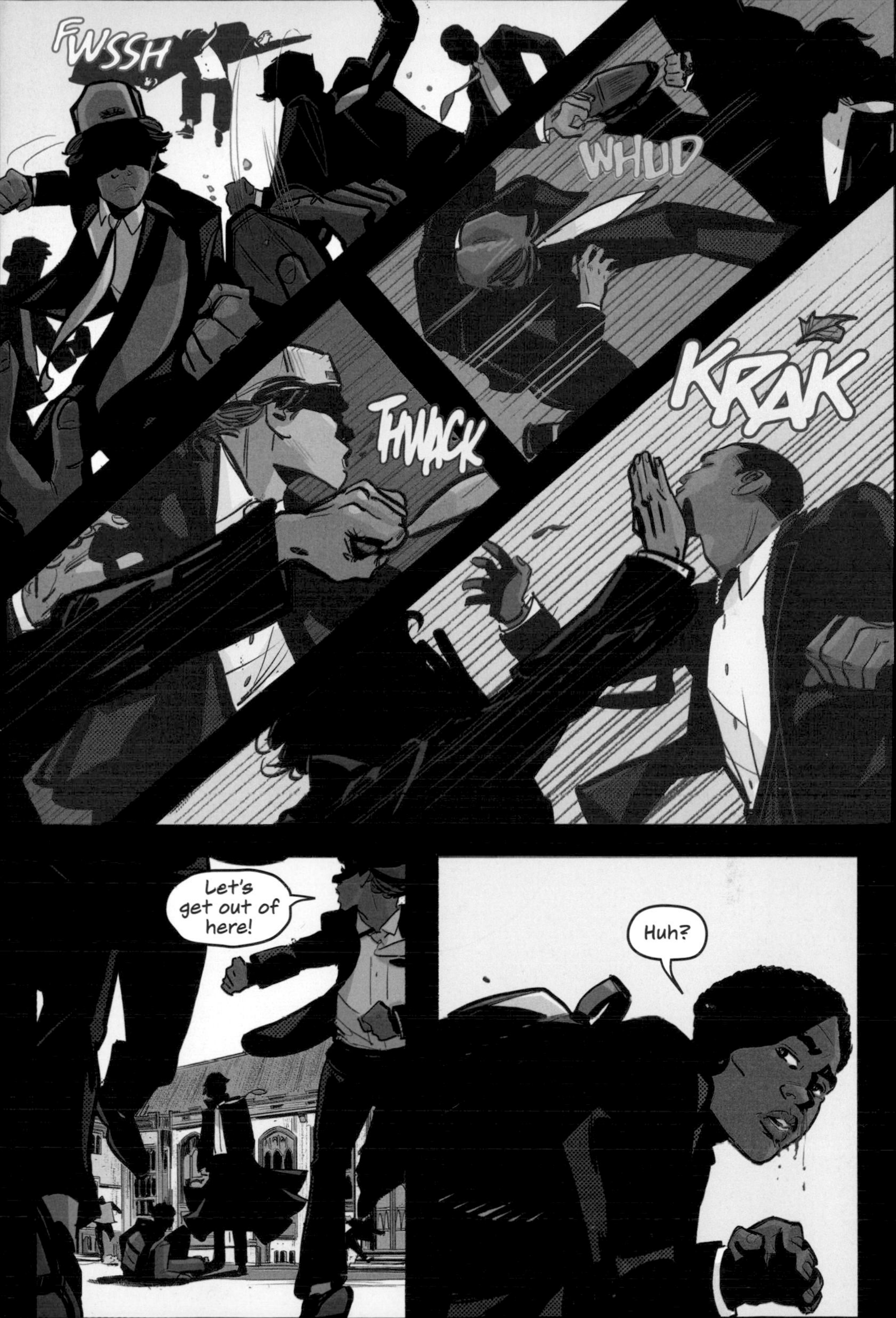
FWSSH
WHUD
THWACK
KRAK
Let's get out of here!
Huh?

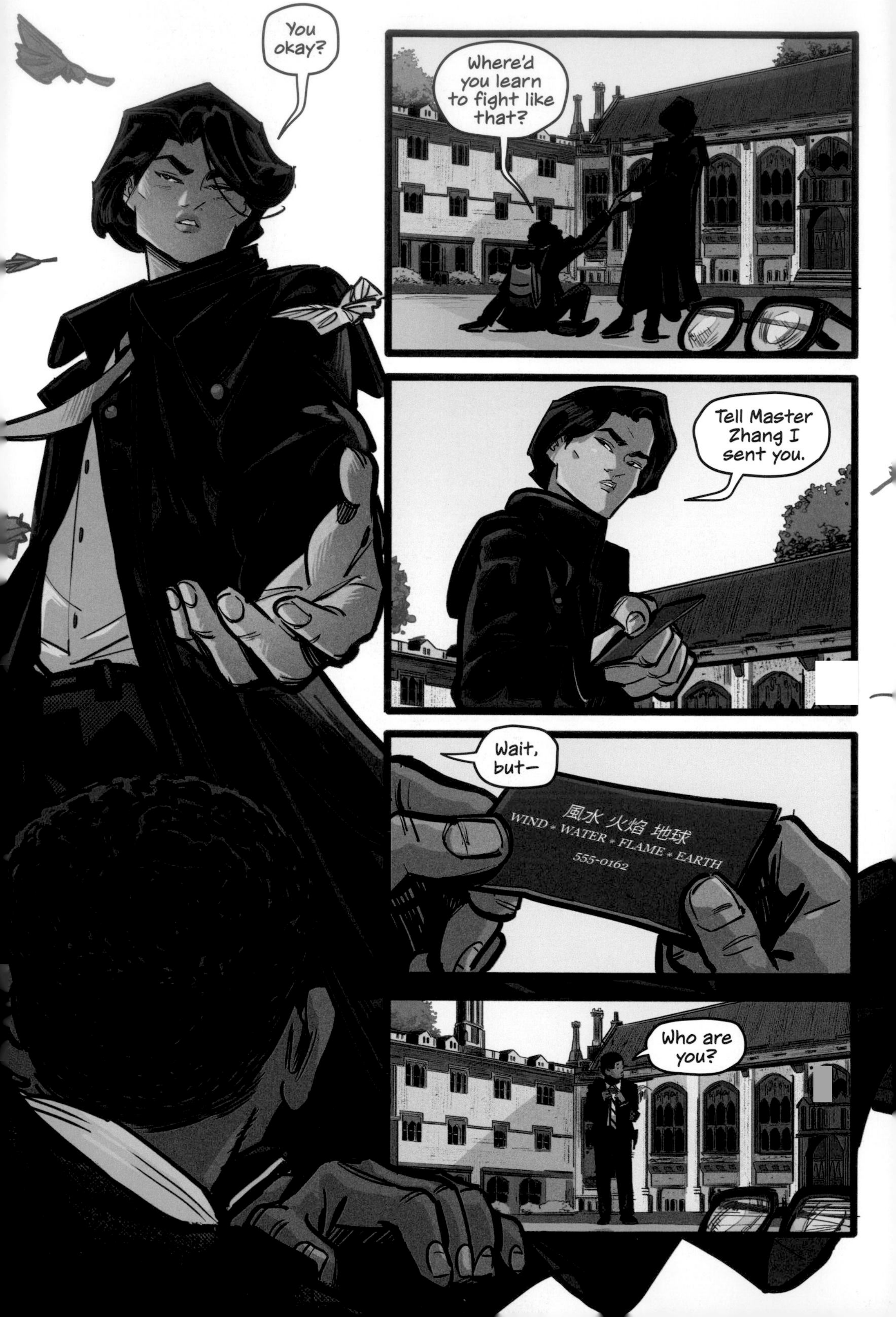
You okay?
Where'd you learn to fight like that?
Tell Master Zhang I sent you.
Wait, but—
風水 火焰 地球
WIND ✻ WATER ✻ FLAME ✻ EARTH
555-0162
Who are you?

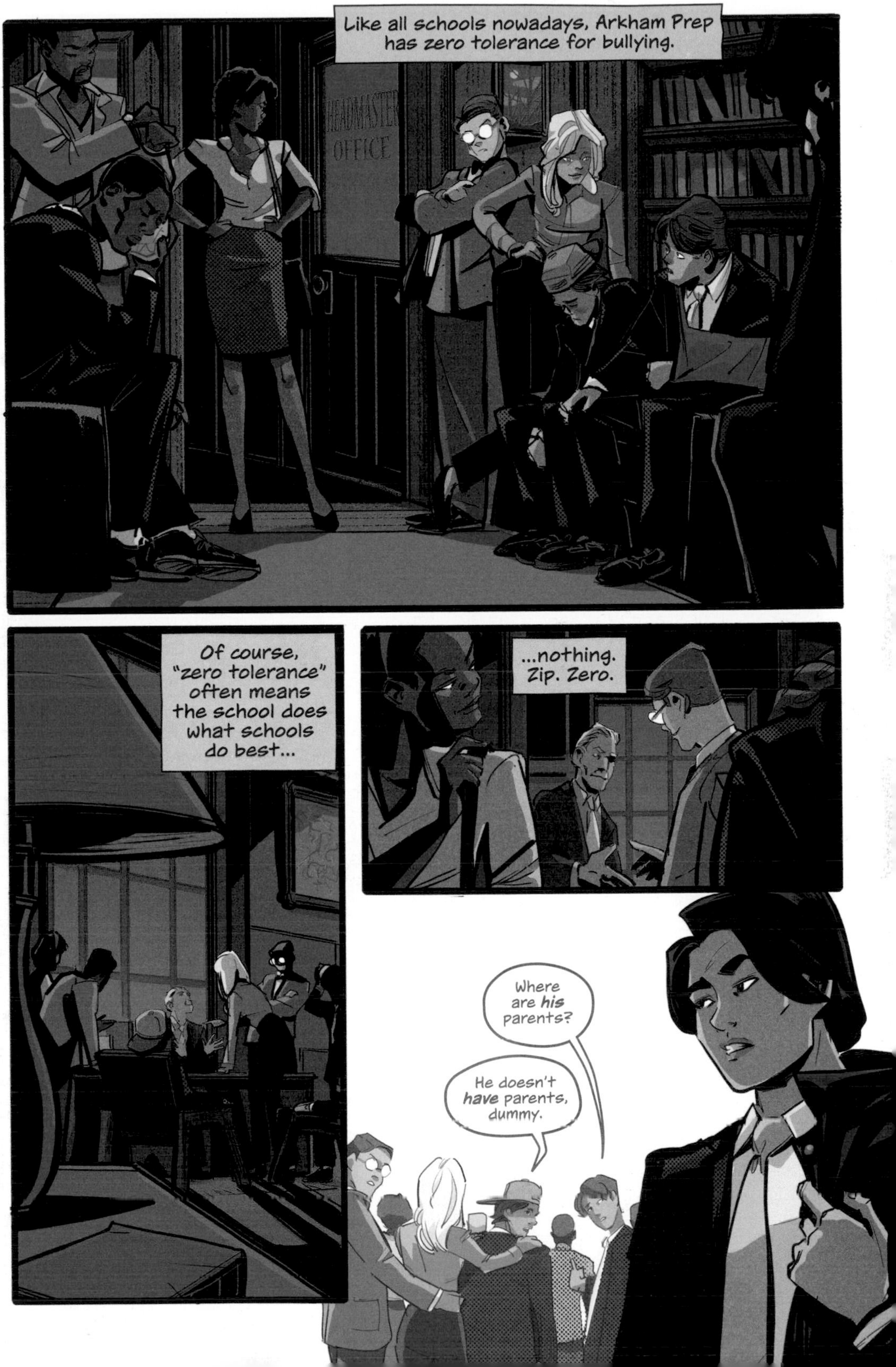
Like all schools nowadays, Arkham Prep has zero tolerance for bullying.
HEADMASTER OFFICE
Of course, "zero tolerance" often means the school does what schools do best...
...nothing. Zip. Zero.
Where are his parents?
He doesn't have parents, dummy.

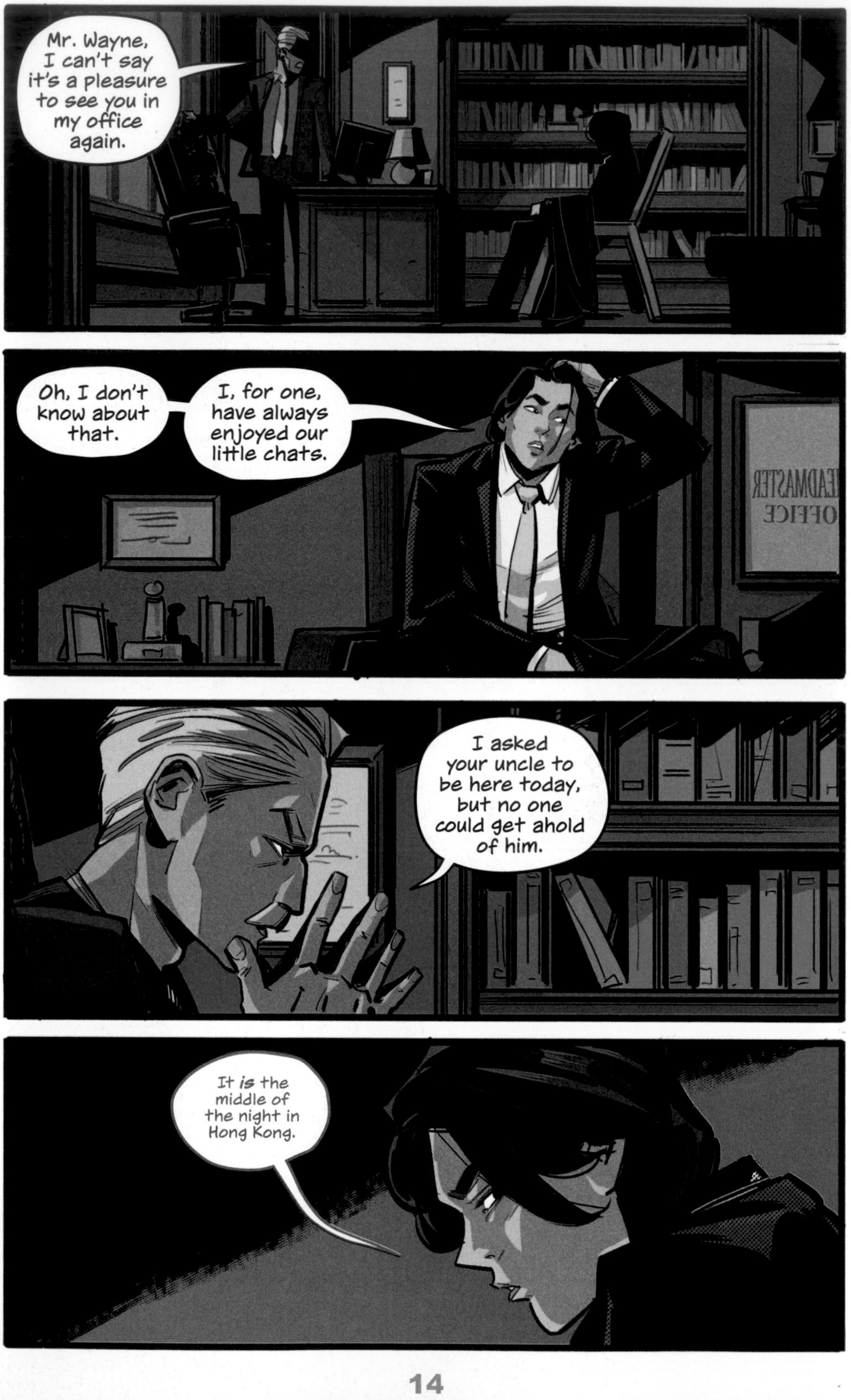
Mr. Wayne, I can't say it's a pleasure to see you in my office again.
Oh, I don't know about that.
I, for one, have always enjoyed our little chats.
I asked your uncle to be here today, but no one could get ahold of him.
It *is* the middle of the night in Hong Kong.

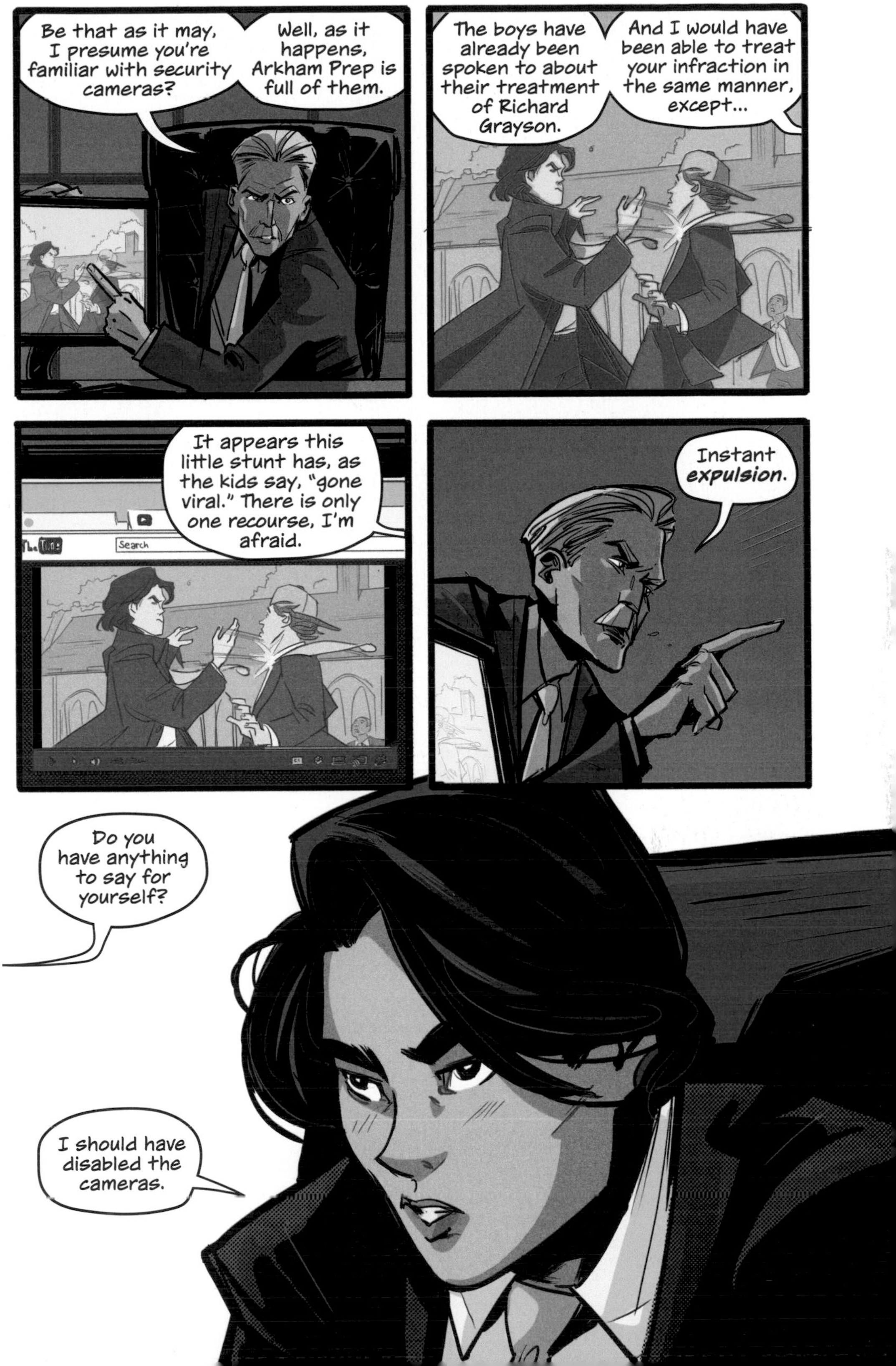
Be that as it may, I presume you're familiar with security cameras?
Well, as it happens, Arkham Prep is full of them.
The boys have already been spoken to about their treatment of Richard Grayson.
And I would have been able to treat your infraction in the same manner, except...
It appears this little stunt has, as the kids say, "gone viral." There is only one recourse, I'm afraid.
Search
Instant *expulsion.*
Do you have anything to say for yourself?
I should have disabled the cameras.

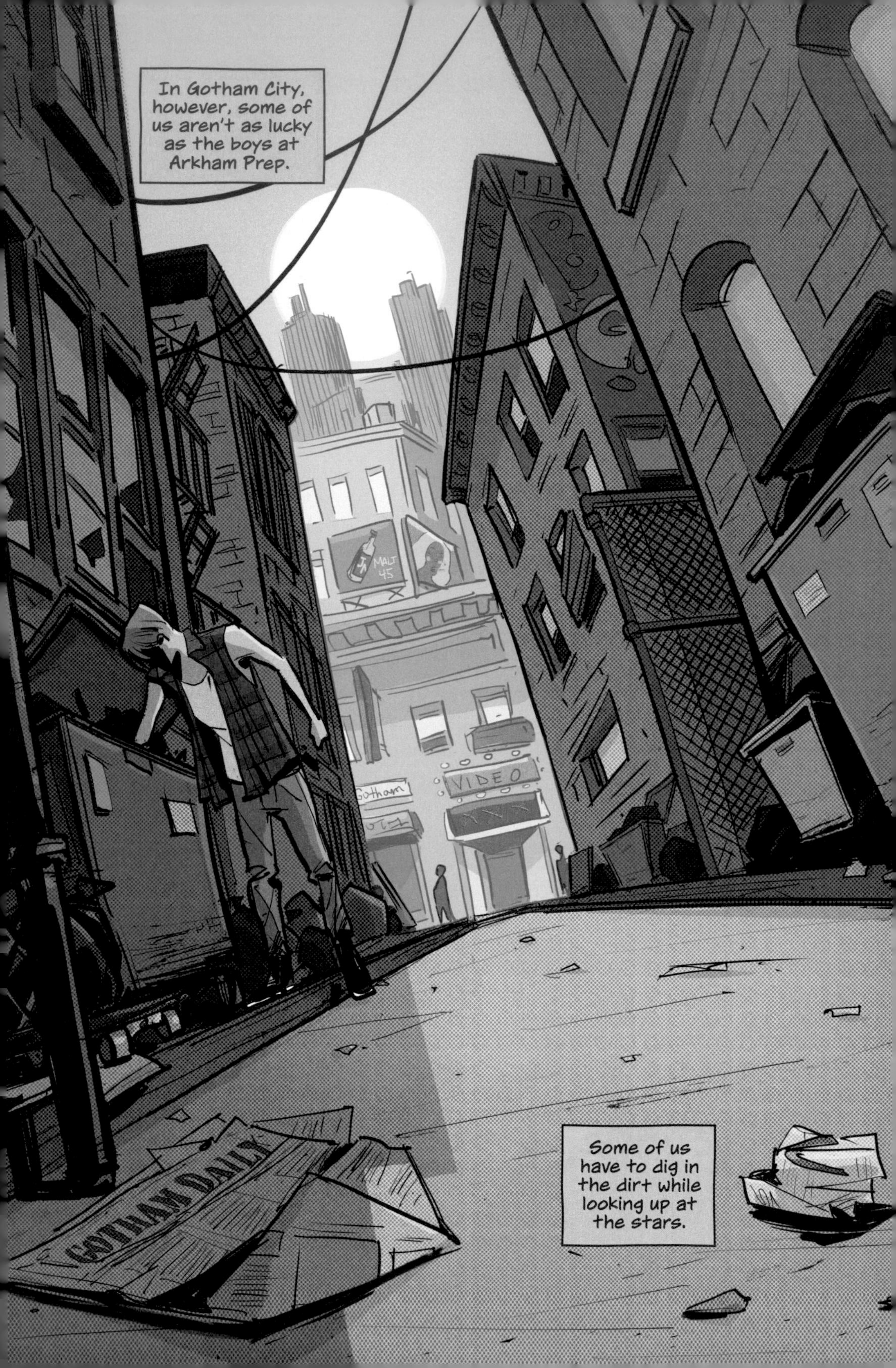
In Gotham City, however, some of us aren't as lucky as the boys at Arkham Prep.
MALT 45
Gotham
VIDEO
GOTHAM DAILY
Some of us have to dig in the dirt while looking up at the stars.

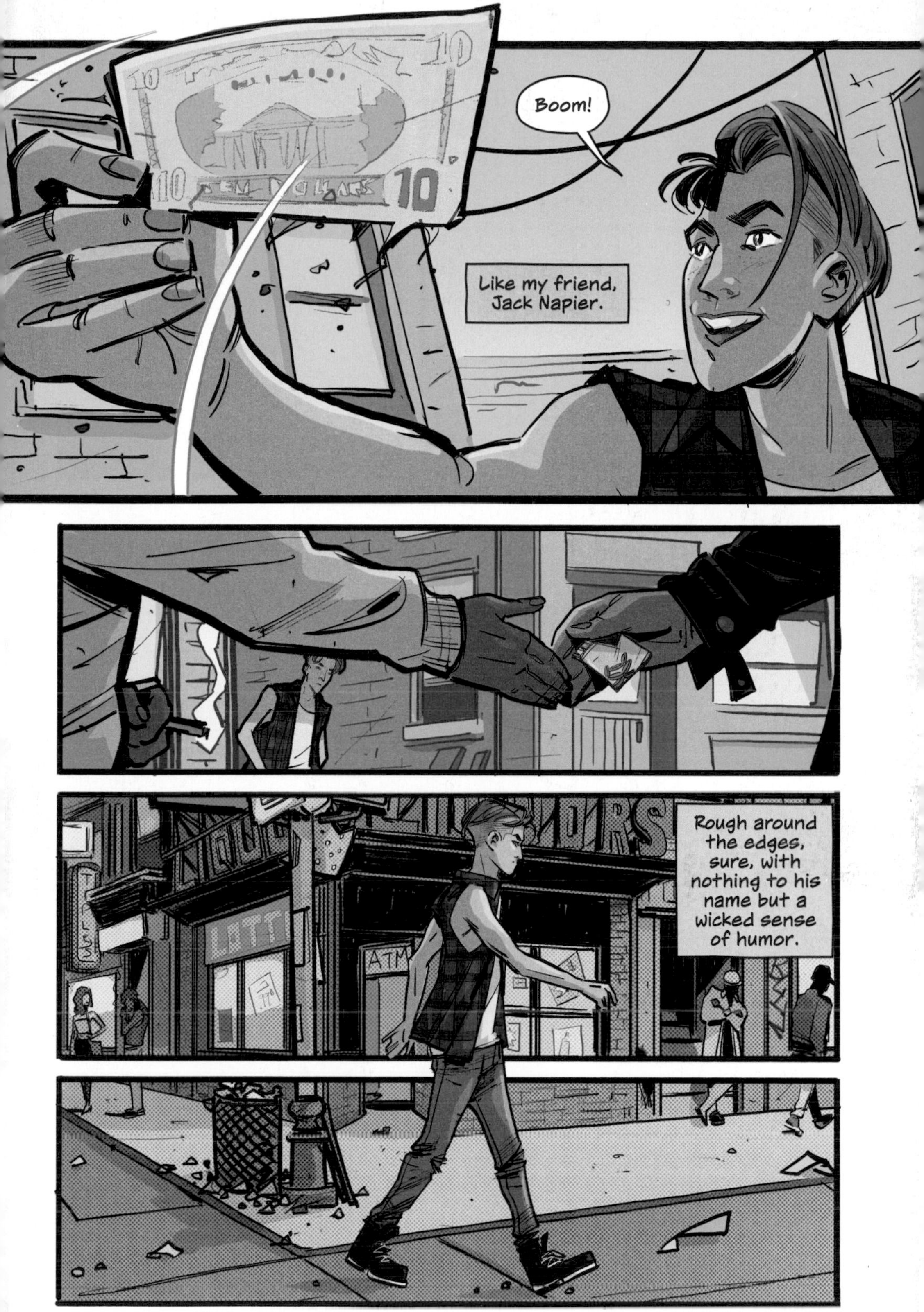
Boom!
Like my friend, Jack Napier.
Rough around the edges, sure, with nothing to his name but a wicked sense of humor.

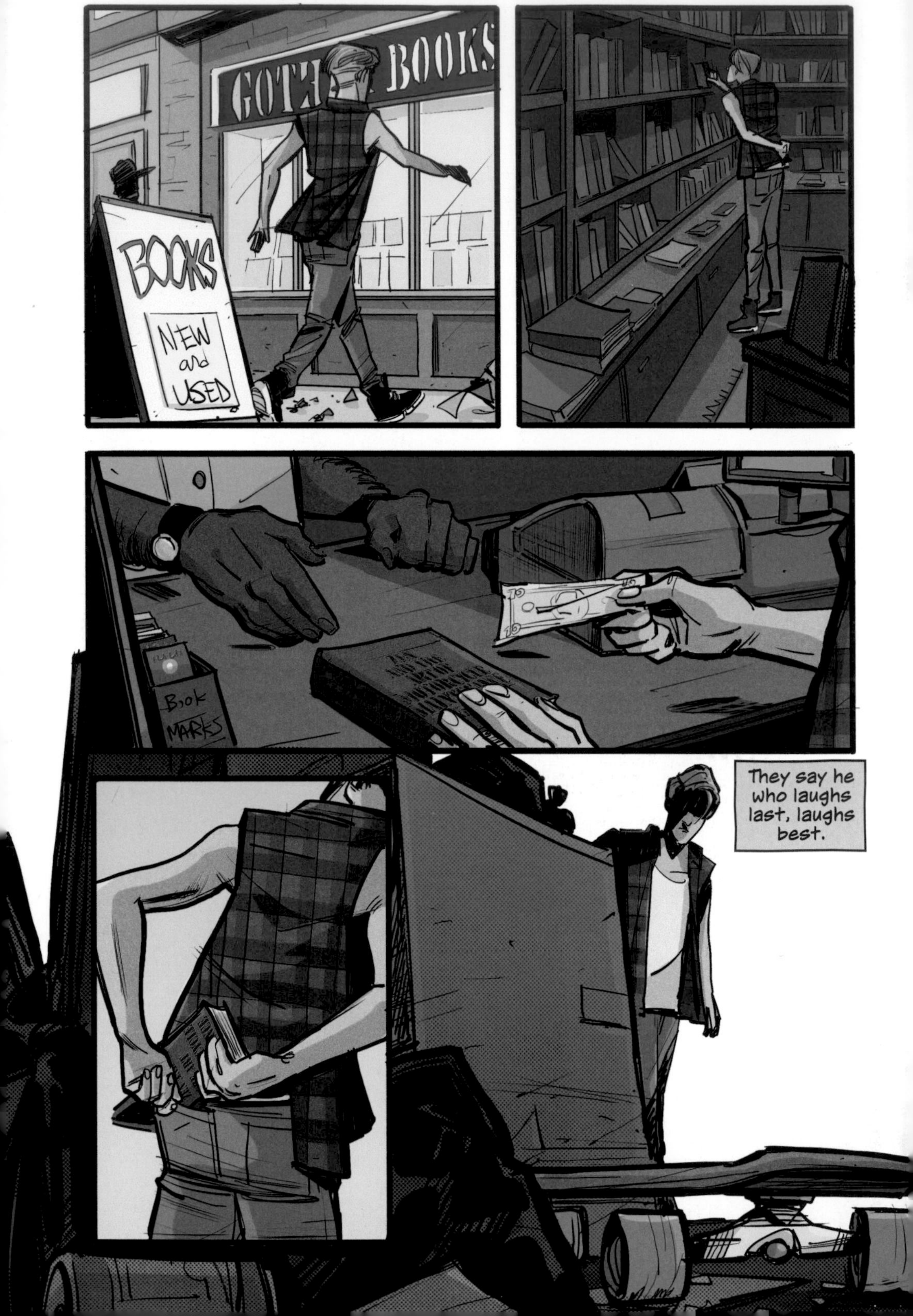
BOOKS
BOOKS
NEW and USED
Book MARKS
They say he who laughs last, laughs best.

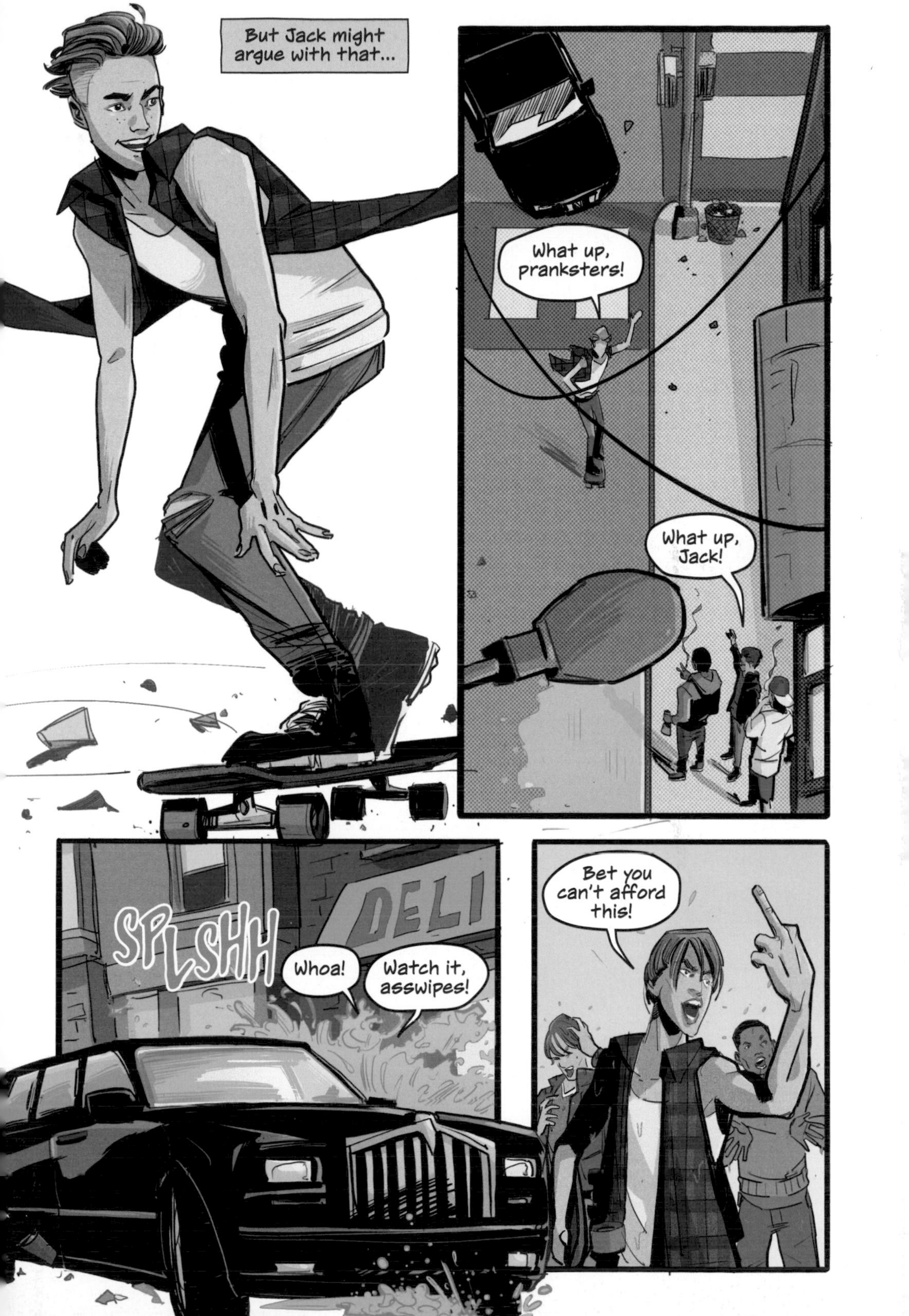
But Jack might argue with that...
What up, pranksters!
What up, Jack!
SPLSHH
Whoa!
Watch it, asswipes!
Bet you can't afford this!
DELI

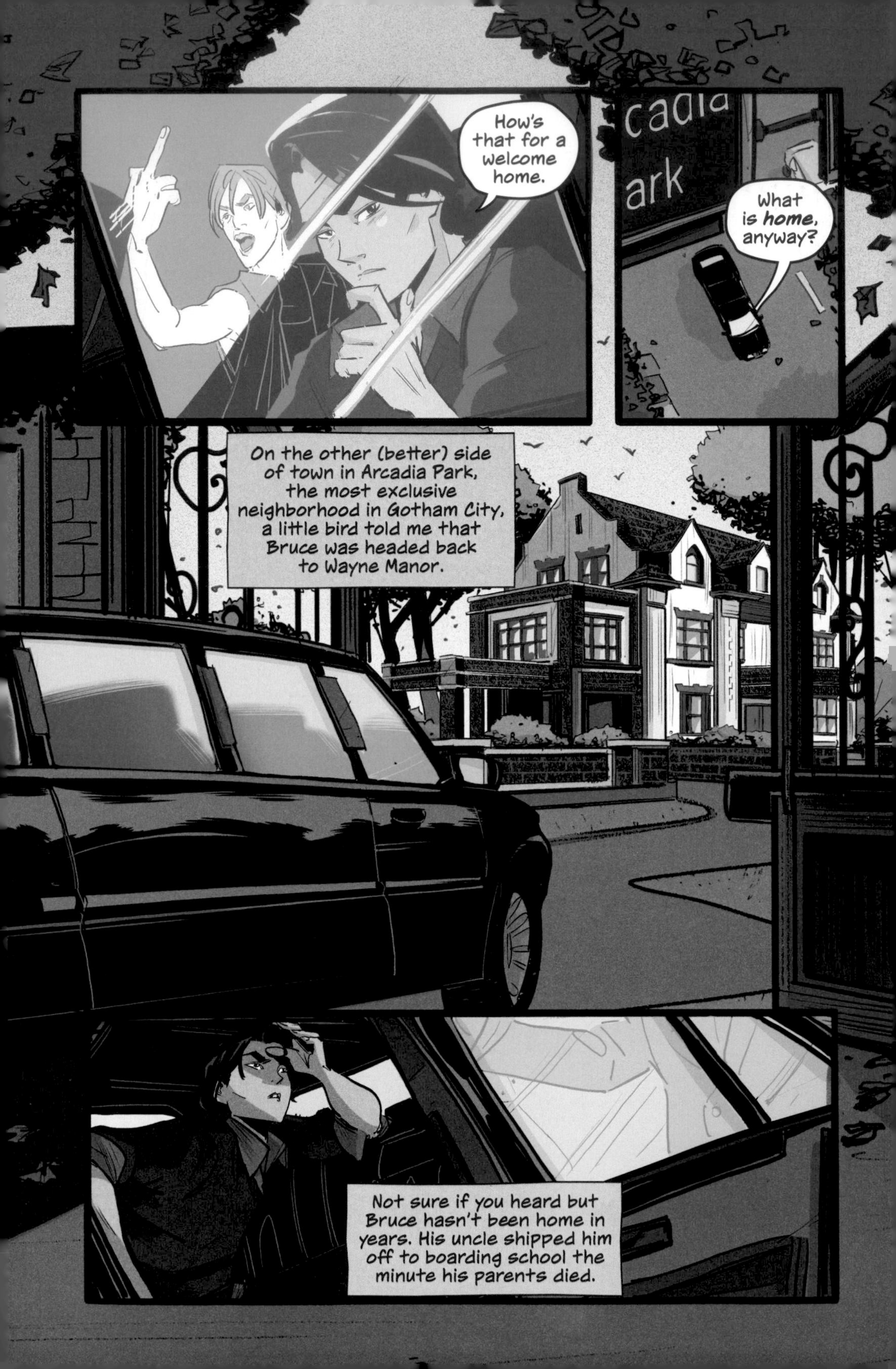
How's that for a welcome home.
cadia
ark
What is **home**, anyway?
On the other (better) side of town in Arcadia Park, the most exclusive neighborhood in Gotham City, a little bird told me that Bruce was headed back to Wayne Manor.
Not sure if you heard but Bruce hasn't been home in years. His uncle shipped him off to boarding school the minute his parents died.

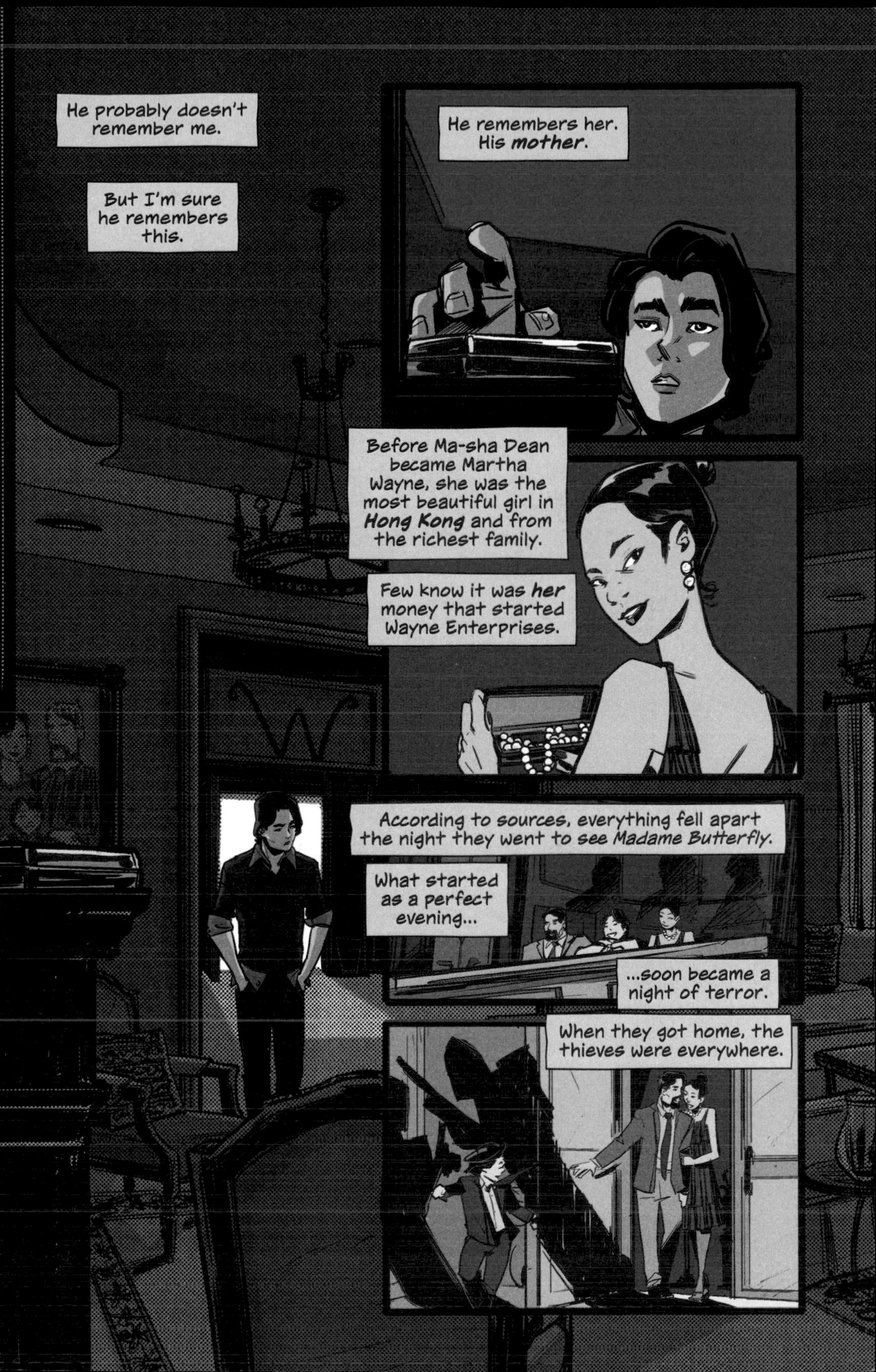
He probably doesn't remember me.
But I'm sure he remembers this.
He remembers her. His *mother*.
Before Ma-sha Dean became Martha Wayne, she was the most beautiful girl in *Hong Kong* and from the richest family.
Few know it was *her* money that started Wayne Enterprises.
According to sources, everything fell apart the night they went to see *Madame Butterfly*.
What started as a perfect evening...
...soon became a night of terror.
When they got home, the thieves were everywhere.

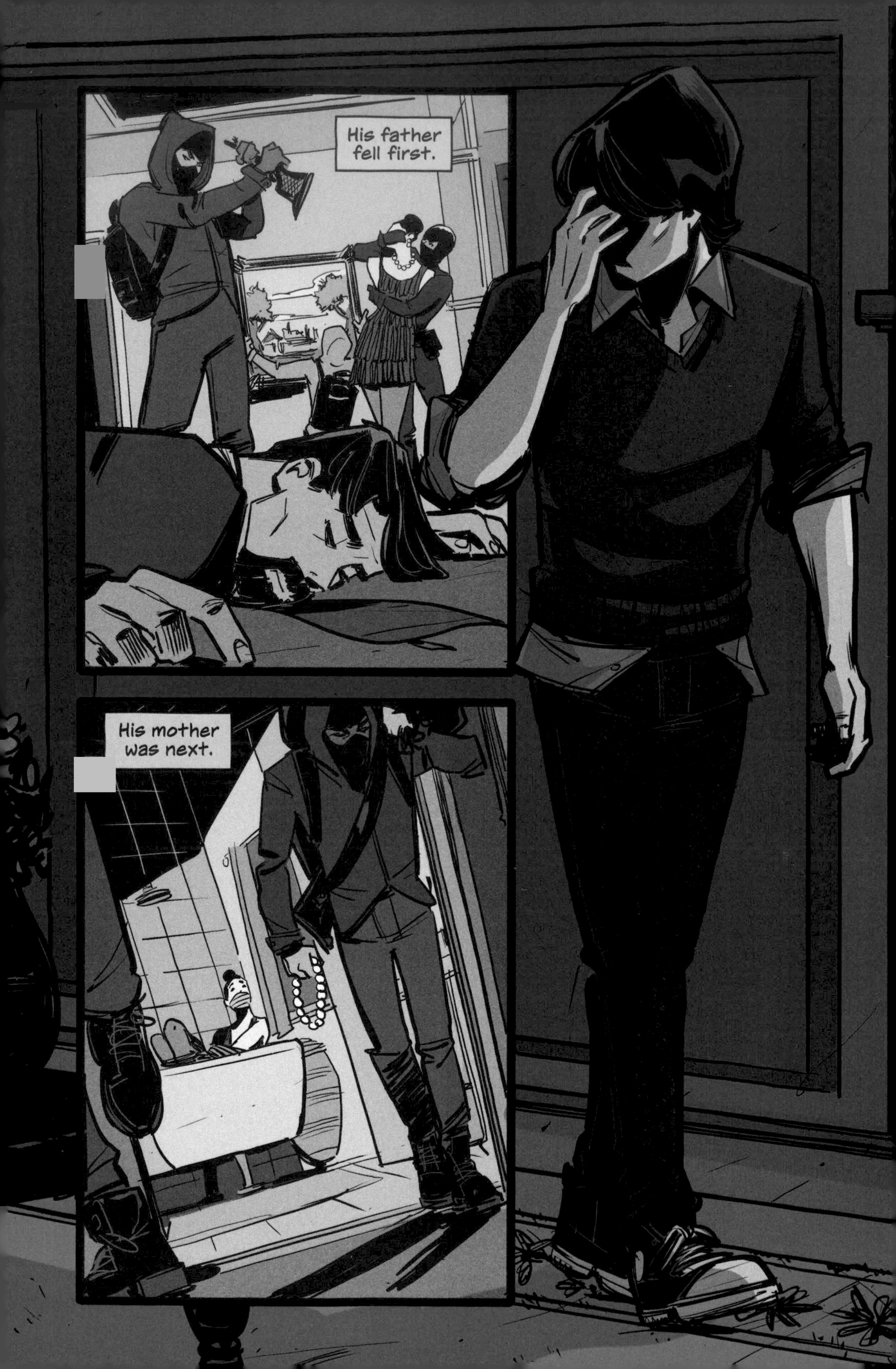
His father fell first.
His mother was next.

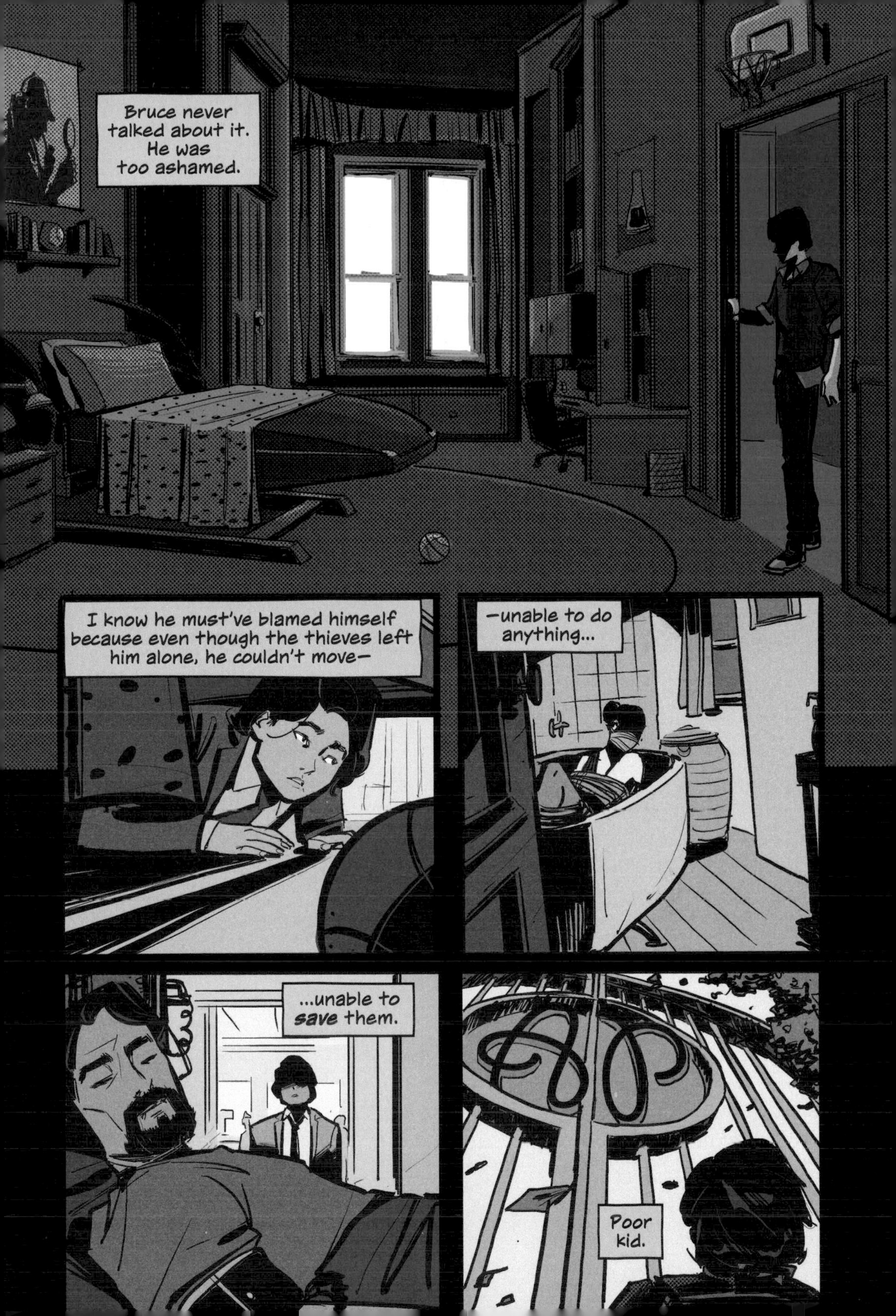
Bruce never talked about it. He was too ashamed.
I know he must've blamed himself because even though the thieves left him alone, he couldn't move—
—unable to do anything...
...unable to save them.
Poor kid.

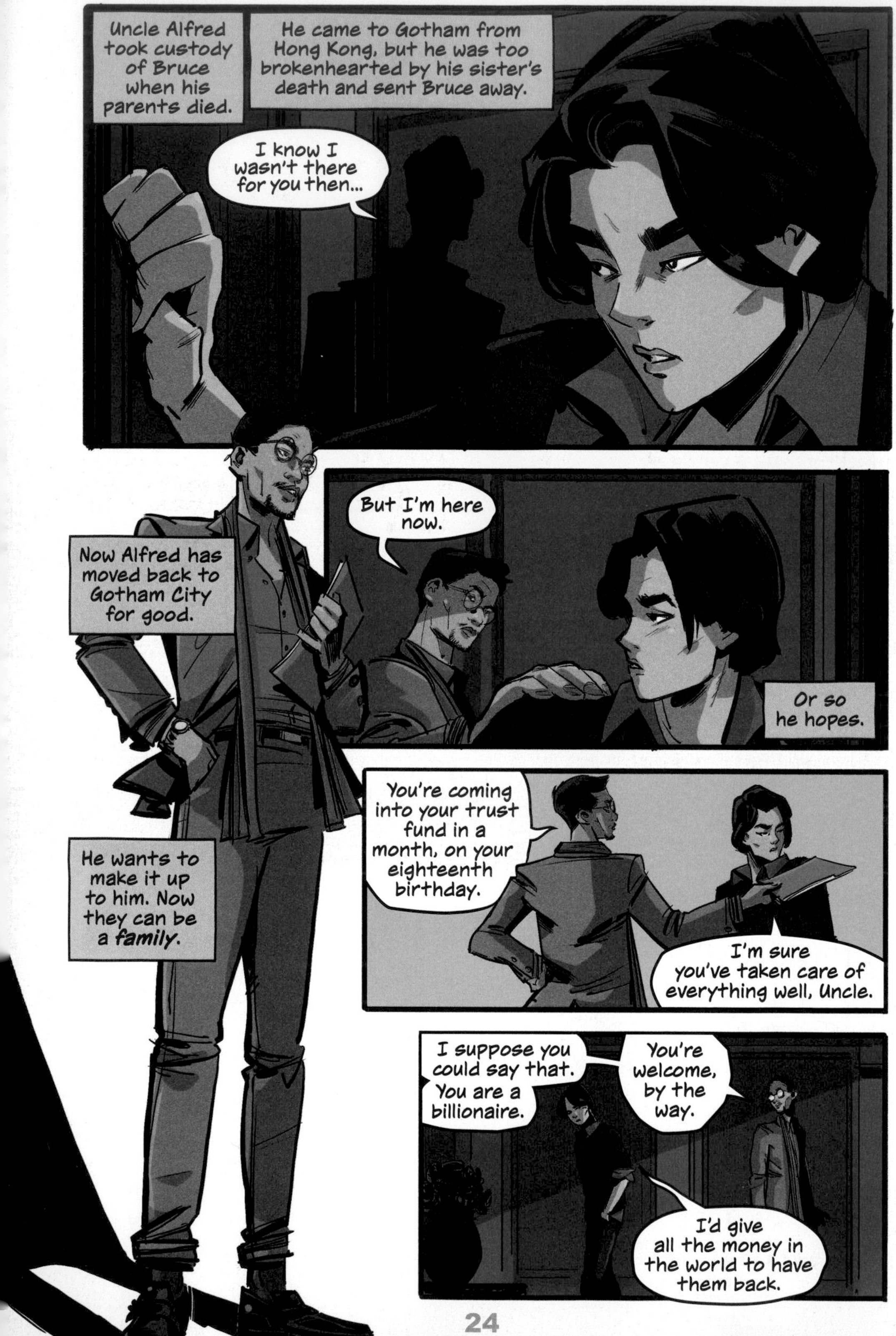
Uncle Alfred took custody of Bruce when his parents died.
He came to Gotham from Hong Kong, but he was too brokenhearted by his sister's death and sent Bruce away.
I know I wasn't there for you then...
Now Alfred has moved back to Gotham City for good.
But I'm here now.
Or so he hopes.
He wants to make it up to him. Now they can be a *family*.
You're coming into your trust fund in a month, on your eighteenth birthday.
I'm sure you've taken care of everything well, Uncle.
I suppose you could say that. You are a billionaire.
You're welcome, by the way.
I'd give all the money in the world to have them back.

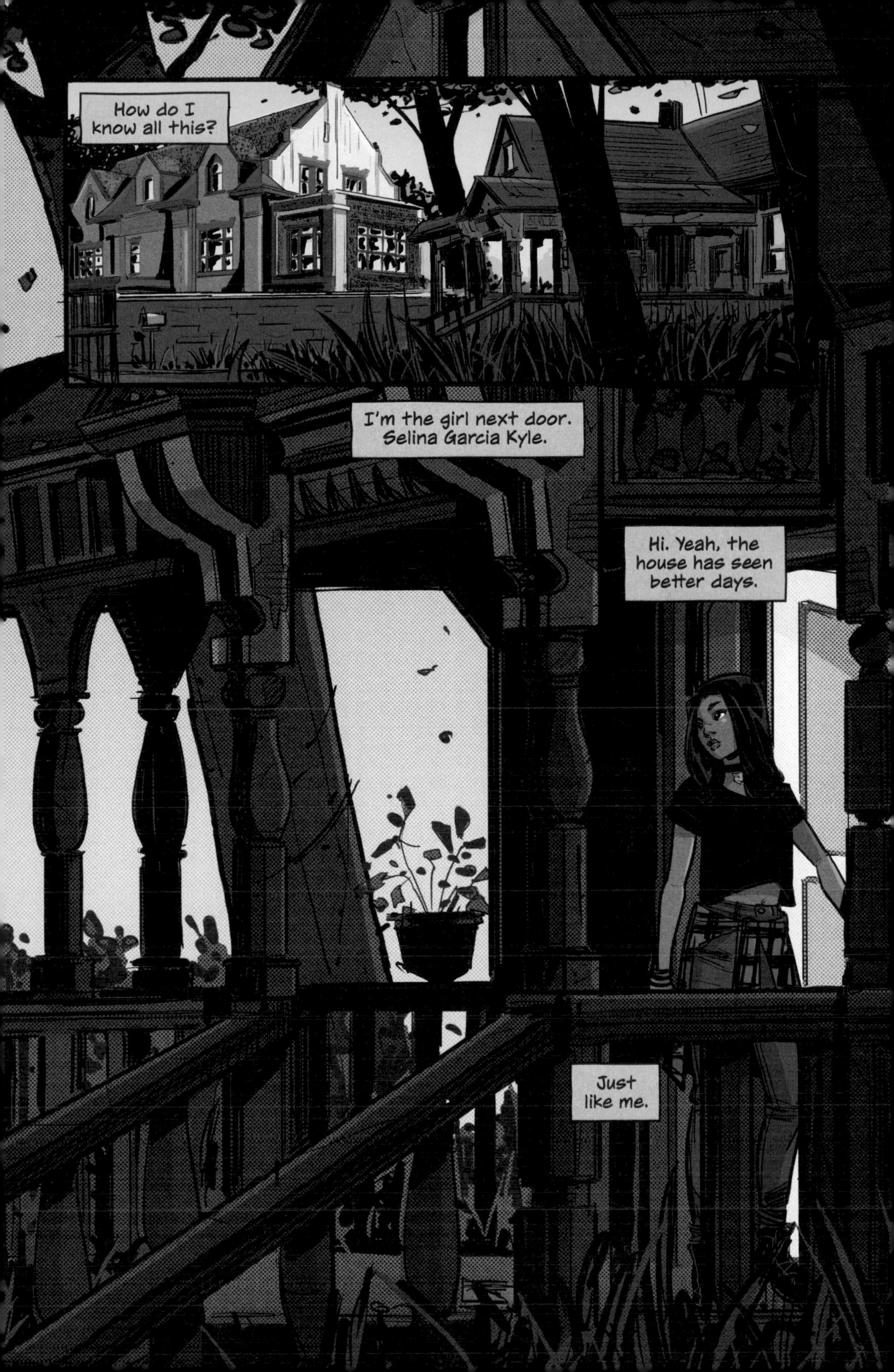
How do I know all this?
I'm the girl next door. Selina Garcia Kyle.
Hi. Yeah, the house has seen better days.
Just like me.

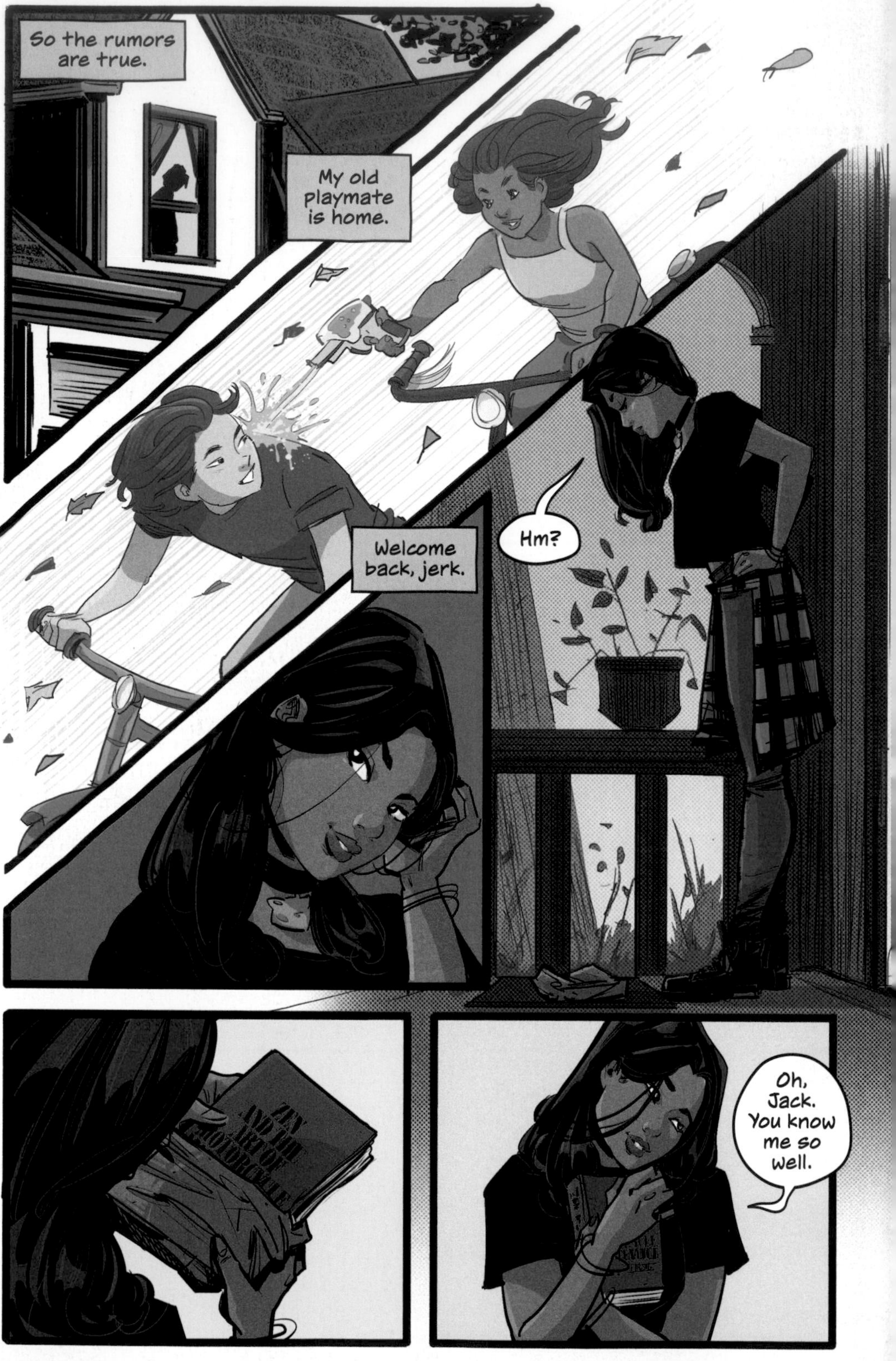
So the rumors are true.
My old playmate is home.
Welcome back, jerk.
Hm?
Oh, Jack. You know me so well.

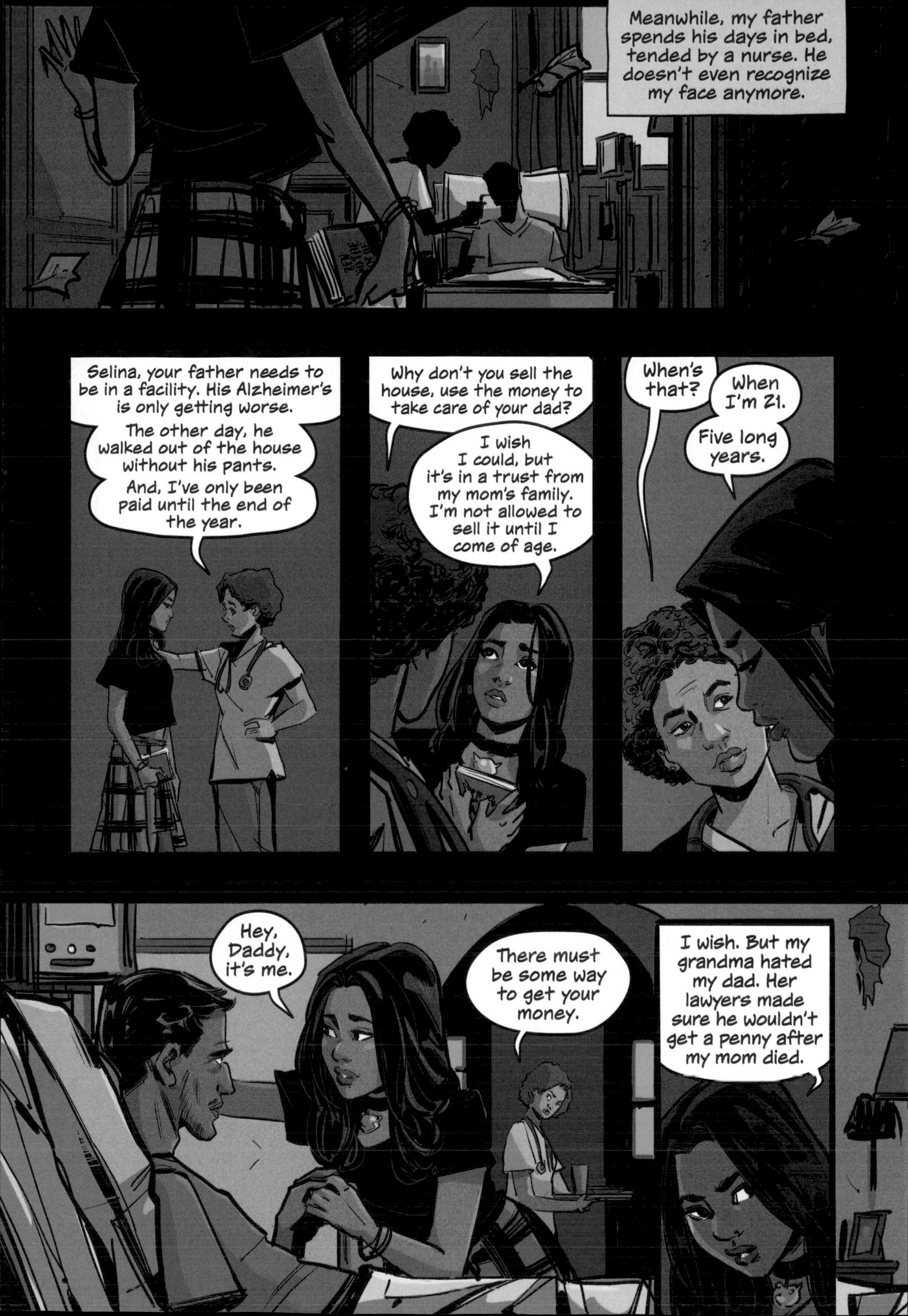
Meanwhile, my father spends his days in bed, tended by a nurse. He doesn't even recognize my face anymore.
Selina, your father needs to be in a facility. His Alzheimer's is only getting worse.
The other day, he walked out of the house without his pants.
And, I've only been paid until the end of the year.
Why don't you sell the house, use the money to take care of your dad?
I wish I could, but it's in a trust from my mom's family. I'm not allowed to sell it until I come of age.
When's that?
When I'm 21.
Five long years.
Hey, Daddy, it's me.
There must be some way to get your money.
I wish. But my grandma hated my dad. Her lawyers made sure he wouldn't get a penny after my mom died.

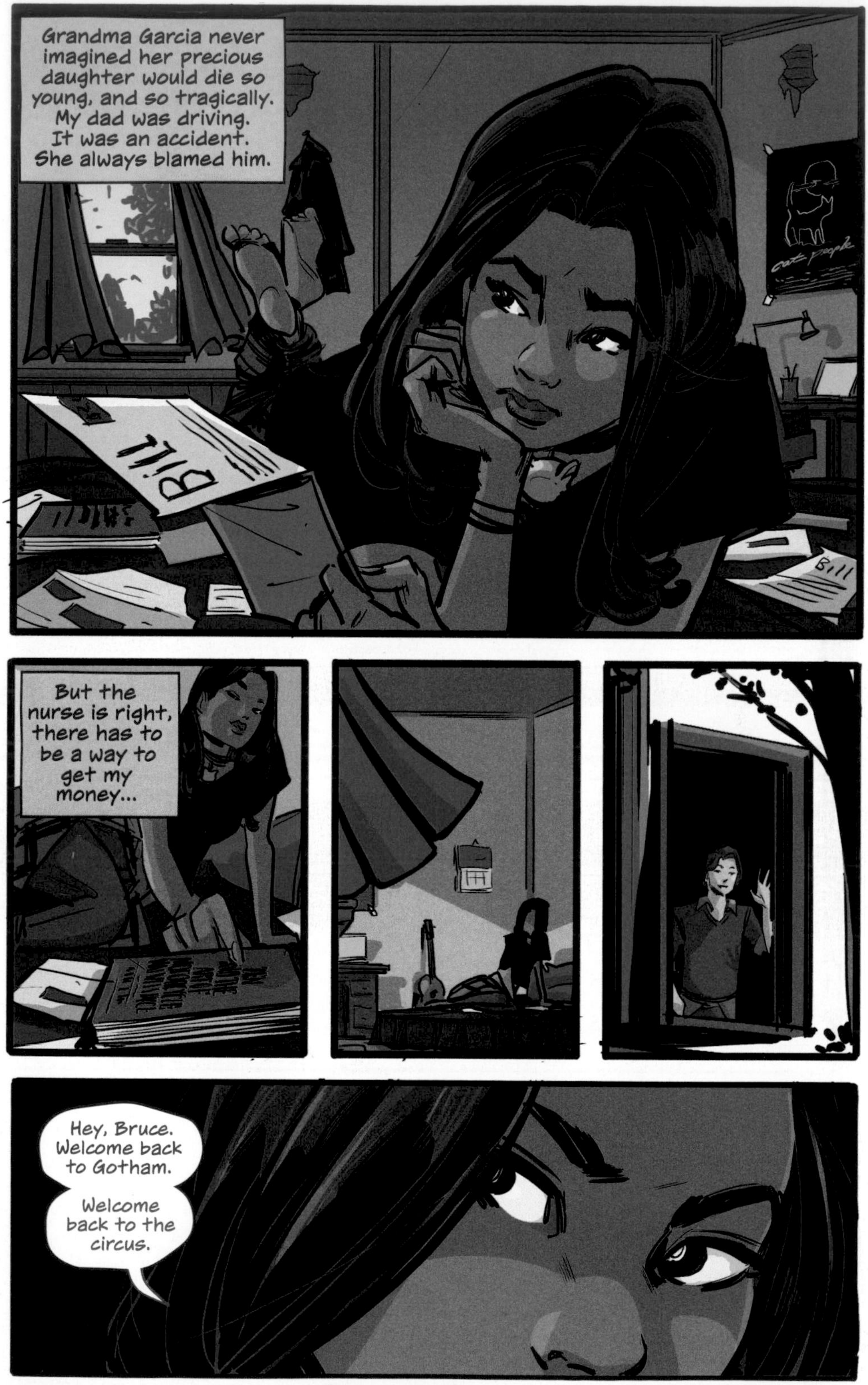
Grandma Garcia never imagined her precious daughter would die so young, and so tragically. My dad was driving. It was an accident. She always blamed him.
BILL
Bill
But the nurse is right, there has to be a way to get my money...
Hey, Bruce. Welcome back to Gotham.
Welcome back to the circus.

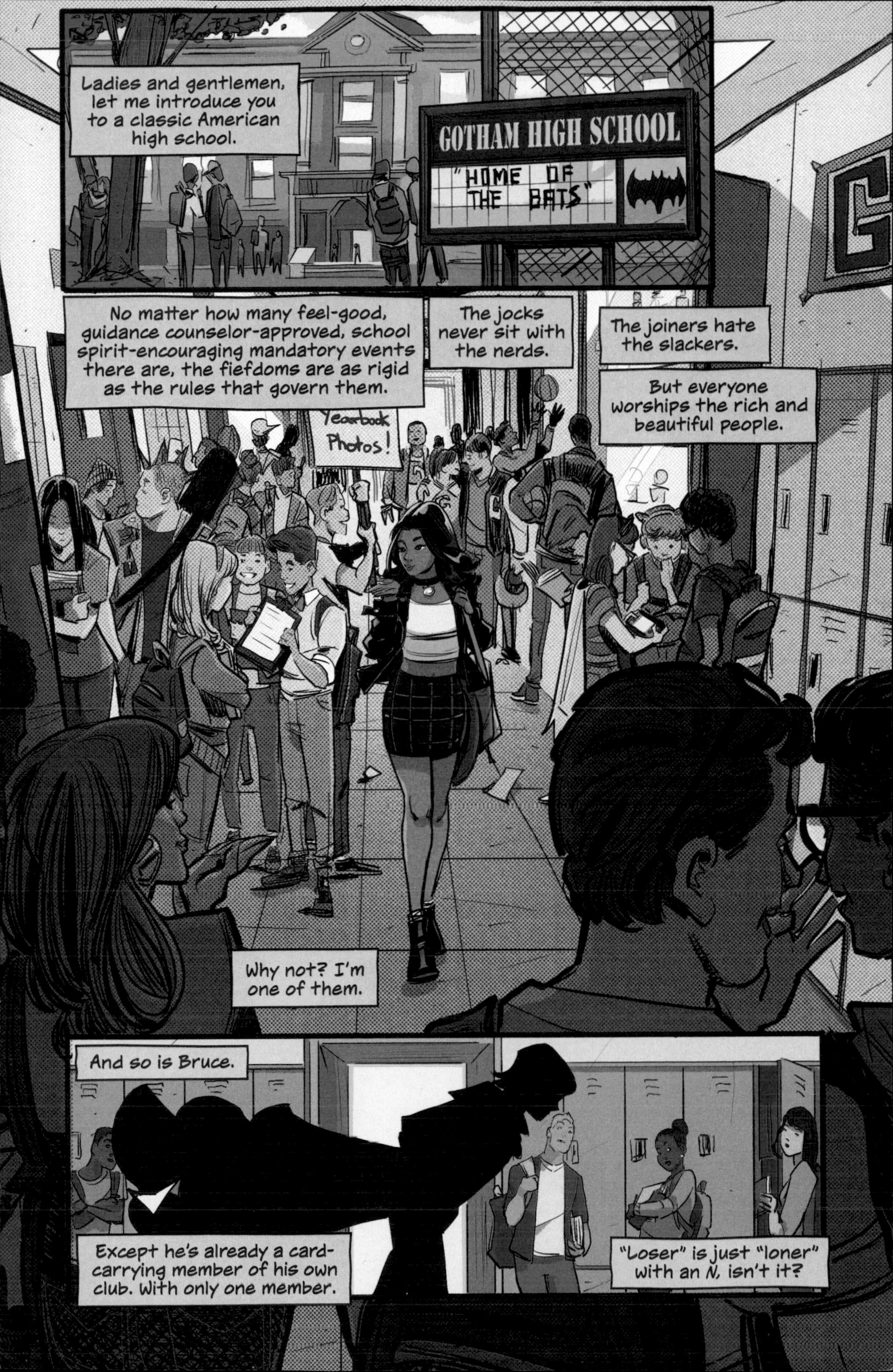
Ladies and gentlemen, let me introduce you to a classic American high school.
GOTHAM HIGH SCHOOL
"HOME OF THE BATS"
No matter how many feel-good, guidance counselor-approved, school spirit-encouraging mandatory events there are, the fiefdoms are as rigid as the rules that govern them.
The jocks never sit with the nerds.
The joiners hate the slackers.
But everyone worships the rich and beautiful people.
Yearbook Photos!
Why not? I'm one of them.
And so is Bruce.
Except he's already a card-carrying member of his own club. With only one member.
"Loser" is just "loner" with an N, isn't it?

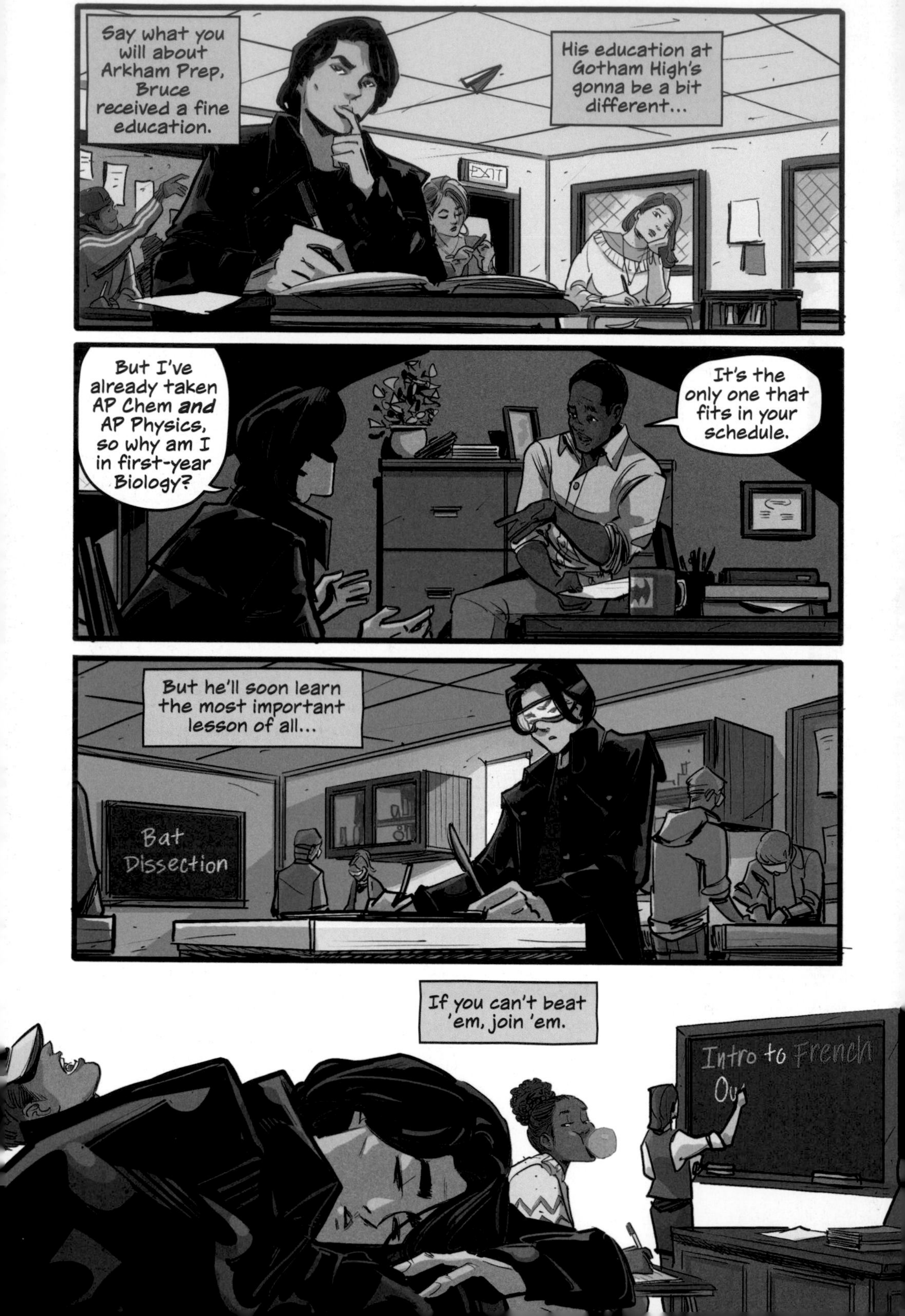
Say what you will about Arkham Prep, Bruce received a fine education.
His education at Gotham High's gonna be a bit different...
EXIT
But I've already taken AP Chem and AP Physics, so why am I in first-year Biology?
It's the only one that fits in your schedule.
But he'll soon learn the most important lesson of all...
Bat Dissection
If you can't beat 'em, join 'em.
Intro to French
Ou

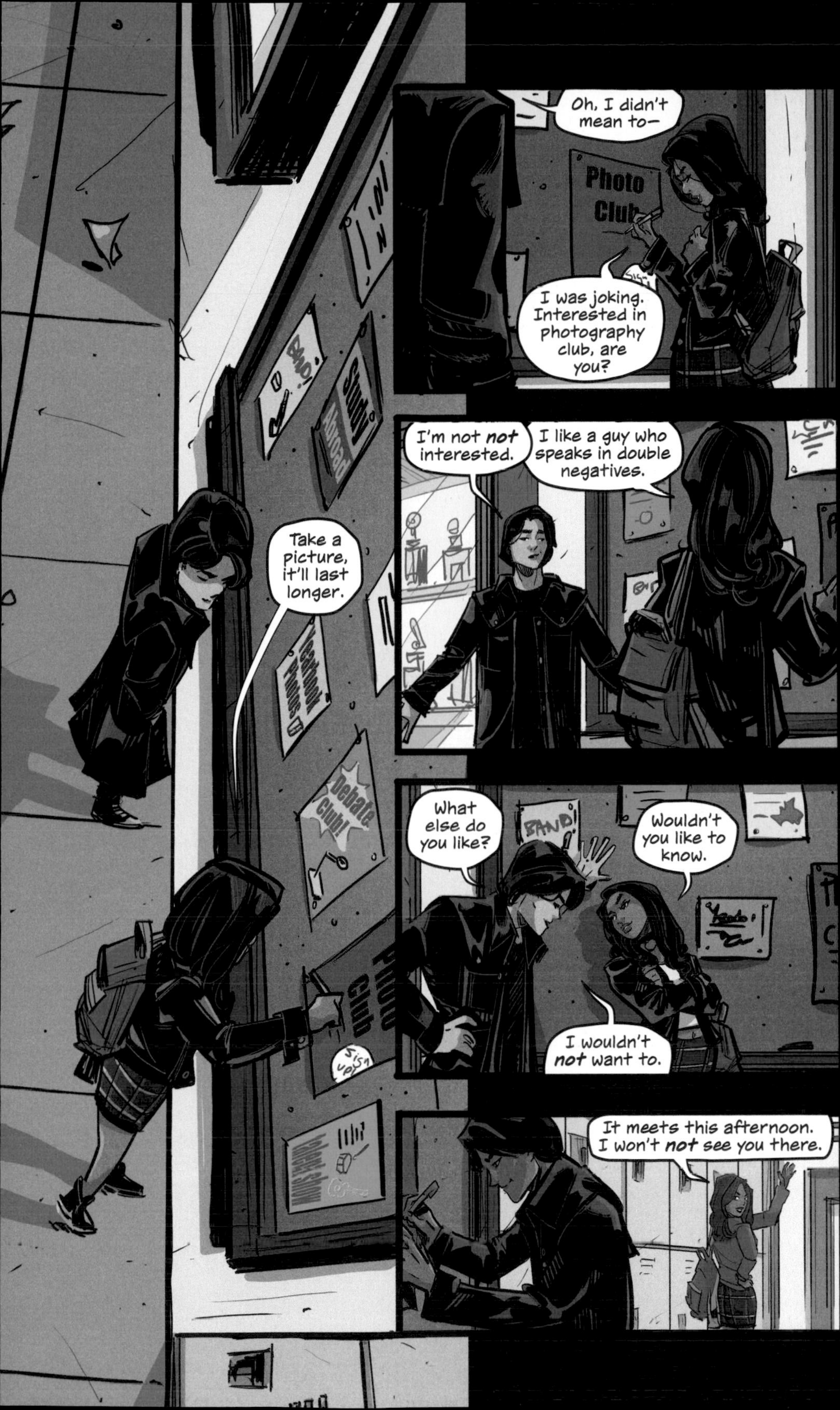
Take a picture, it'll last longer.
Oh, I didn't mean to—
I was joking. Interested in photography club, are you?
I'm not *not* interested.
I like a guy who speaks in double negatives.
What else do you like?
Wouldn't you like to know.
I wouldn't *not* want to.
It meets this afternoon. I won't *not* see you there.

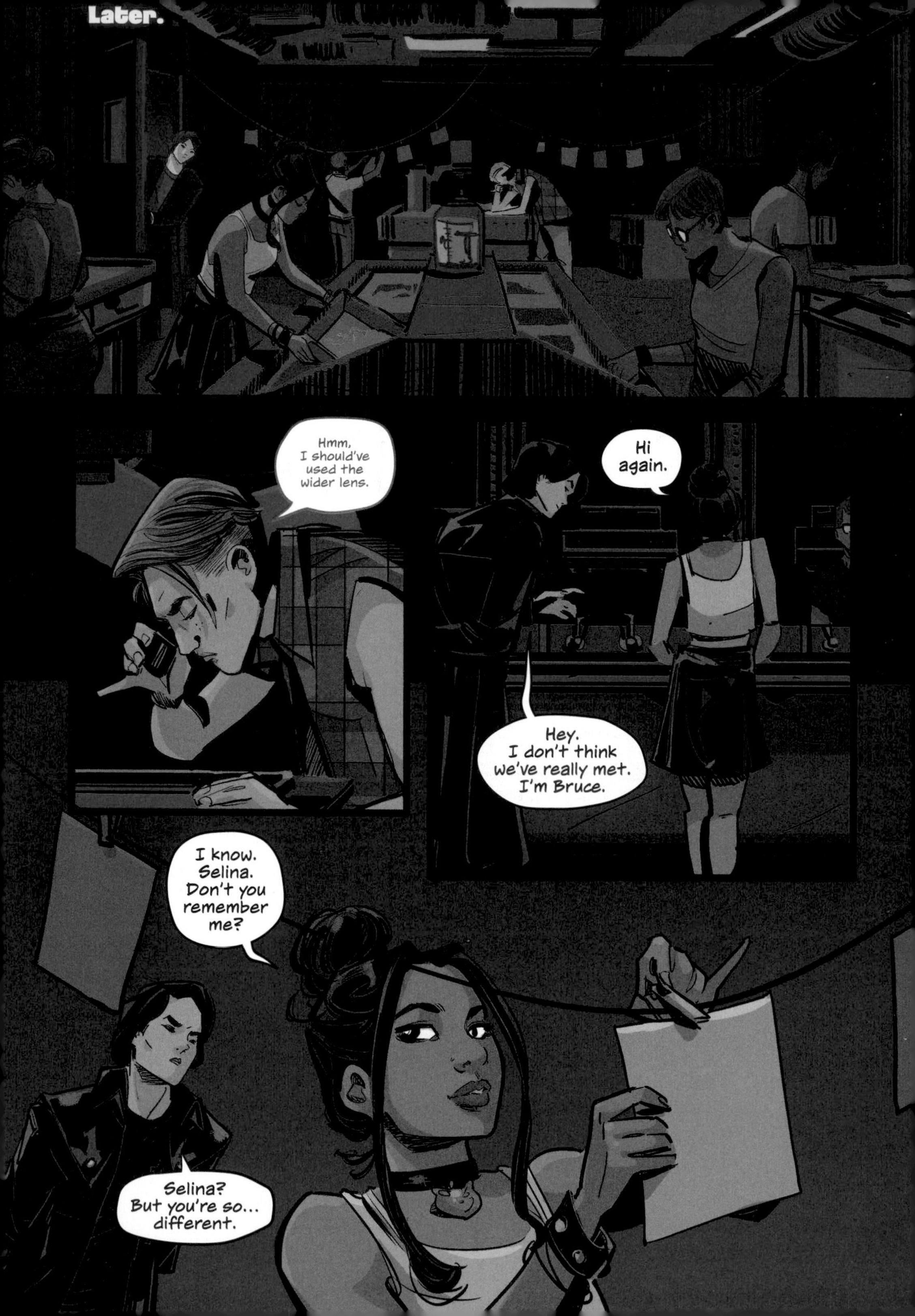
Later.
Hmm, I should've used the wider lens.
Hi again.
Hey. I don't think we've really met. I'm Bruce.
I know. Selina. Don't you remember me?
Selina? But you're so... different.

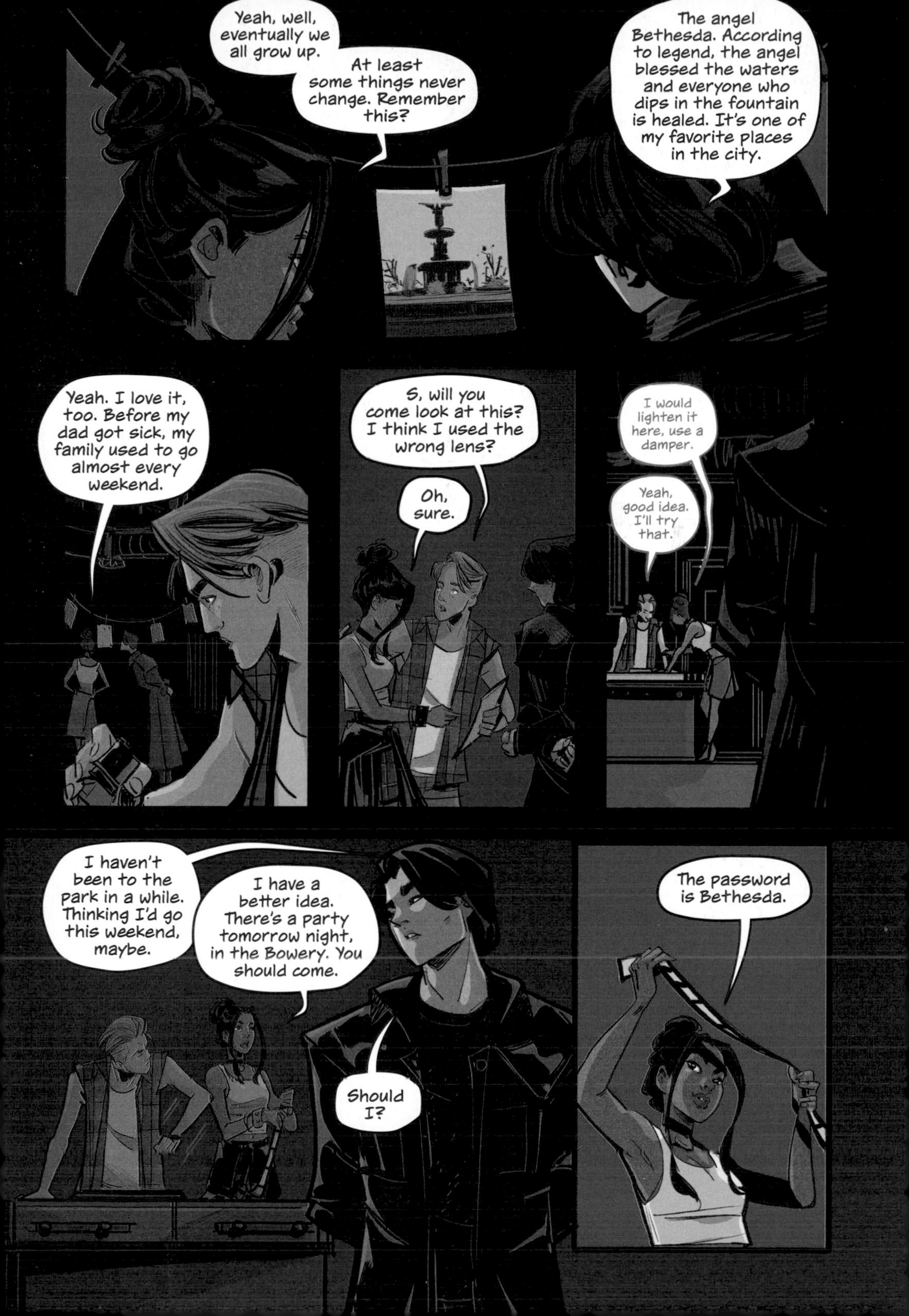
Yeah, well, eventually we all grow up.
At least some things never change. Remember this?
The angel Bethesda. According to legend, the angel blessed the waters and everyone who dips in the fountain is healed. It's one of my favorite places in the city.
Yeah. I love it, too. Before my dad got sick, my family used to go almost every weekend.
S, will you come look at this? I think I used the wrong lens?
Oh, sure.
I would lighten it here, use a damper.
Yeah, good idea. I'll try that.
I haven't been to the park in a while. Thinking I'd go this weekend, maybe.
I have a better idea. There's a party tomorrow night, in the Bowery. You should come.
Should I?
The password is Bethesda.

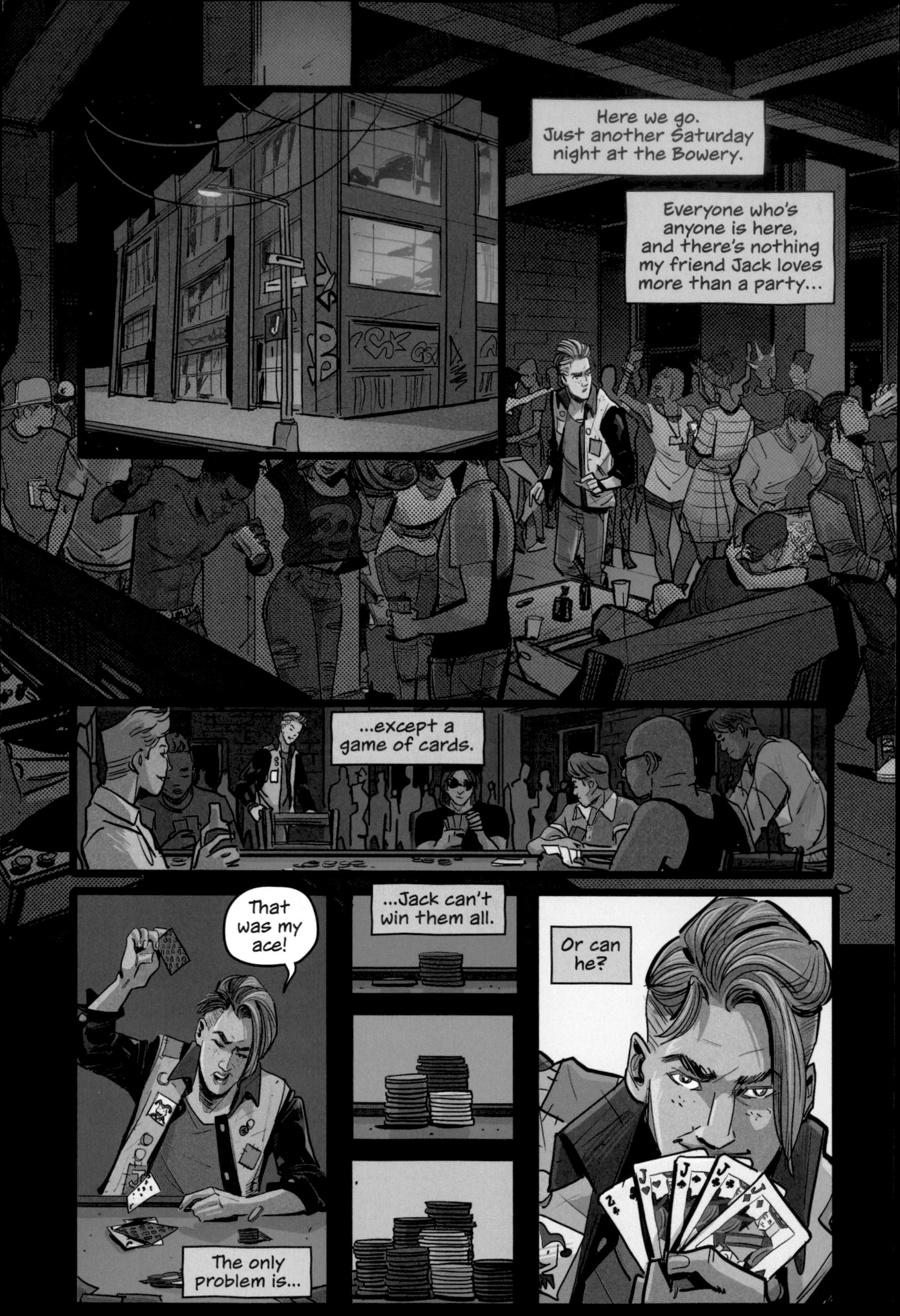
Here we go.
Just another Saturday night at the Bowery.
Everyone who's anyone is here, and there's nothing my friend Jack loves more than a party...
...except a game of cards.
That was my ace!
The only problem is...
...Jack can't win them all.
Or can he?

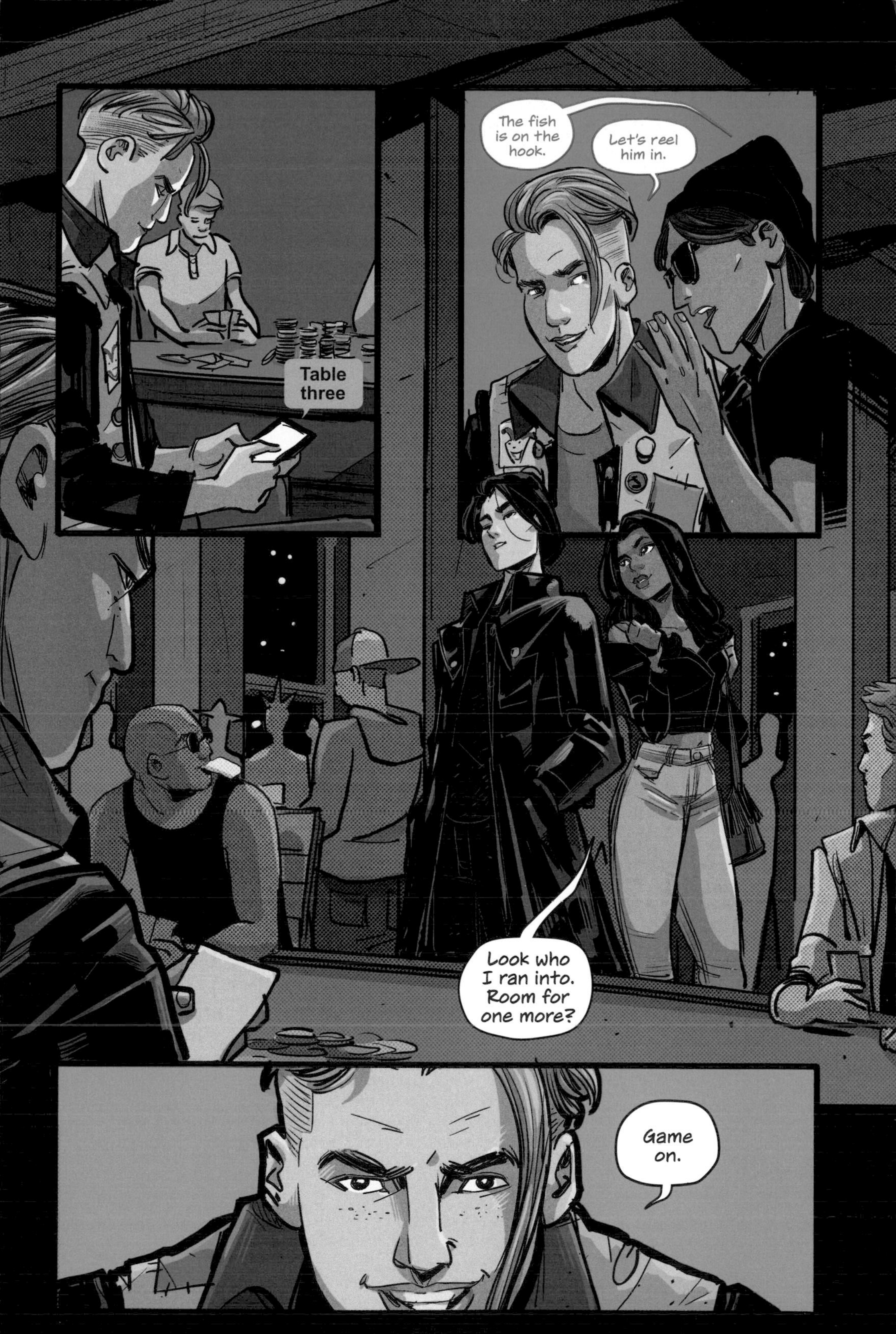

Table three
The fish is on the hook.
Let's reel him in.
Look who I ran into. Room for one more?
Game on.

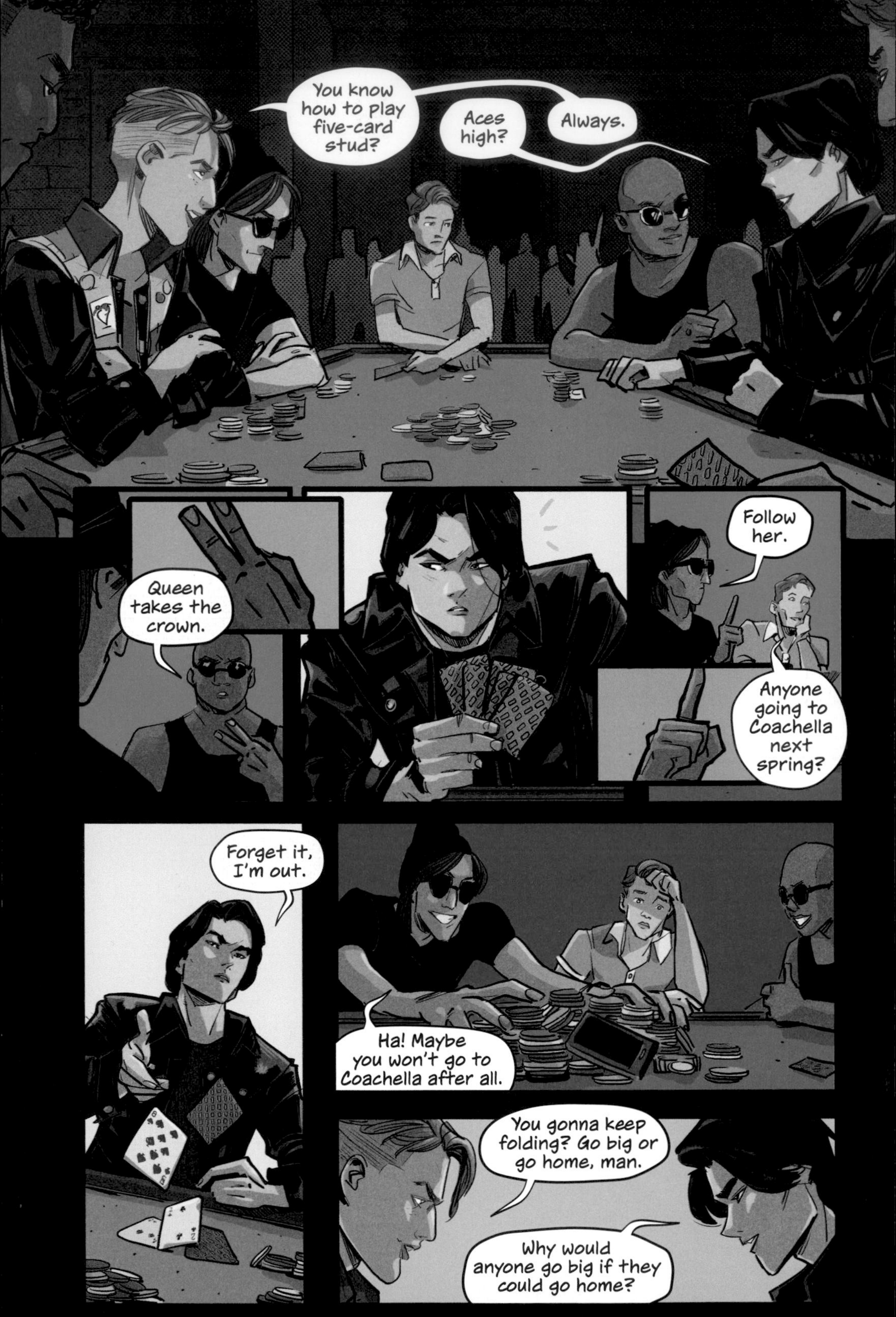
You know how to play five-card stud?
Aces high?
Always.
Queen takes the crown.
Follow her.
Anyone going to Coachella next spring?
Forget it, I'm out.
Ha! Maybe you won't go to Coachella after all.
You gonna keep folding? Go big or go home, man.
Why would anyone go big if they could go home?

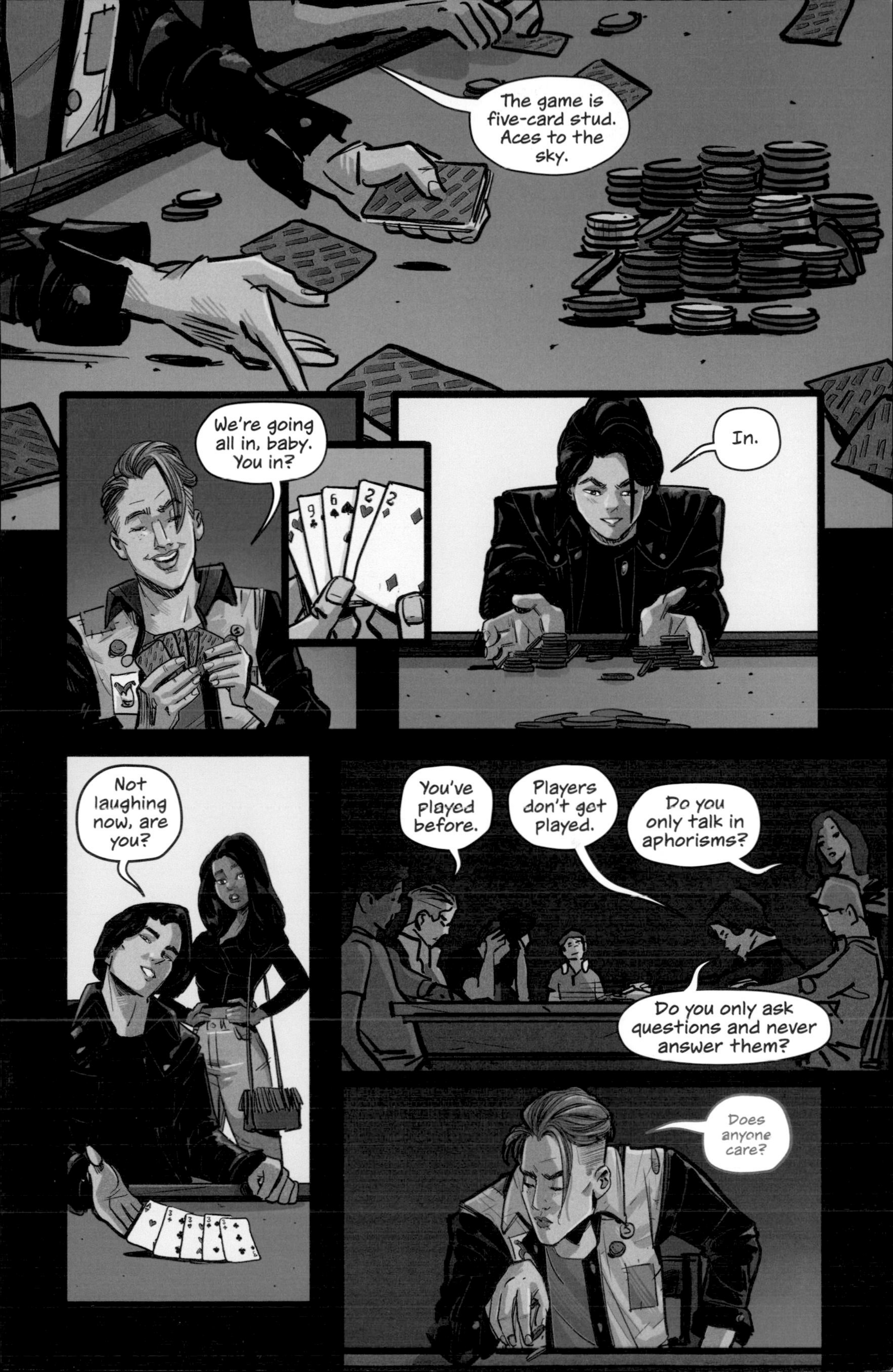
The game is five-card stud. Aces to the sky.
We're going all in, baby. You in?
In.
Not laughing now, are you?
You've played before.
Players don't get played.
Do you only talk in aphorisms?
Do you only ask questions and never answer them?
Does anyone care?

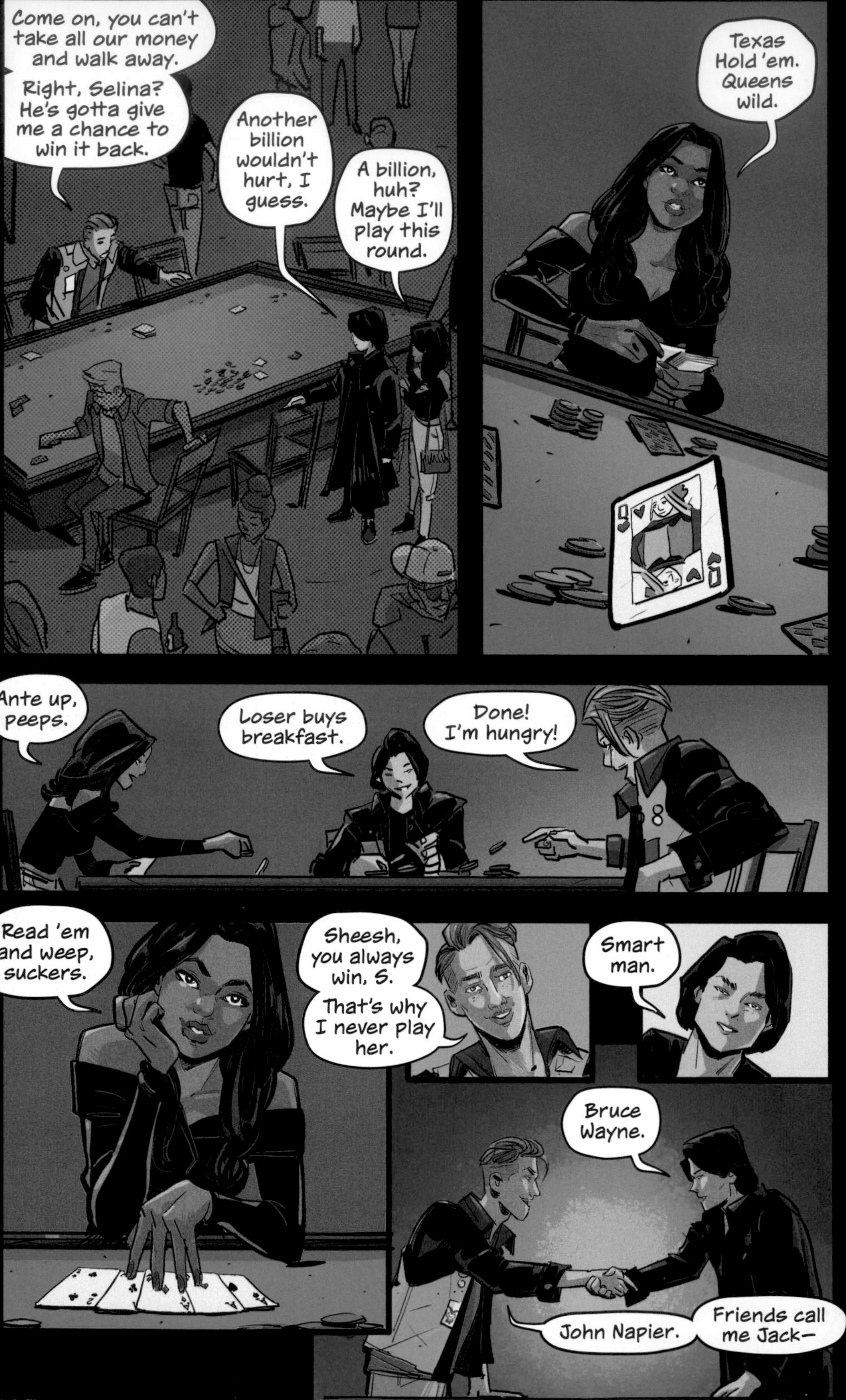
Come on, you can't take all our money and walk away.
Right, Selina? He's gotta give me a chance to win it back.
Another billion wouldn't hurt, I guess.
A billion, huh? Maybe I'll play this round.
Texas Hold 'em. Queens wild.
Ante up, peeps.
Loser buys breakfast.
Done! I'm hungry!
Read 'em and weep, suckers.
Sheesh, you always win, S.
That's why I never play her.
Smart man.
Bruce Wayne.
John Napier.
Friends call me Jack—

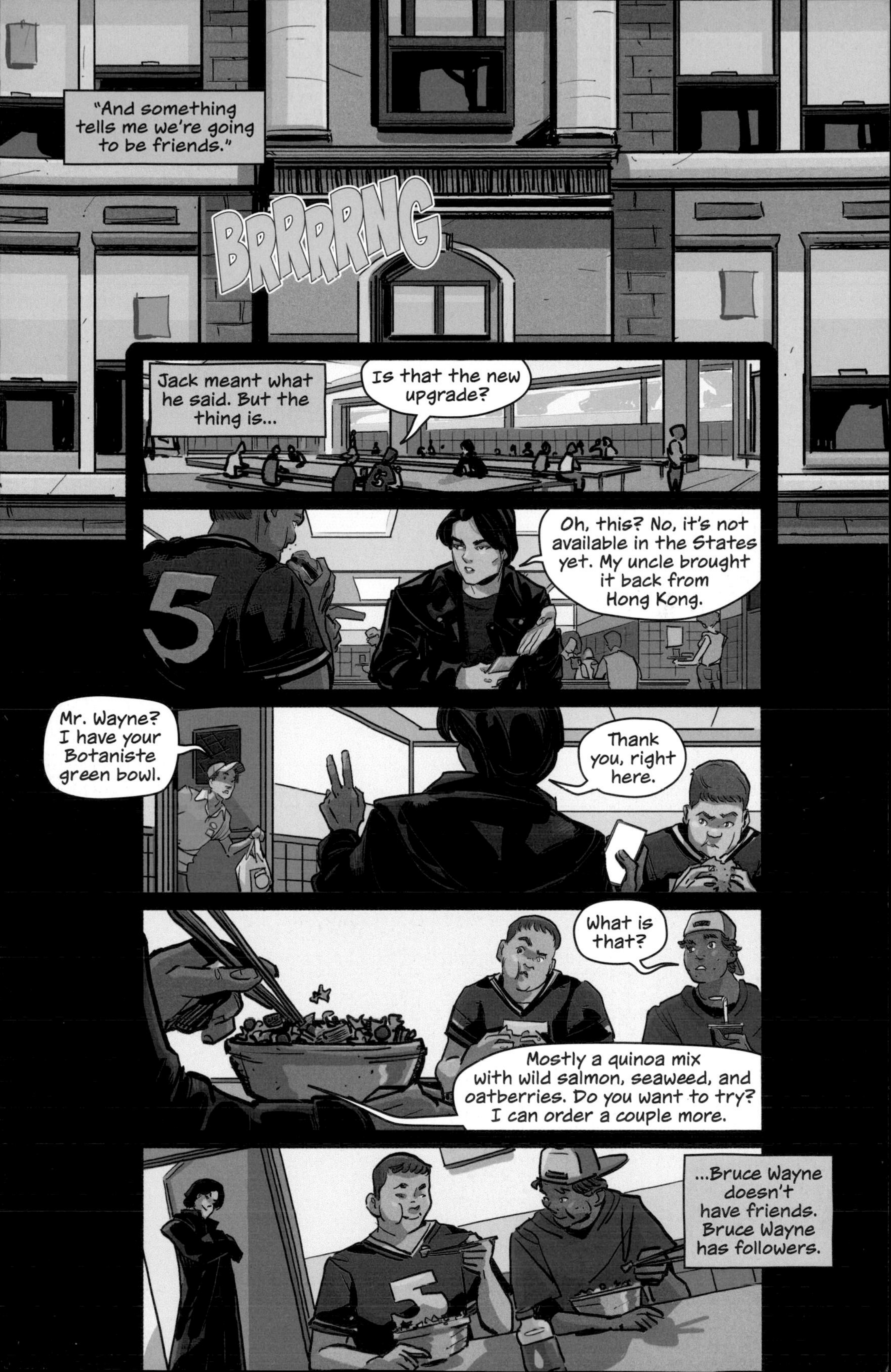
"And something tells me we're going to be friends."
BRRRRNG
Jack meant what he said. But the thing is...
Is that the new upgrade?
Oh, this? No, it's not available in the States yet. My uncle brought it back from Hong Kong.
Mr. Wayne? I have your Botaniste green bowl.
Thank you, right here.
What is that?
Mostly a quinoa mix with wild salmon, seaweed, and oatberries. Do you want to try? I can order a couple more.
...Bruce Wayne doesn't have friends. Bruce Wayne has followers.

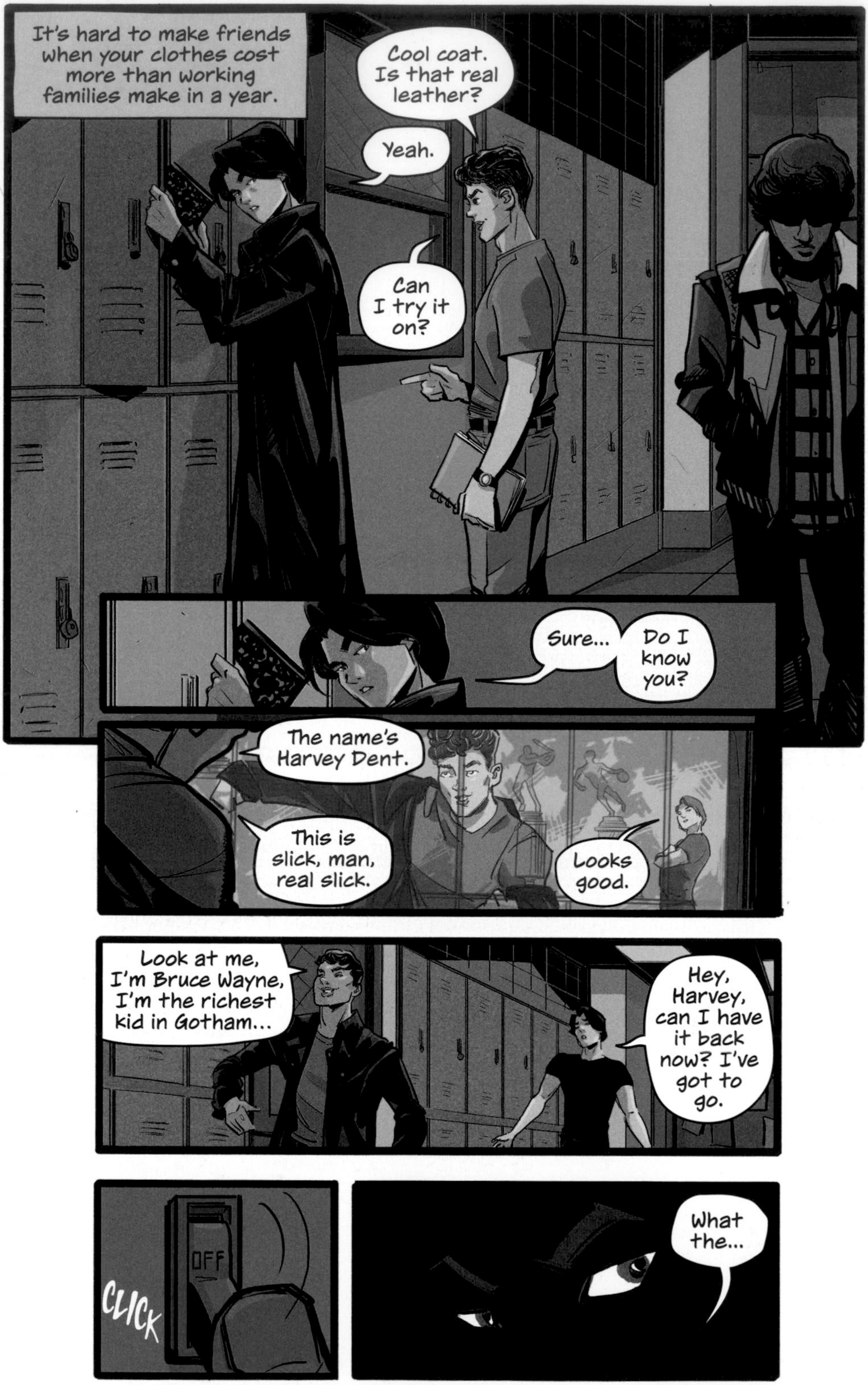
It's hard to make friends when your clothes cost more than working families make in a year.
Cool coat. Is that real leather?
Yeah.
Can I try it on?
Sure...
Do I know you?
The name's Harvey Dent.
This is slick, man, real slick.
Looks good.
Look at me, I'm Bruce Wayne, I'm the richest kid in Gotham...
Hey, Harvey, can I have it back now? I've got to go.
OFF
CLICK
What the...

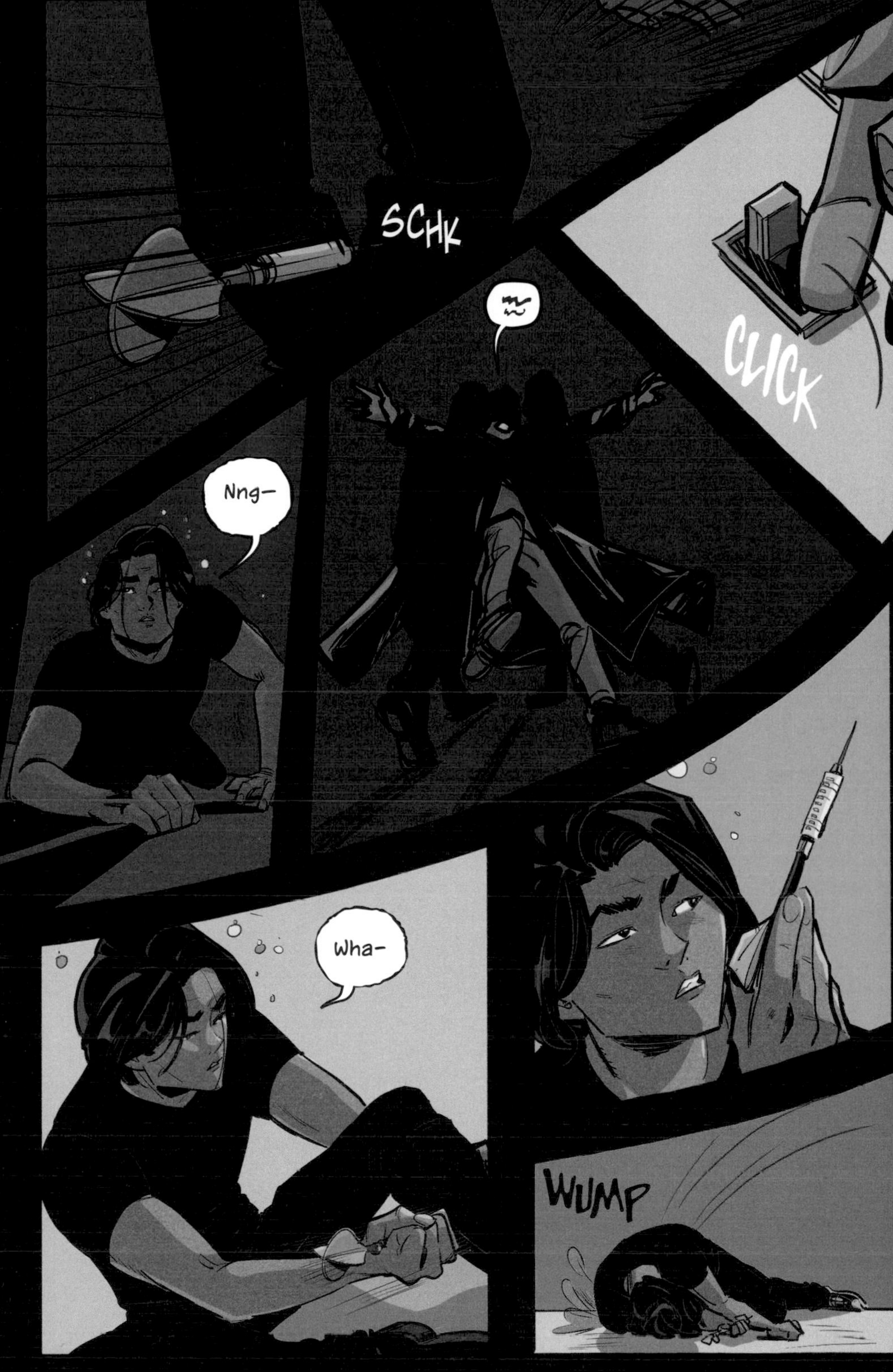
SCHK
CLICK
Nng-
Wha-
WUMP

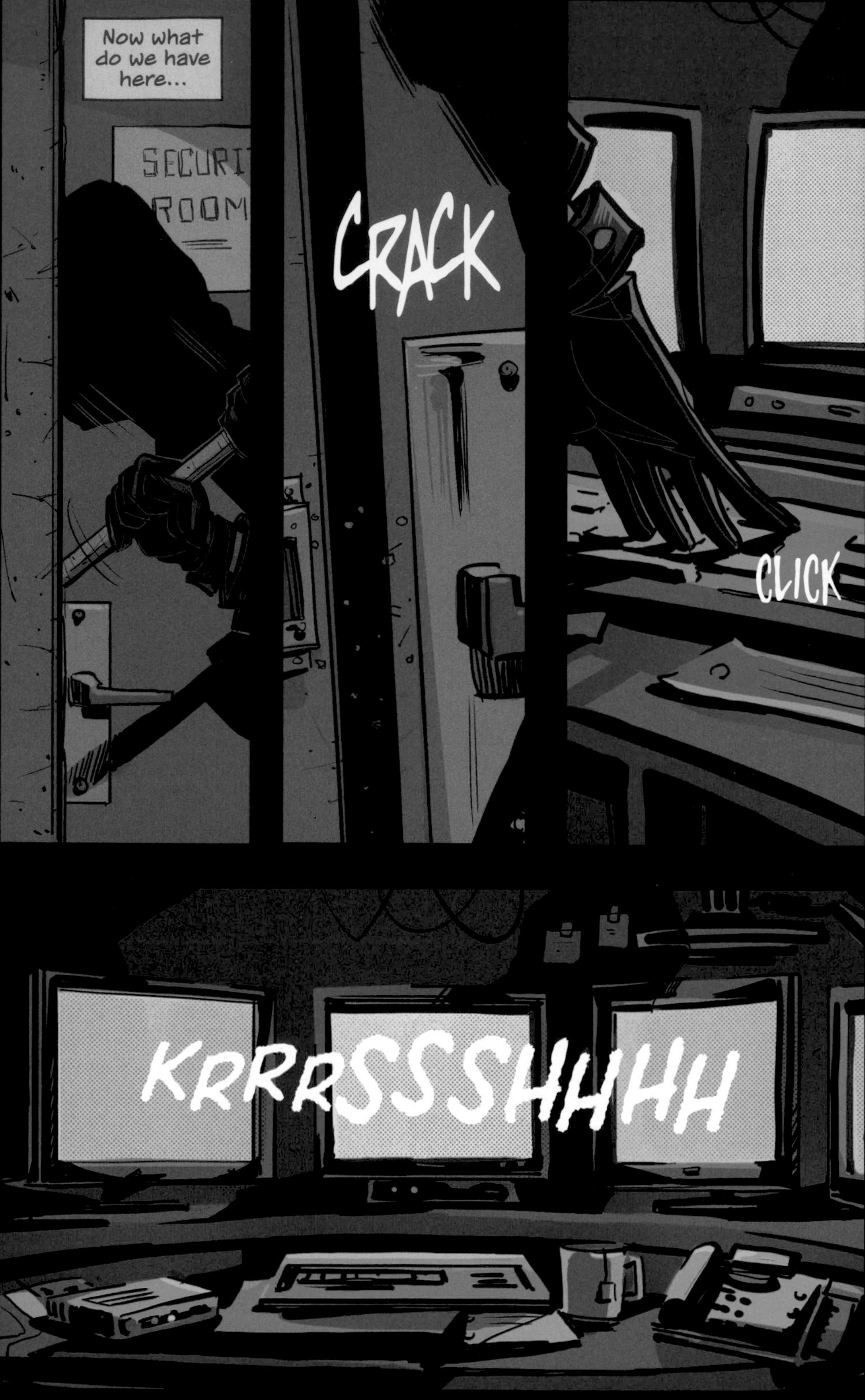
Now what do we have here...
SECURI
ROOM
CRACK
CLICK
KRRRSSSHHHH

PLAY

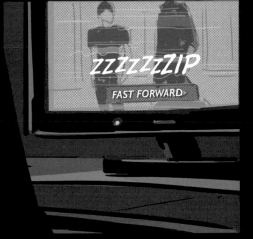

ZZZZZZZIP

FAST FORWARD

PAUSE

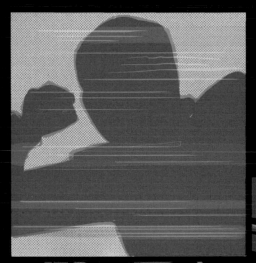

Uh-oh, I think someone forgot to disable the security cameras.

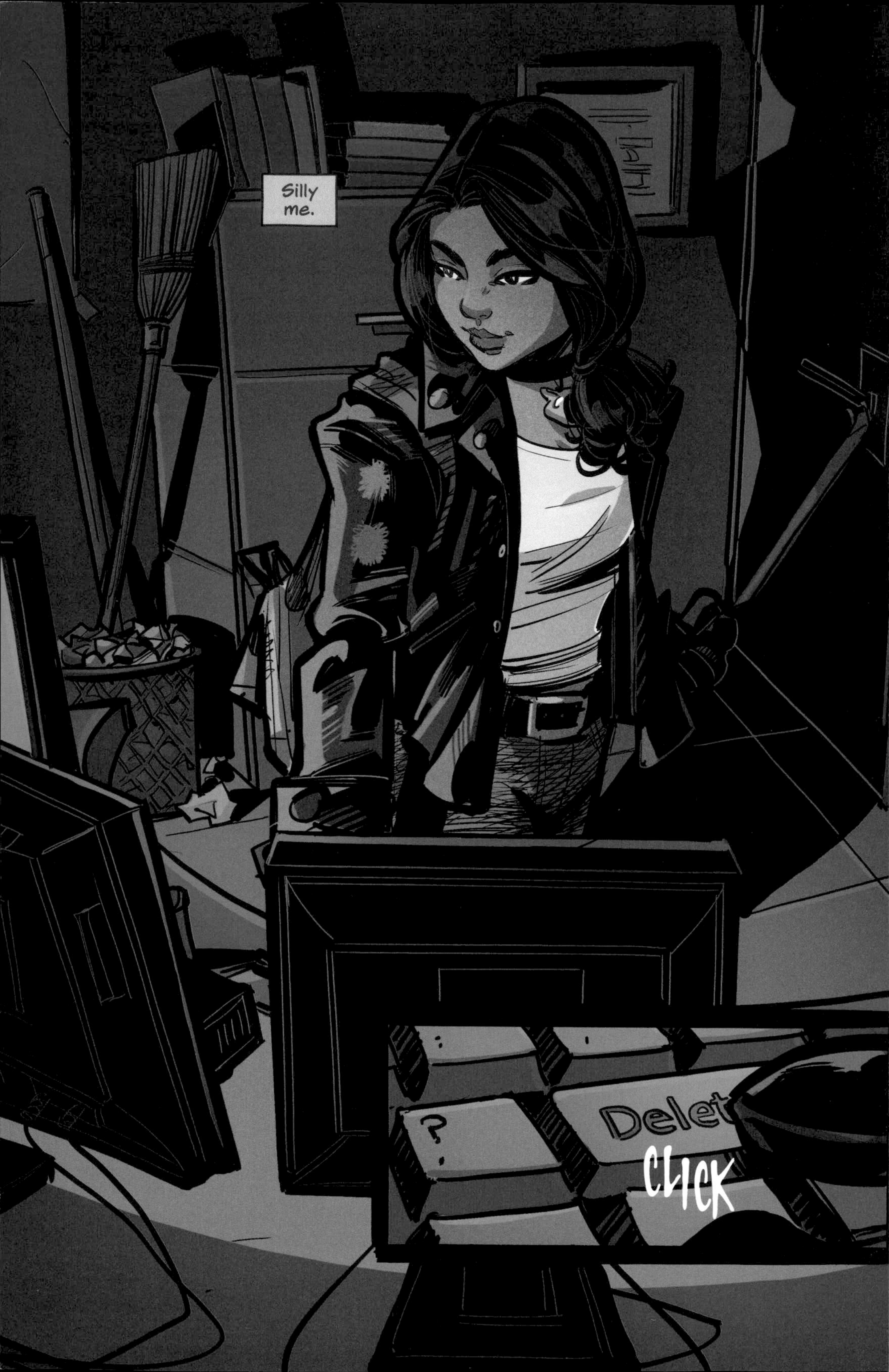
Silly me.
Delet
CLICK

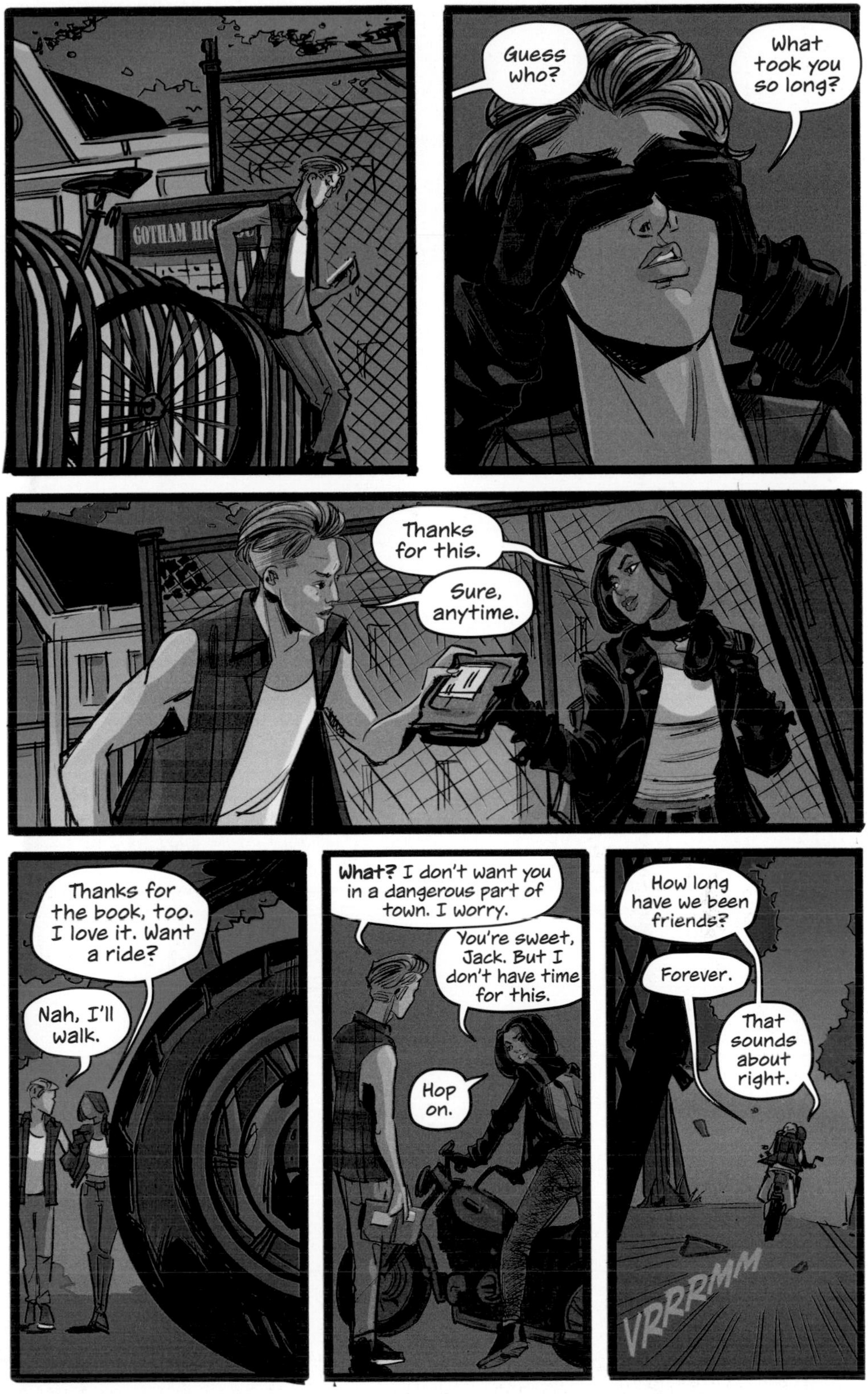
GOTHAM HIG
Guess who?
What took you so long?
Thanks for this.
Sure, anytime.
Thanks for the book, too. I love it. Want a ride?
Nah, I'll walk.
What? I don't want you in a dangerous part of town. I worry.
You're sweet, Jack. But I don't have time for this.
Hop on.
How long have we been friends?
Forever.
That sounds about right.
VRRRMM

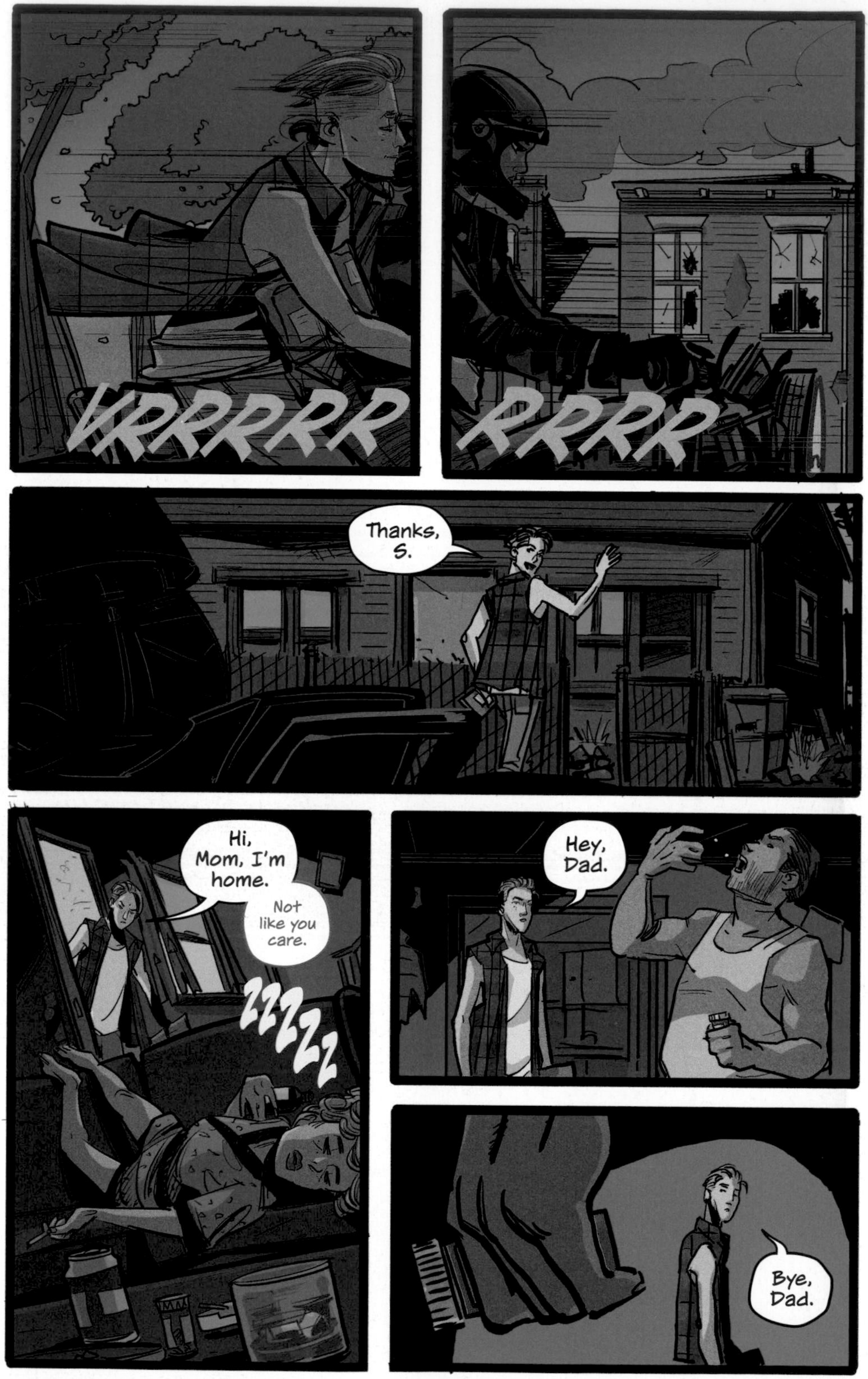
VRRRRR
RRRR
Thanks, S.
Hi, Mom, I'm home.
Not like you care.
ZZZZZ
Hey, Dad.
Bye, Dad.

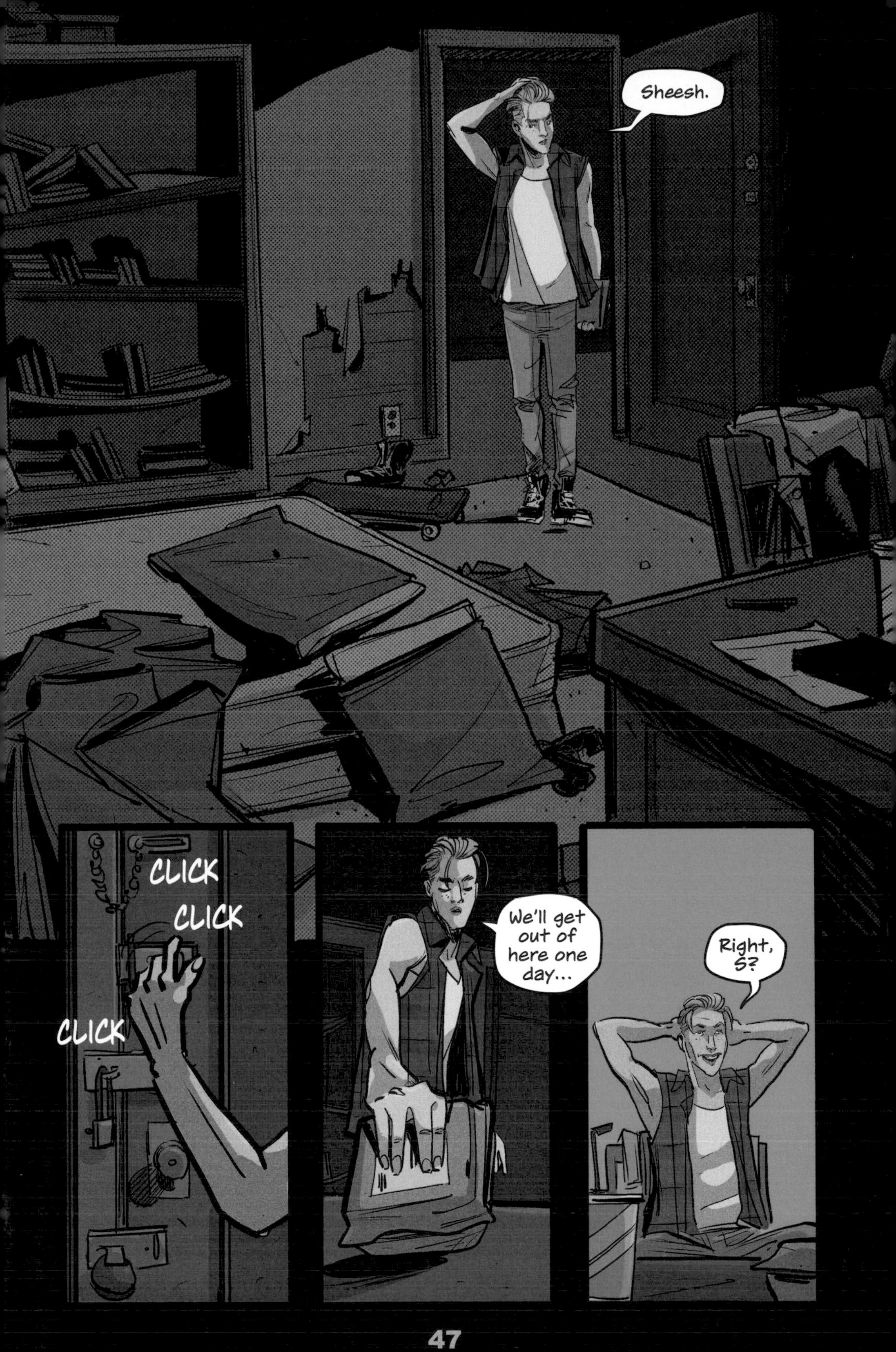
Sheesh.
CLICK
CLICK
CLICK
We'll get out of here one day...
Right, S?

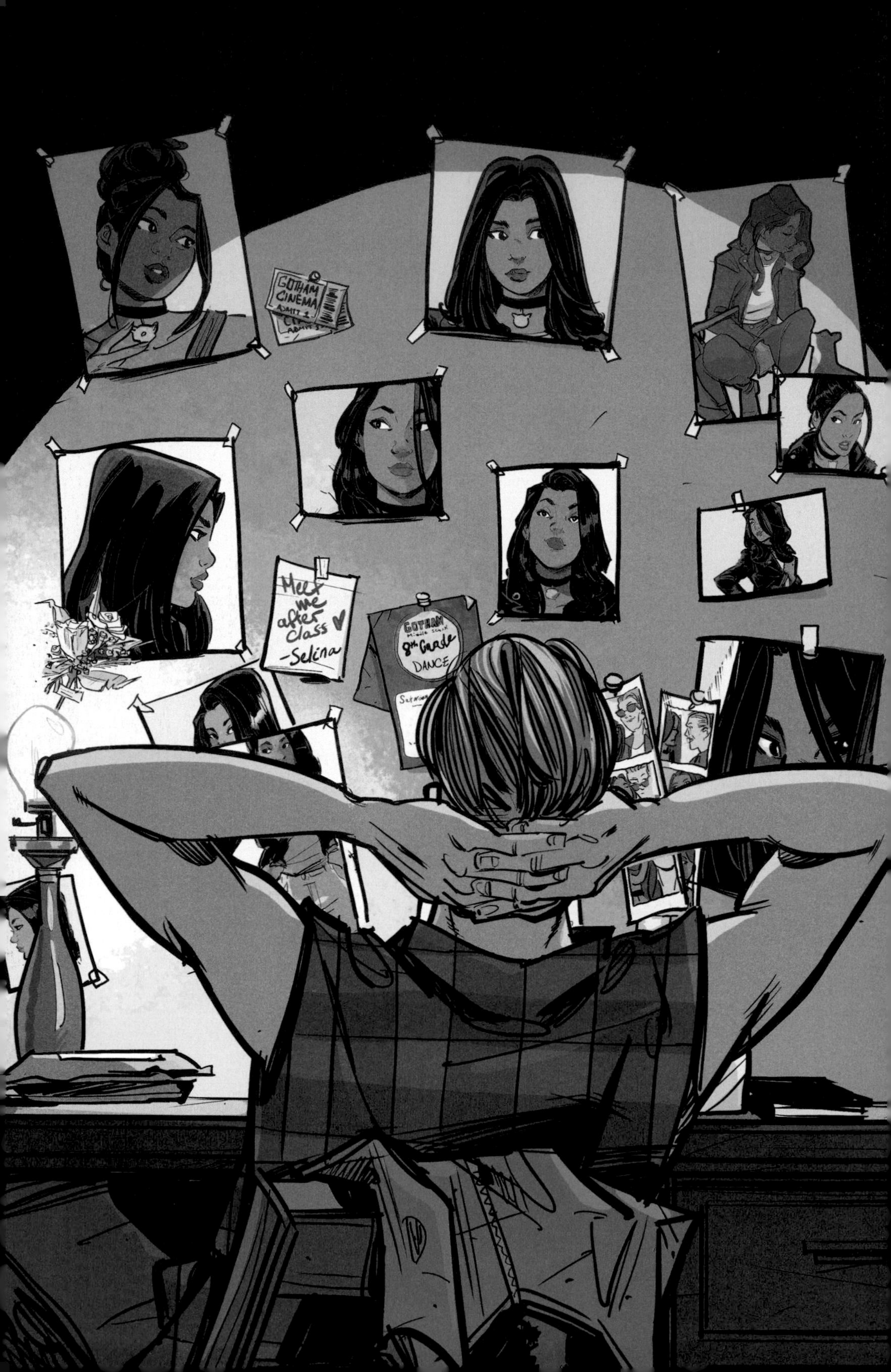
GOTHAM CINEMA
ADMIT 1
Meet me after class ♥ -Selina
GOTHAM Middle School
8th Grade DANCE

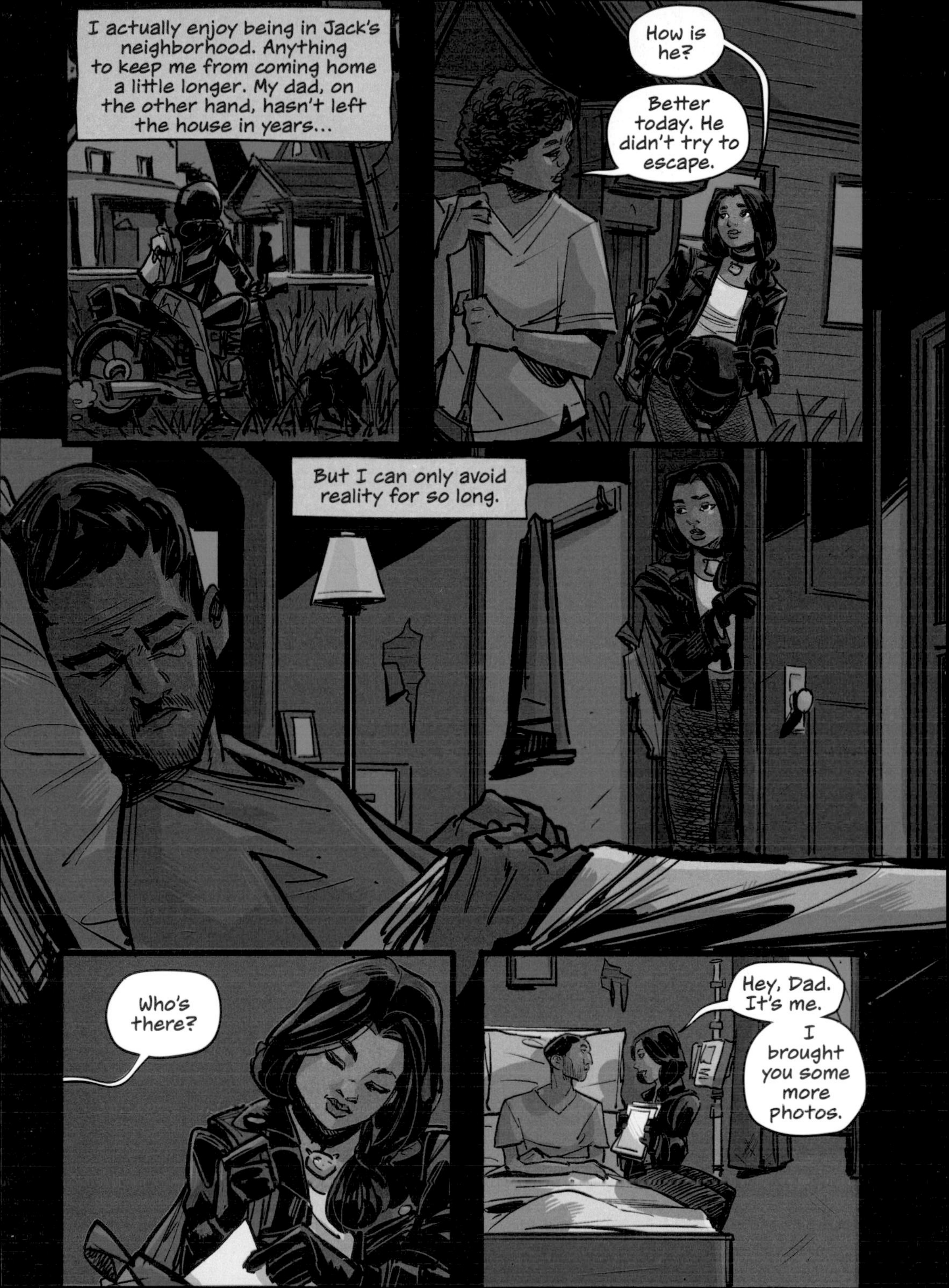
I actually enjoy being in Jack's neighborhood. Anything to keep me from coming home a little longer. My dad, on the other hand, hasn't left the house in years...
How is he?
Better today. He didn't try to escape.
But I can only avoid reality for so long.
Who's there?
Hey, Dad. It's me.
I brought you some more photos.

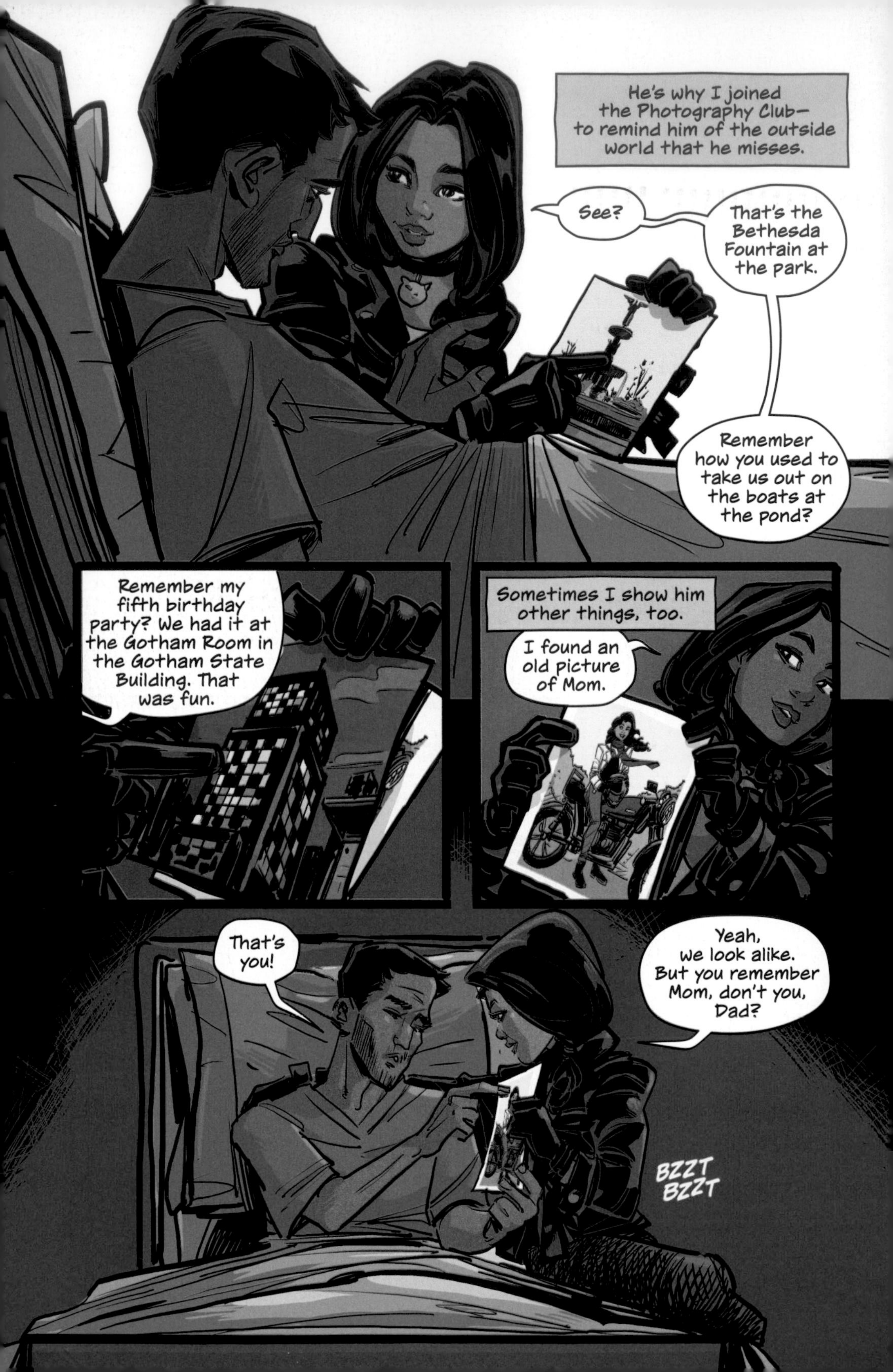
He's why I joined the Photography Club— to remind him of the outside world that he misses.
See?
That's the Bethesda Fountain at the park.
Remember how you used to take us out on the boats at the pond?
Remember my fifth birthday party? We had it at the Gotham Room in the Gotham State Building. That was fun.
Sometimes I show him other things, too.
I found an old picture of Mom.
That's you!
Yeah, we look alike. But you remember Mom, don't you, Dad?
BZZT BZZT

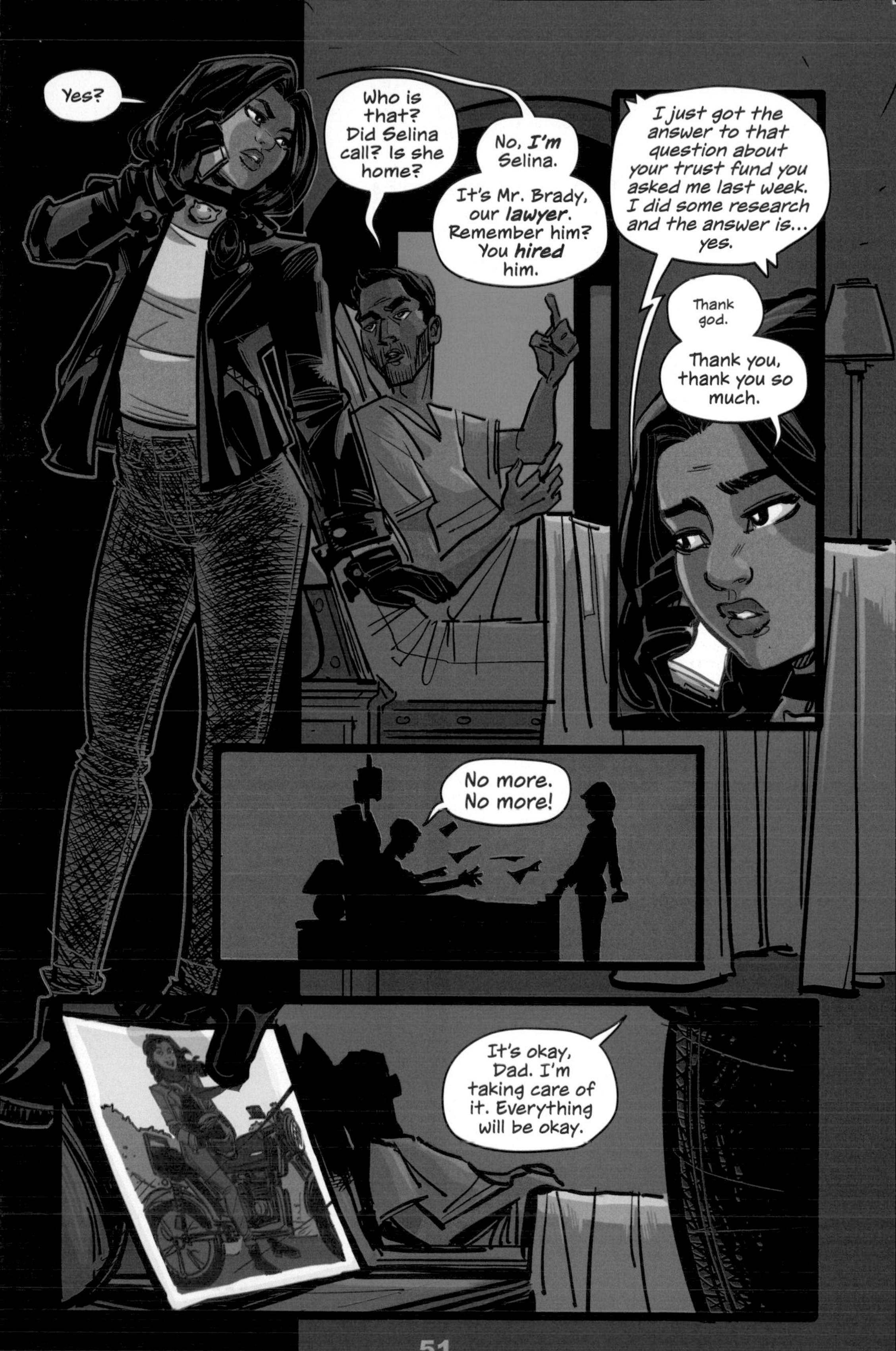
Yes?
Who is that? Did Selina call? Is she home?
No, I'm Selina.
It's Mr. Brady, our lawyer. Remember him? You hired him.
I just got the answer to that question about your trust fund you asked me last week. I did some research and the answer is... yes.
Thank god.
Thank you, thank you so much.
No more. No more!
It's okay, Dad. I'm taking care of it. Everything will be okay.

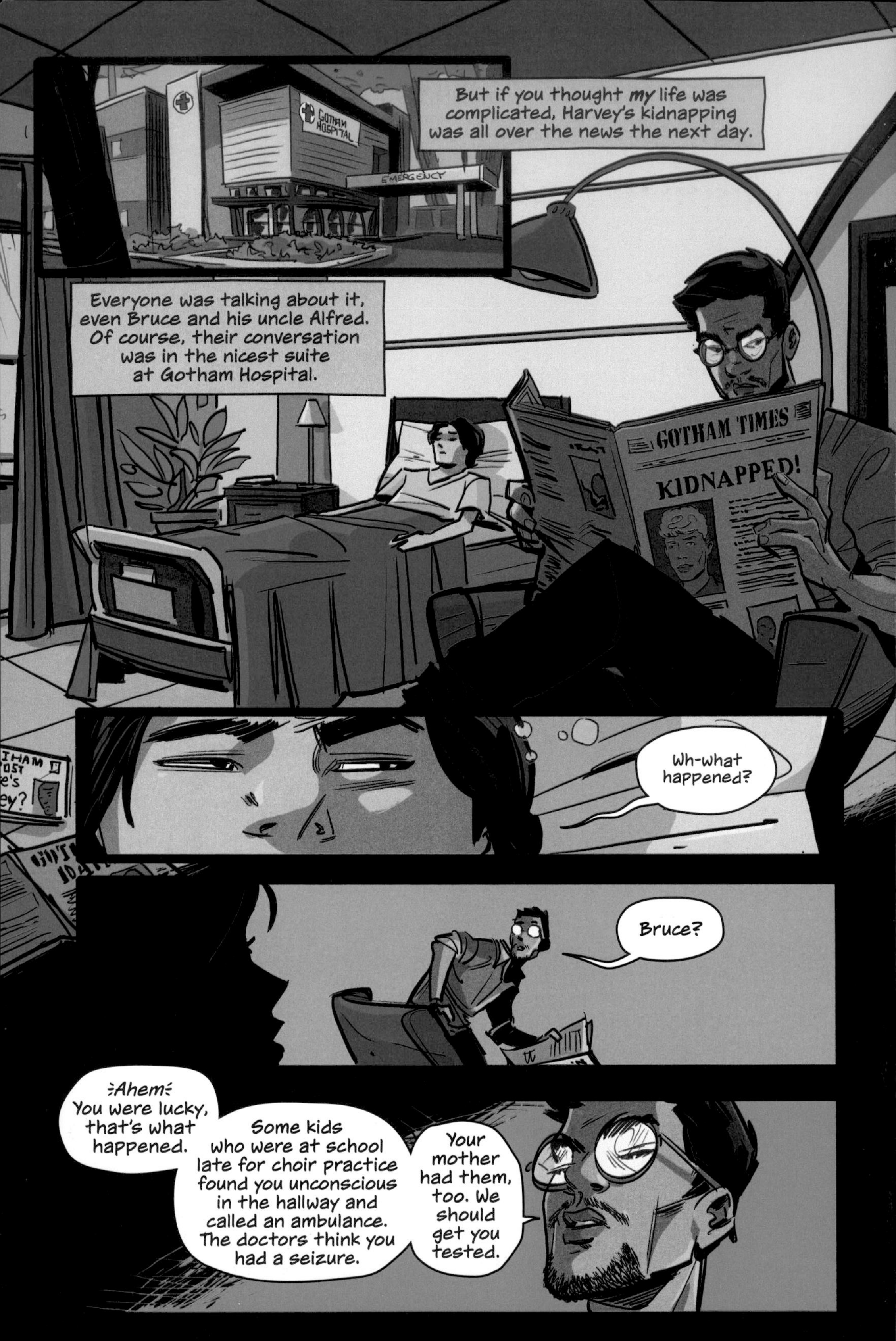
GOTHAM HOSPITAL
EMERGENCY
But if you thought *my* life was complicated, Harvey's kidnapping was all over the news the next day.
Everyone was talking about it, even Bruce and his uncle Alfred. Of course, their conversation was in the nicest suite at Gotham Hospital.
GOTHAM TIMES
KIDNAPPED!
Wh-what happened?
Bruce?
Ahem You were lucky, that's what happened.
Some kids who were at school late for choir practice found you unconscious in the hallway and called an ambulance. The doctors think you had a seizure.
Your mother had them, too. We should get you tested.

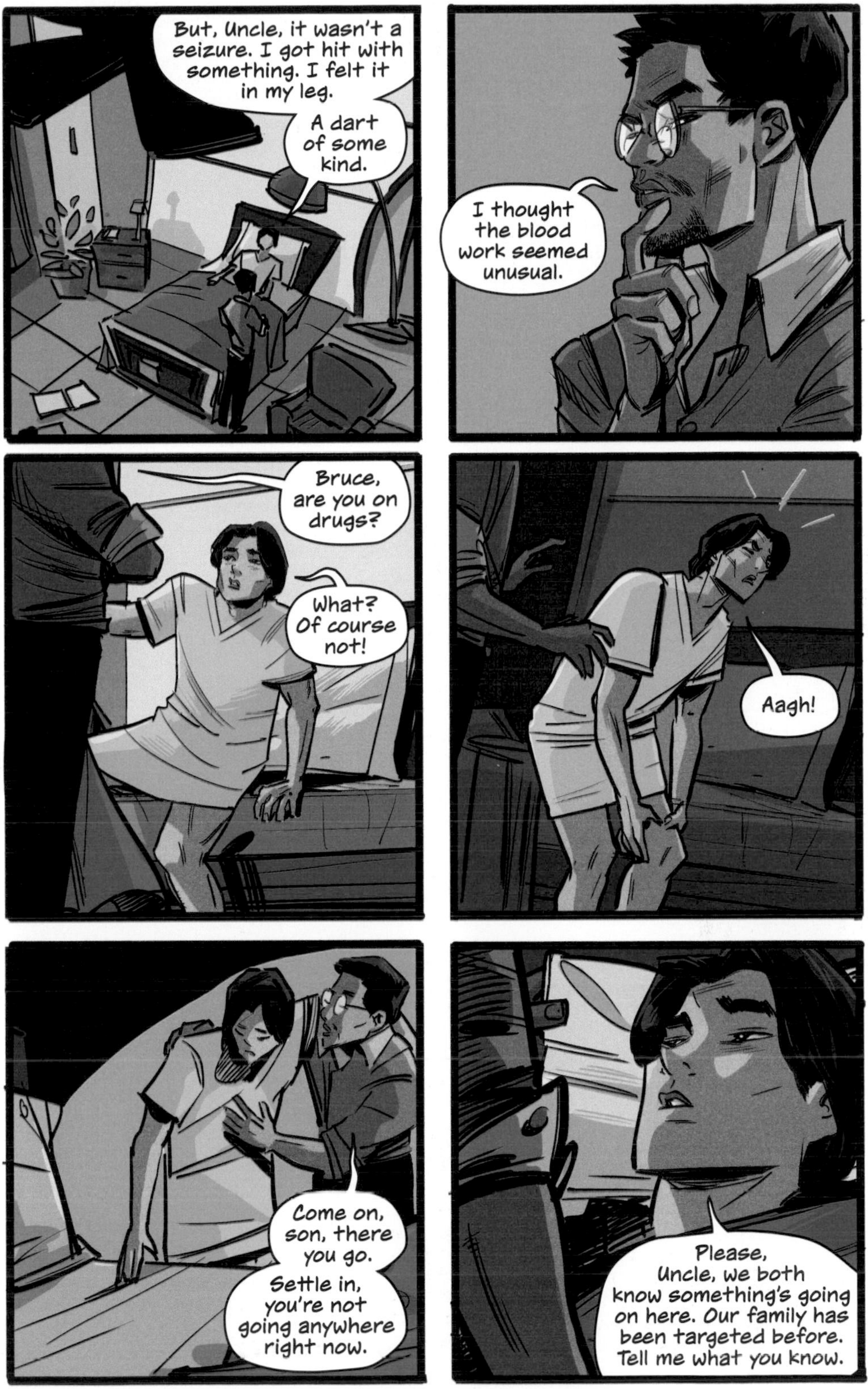
But, Uncle, it wasn't a seizure. I got hit with something. I felt it in my leg.
A dart of some kind.
I thought the blood work seemed unusual.
Bruce, are you on drugs?
What? Of course not!
Aagh!
Come on, son, there you go.
Settle in, you're not going anywhere right now.
Please, Uncle, we both know something's going on here. Our family has been targeted before. Tell me what you know.

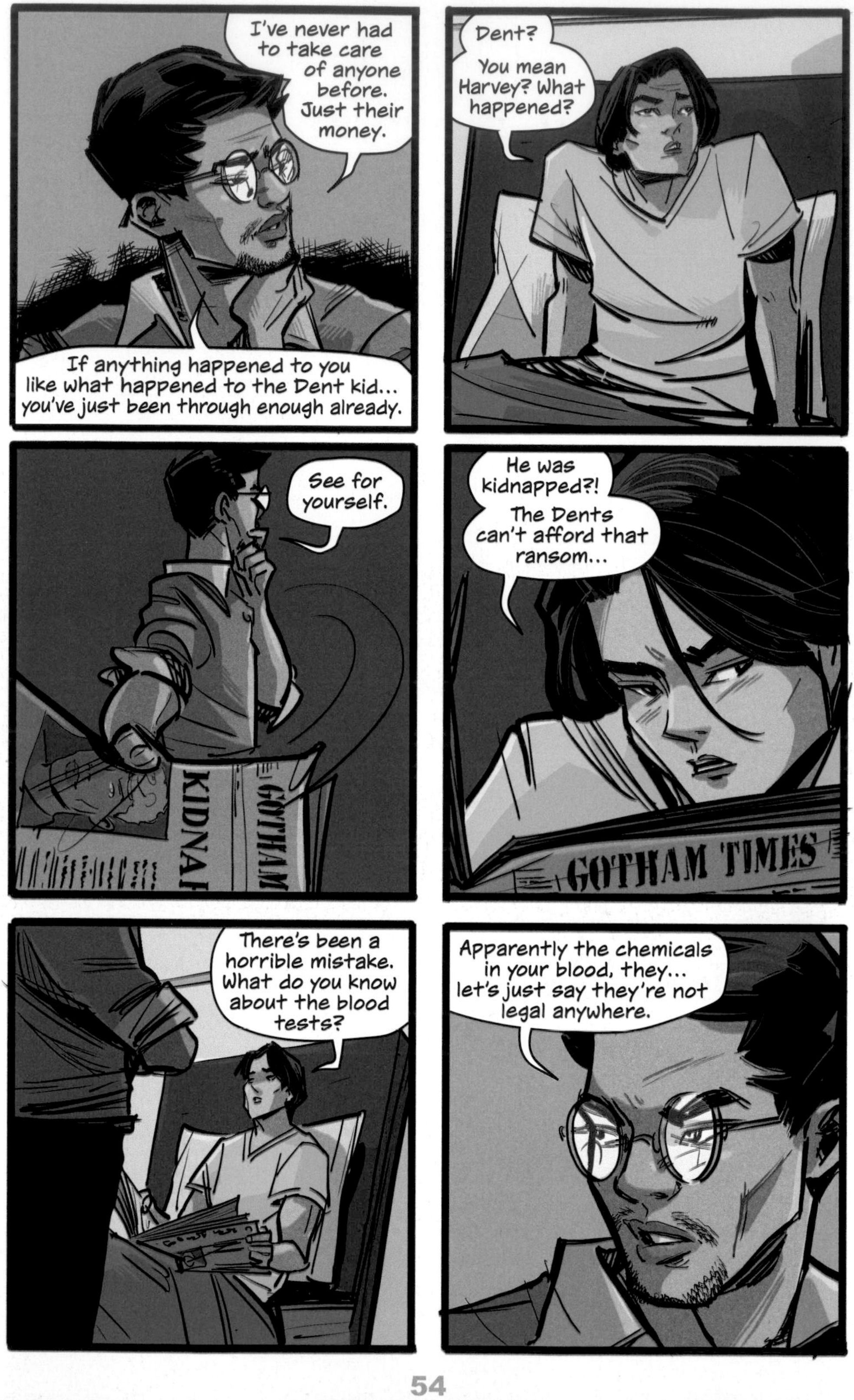

I've never had to take care of anyone before. Just their money.
If anything happened to you like what happened to the Dent kid... you've just been through enough already.
Dent?
You mean Harvey? What happened?
See for yourself.
GOTHAM
KIDNA
He was kidnapped?!
The Dents can't afford that ransom...
GOTHAM TIMES
There's been a horrible mistake. What do you know about the blood tests?
Apparently the chemicals in your blood, they... let's just say they're not legal anywhere.

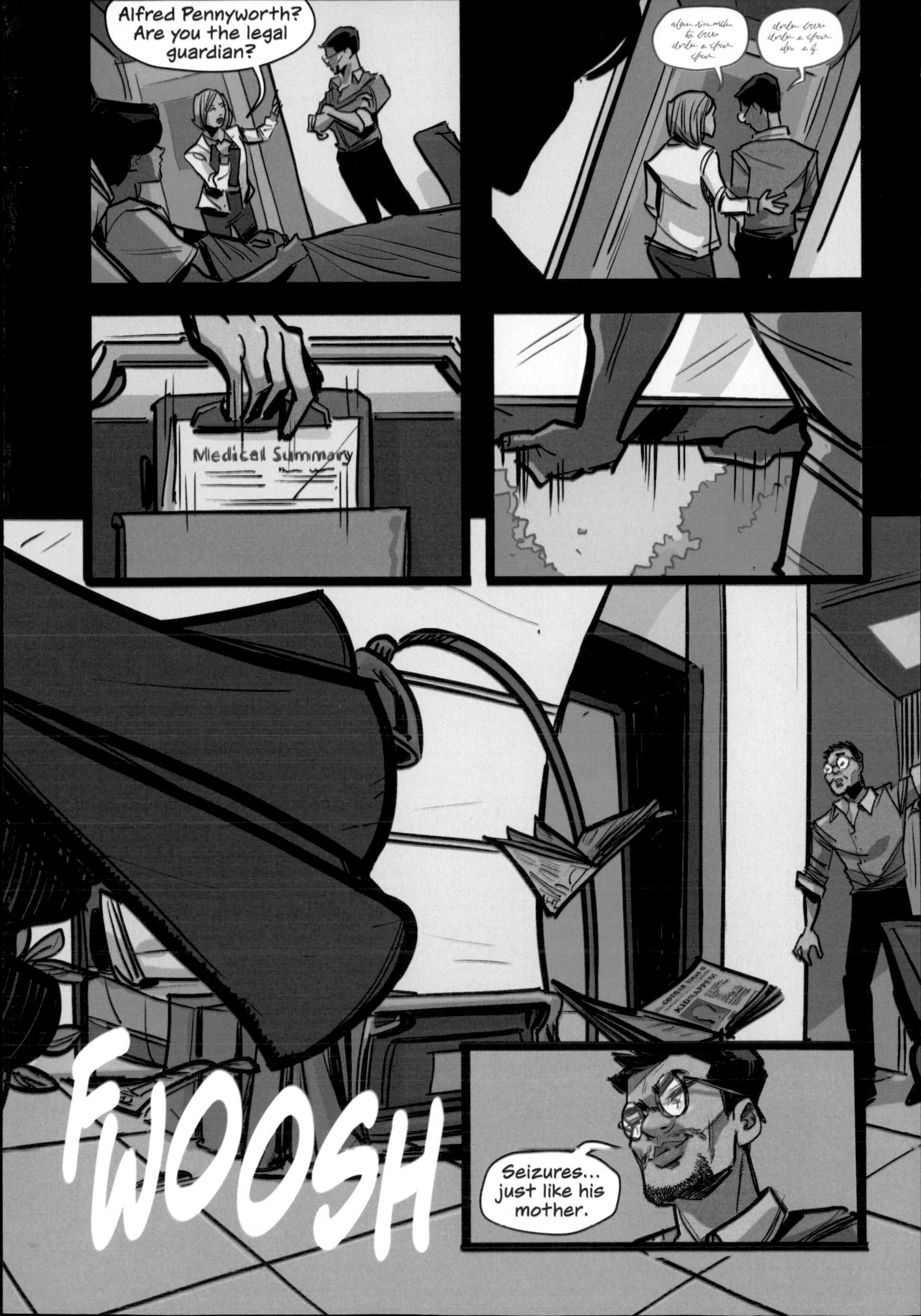
Alfred Pennyworth? Are you the legal guardian?
Medical Summary
KIDNAPPED!
FWOOSH
Seizures... just like his mother.

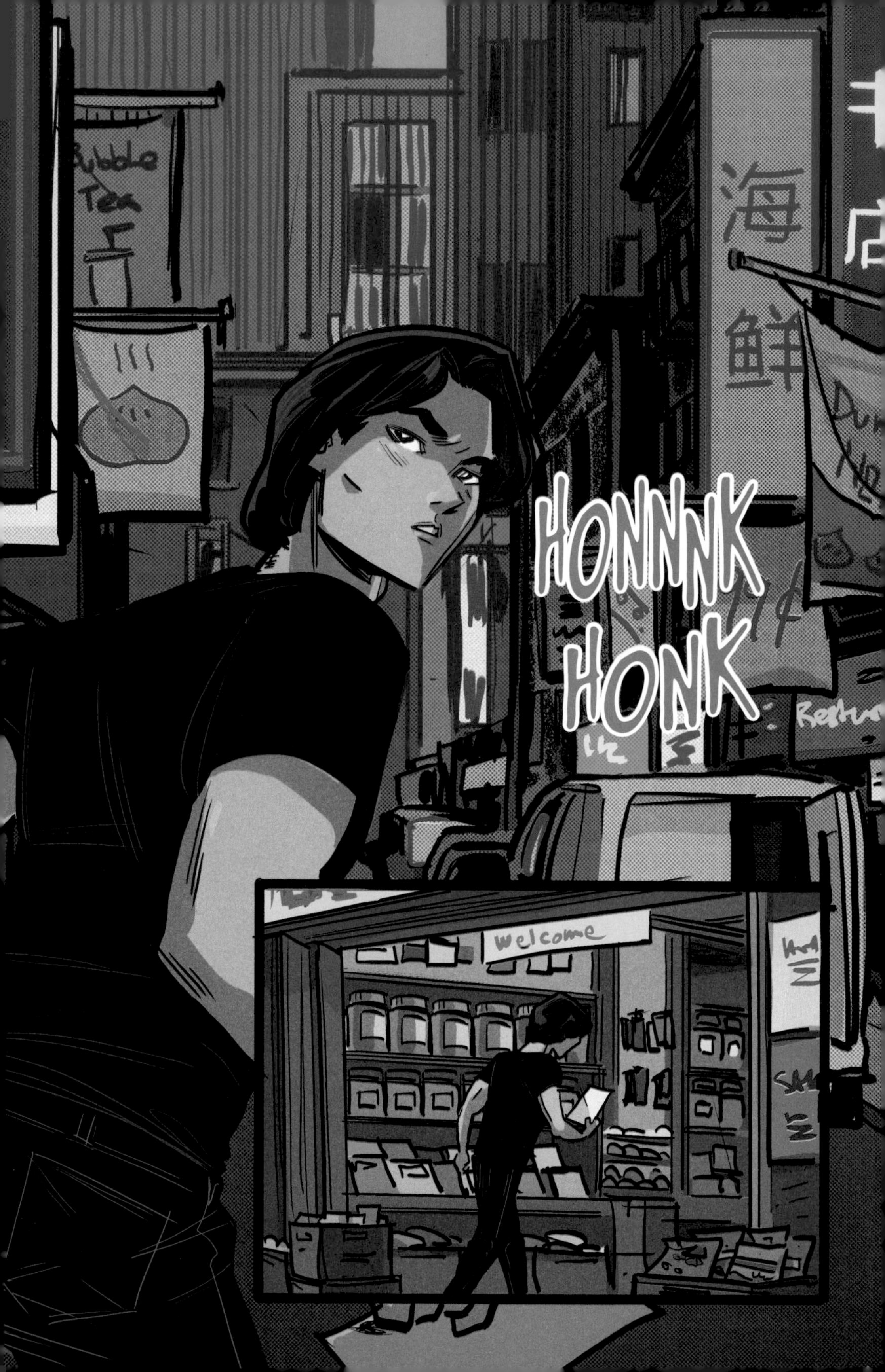
Bubble Tea
海
鲜
店
HONNNK
HONK
welcome

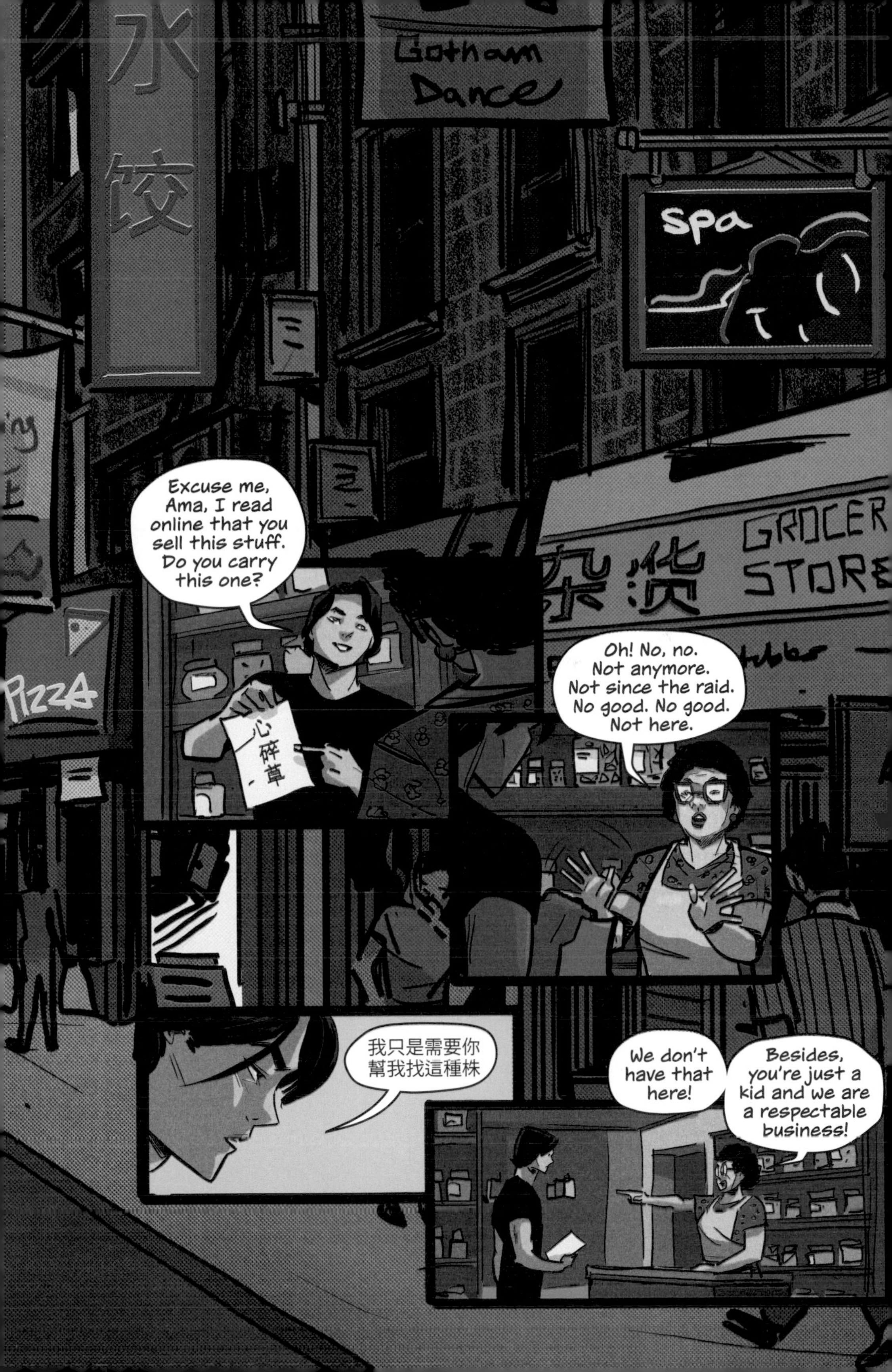

水饺
Gotham Dance
Spa
GROCER
STORE
杂货
PIZZA
Excuse me, Ama, I read online that you sell this stuff. Do you carry this one?
心碎草
Oh! No, no. Not anymore. Not since the raid. No good. No good. Not here.
我只是需要你幫我找這種株
We don't have that here!
Besides, you're just a kid and we are a respectable business!

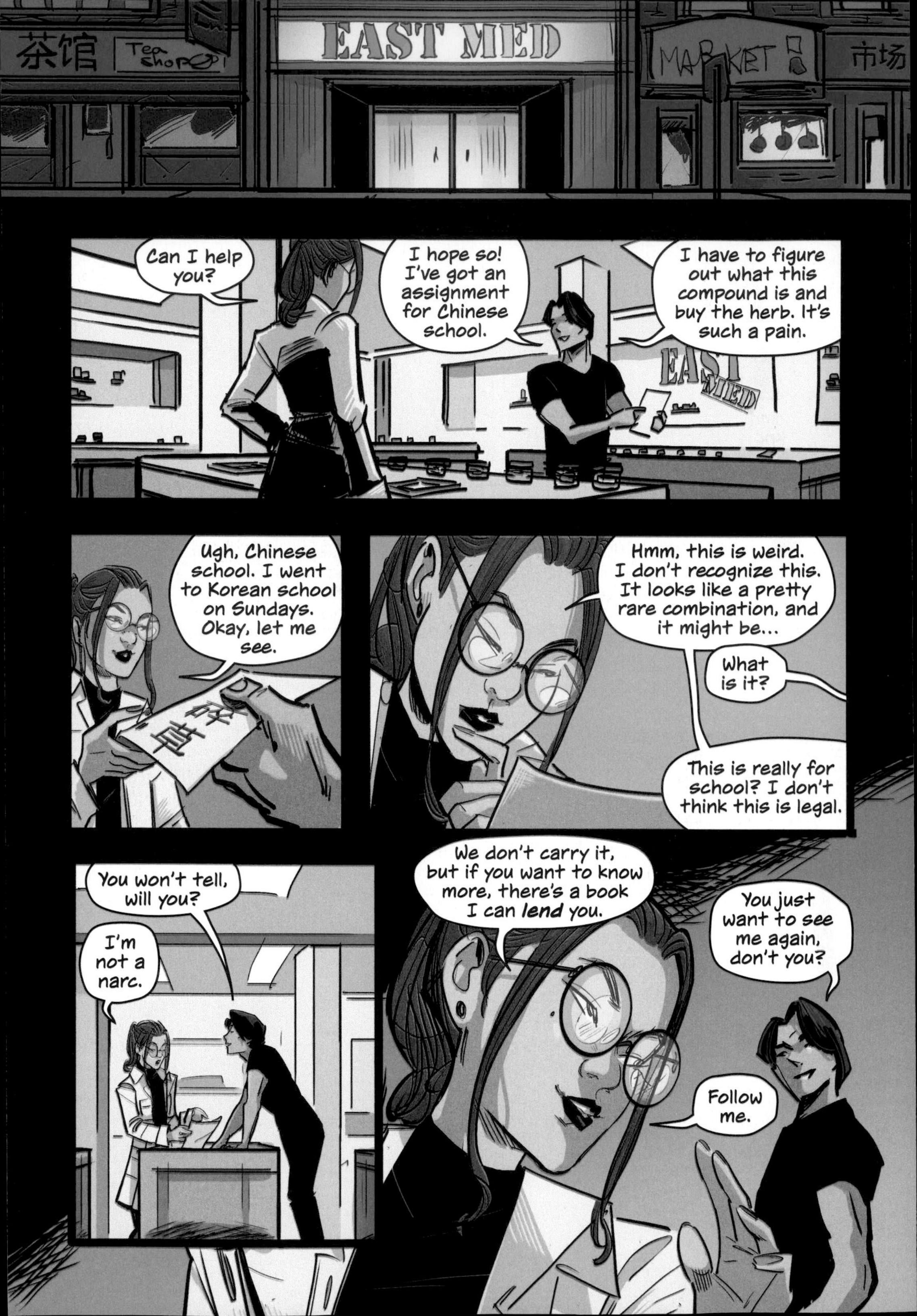
茶馆
Tea shop
EAST MED
MARKET
市场
Can I help you?
I hope so! I've got an assignment for Chinese school.
I have to figure out what this compound is and buy the herb. It's such a pain.
EAST MED
Ugh, Chinese school. I went to Korean school on Sundays. Okay, let me see.
Hmm, this is weird. I don't recognize this. It looks like a pretty rare combination, and it might be...
What is it?
This is really for school? I don't think this is legal.
You won't tell, will you?
I'm not a narc.
We don't carry it, but if you want to know more, there's a book I can *lend* you.
You just want to see me again, don't you?
Follow me.

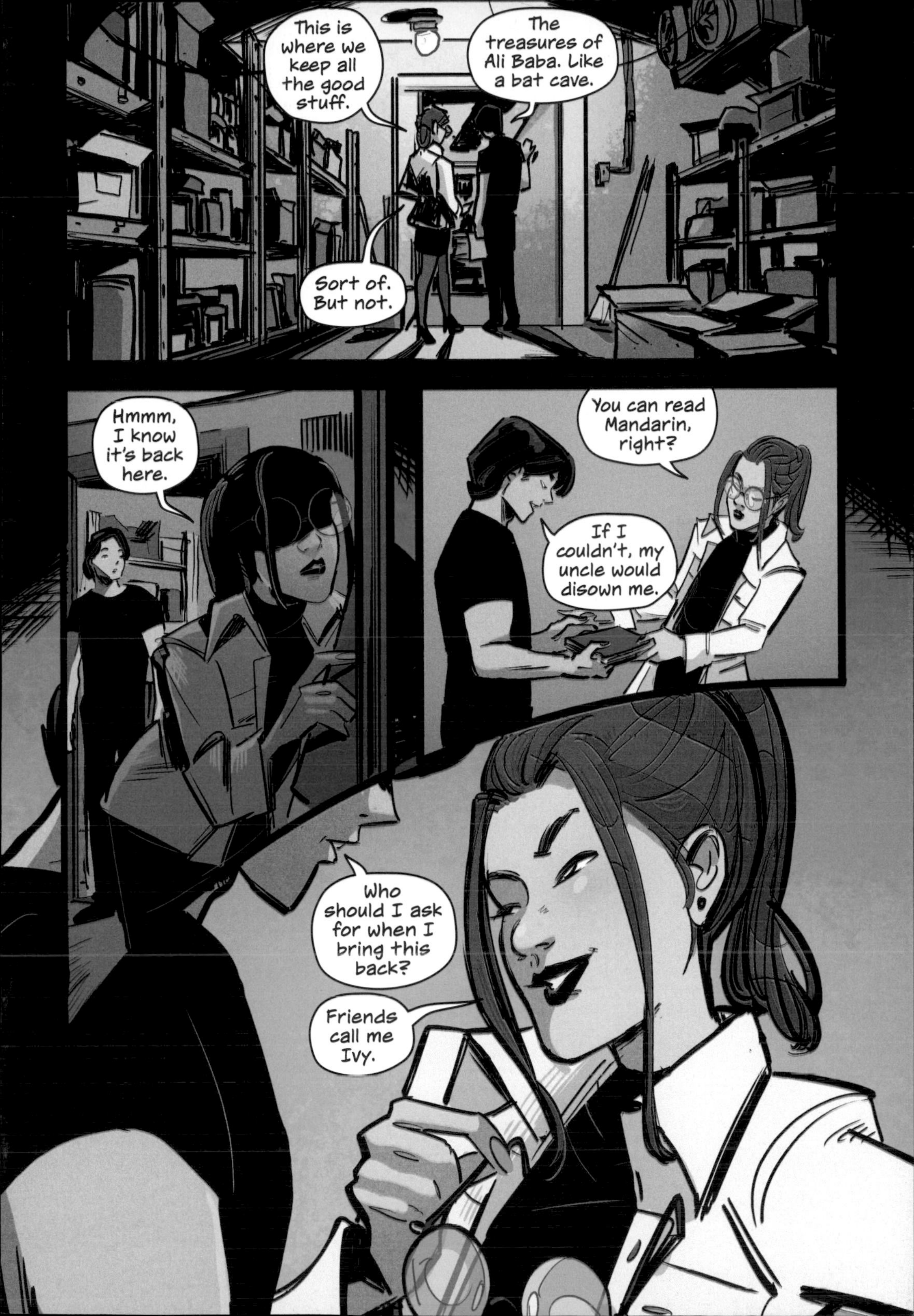
This is where we keep all the good stuff.
The treasures of Ali Baba. Like a bat cave.
Sort of. But not.
Hmmm, I know it's back here.
You can read Mandarin, right?
If I couldn't, my uncle would disown me.
Who should I ask for when I bring this back?
Friends call me Ivy.

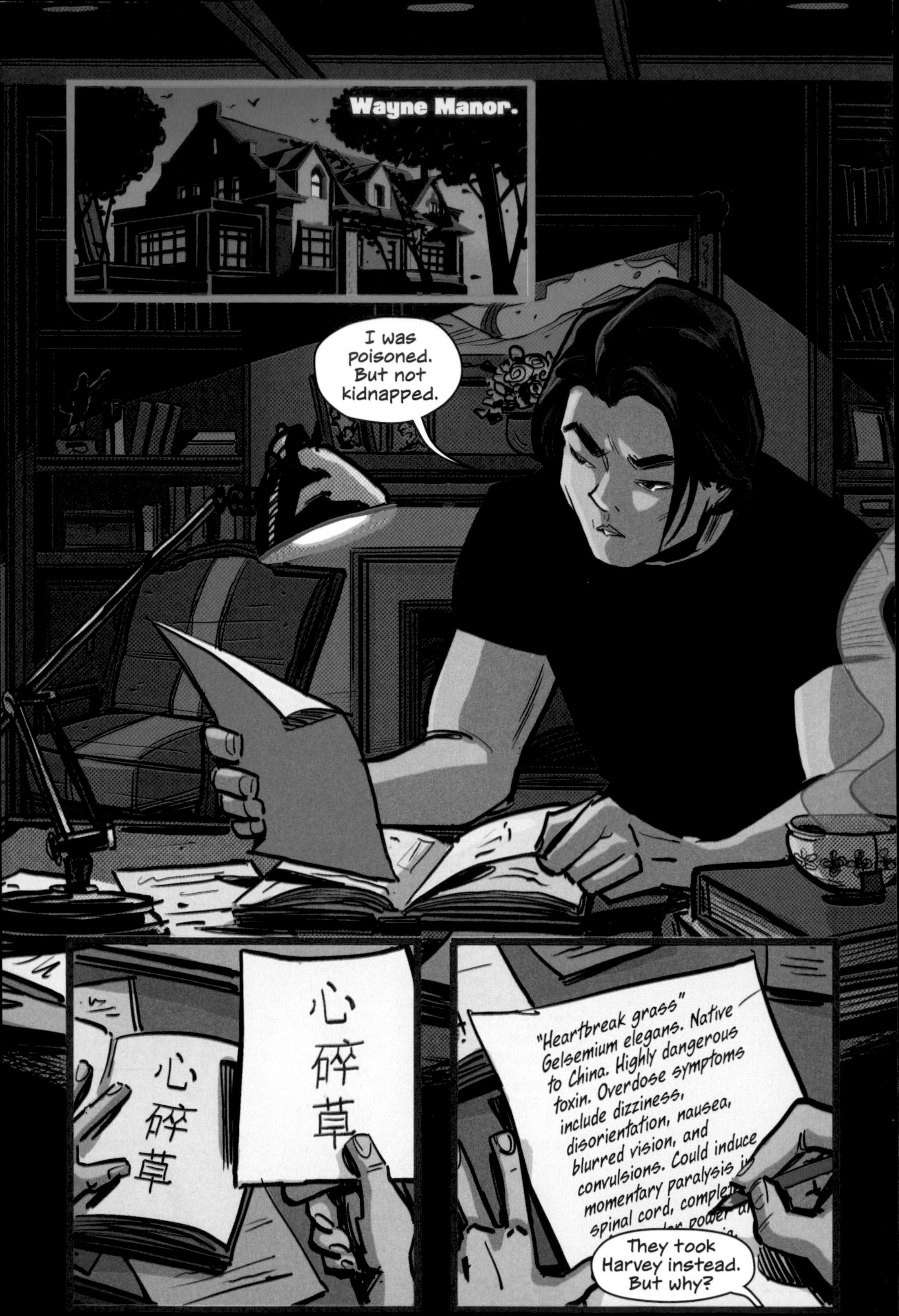
Wayne Manor.
I was poisoned. But not kidnapped.
心碎草
心碎草
"Heartbreak grass"
Gelsemium elegans. Native
to China. Highly dangerous
toxin. Overdose symptoms
include dizziness,
disorientation, nausea,
blurred vision, and
convulsions. Could induce
momentary paralysis
spinal cord, complete
They took Harvey instead. But why?

PART TWO

The Party
of the Century

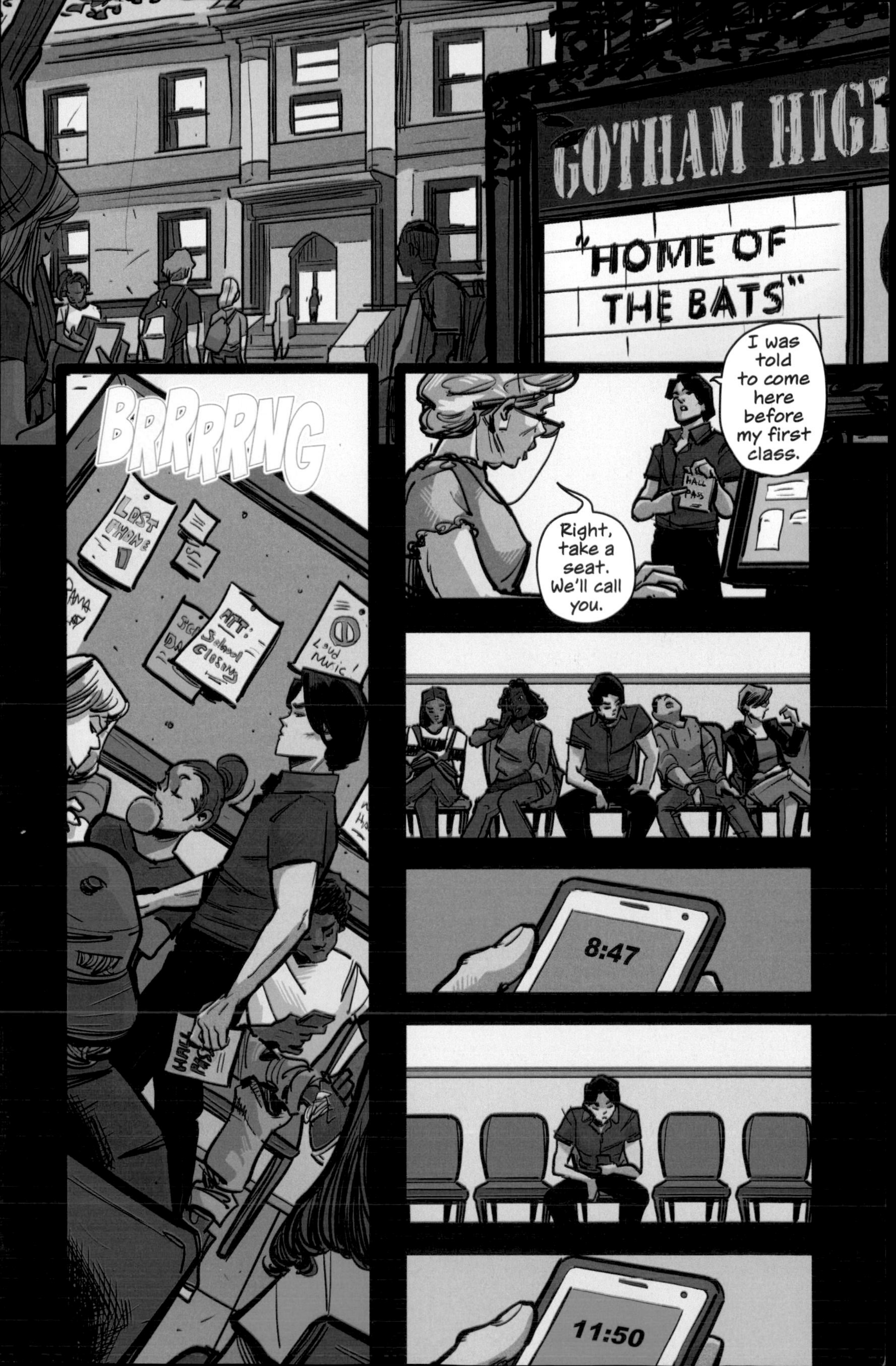
GOTHAM HIG
"HOME OF THE BATS"
BRRRRRNG
LOST PHONE
ATT: School Closing
Loud Music
I was told to come here before my first class.
HALL PASS
Right, take a seat. We'll call you.
8:47
11:50

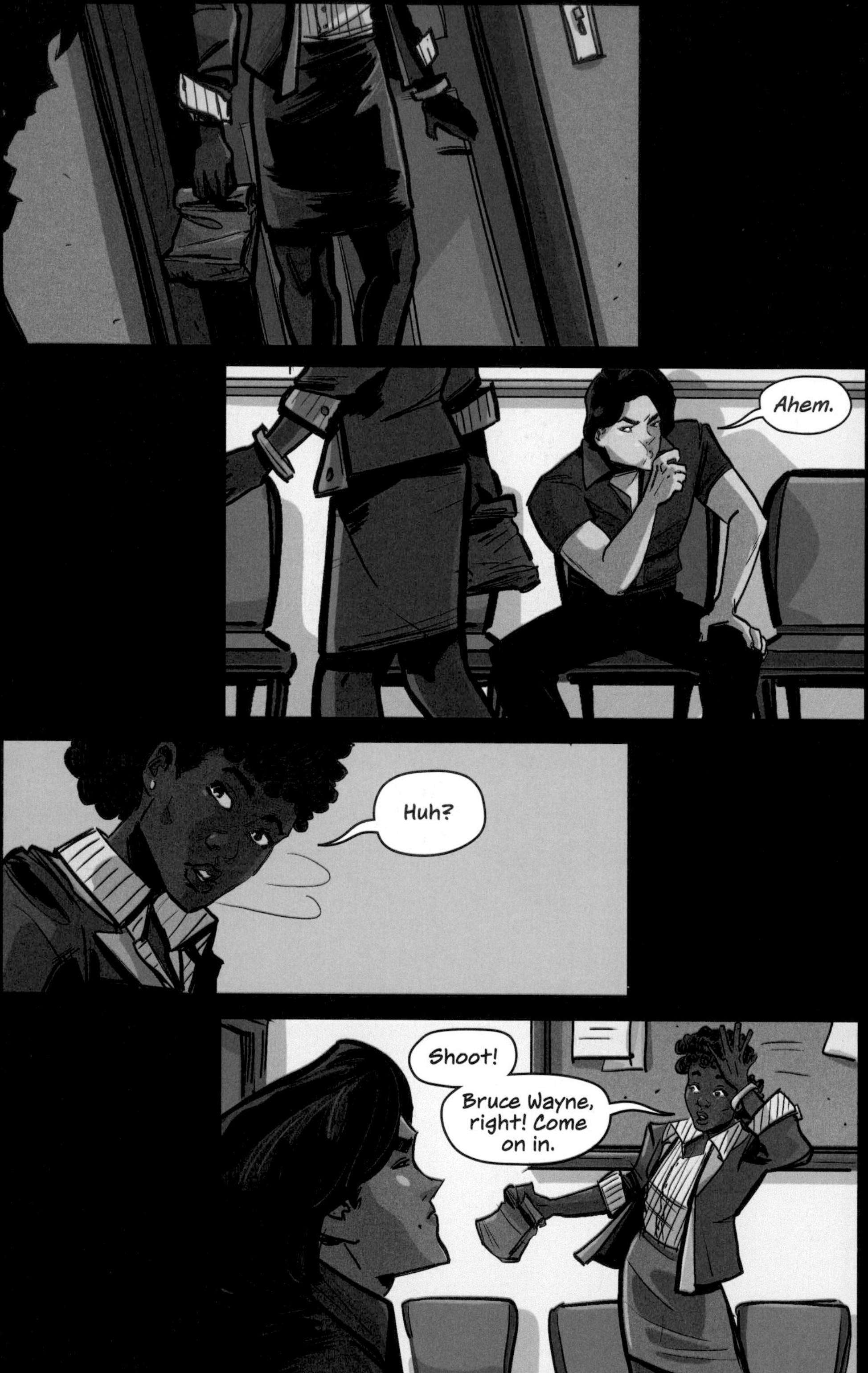
Ahem.
Huh?
Shoot!
Bruce Wayne, right! Come on in.

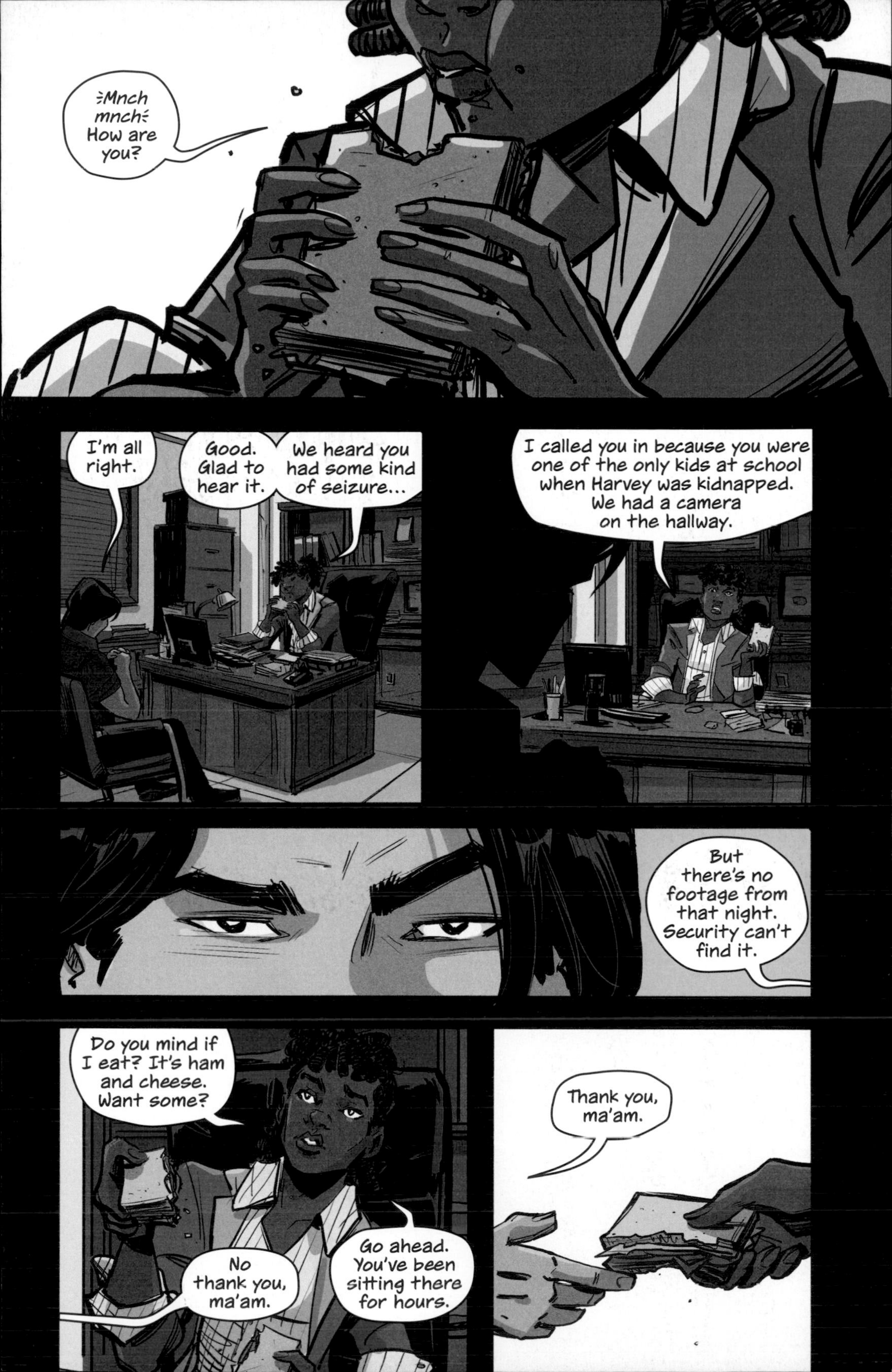

:Mnch mnch: How are you?
I'm all right.
Good. Glad to hear it.
We heard you had some kind of seizure...
I called you in because you were one of the only kids at school when Harvey was kidnapped. We had a camera on the hallway.
But there's no footage from that night. Security can't find it.
Do you mind if I eat? It's ham and cheese. Want some?
No thank you, ma'am.
Go ahead. You've been sitting there for hours.
Thank you, ma'am.

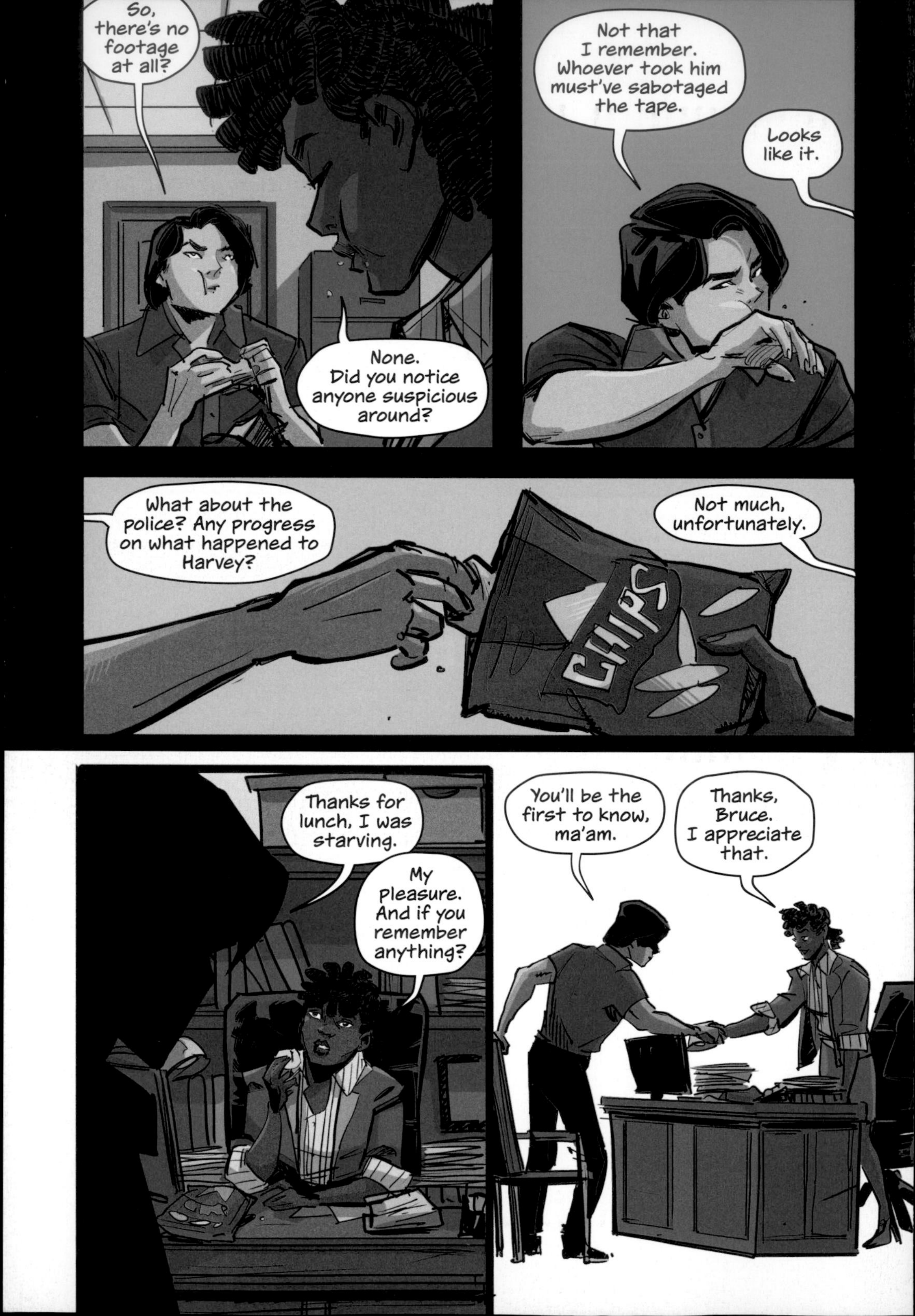
So, there's no footage at all?
None. Did you notice anyone suspicious around?
Not that I remember. Whoever took him must've sabotaged the tape.
Looks like it.
What about the police? Any progress on what happened to Harvey?
Not much, unfortunately.
CHIPS
Thanks for lunch, I was starving.
My pleasure. And if you remember anything?
You'll be the first to know, ma'am.
Thanks, Bruce. I appreciate that.

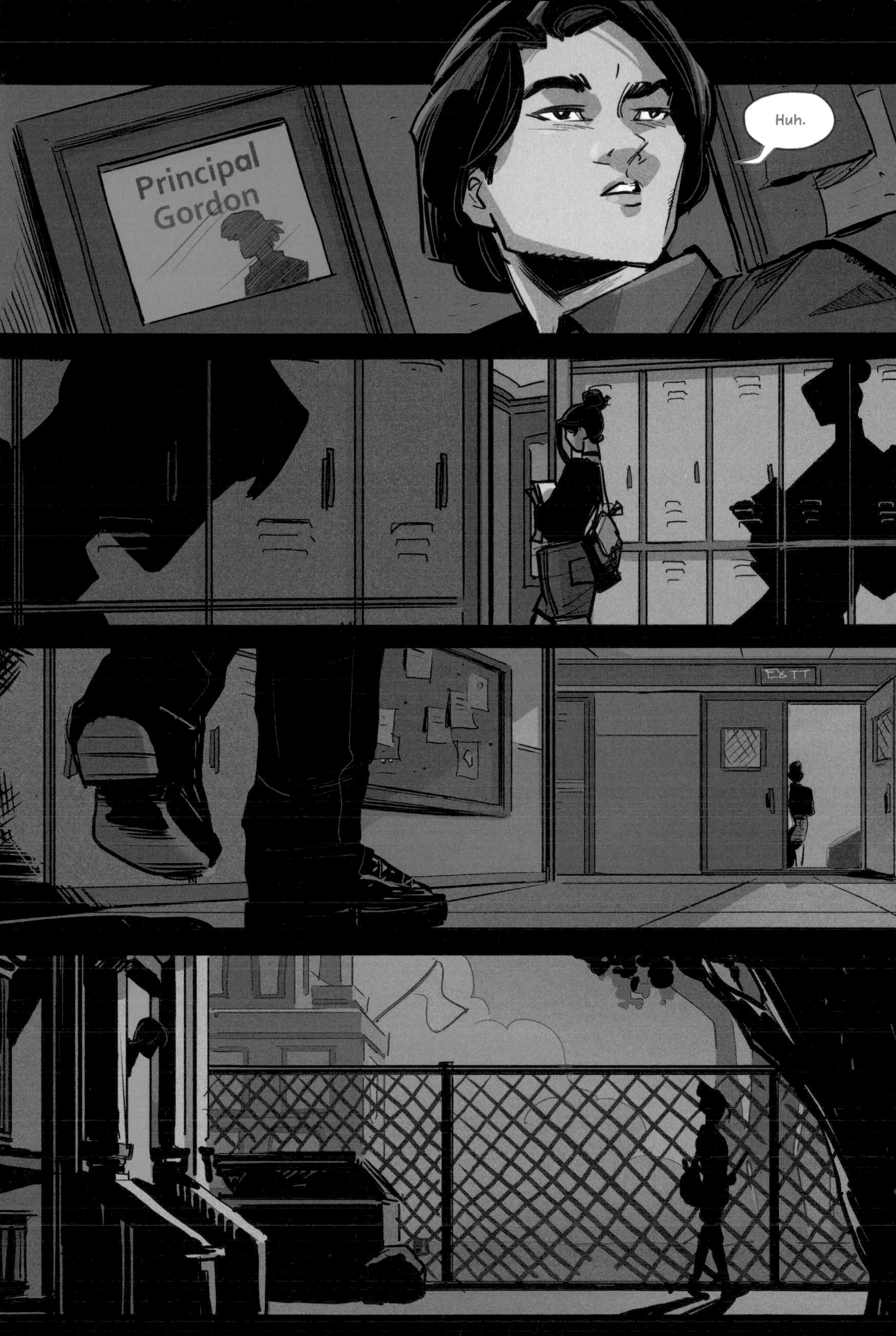
Principal
Gordon
Huh.

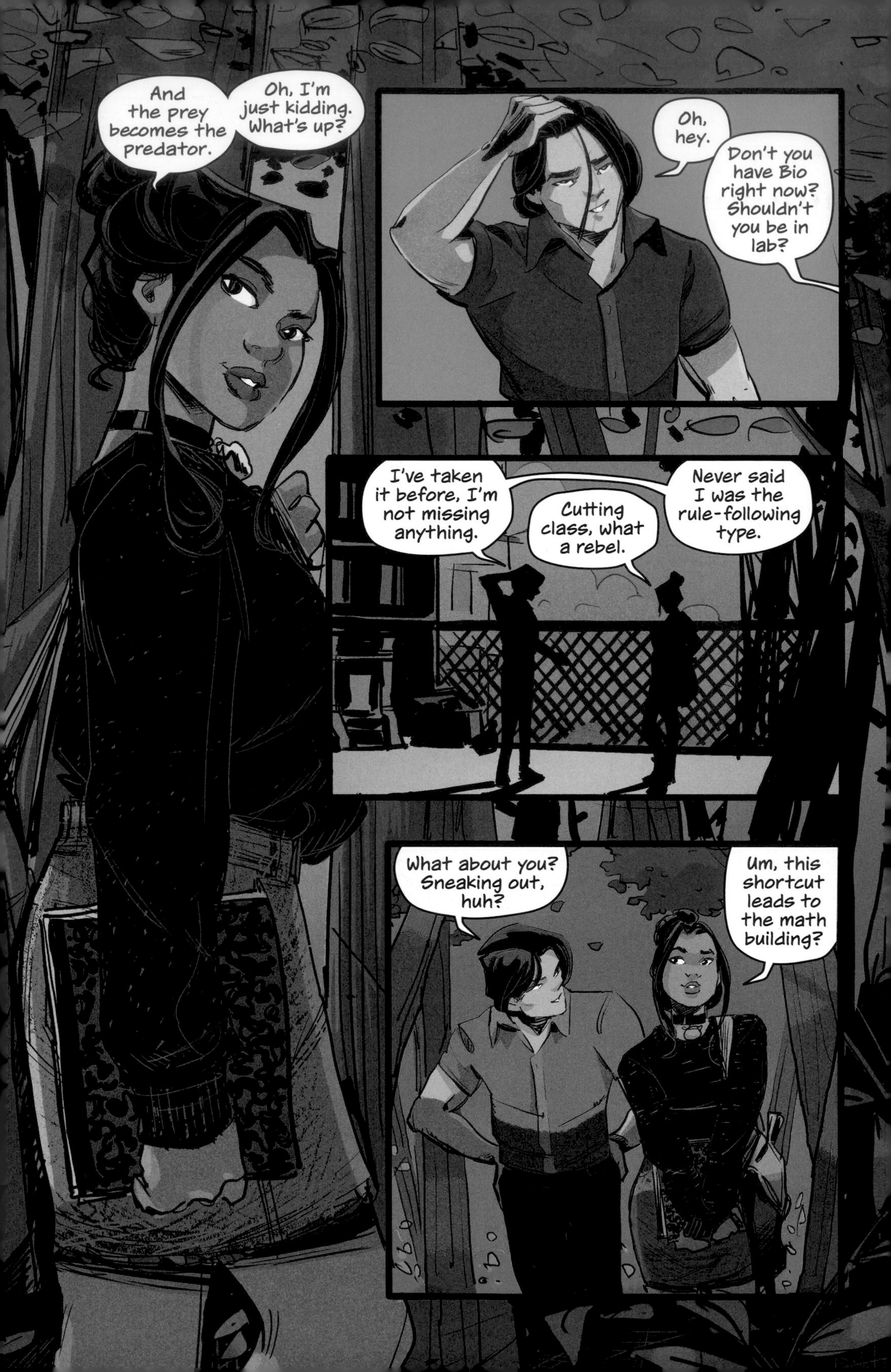

And the prey becomes the predator.
Oh, I'm just kidding. What's up?
Oh, hey.
Don't you have Bio right now? Shouldn't you be in lab?
I've taken it before, I'm not missing anything.
Cutting class, what a rebel.
Never said I was the rule-following type.
What about you? Sneaking out, huh?
Um, this shortcut leads to the math building?

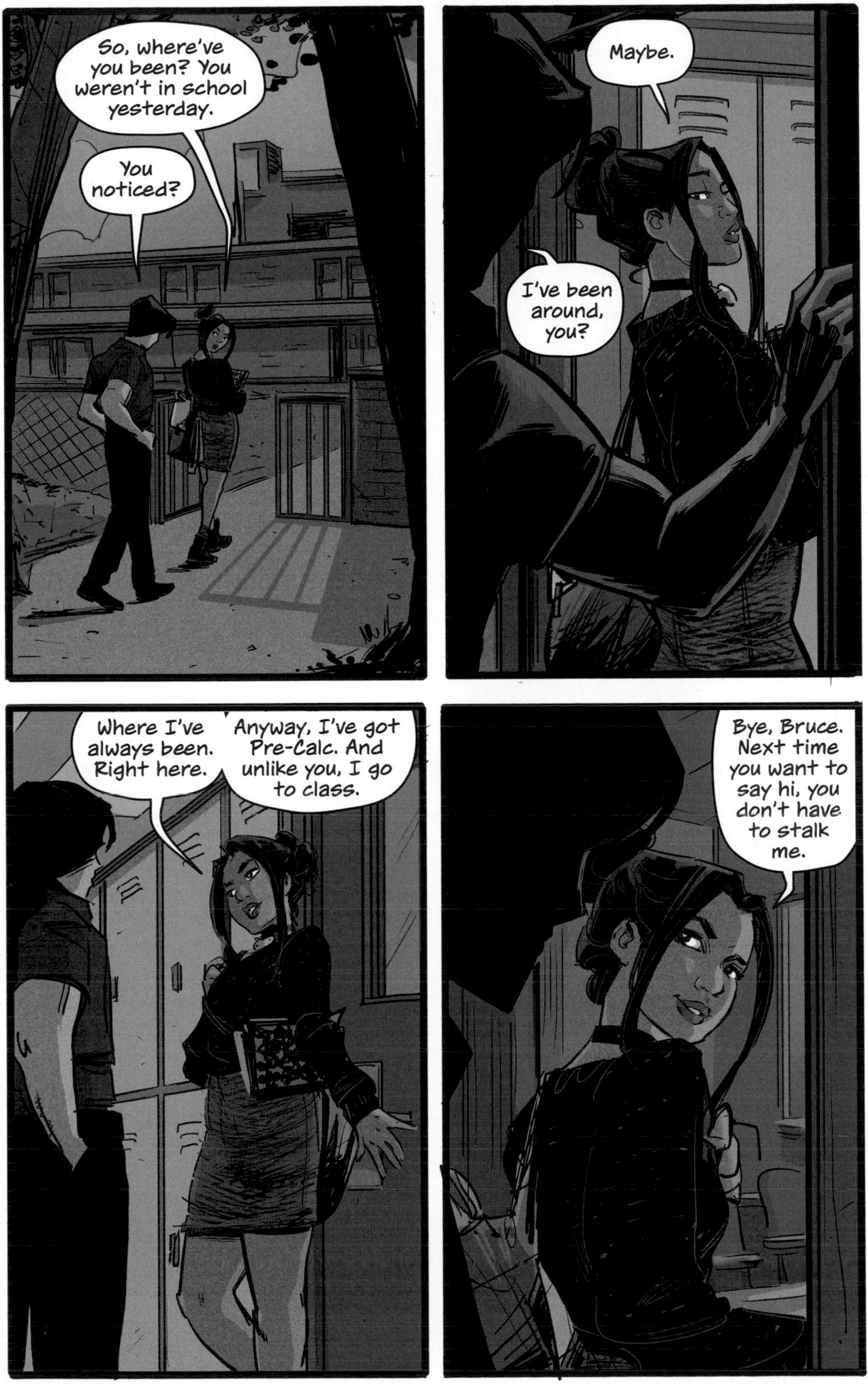
So, where've you been? You weren't in school yesterday.
You noticed?
Maybe.
I've been around, you?
Where I've always been. Right here.
Anyway, I've got Pre-Calc. And unlike you, I go to class.
Bye, Bruce. Next time you want to say hi, you don't have to stalk me.

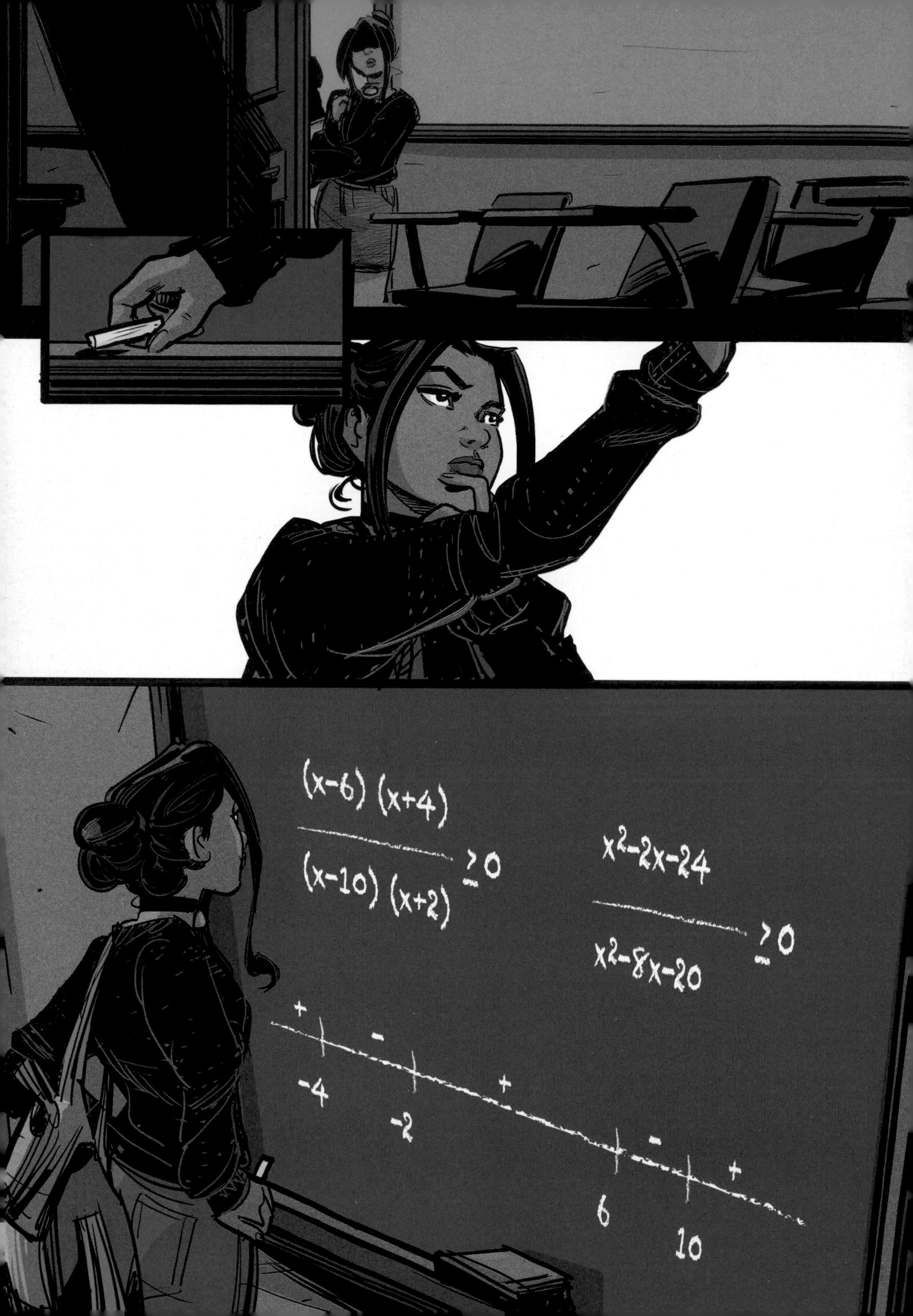

(x-6) (x+4) / (x-10) (x+2) ≥ 0
x²-2x-24 / x²-8x-20 ≥ 0
+ - + - +
-4 -2 6 10

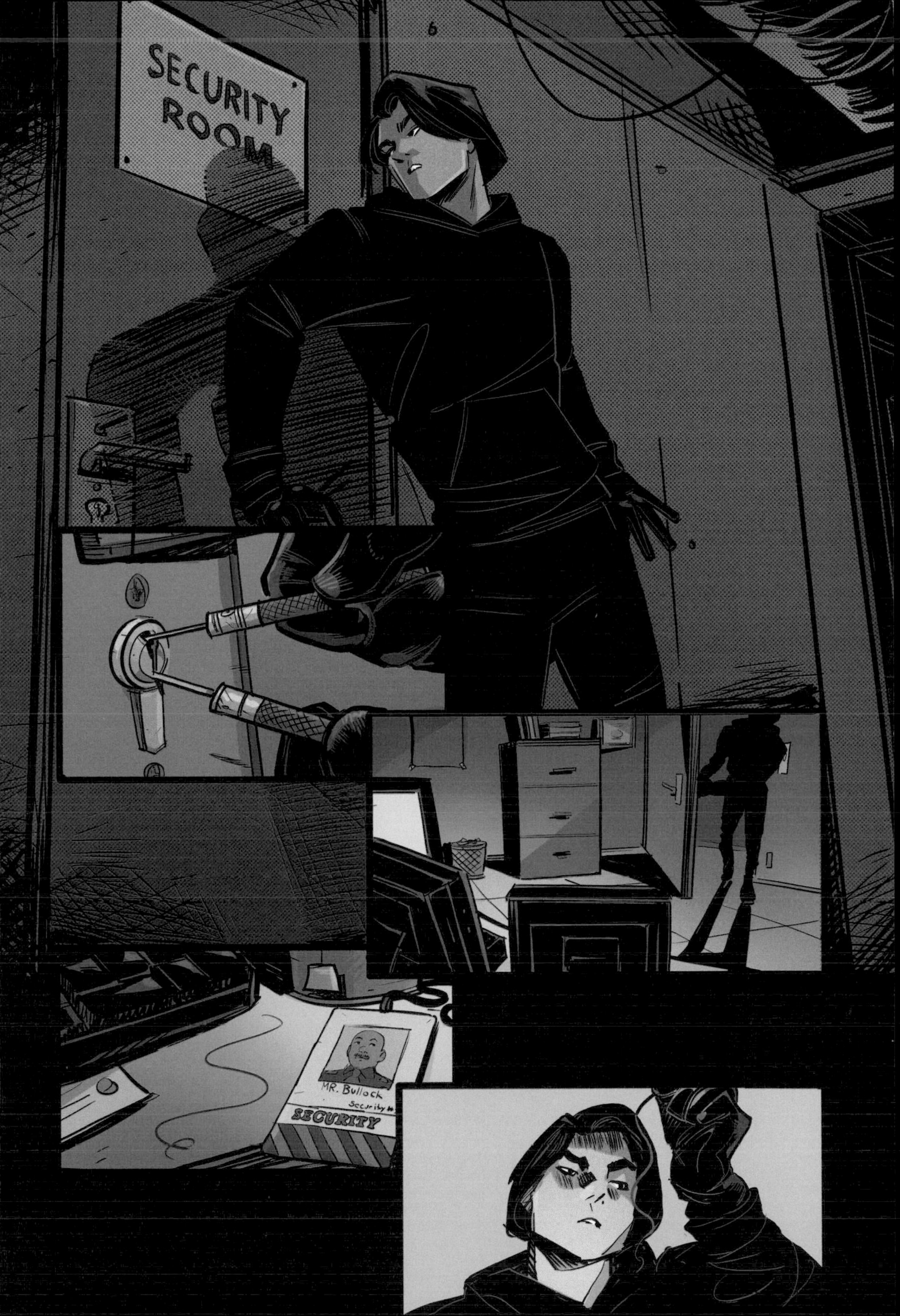
SECURITY ROOM
MR. Bullock
Security
SECURITY

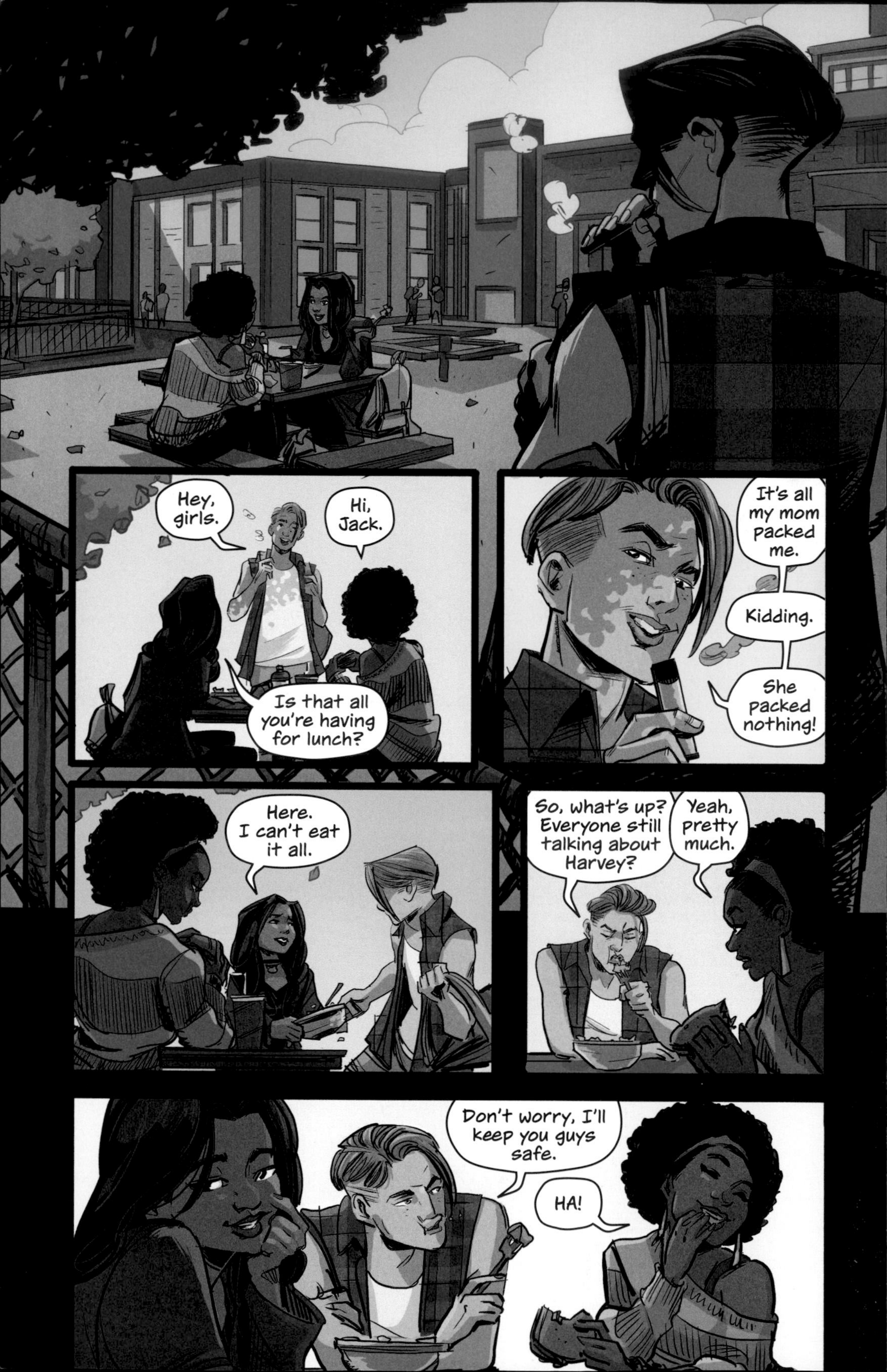

Hey, girls.
Hi, Jack.
Is that all you're having for lunch?
It's all my mom packed me.
Kidding.
She packed nothing!
Here. I can't eat it all.
So, what's up? Everyone still talking about Harvey?
Yeah, pretty much.
Don't worry, I'll keep you guys safe.
HA!

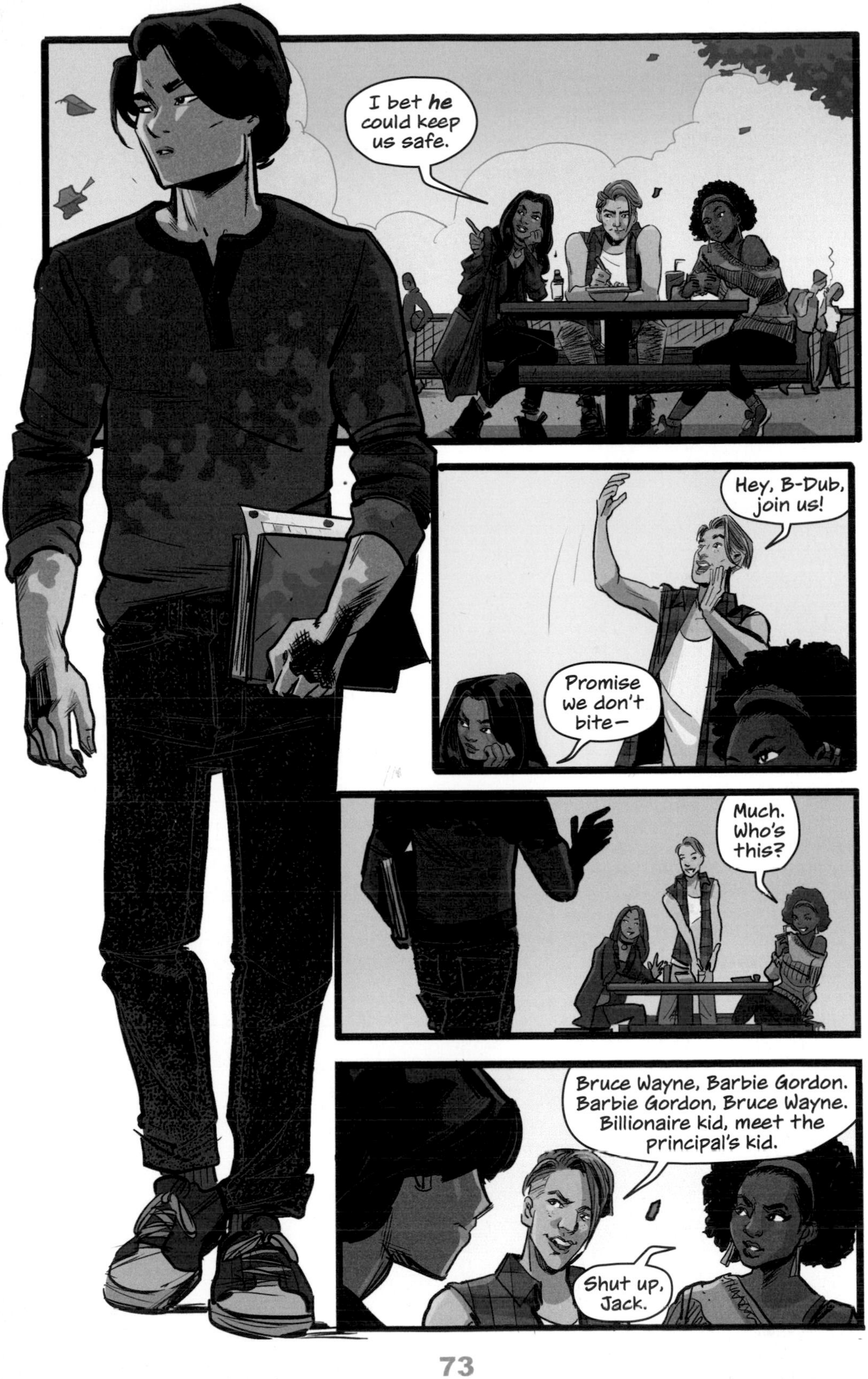
I bet he could keep us safe.
Hey, B-Dub, join us!
Promise we don't bite—
Much. Who's this?
Bruce Wayne, Barbie Gordon. Barbie Gordon, Bruce Wayne. Billionaire kid, meet the principal's kid.
Shut up, Jack.

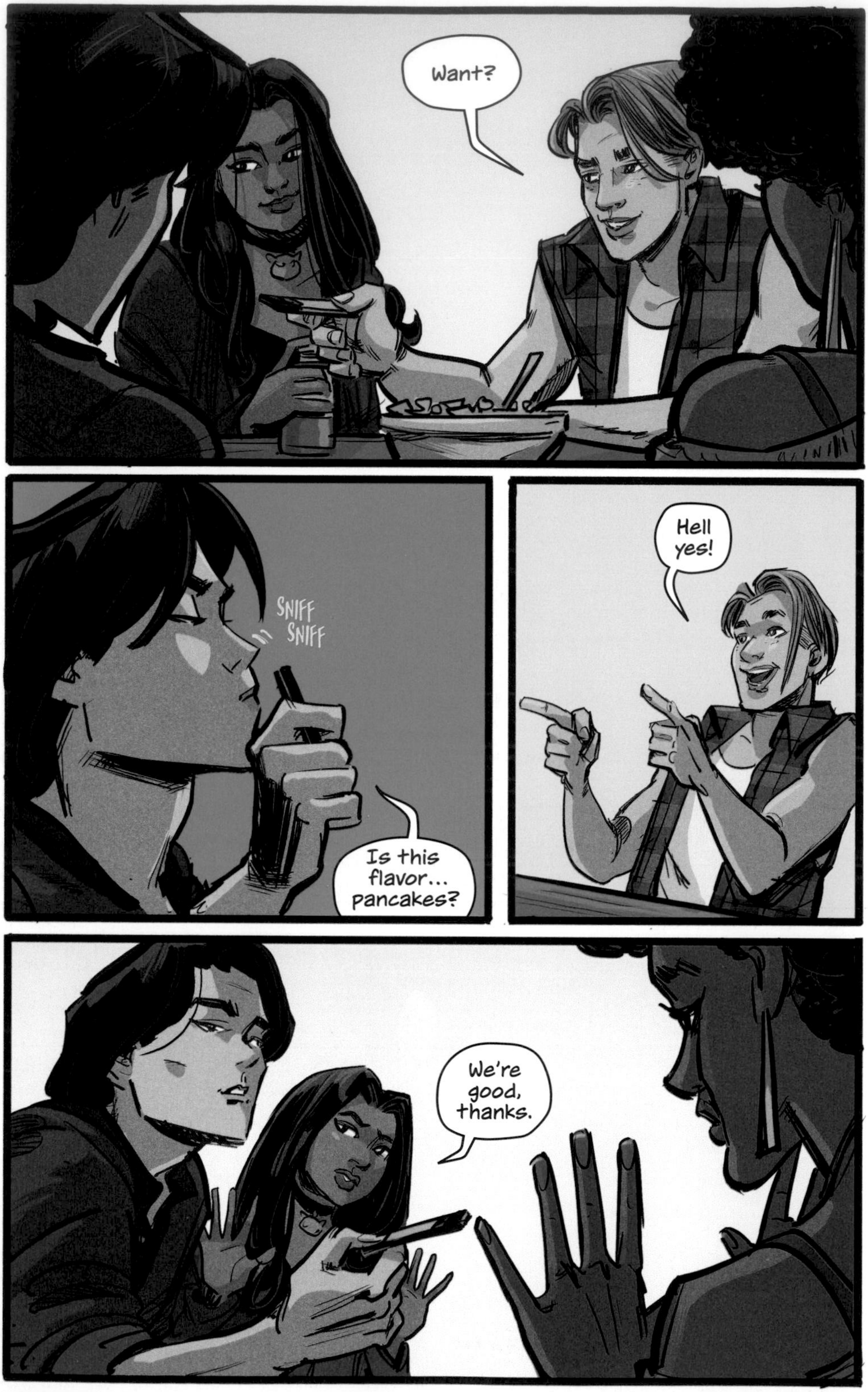
Want?
SNIFF SNIFF
Is this flavor... pancakes?
Hell yes!
We're good, thanks.

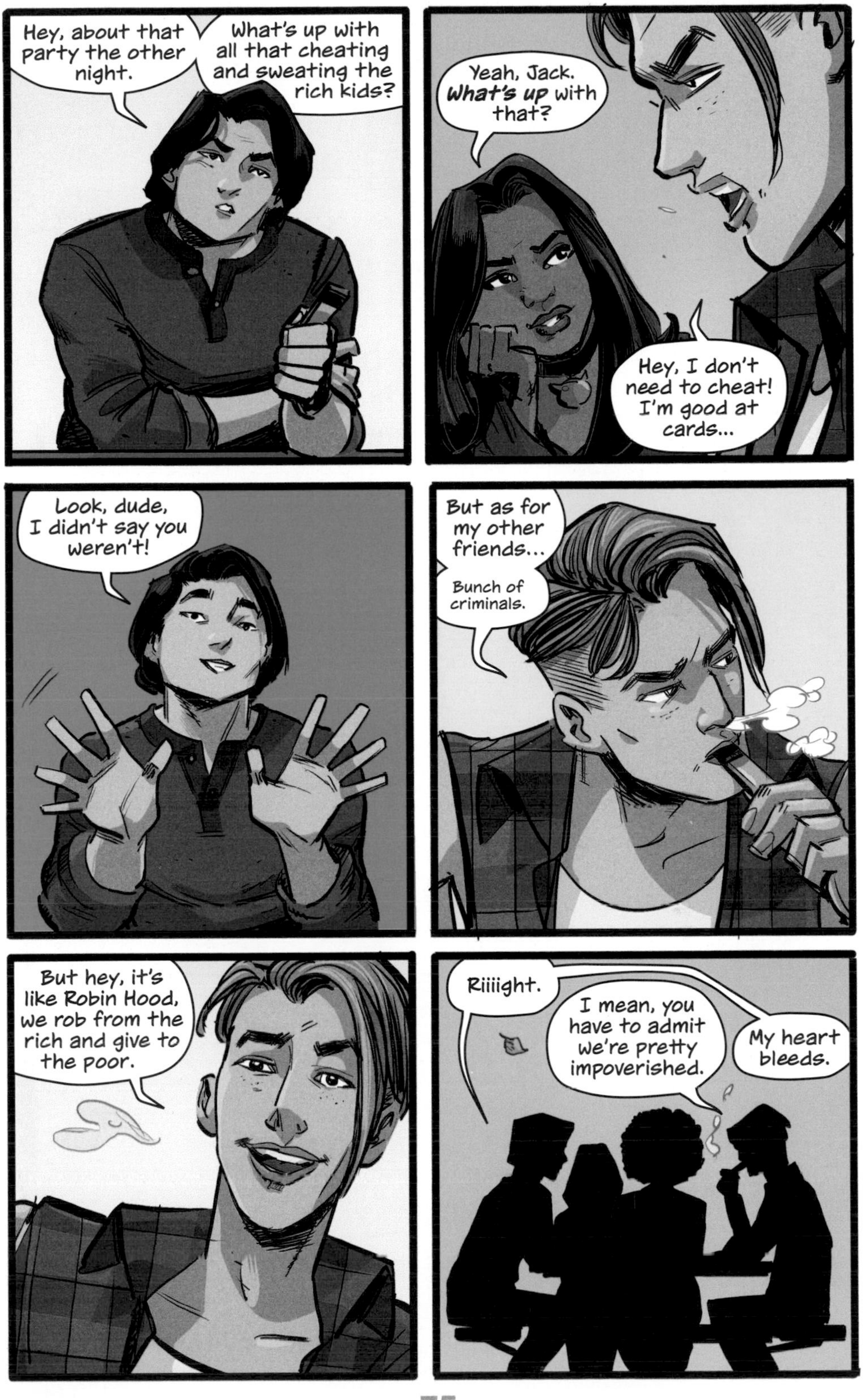
Hey, about that party the other night.
What's up with all that cheating and sweating the rich kids?
Yeah, Jack. *What's up* with that?
Hey, I don't need to cheat! I'm good at cards...
Look, dude, I didn't say you weren't!
But as for my other friends...
Bunch of criminals.
But hey, it's like Robin Hood, we rob from the rich and give to the poor.
Riiiight.
I mean, you have to admit we're pretty impoverished.
My heart bleeds.

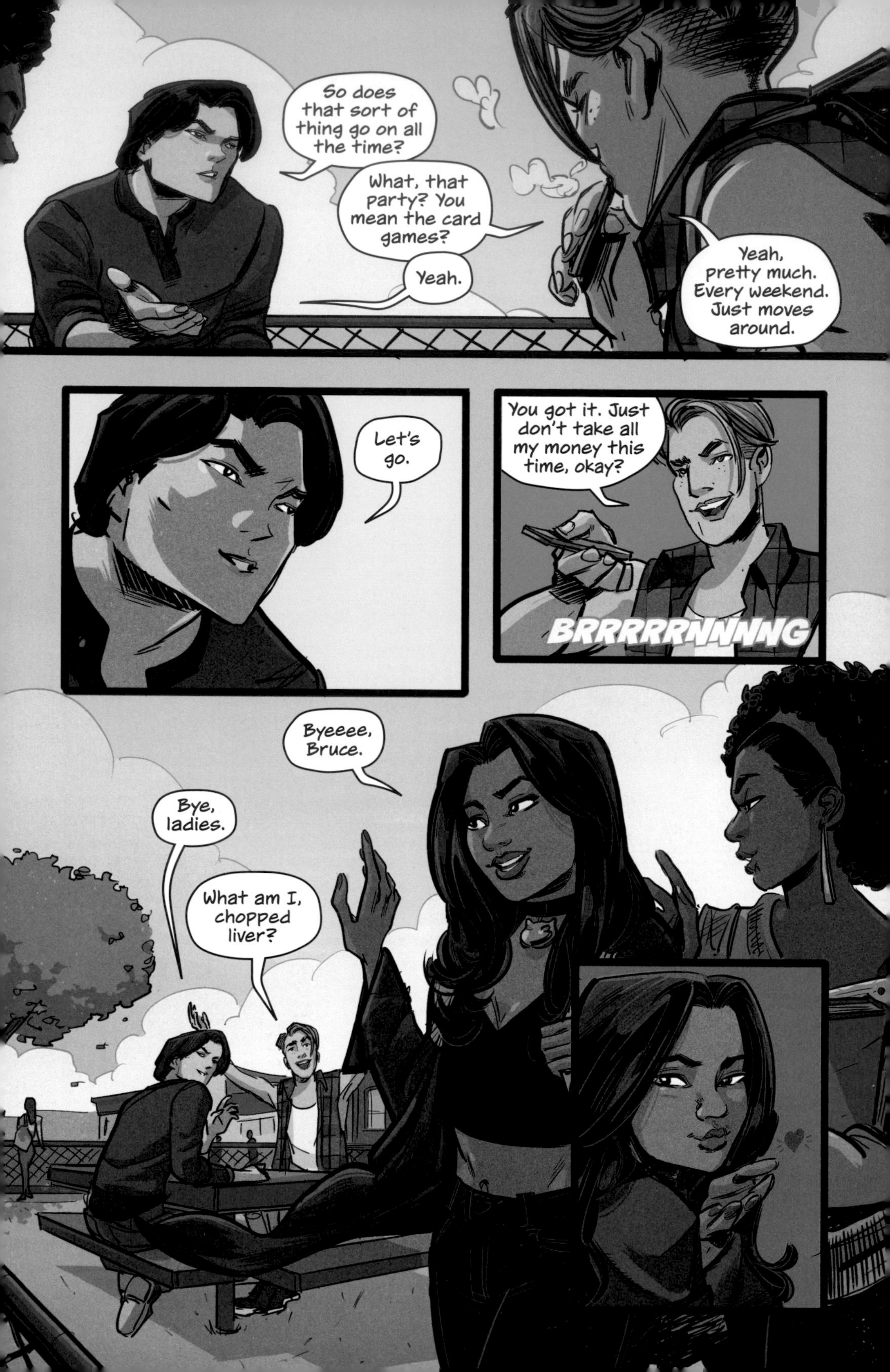
So does that sort of thing go on all the time?
What, that party? You mean the card games?
Yeah.
Yeah, pretty much. Every weekend. Just moves around.
Let's go.
You got it. Just don't take all my money this time, okay?
BRRRRRNNNNG
Byeeee, Bruce.
Bye, ladies.
What am I, chopped liver?

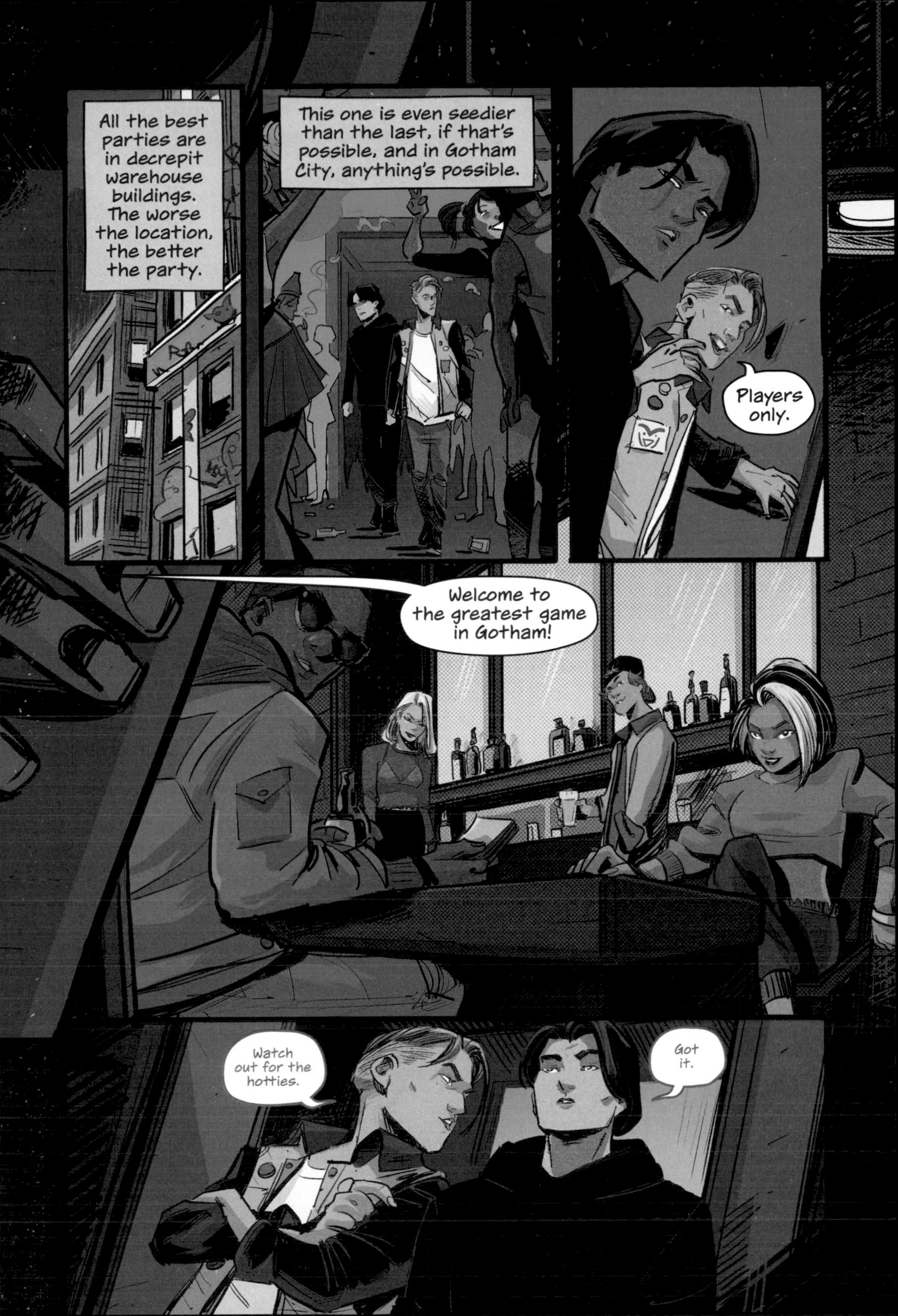
All the best parties are in decrepit warehouse buildings. The worse the location, the better the party.
This one is even seedier than the last, if that's possible, and in Gotham City, anything's possible.
Players only.
Welcome to the greatest game in Gotham!
Watch out for the hotties.
Got it.

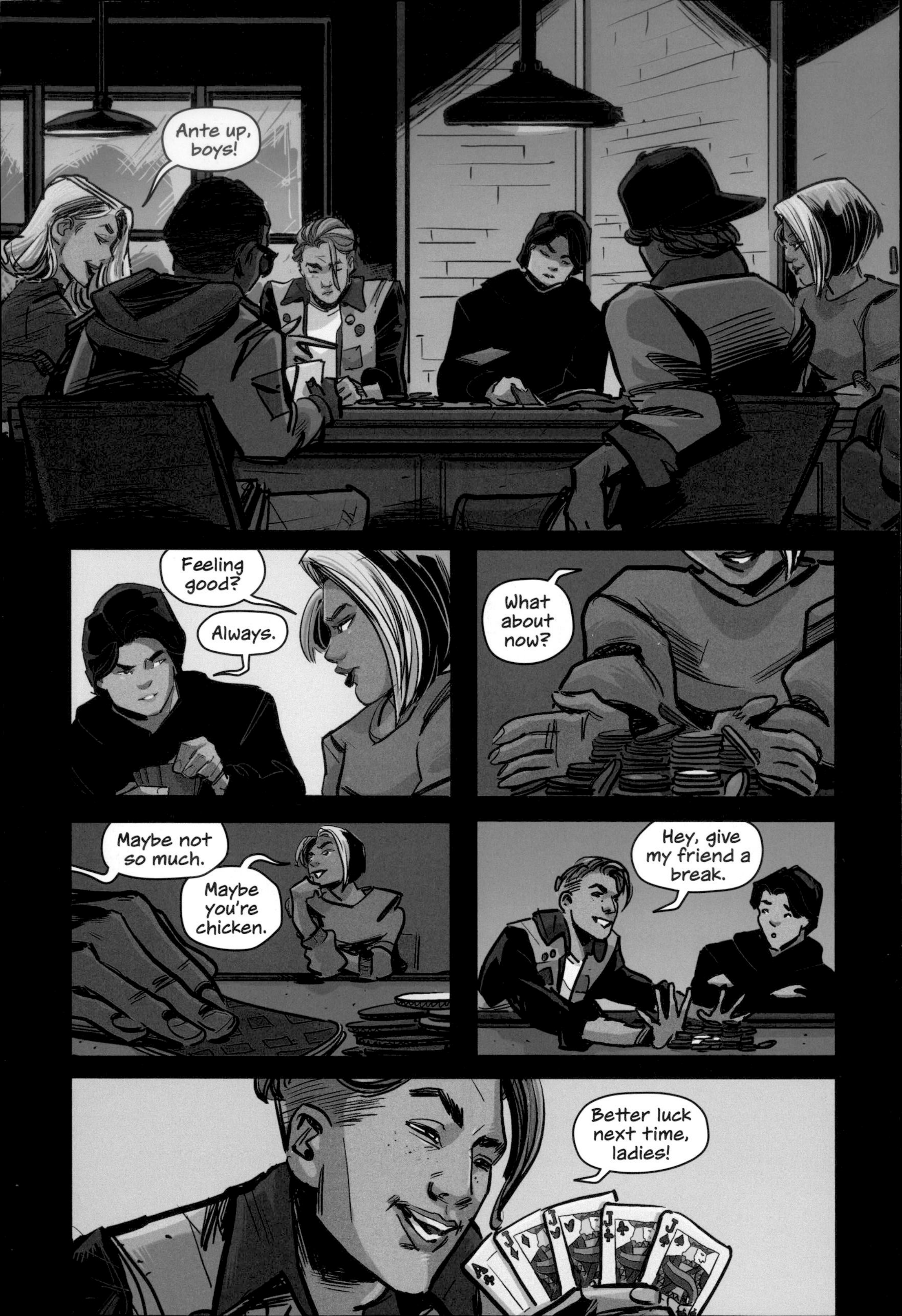
Ante up, boys!
Feeling good?
Always.
What about now?
Maybe not so much.
Maybe you're chicken.
Hey, give my friend a break.
Better luck next time, ladies!

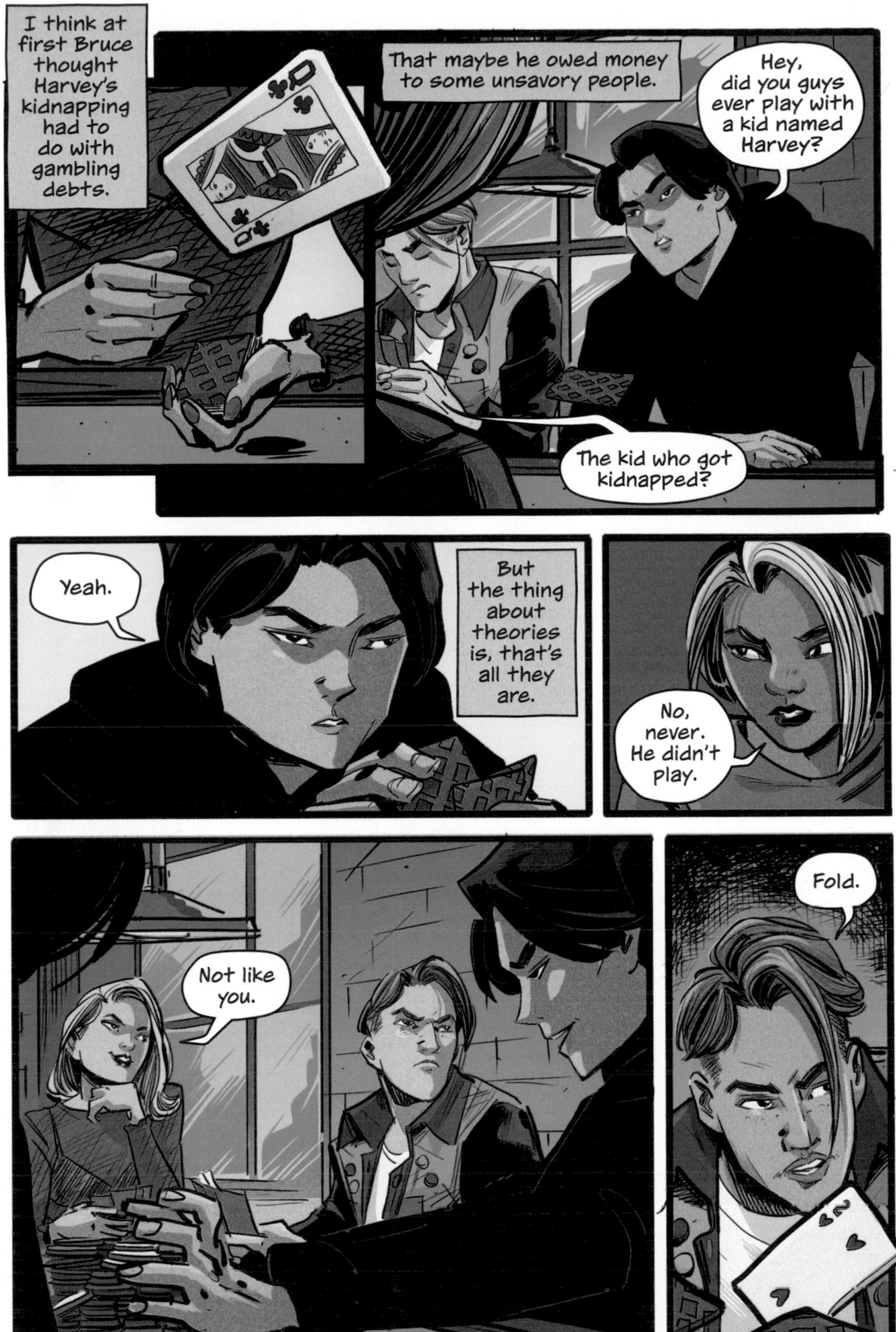

I think at first Bruce thought Harvey's kidnapping had to do with gambling debts.
That maybe he owed money to some unsavory people.
Hey, did you guys ever play with a kid named Harvey?
The kid who got kidnapped?
Yeah.
But the thing about theories is, that's all they are.
No, never. He didn't play.
Not like you.
Fold.

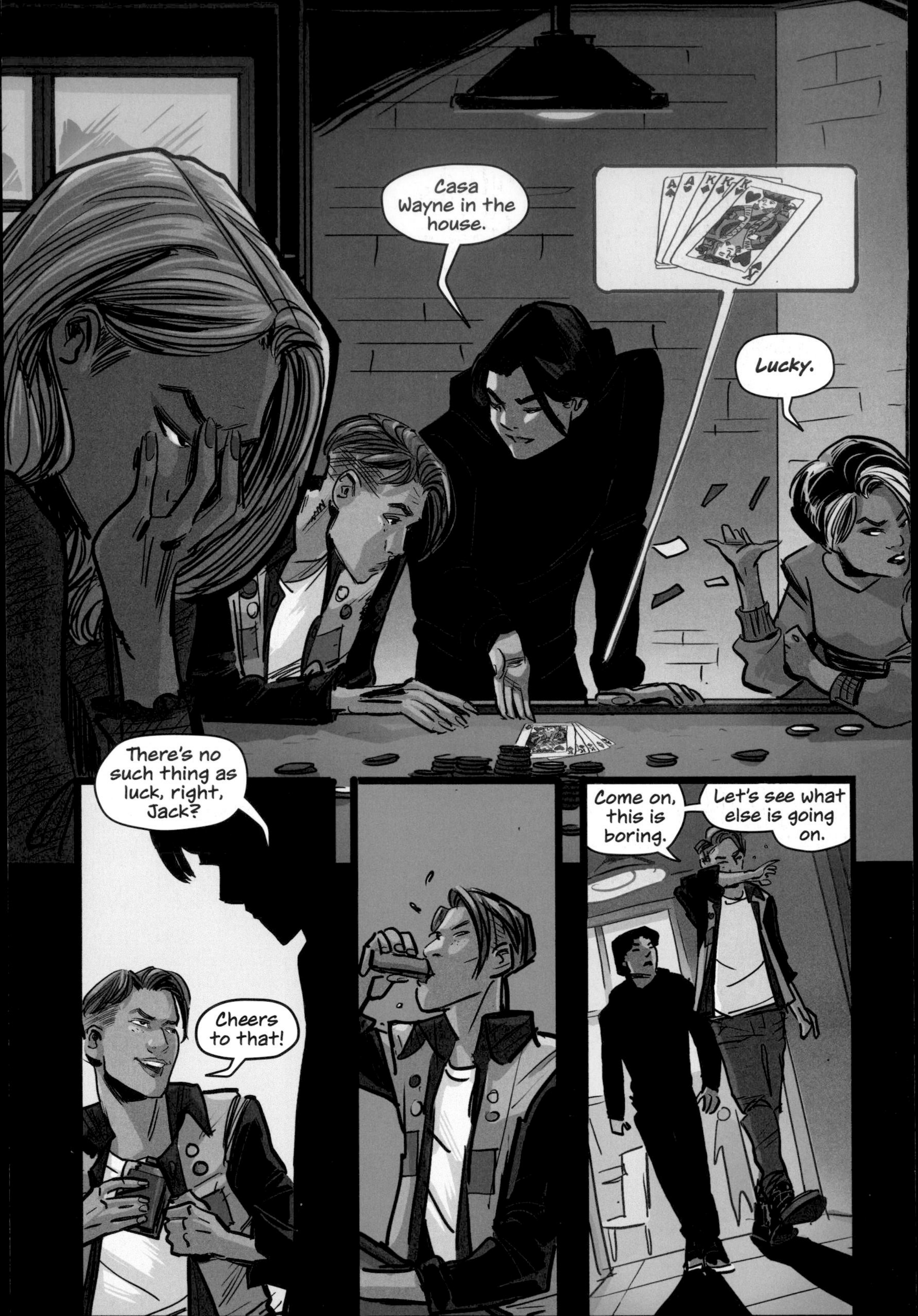
Casa Wayne in the house.
Lucky.
There's no such thing as luck, right, Jack?
Cheers to that!
Come on, this is boring.
Let's see what else is going on.

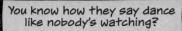
You know how they say dance like nobody's watching?

Well, that's bullshit. I dance like everyone's watching, always.

I need some fresh air. Wanna get out of here?

I know just the place.

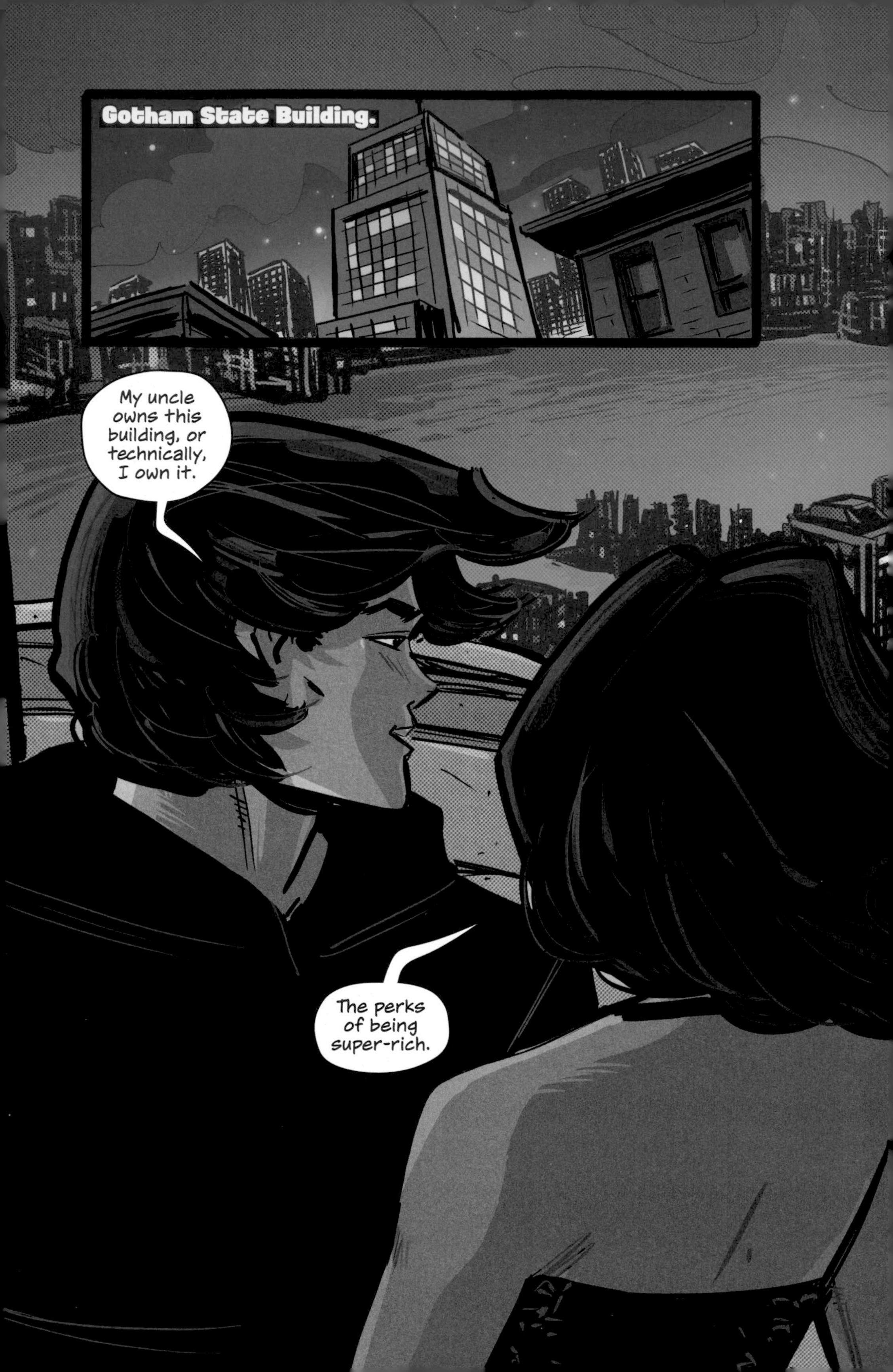
Gotham State Building.
My uncle owns this building, or technically, I own it.
The perks of being super-rich.

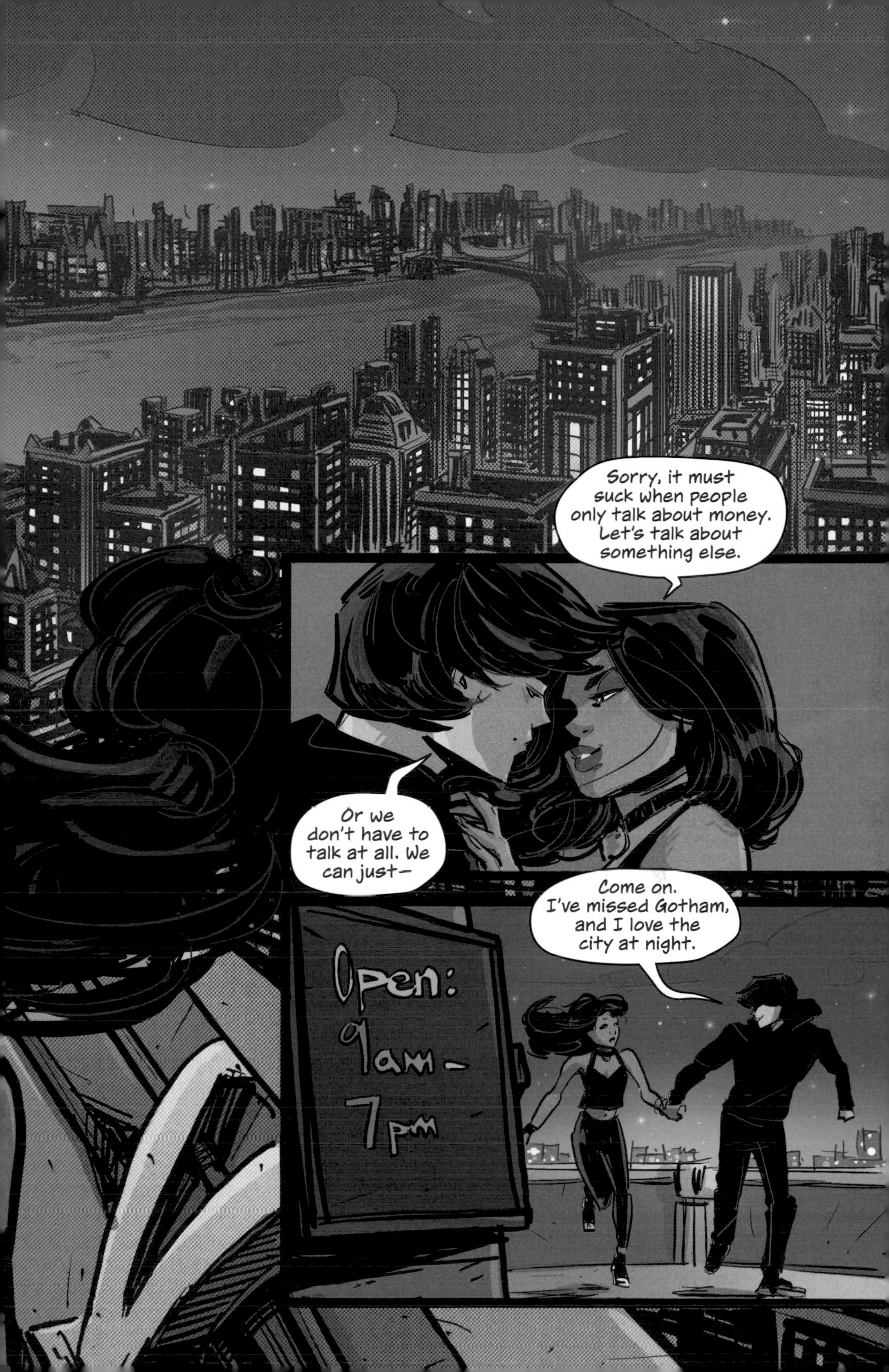

Sorry, it must suck when people only talk about money. Let's talk about something else.
Or we don't have to talk at all. We can just—
Come on. I've missed Gotham, and I love the city at night.
Open: 9am - 7pm

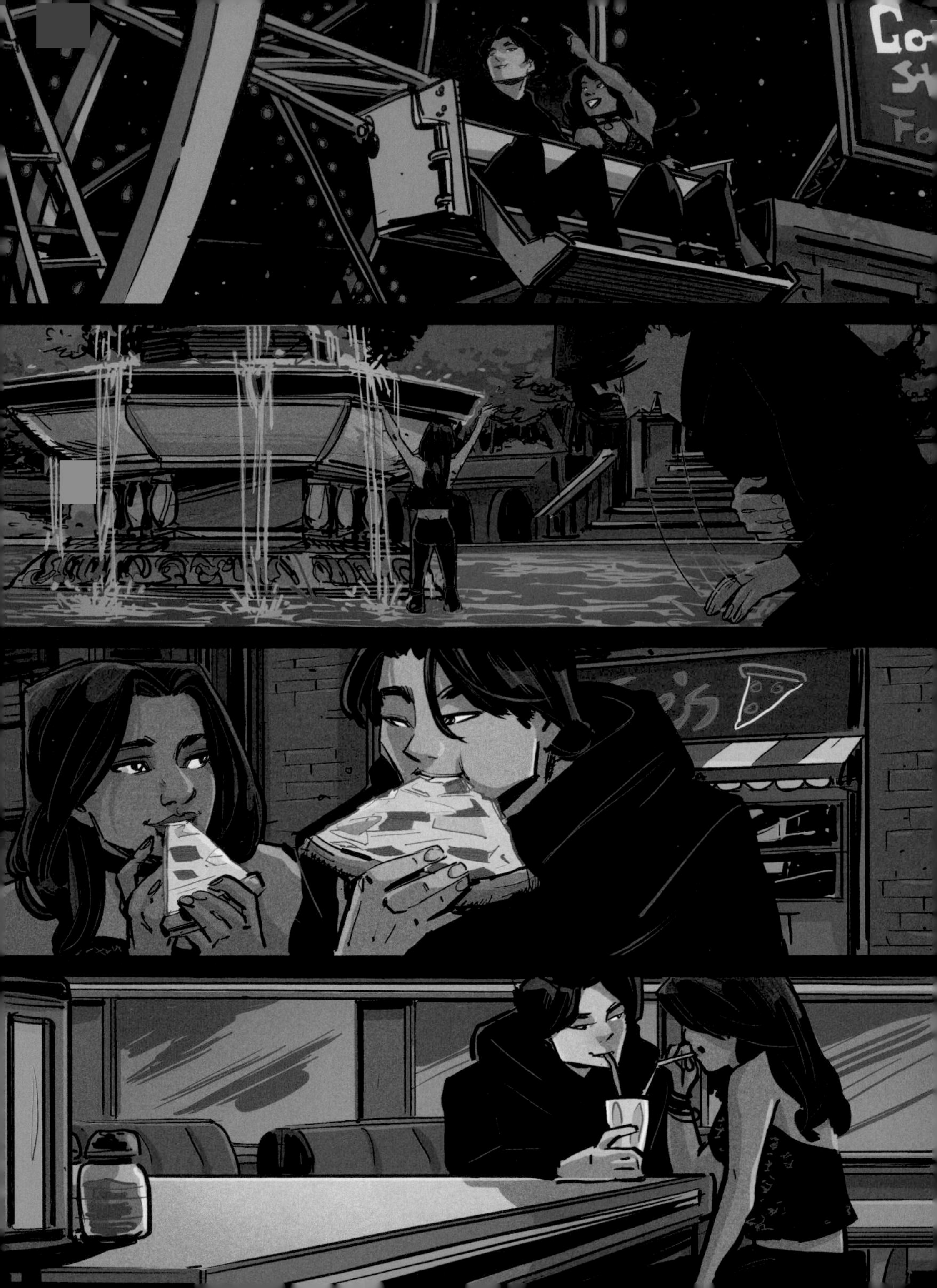

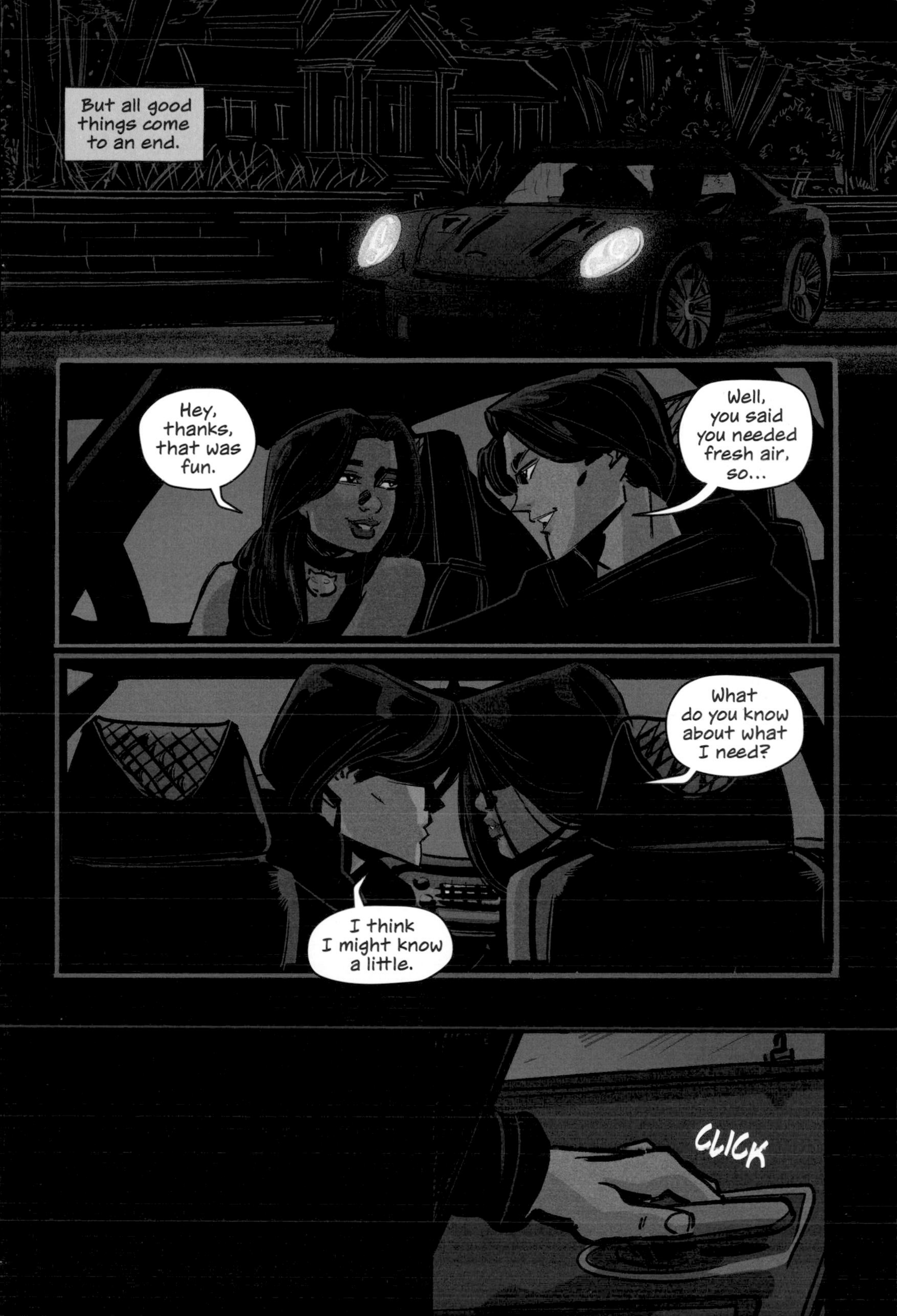
But all good things come to an end.
Hey, thanks, that was fun.
Well, you said you needed fresh air, so...
What do you know about what I need?
I think I might know a little.
CLICK

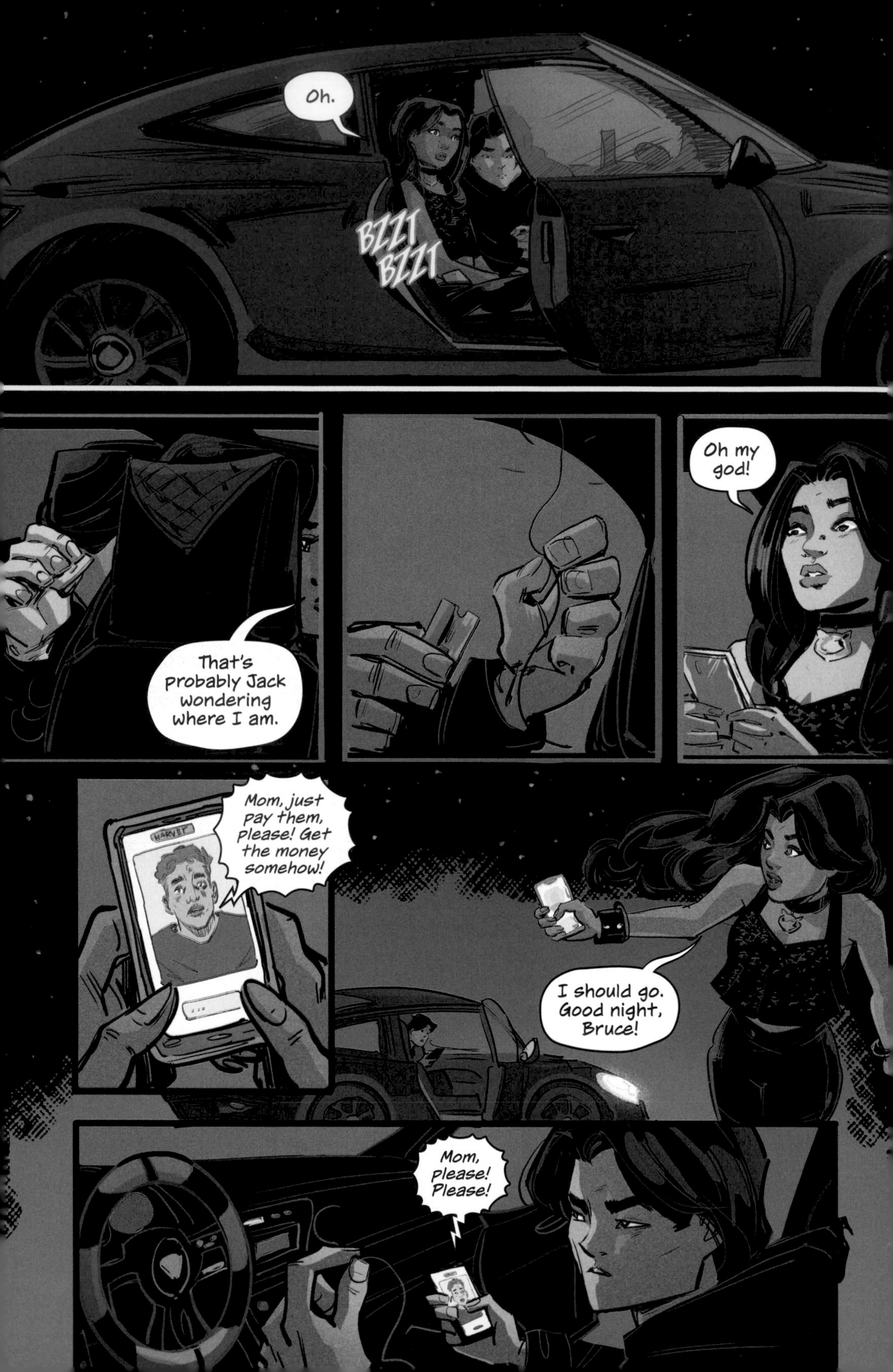

Oh.
BZZT
BZZT
That's probably Jack wondering where I am.
Oh my god!
HARVEY
Mom, just pay them, please! Get the money somehow!
I should go. Good night, Bruce!
Mom, please! Please!

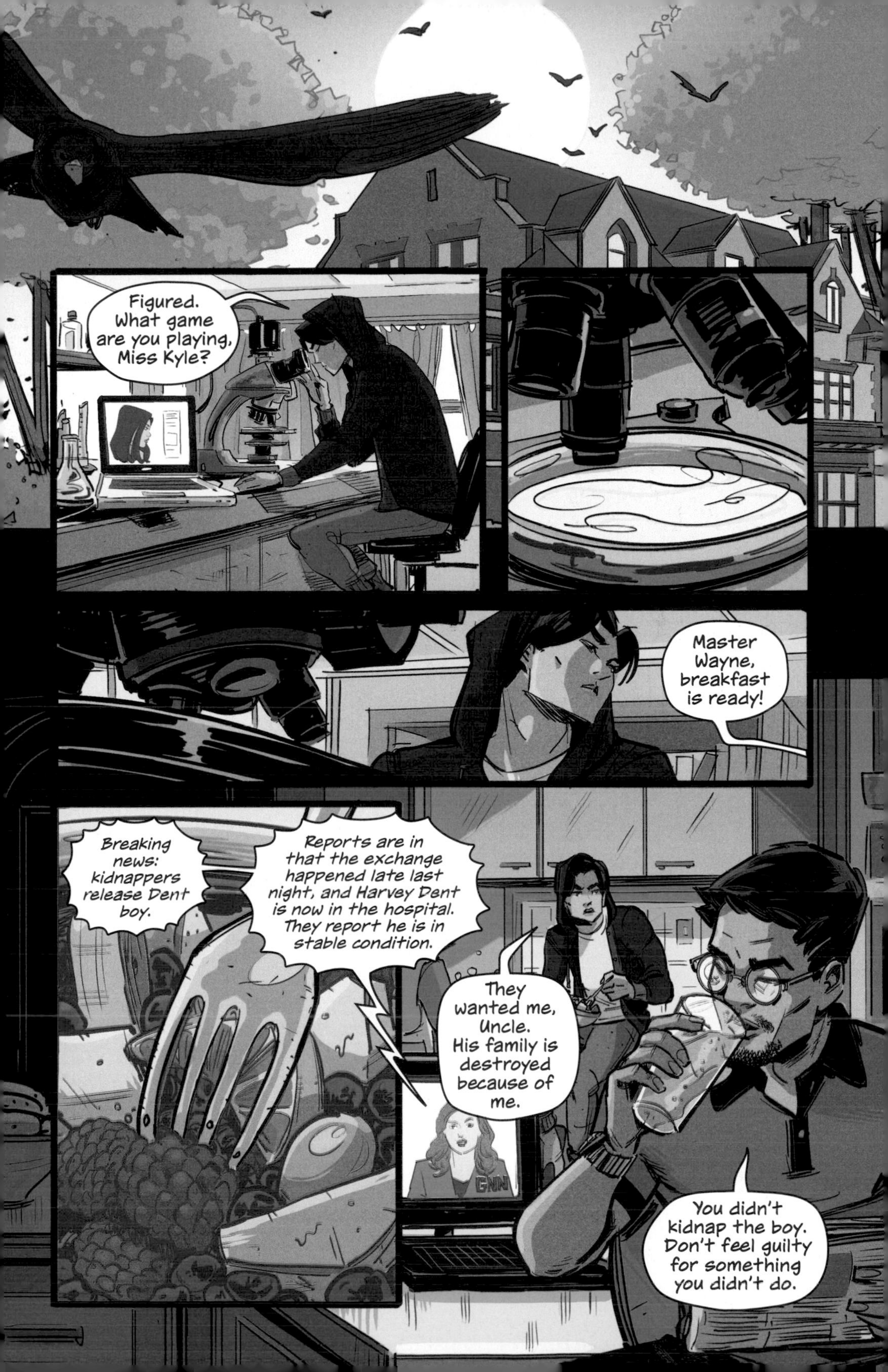
Figured. What game are you playing, Miss Kyle?
Master Wayne, breakfast is ready!
Breaking news: kidnappers release Dent boy.
Reports are in that the exchange happened late last night, and Harvey Dent is now in the hospital. They report he is in stable condition.
They wanted me, Uncle. His family is destroyed because of me.
You didn't kidnap the boy. Don't feel guilty for something you didn't do.
GNN

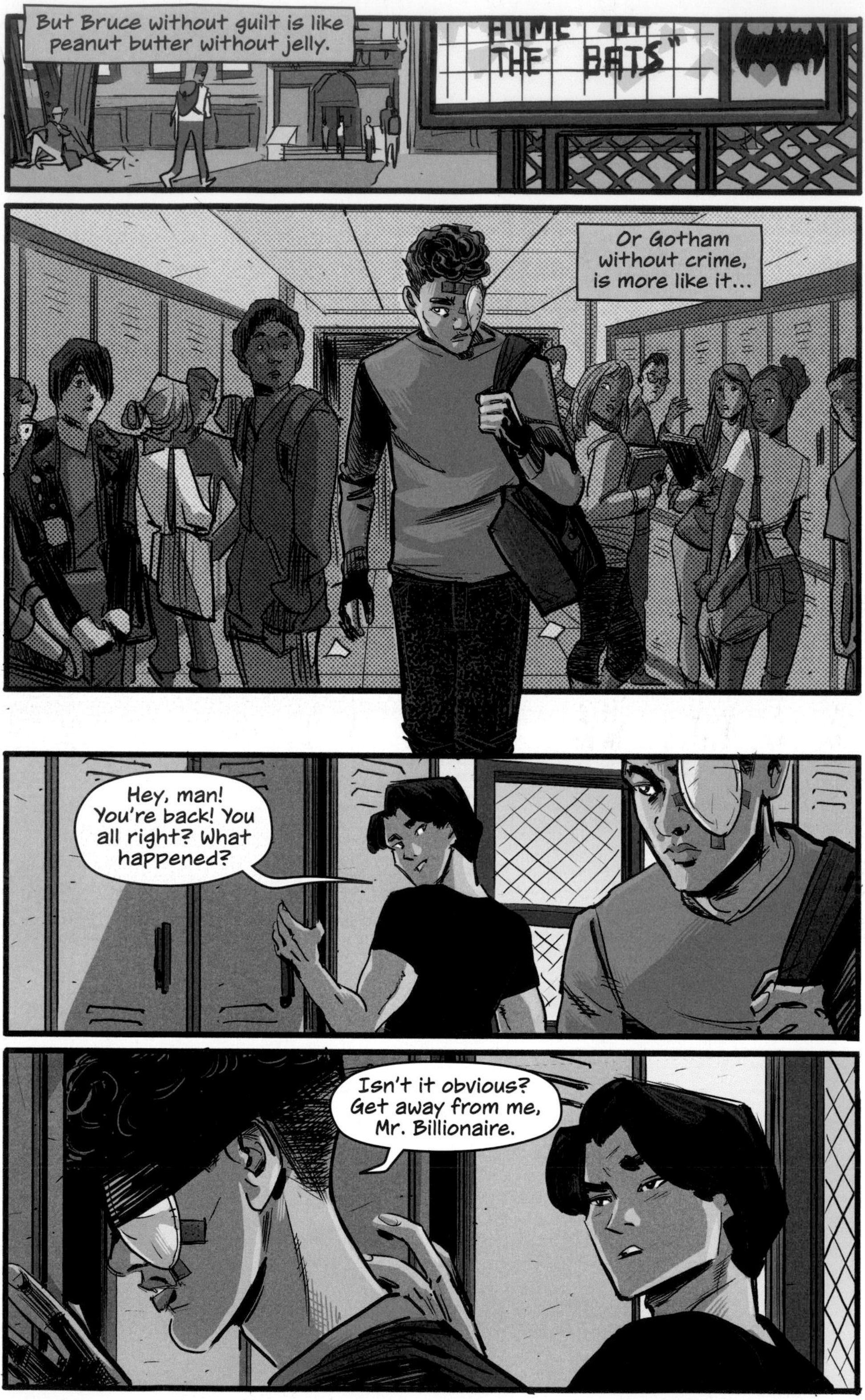

But Bruce without guilt is like peanut butter without jelly.
Or Gotham without crime, is more like it...
Hey, man! You're back! You all right? What happened?
Isn't it obvious? Get away from me, Mr. Billionaire.

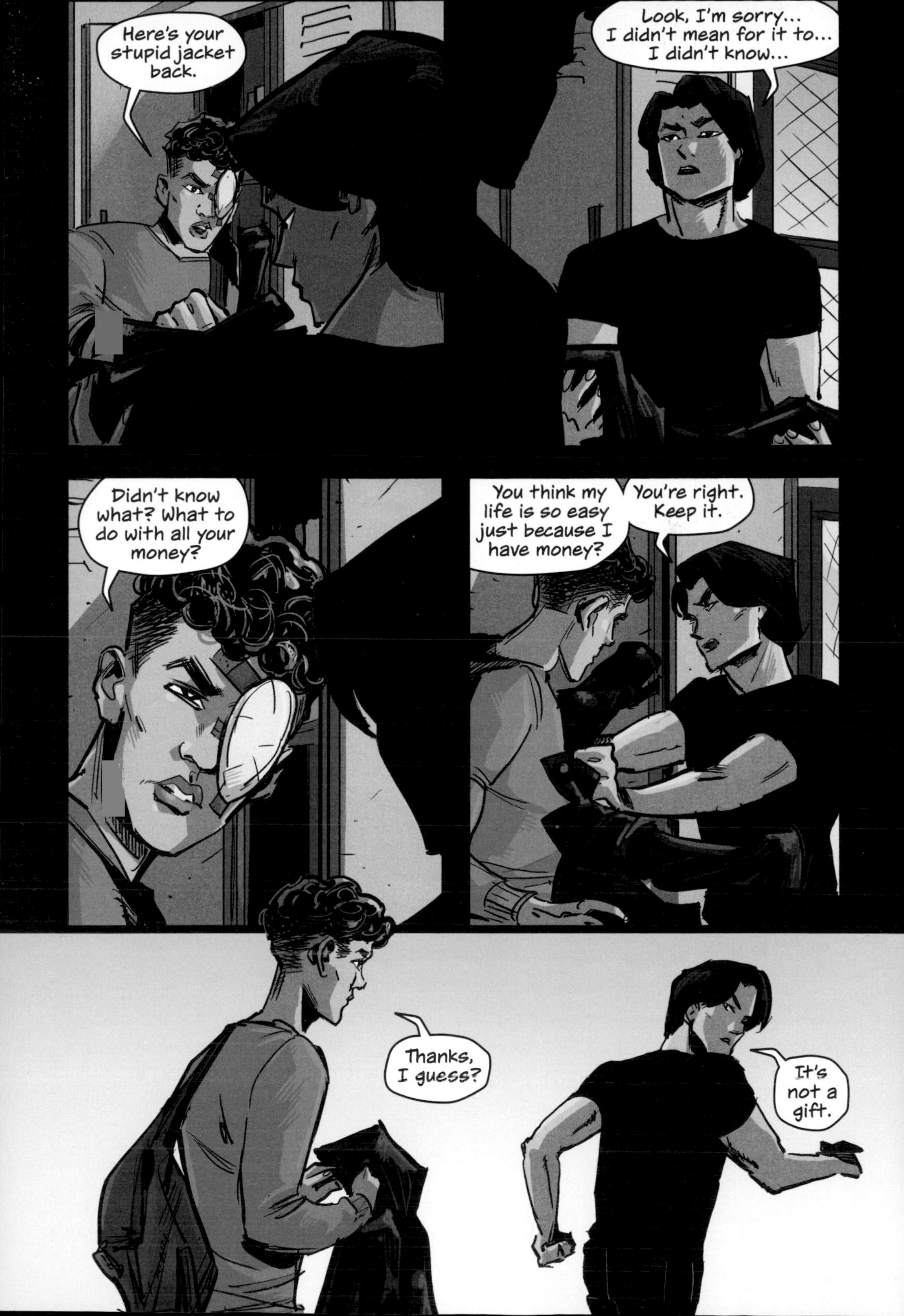
Here's your stupid jacket back.
Look, I'm sorry... I didn't mean for it to... I didn't know...
Didn't know what? What to do with all your money?
You think my life is so easy just because I have money?
You're right. Keep it.
Thanks, I guess?
It's not a gift.

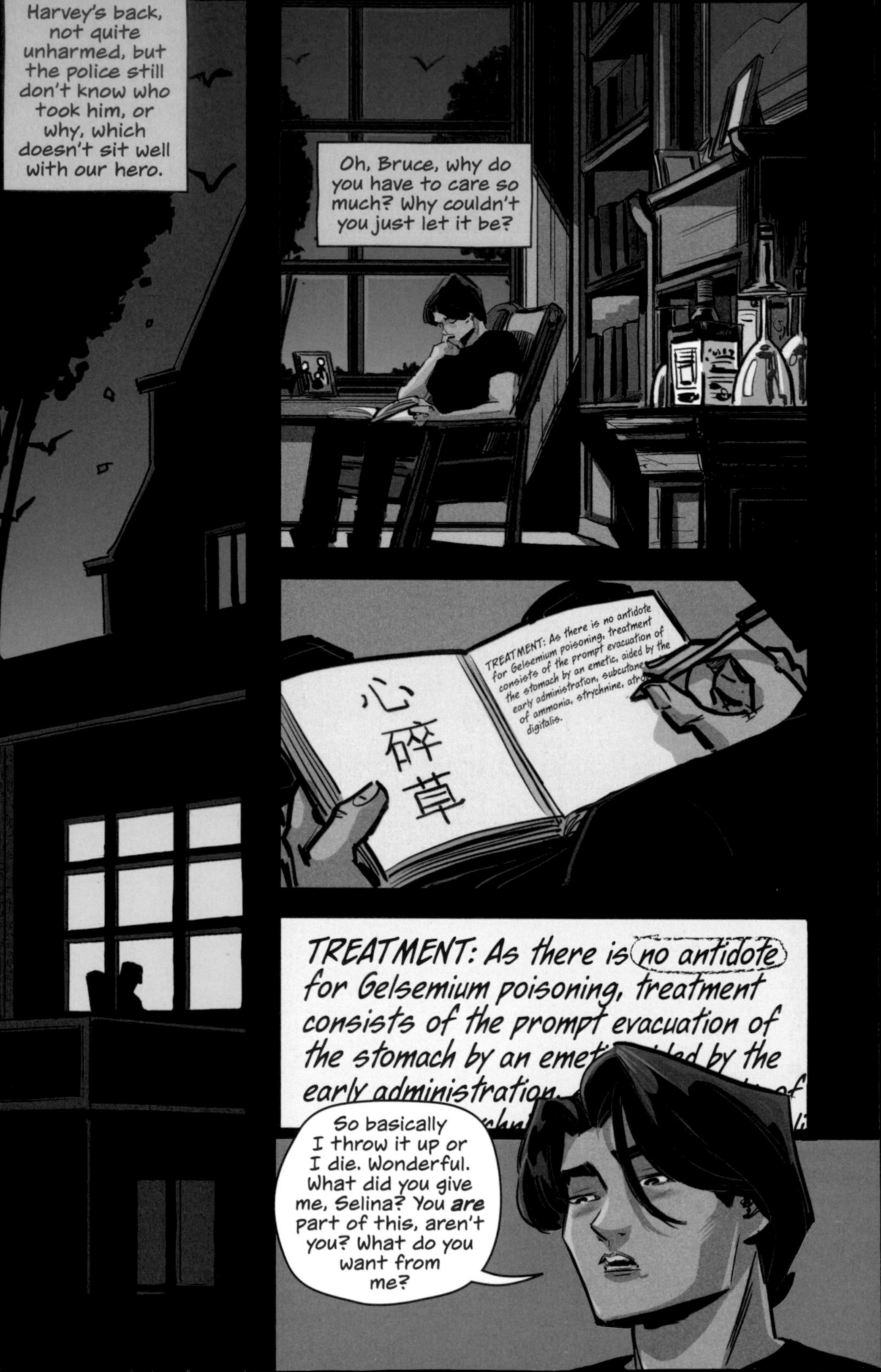

Harvey's back, not quite unharmed, but the police still don't know who took him, or why, which doesn't sit well with our hero.
Oh, Bruce, why do you have to care so much? Why couldn't you just let it be?
心碎草
TREATMENT: As there is no antidote for Gelsemium poisoning, treatment consists of the prompt evacuation of the stomach by an emetic, aided by the early administration, subcutane of ammonia, strychnine, atro digitalis.
TREATMENT: As there is no antidote for Gelsemium poisoning, treatment consists of the prompt evacuation of the stomach by an emet
early administration
So basically I throw it up or I die. Wonderful. What did you give me, Selina? You are part of this, aren't you? What do you want from me?

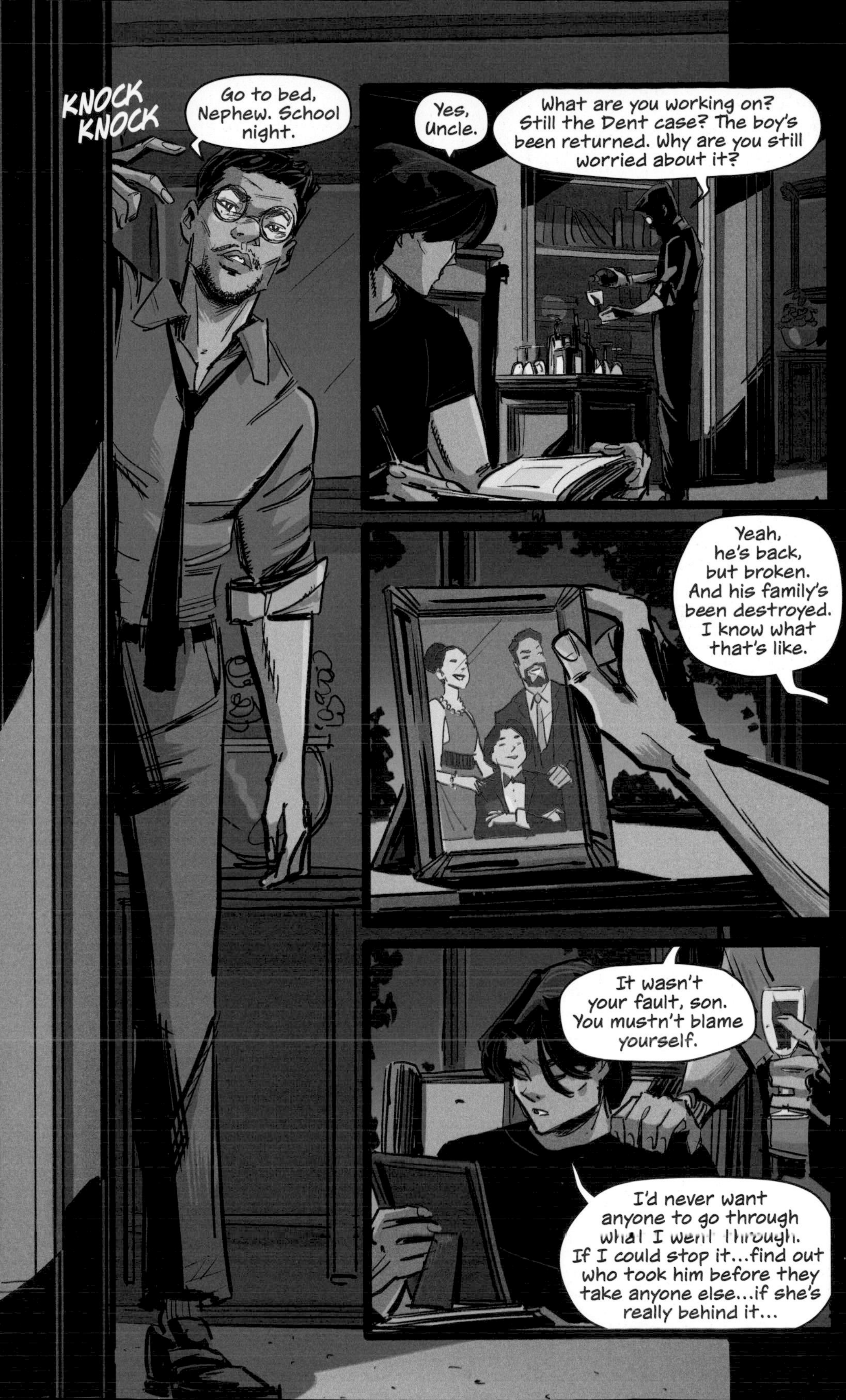
KNOCK KNOCK
Go to bed, Nephew. School night.
Yes, Uncle.
What are you working on? Still the Dent case? The boy's been returned. Why are you still worried about it?
Yeah, he's back, but broken. And his family's been destroyed. I know what that's like.
It wasn't your fault, son. You mustn't blame yourself.
I'd never want anyone to go through what I went through. If I could stop it...find out who took him before they take anyone else...if she's really behind it...

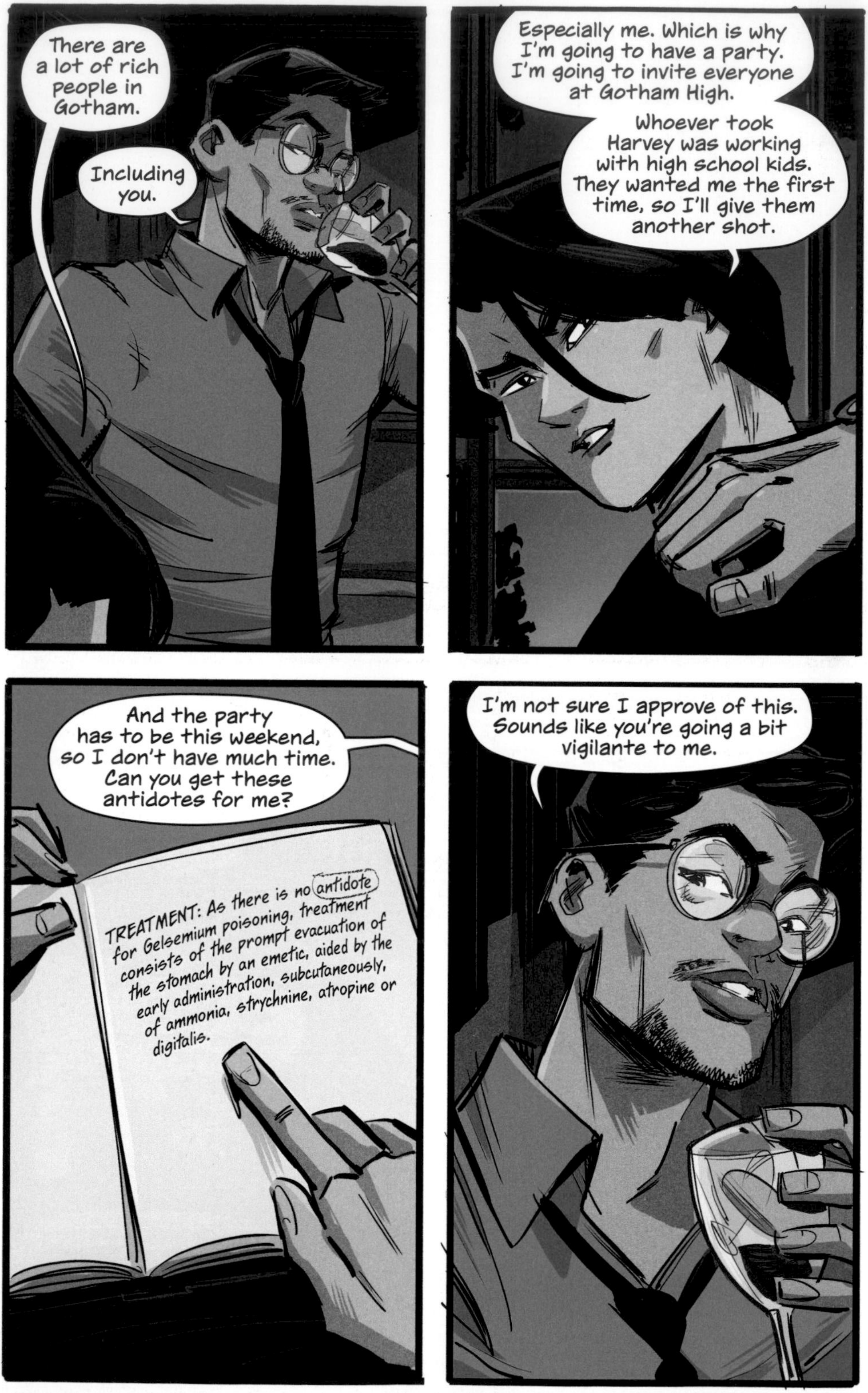
There are a lot of rich people in Gotham.
Including you.
Especially me. Which is why I'm going to have a party. I'm going to invite everyone at Gotham High.
Whoever took Harvey was working with high school kids. They wanted me the first time, so I'll give them another shot.
And the party has to be this weekend, so I don't have much time. Can you get these antidotes for me?
TREATMENT: As there is no antidote for Gelsemium poisoning, treatment consists of the prompt evacuation of the stomach by an emetic, aided by the early administration, subcutaneously, of ammonia, strychnine, atropine or digitalis.
I'm not sure I approve of this. Sounds like you're going a bit vigilante to me.

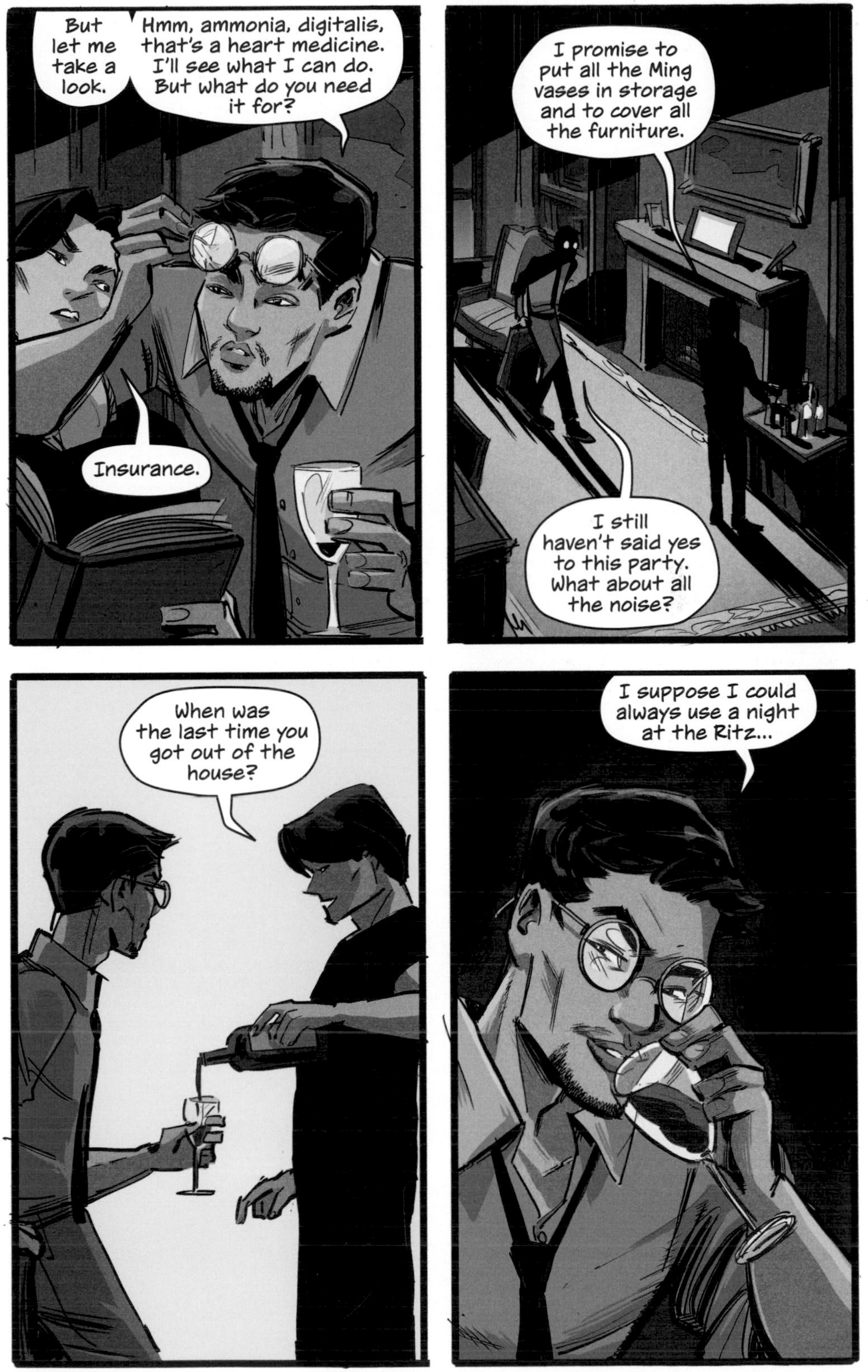

But let me take a look.
Hmm, ammonia, digitalis, that's a heart medicine. I'll see what I can do. But what do you need it for?
Insurance.
I promise to put all the Ming vases in storage and to cover all the furniture.
I still haven't said yes to this party. What about all the noise?
When was the last time you got out of the house?
I suppose I could always use a night at the Ritz...

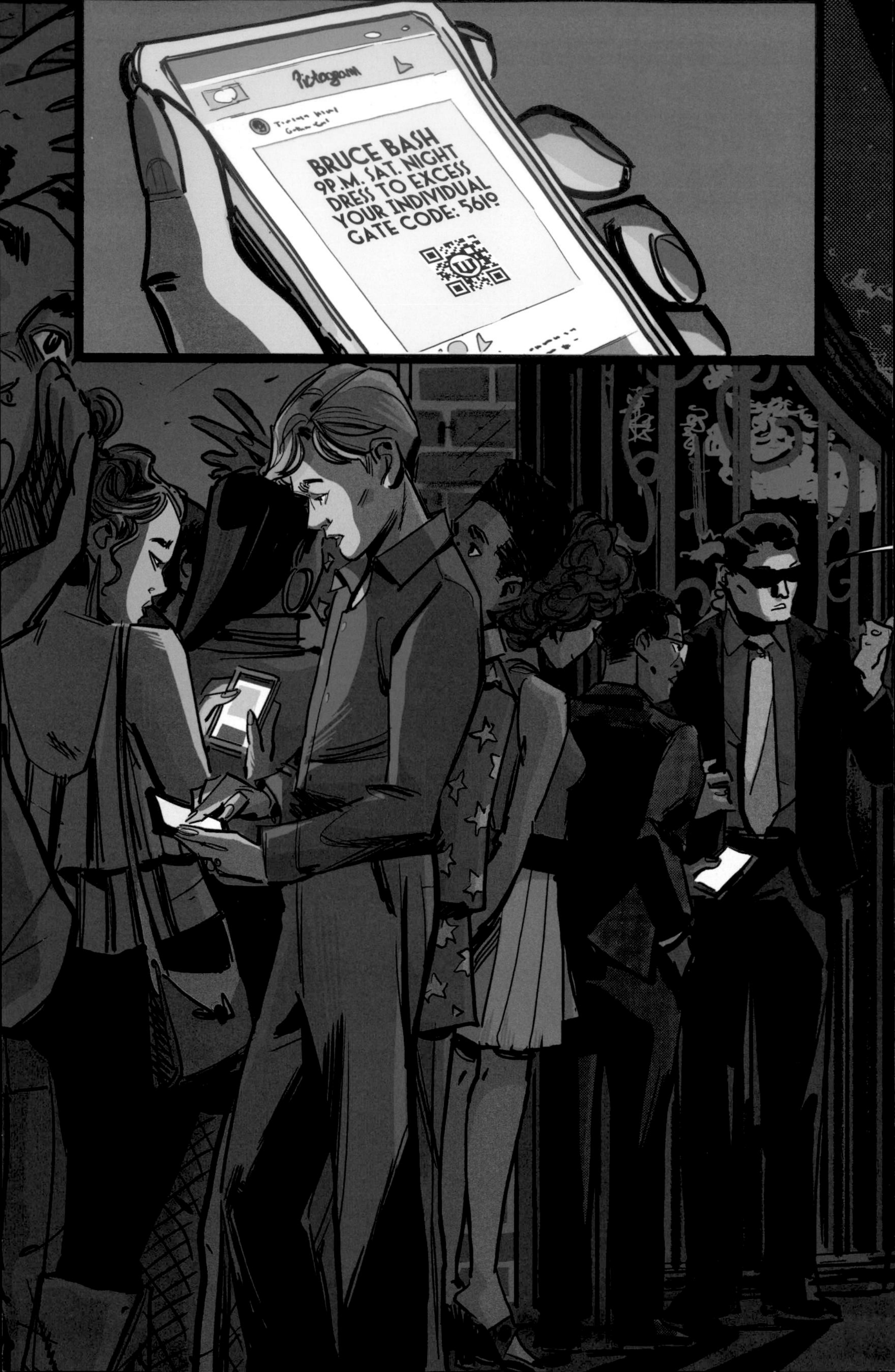
Pictogram
BRUCE BASH
9P.M. SAT. NIGHT
DRESS TO EXCESS
YOUR INDIVIDUAL
GATE CODE: 5610.

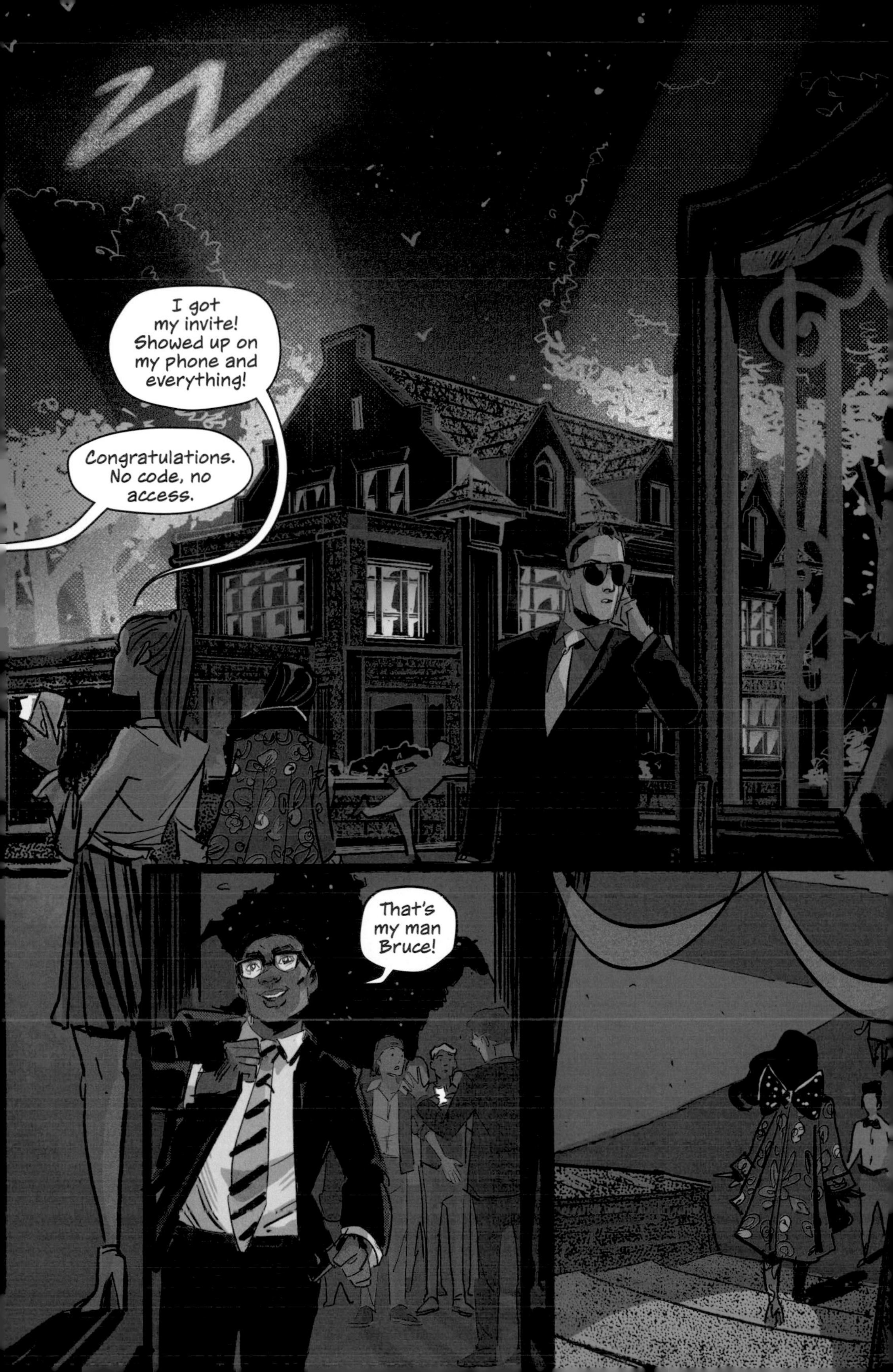
I got my invite! Showed up on my phone and everything!
Congratulations. No code, no access.
That's my man Bruce!

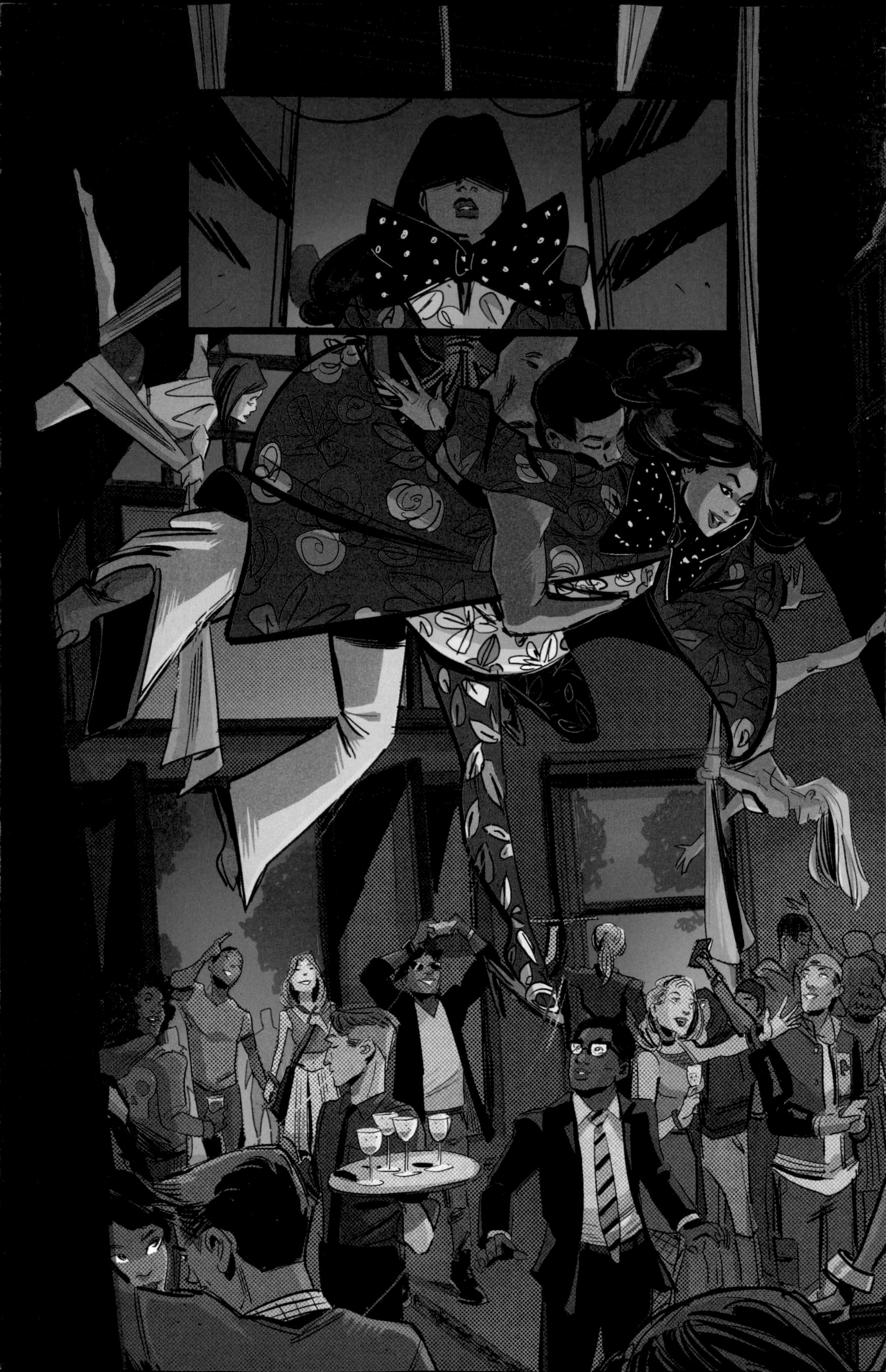

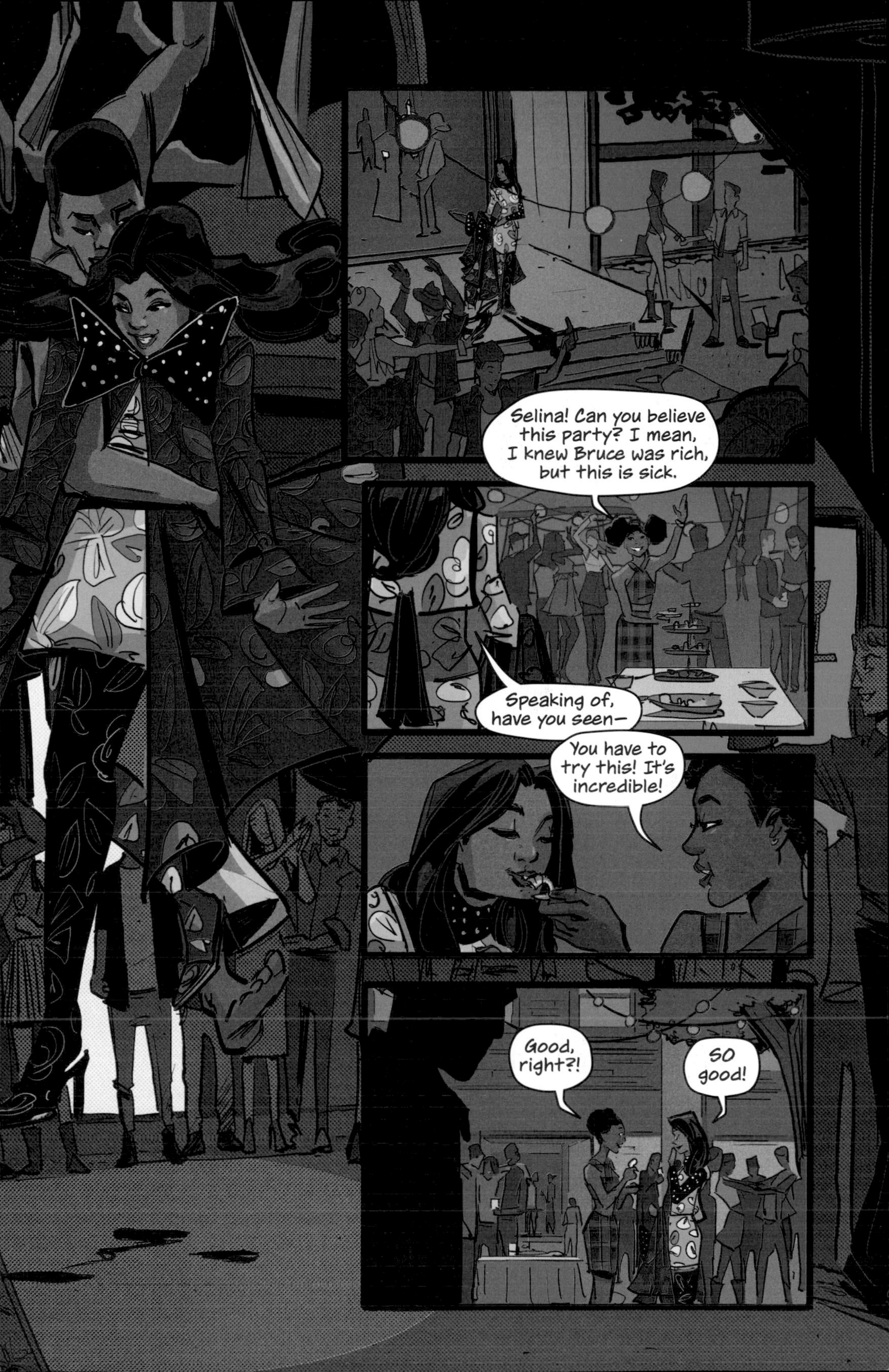
Selina! Can you believe this party? I mean, I knew Bruce was rich, but this is sick.
Speaking of, have you seen—
You have to try this! It's incredible!
Good, right?!
SO good!

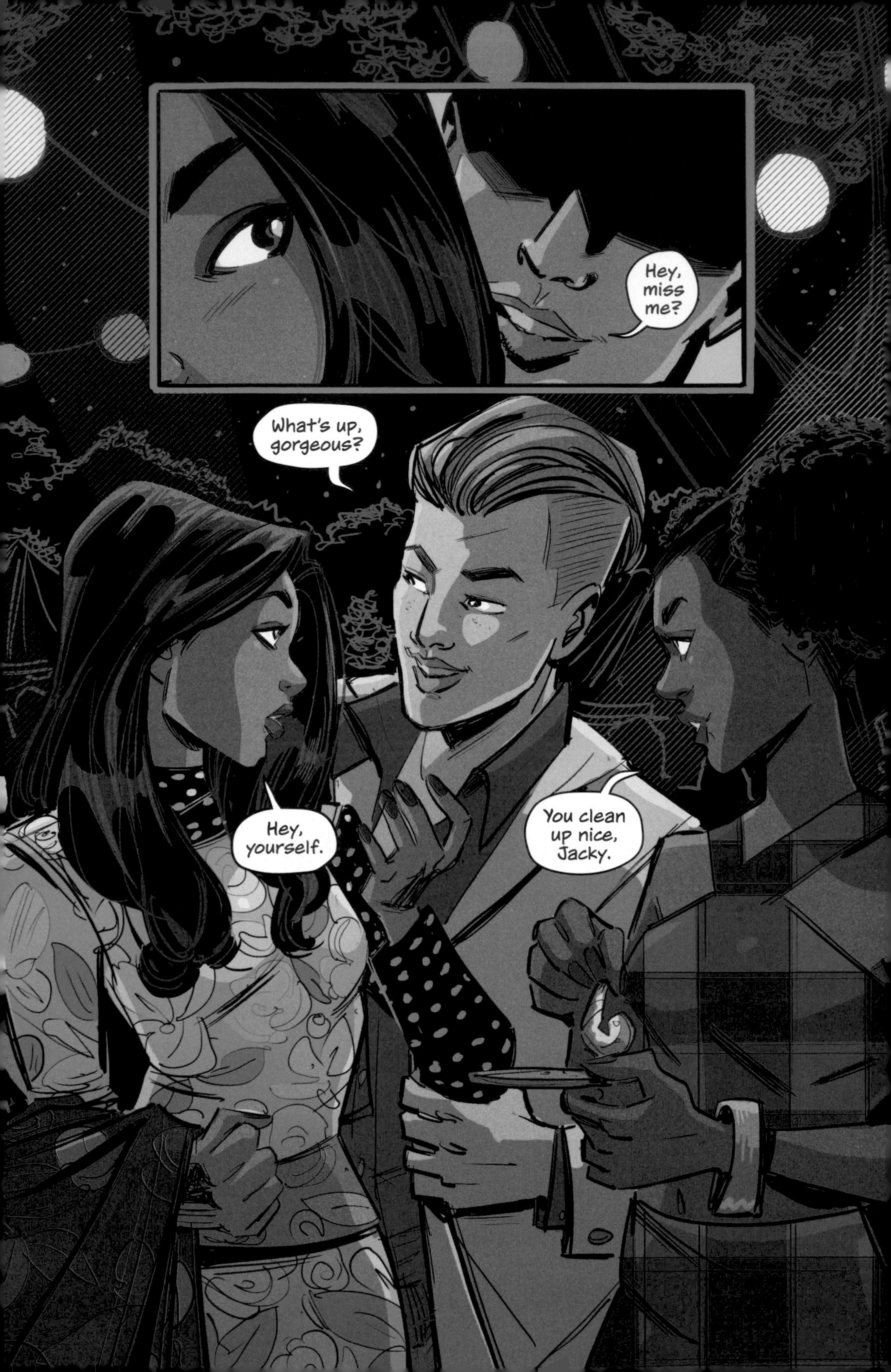
Hey, miss me?
What's up, gorgeous?
Hey, yourself.
You clean up nice, Jacky.

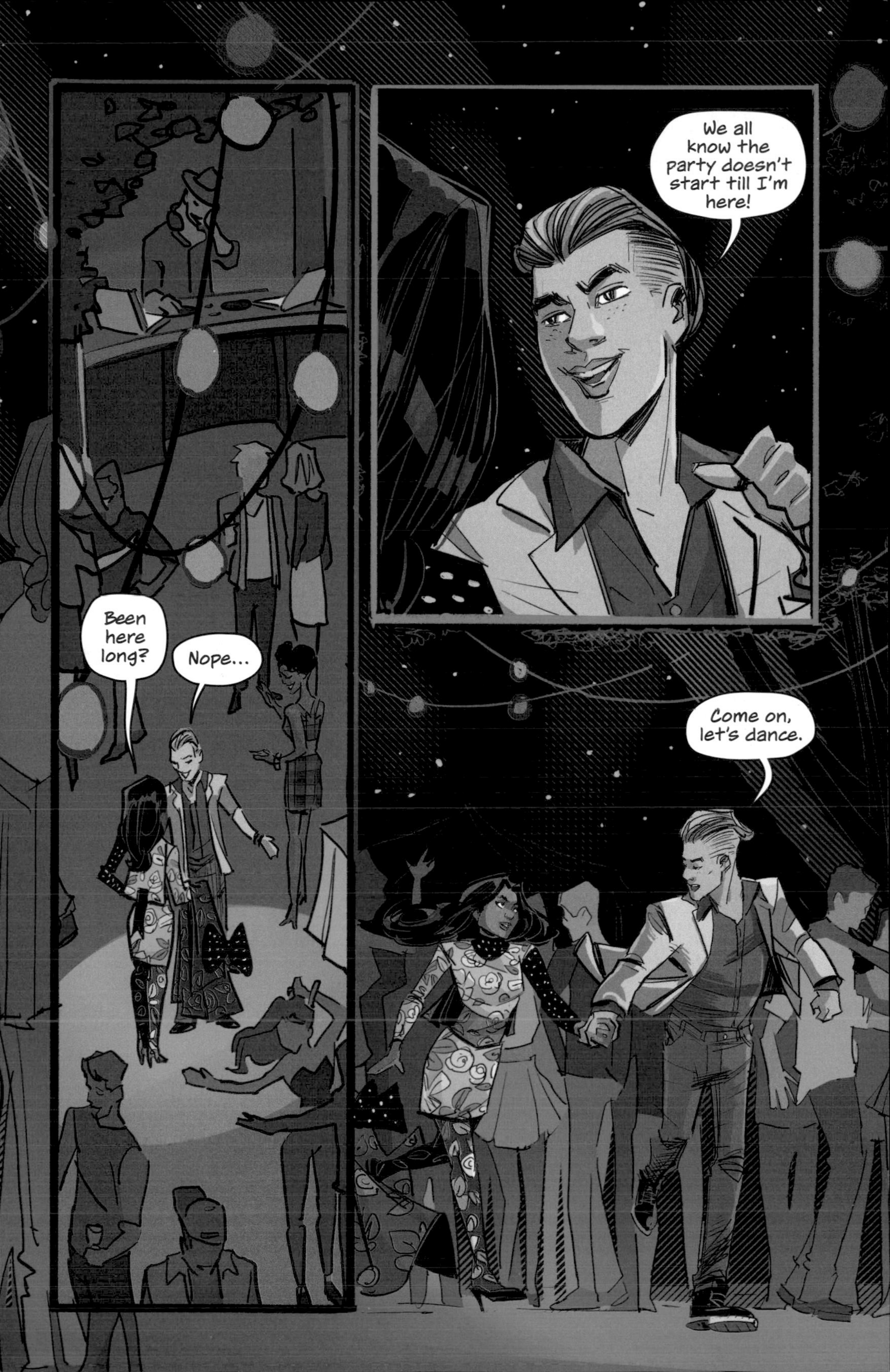
We all know the party doesn't start till I'm here!
Been here long?
Nope...
Come on, let's dance.

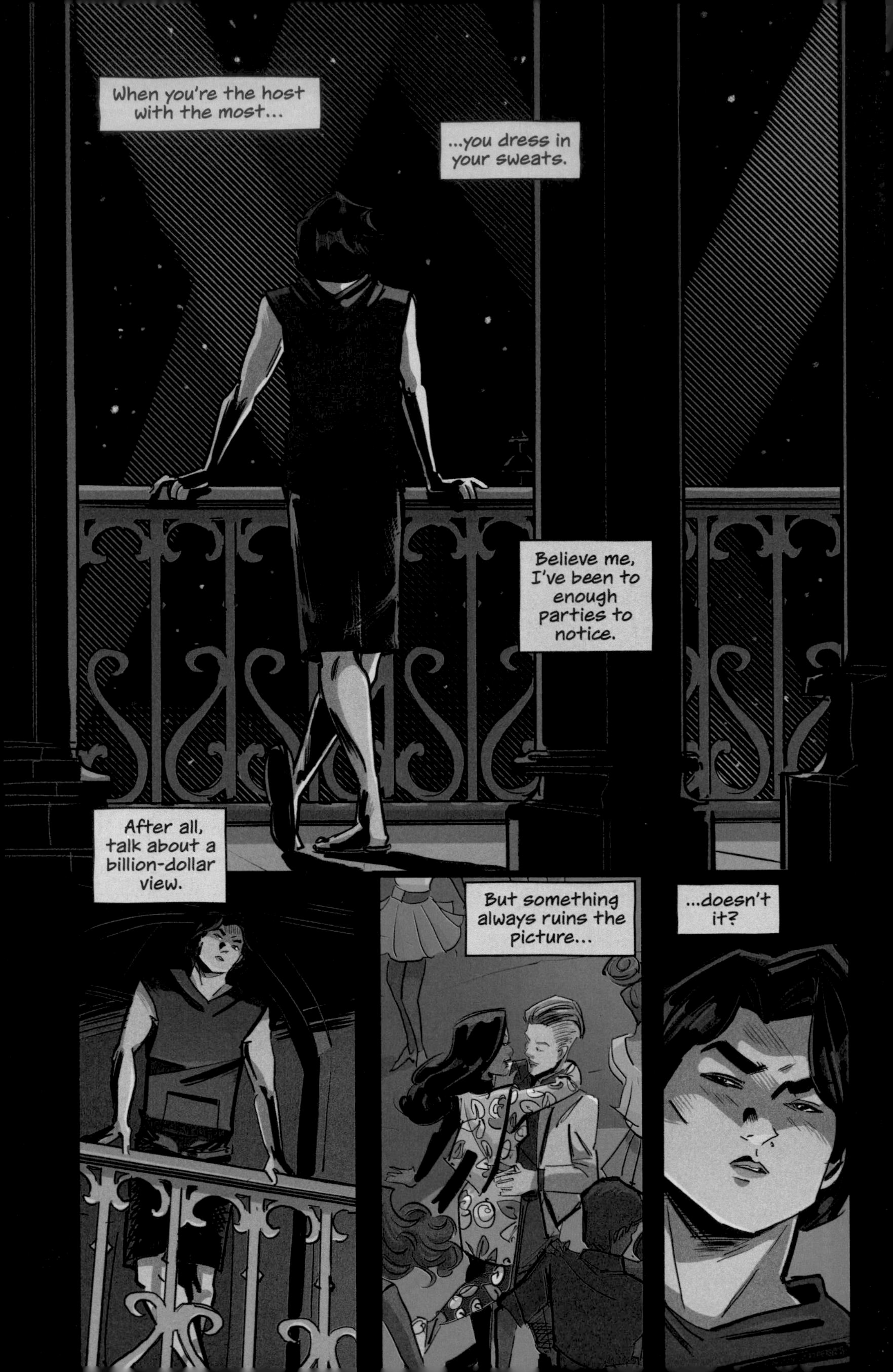
When you're the host with the most...
...you dress in your sweats.
Believe me, I've been to enough parties to notice.
After all, talk about a billion-dollar view.
But something always ruins the picture...
...doesn't it?

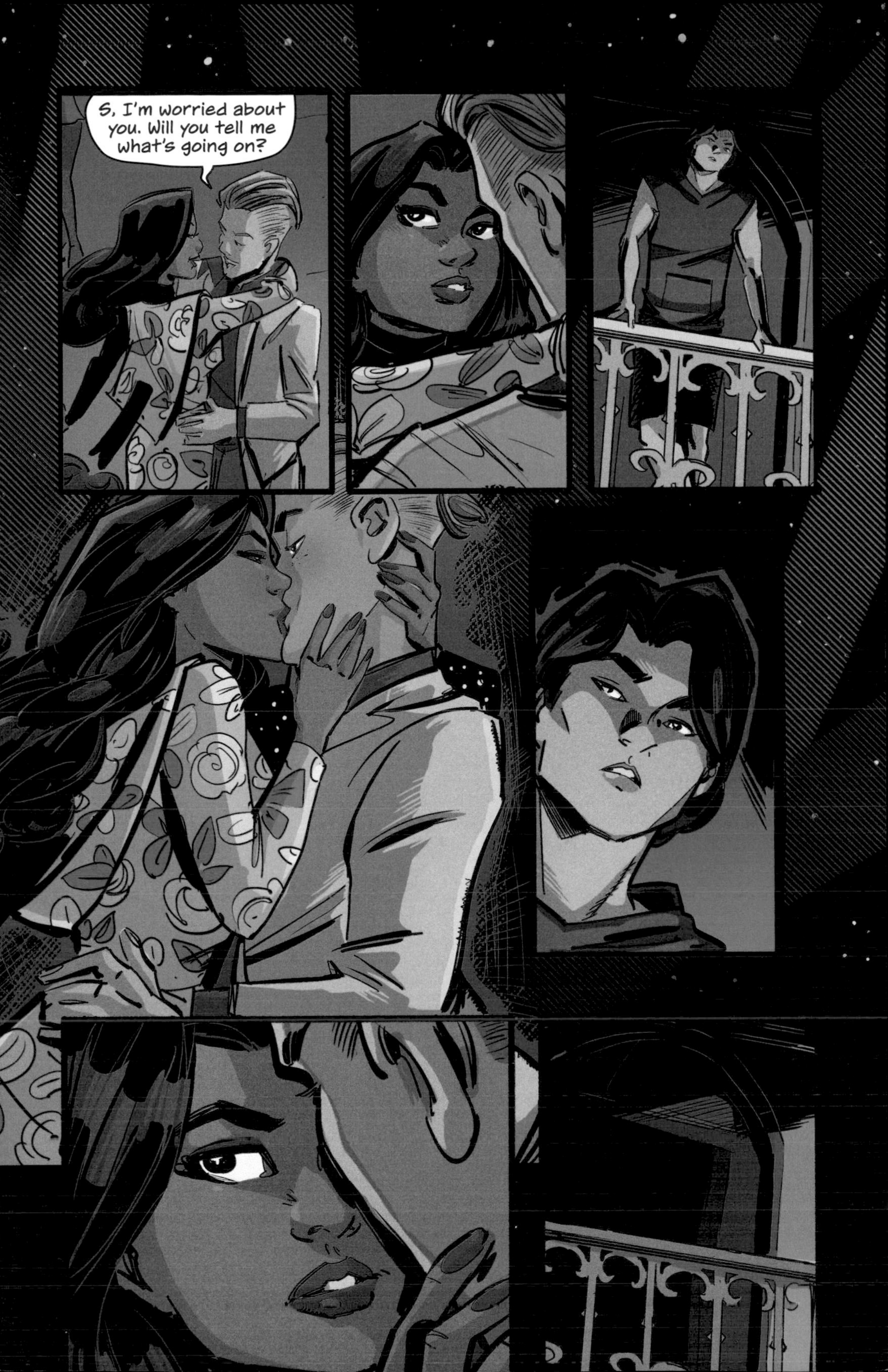
S, I'm worried about you. Will you tell me what's going on?

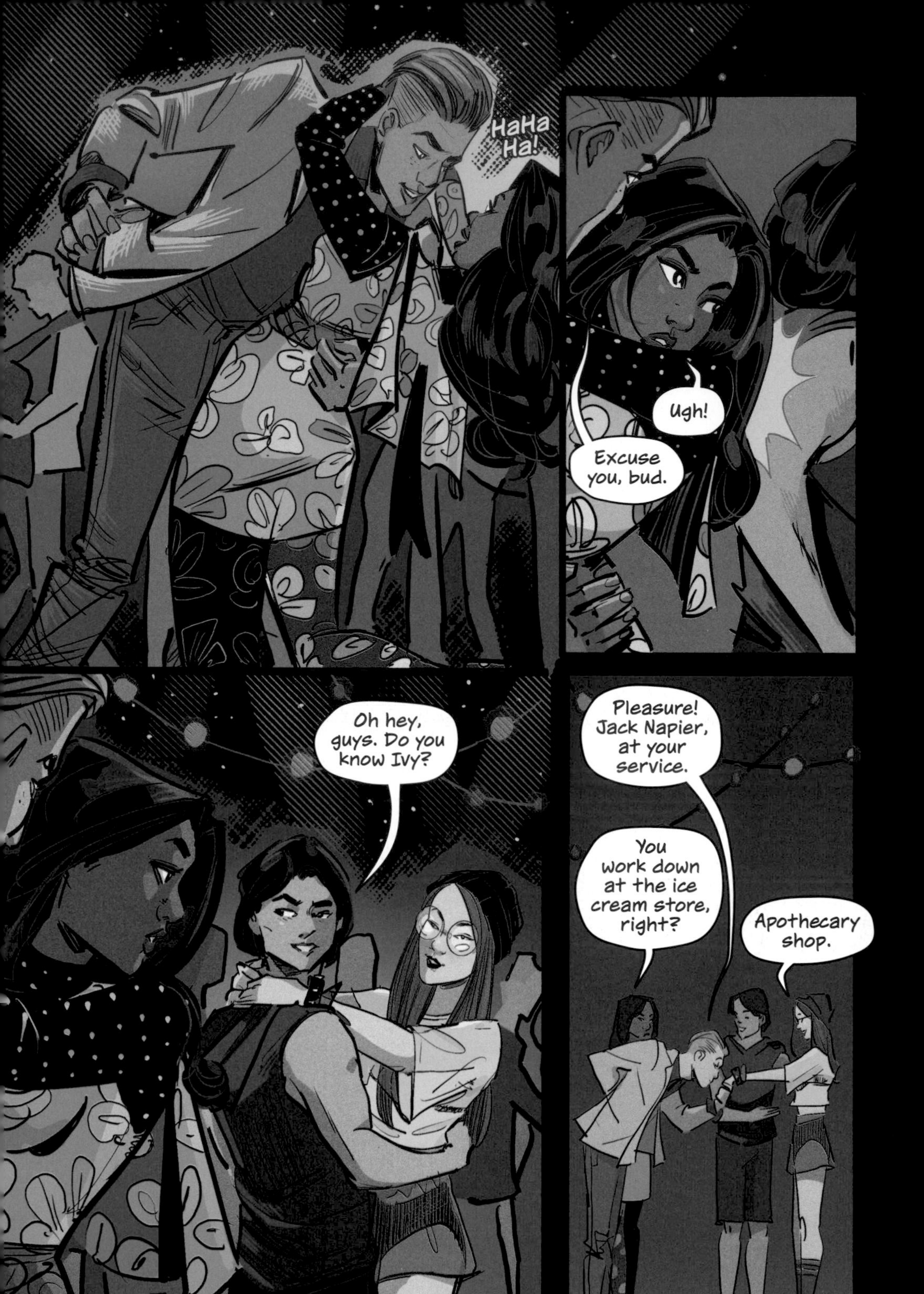
HaHa Ha!
Ugh!
Excuse you, bud.
Oh hey, guys. Do you know Ivy?
Pleasure! Jack Napier, at your service.
You work down at the ice cream store, right?
Apothecary shop.

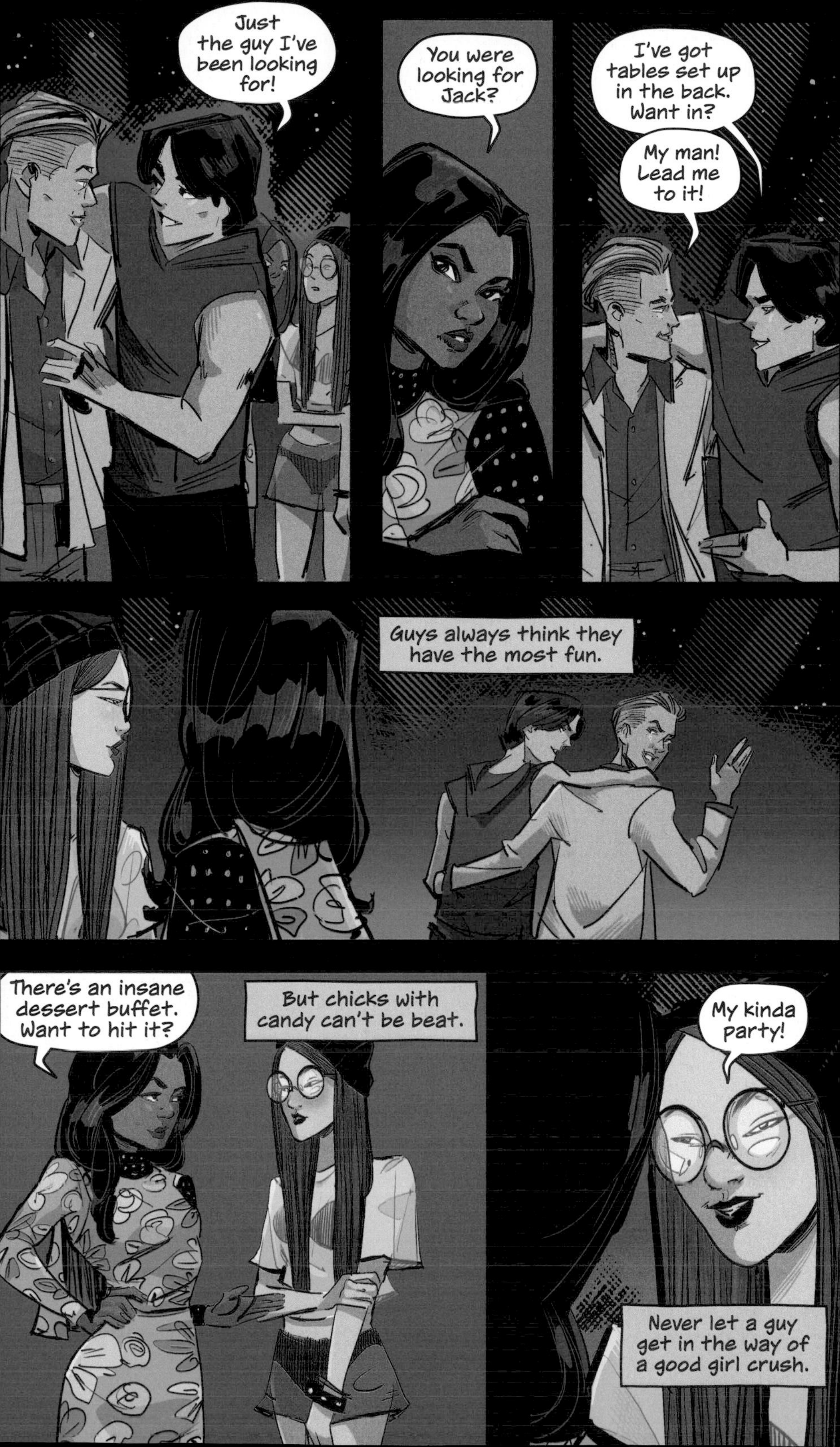
Just the guy I've been looking for!
You were looking for Jack?
I've got tables set up in the back. Want in?
My man! Lead me to it!
Guys always think they have the most fun.
There's an insane dessert buffet. Want to hit it?
But chicks with candy can't be beat.
My kinda party!
Never let a guy get in the way of a good girl crush.

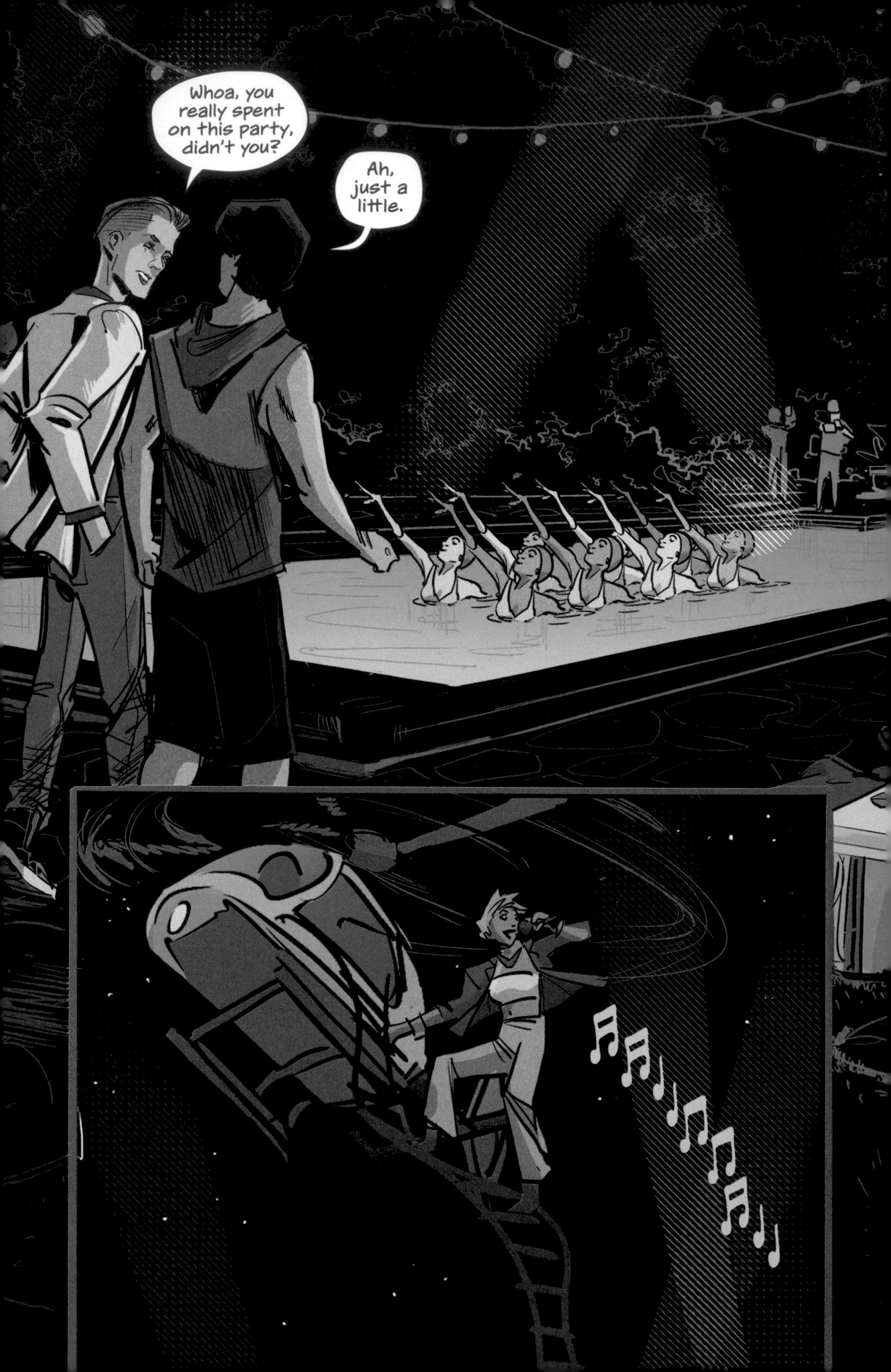
Whoa, you really spent on this party, didn't you?
Ah, just a little.

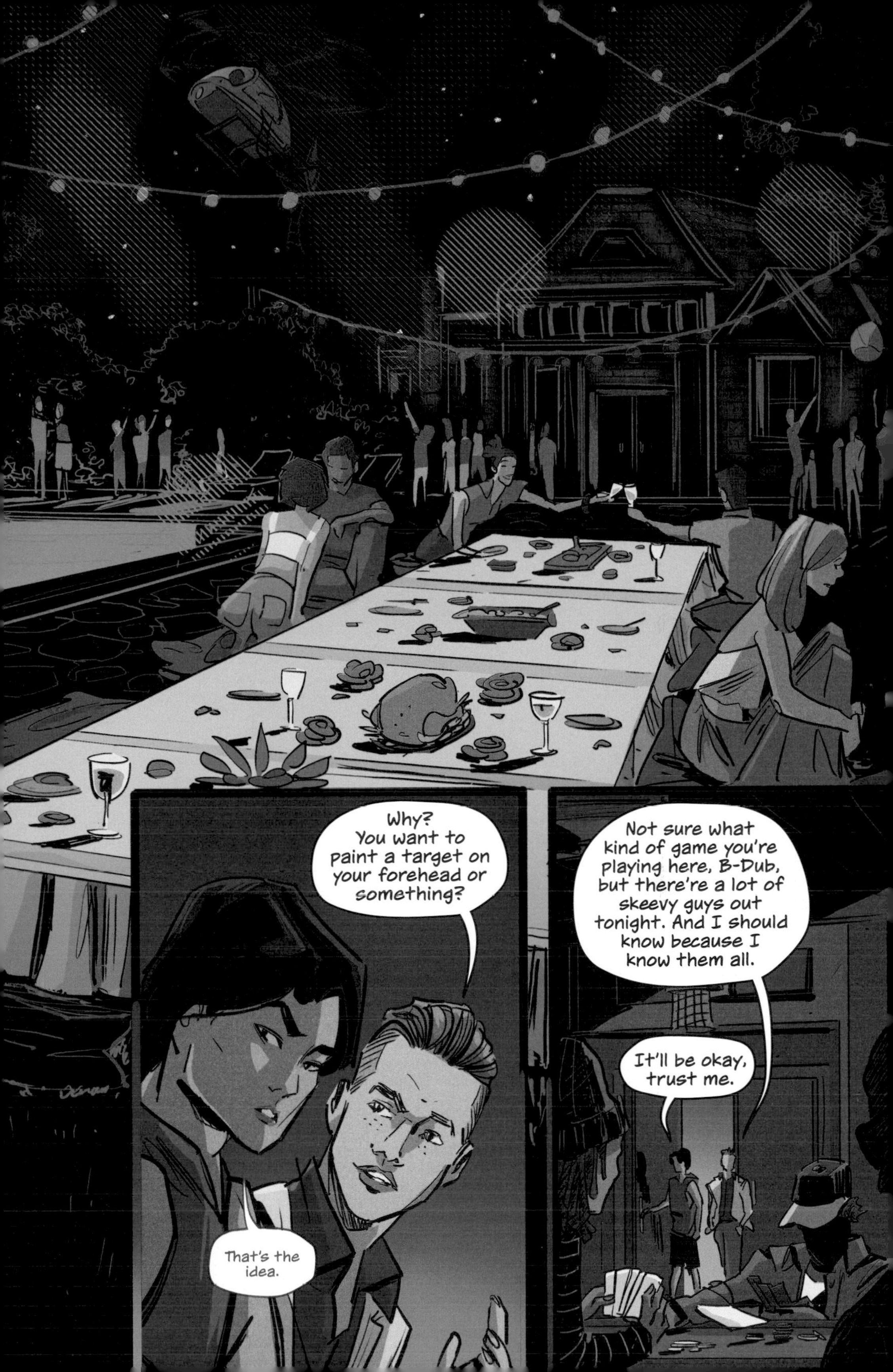
Why? You want to paint a target on your forehead or something?
That's the idea.
Not sure what kind of game you're playing here, B-Dub, but there're a lot of skeevy guys out tonight. And I should know because I know them all.
It'll be okay, trust me.

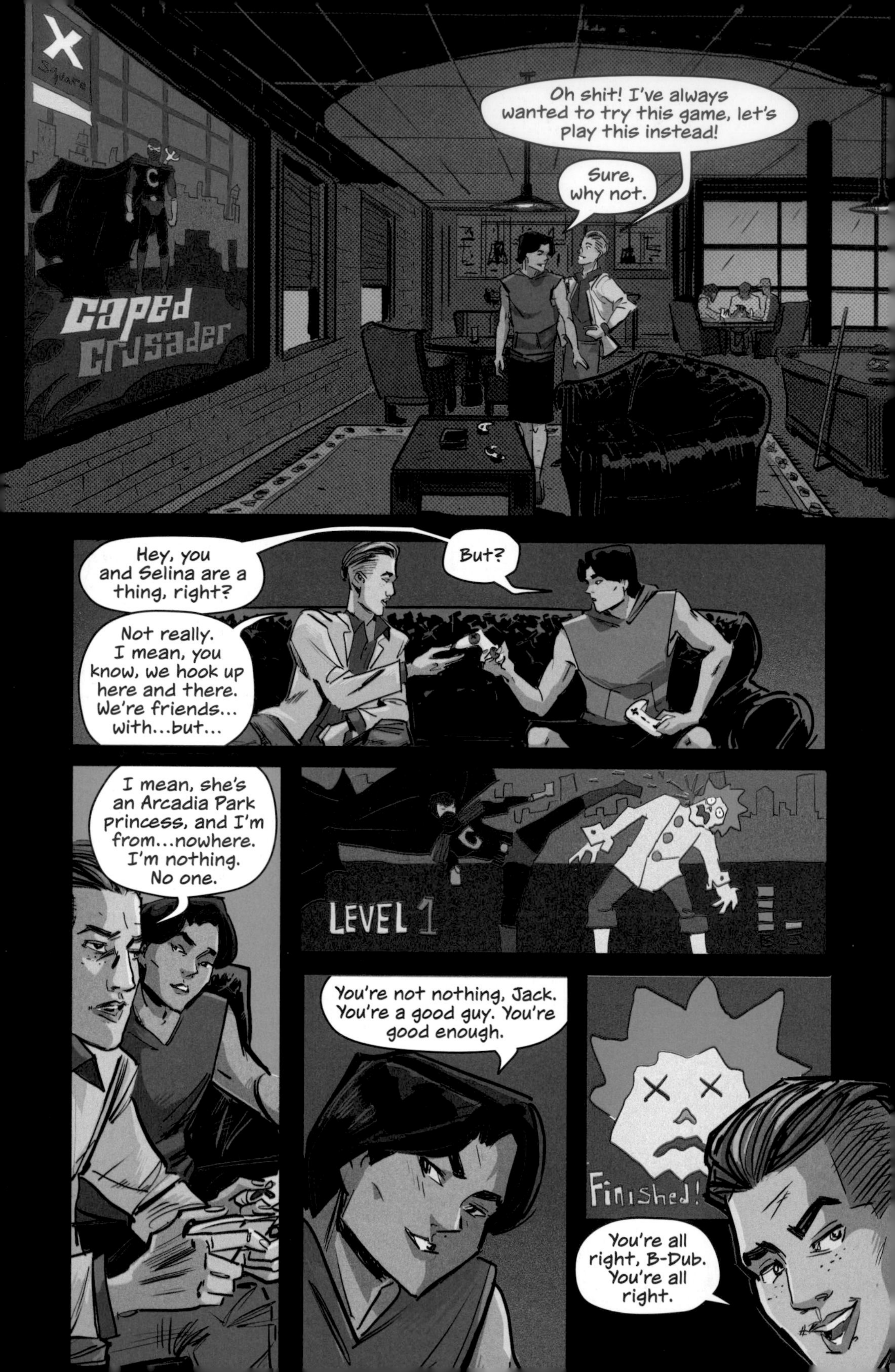
X
Square
Caped Crusader
Oh shit! I've always wanted to try this game, let's play this instead!
Sure, why not.
Hey, you and Selina are a thing, right?
But?
Not really. I mean, you know, we hook up here and there. We're friends... with...but...
I mean, she's an Arcadia Park princess, and I'm from...nowhere. I'm nothing. No one.
LEVEL 1
You're not nothing, Jack. You're a good guy. You're good enough.
Finished!
You're all right, B-Dub. You're all right.

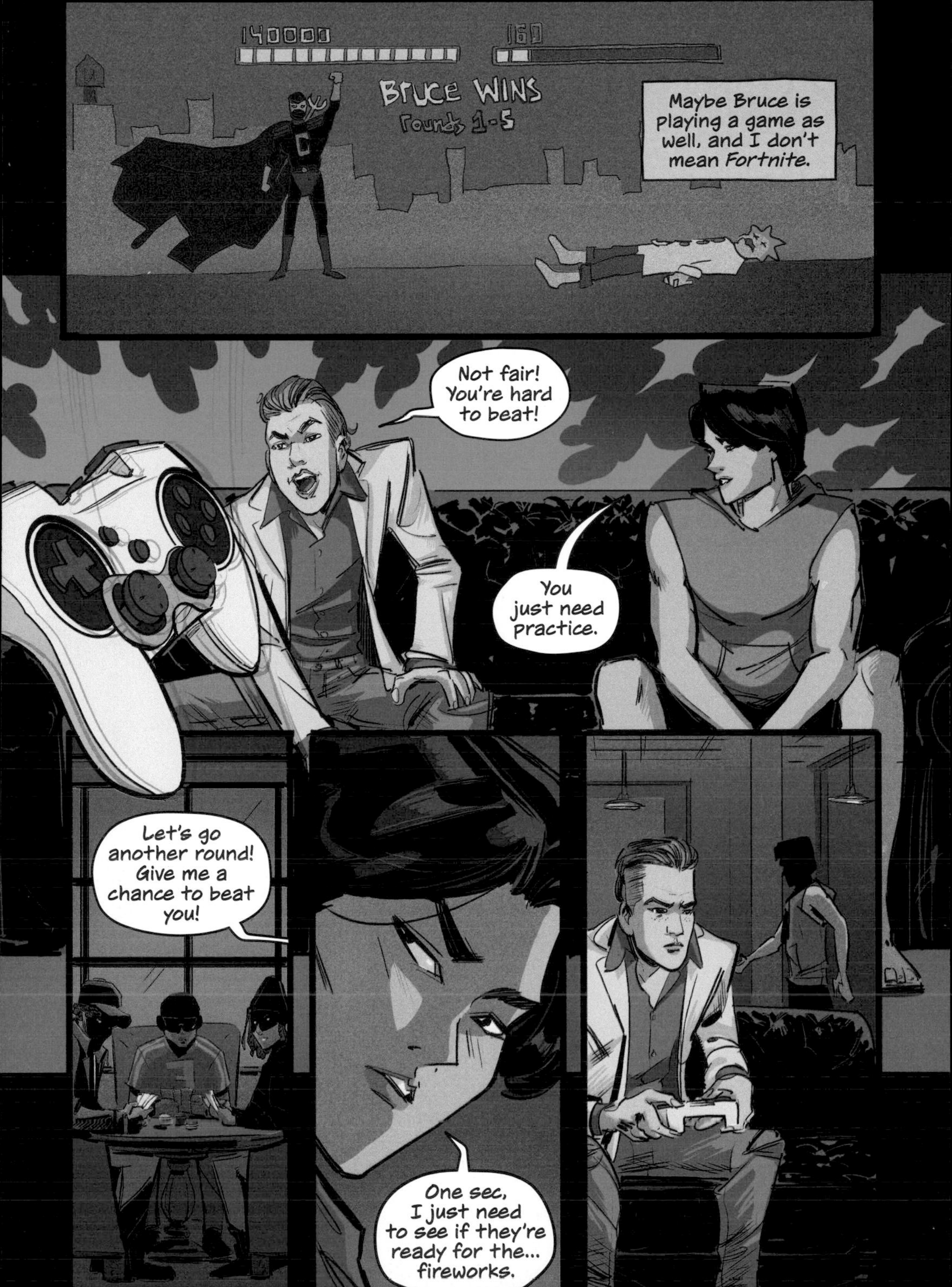
140000
160
Bruce WINS
rounds 1-5
Maybe Bruce is playing a game as well, and I don't mean *Fortnite*.
Not fair! You're hard to beat!
You just need practice.
Let's go another round! Give me a chance to beat you!
One sec, I just need to see if they're ready for the... fireworks.

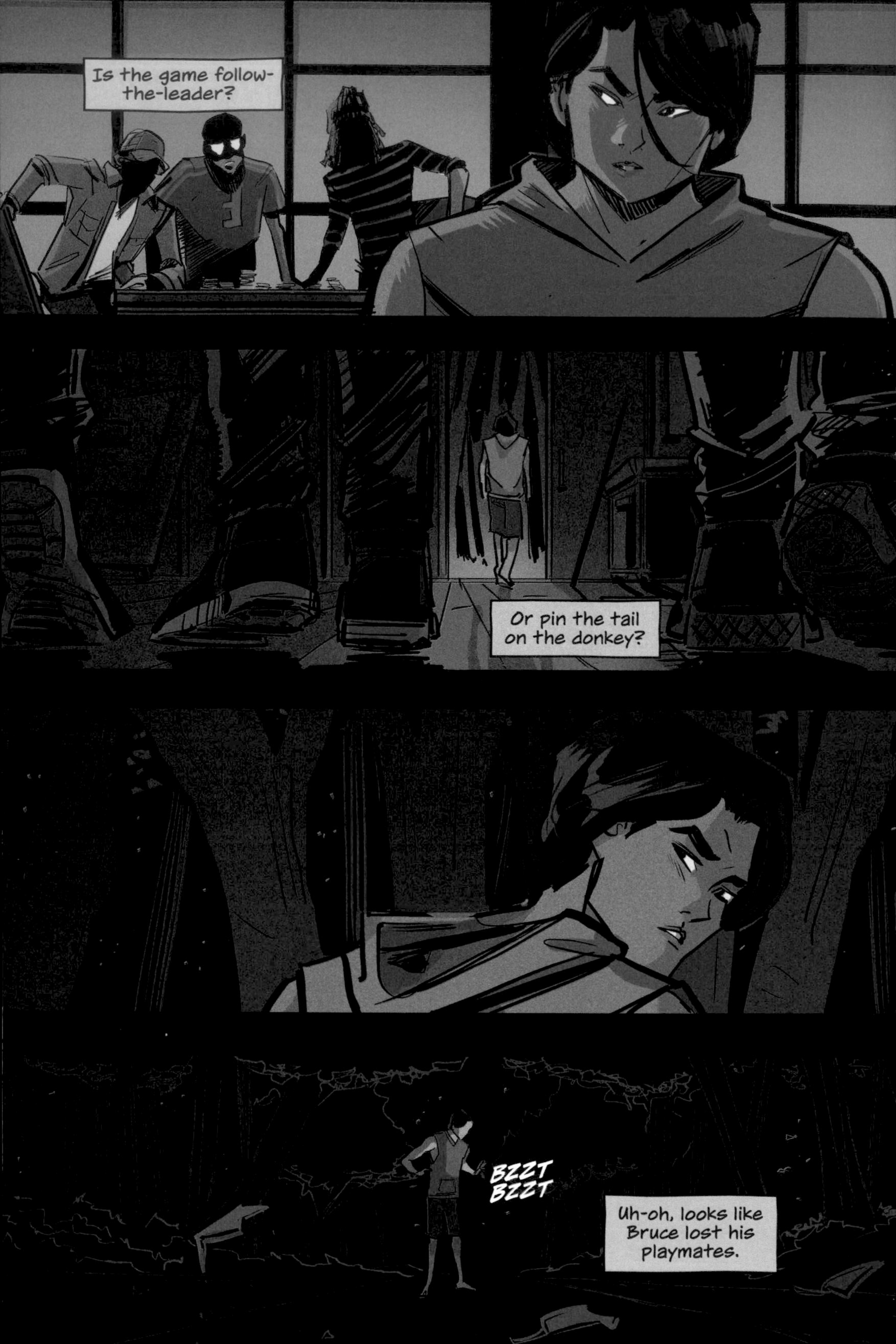
Is the game follow-the-leader?
Or pin the tail on the donkey?
BZZT BZZT
Uh-oh, looks like Bruce lost his playmates.

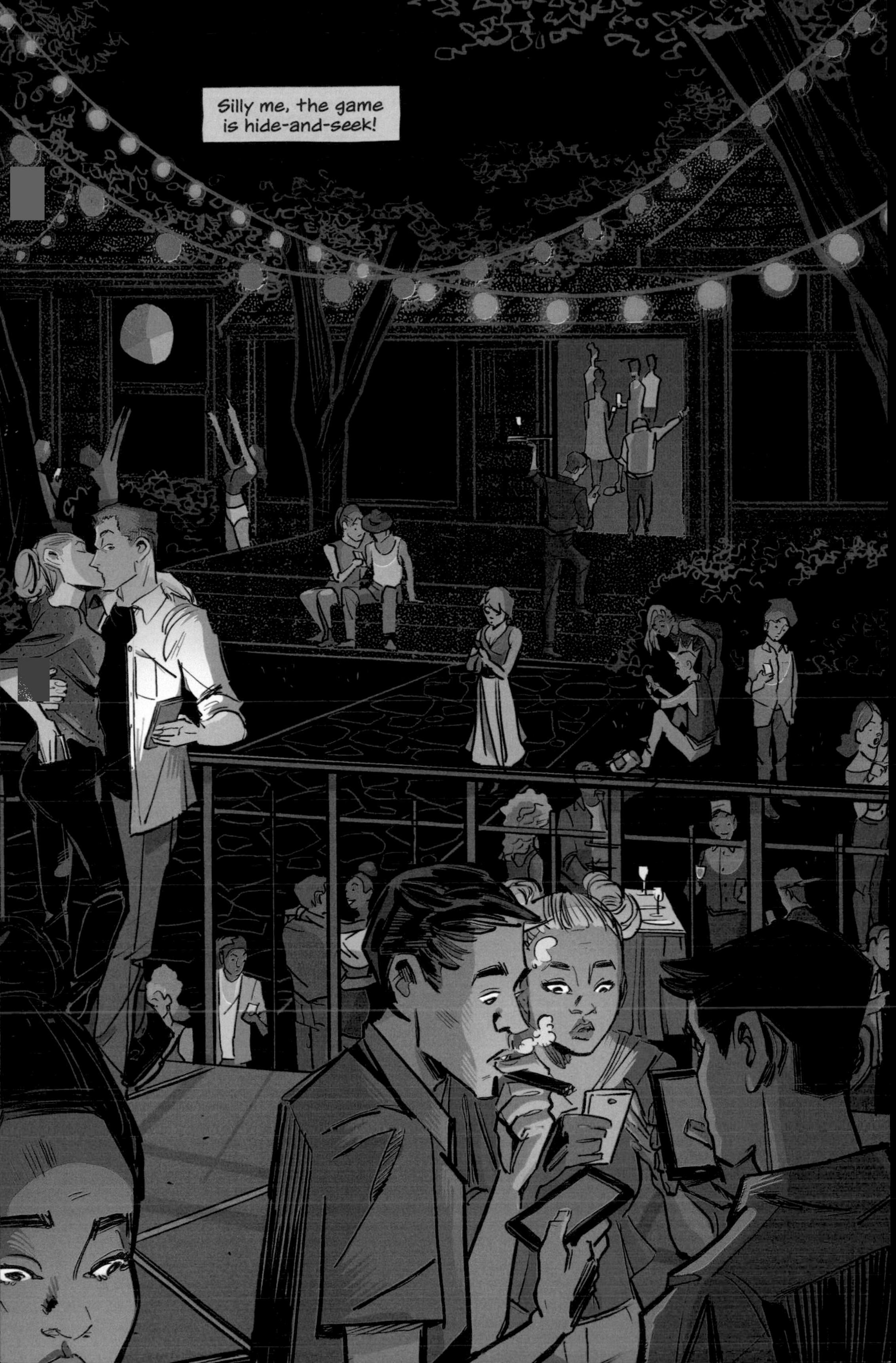
Silly me, the game
is hide-and-seek!

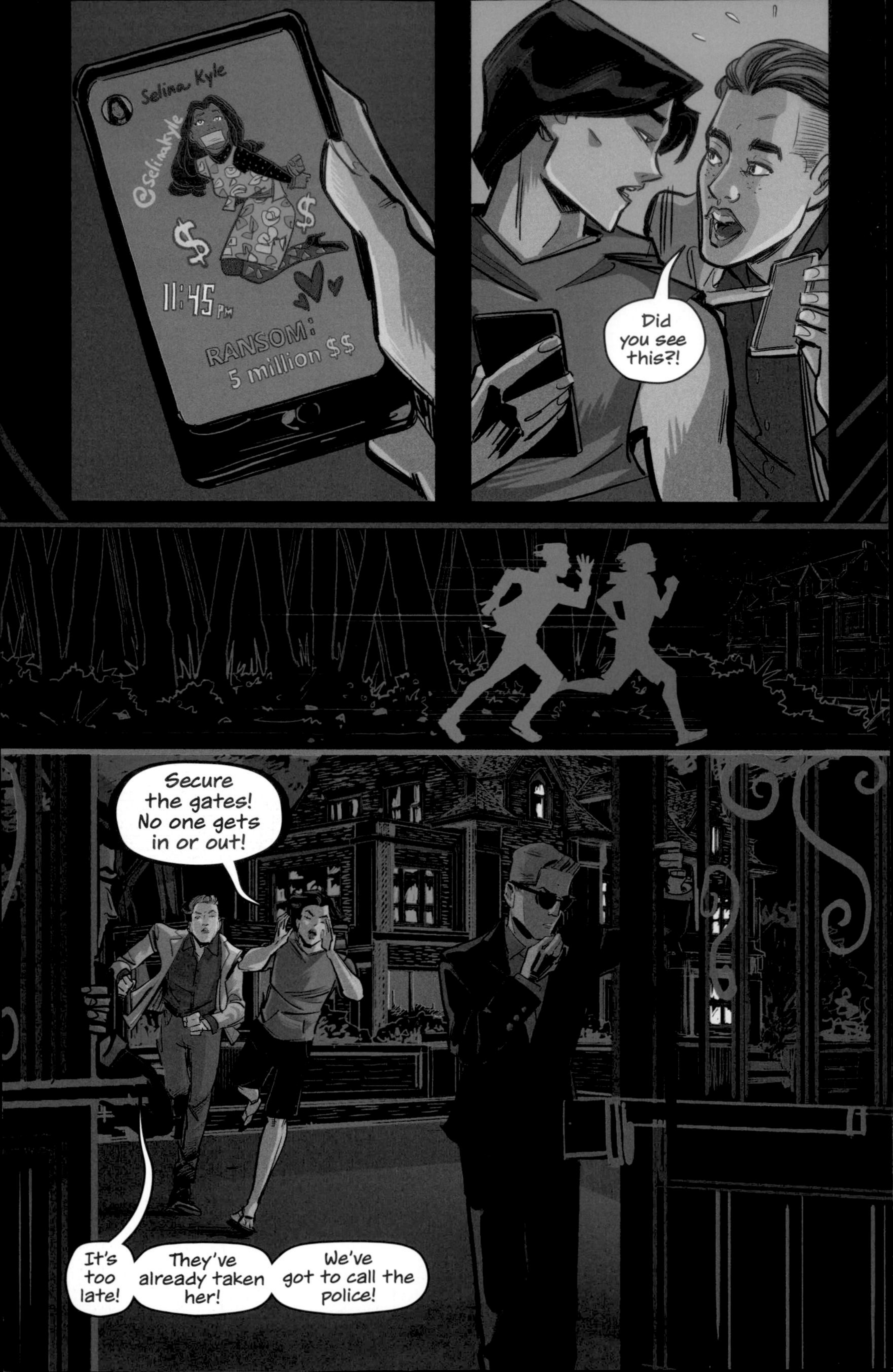
Selina Kyle
@selinakyle
11:45 PM
RANSOM: 5 million $$
Did you see this?!
Secure the gates! No one gets in or out!
It's too late!
They've already taken her!
We've got to call the police!

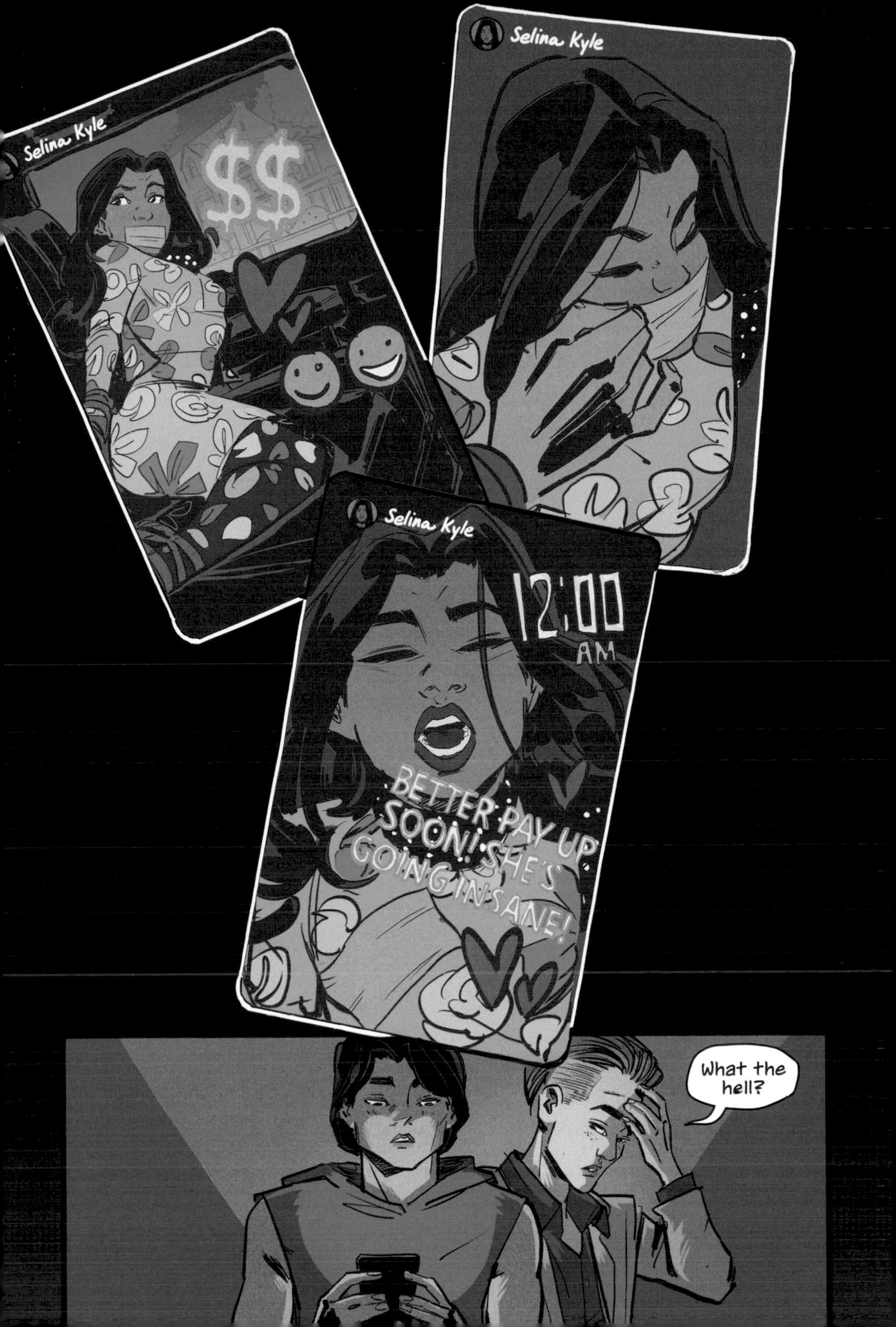
Selina Kyle
$$
Selina Kyle
Selina Kyle
12:00 AM
BETTER PAY UP SOON! SHE'S GOING INSANE!
What the hell?

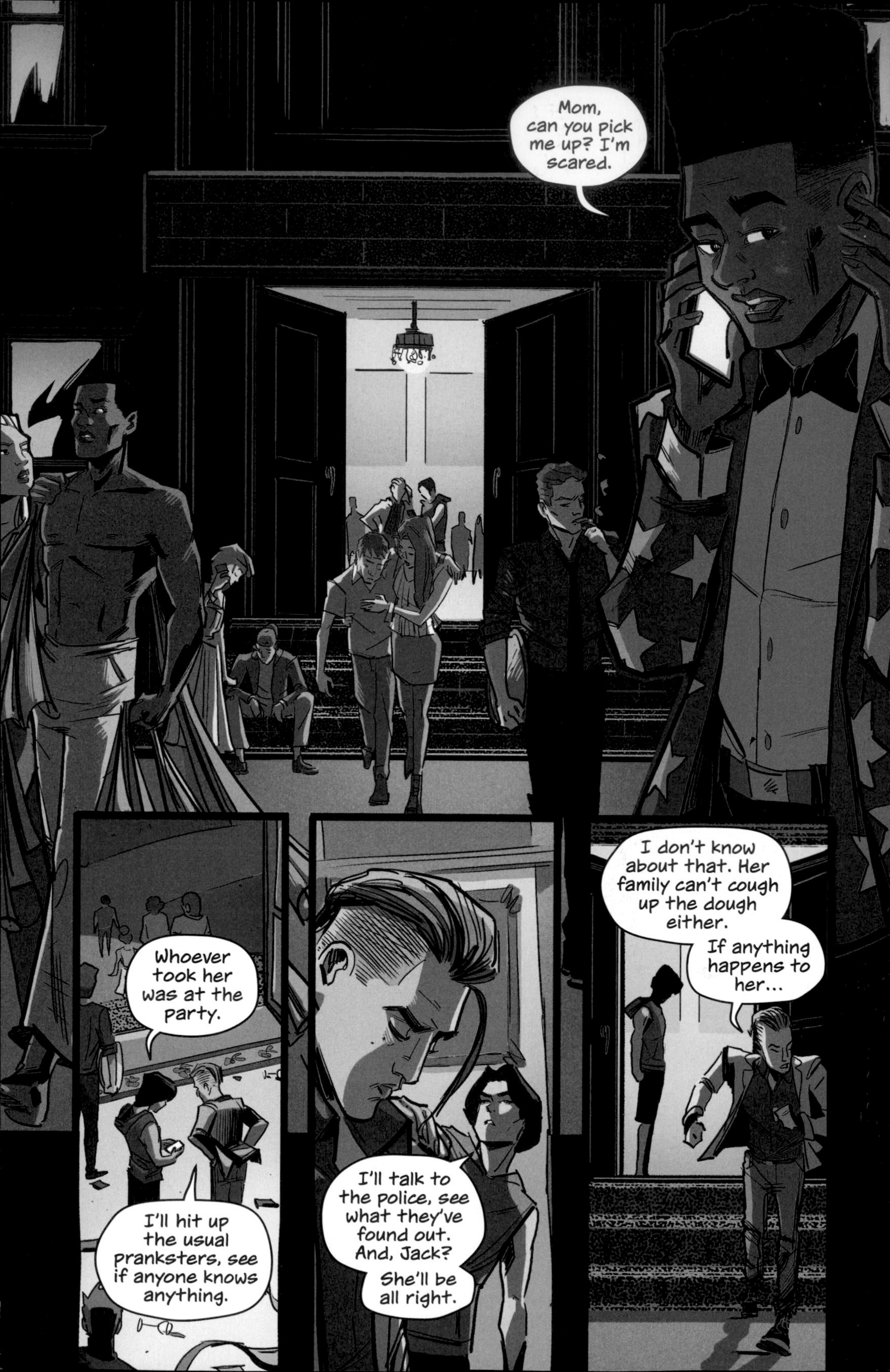
Mom, can you pick me up? I'm scared.
Whoever took her was at the party.
I'll hit up the usual pranksters, see if anyone knows anything.
I'll talk to the police, see what they've found out. And, Jack?
She'll be all right.
I don't know about that. Her family can't cough up the dough either.
If anything happens to her...

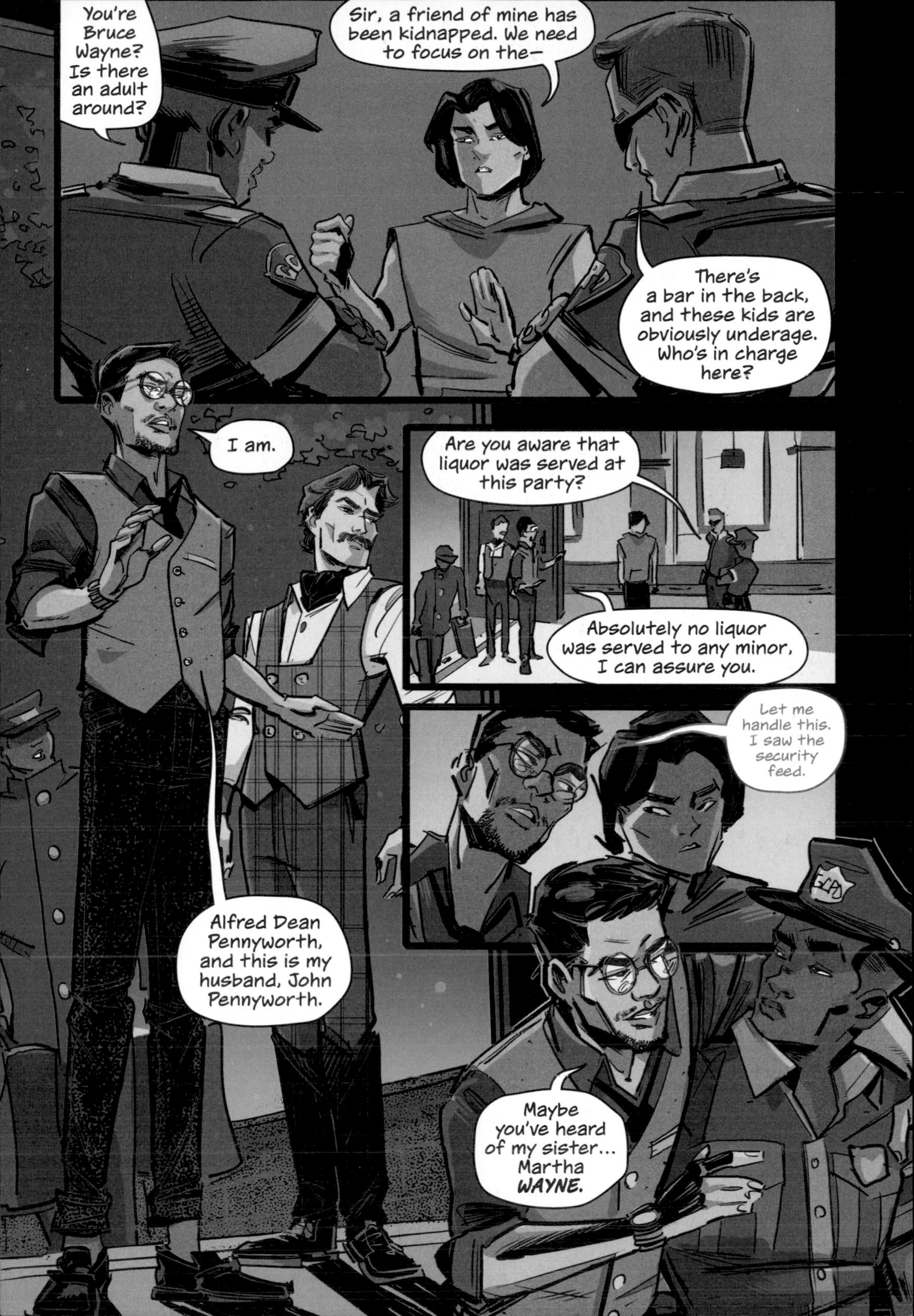
You're Bruce Wayne? Is there an adult around?
Sir, a friend of mine has been kidnapped. We need to focus on the—
There's a bar in the back, and these kids are obviously underage. Who's in charge here?
I am.
Are you aware that liquor was served at this party?
Absolutely no liquor was served to any minor, I can assure you.
Alfred Dean Pennyworth, and this is my husband, John Pennyworth.
Let me handle this. I saw the security feed.
Maybe you've heard of my sister... Martha **WAYNE.**

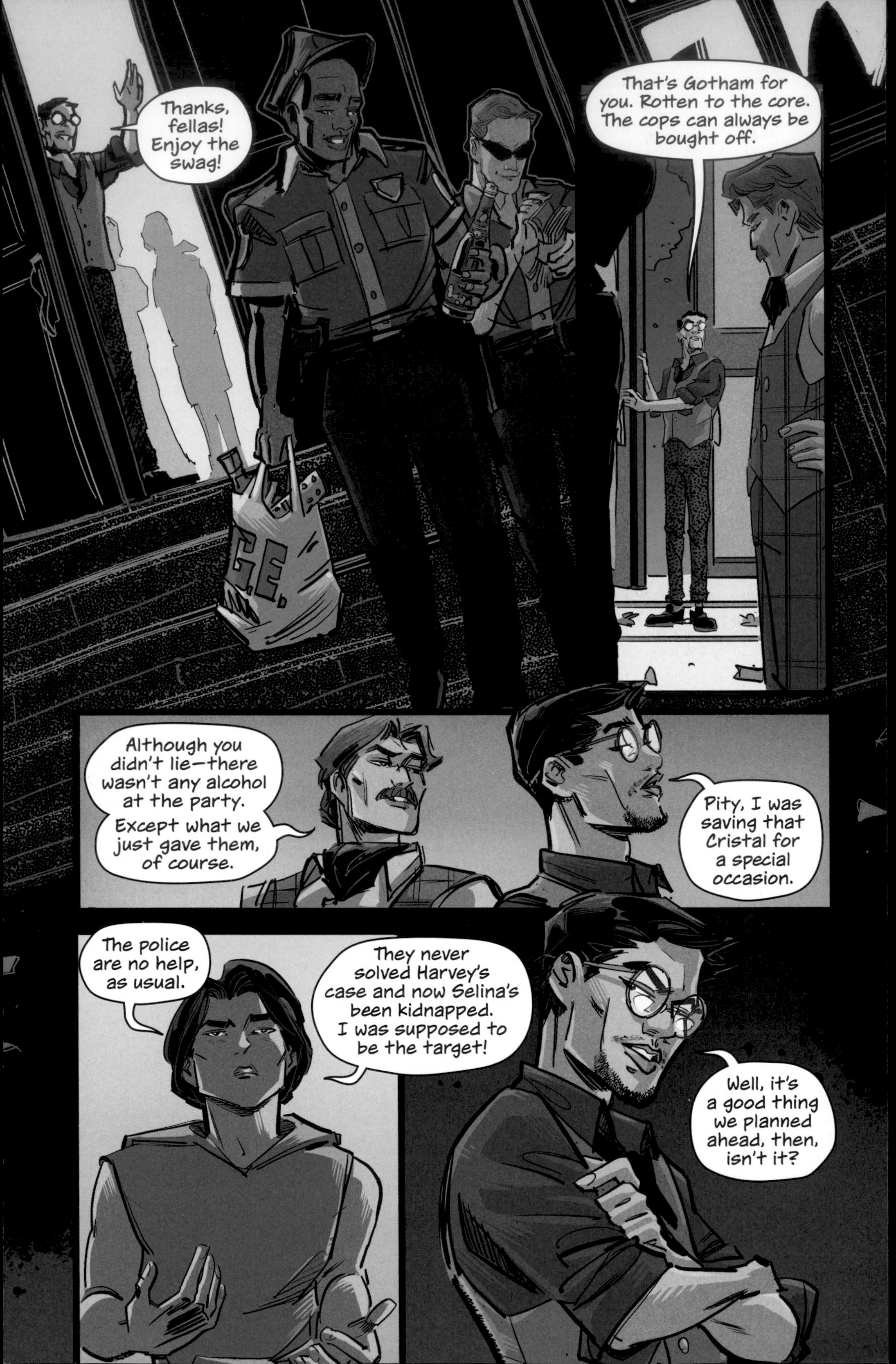
Thanks, fellas! Enjoy the swag!
That's Gotham for you. Rotten to the core. The cops can always be bought off.
G.E.
Although you didn't lie—there wasn't any alcohol at the party.
Except what we just gave them, of course.
Pity, I was saving that Cristal for a special occasion.
The police are no help, as usual.
They never solved Harvey's case and now Selina's been kidnapped. I was supposed to be the target!
Well, it's a good thing we planned ahead, then, isn't it?

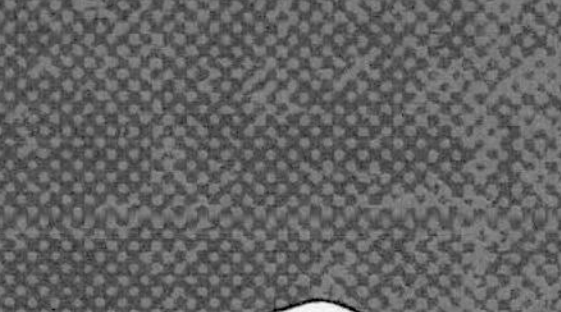

PART THREE

Behind the Mask

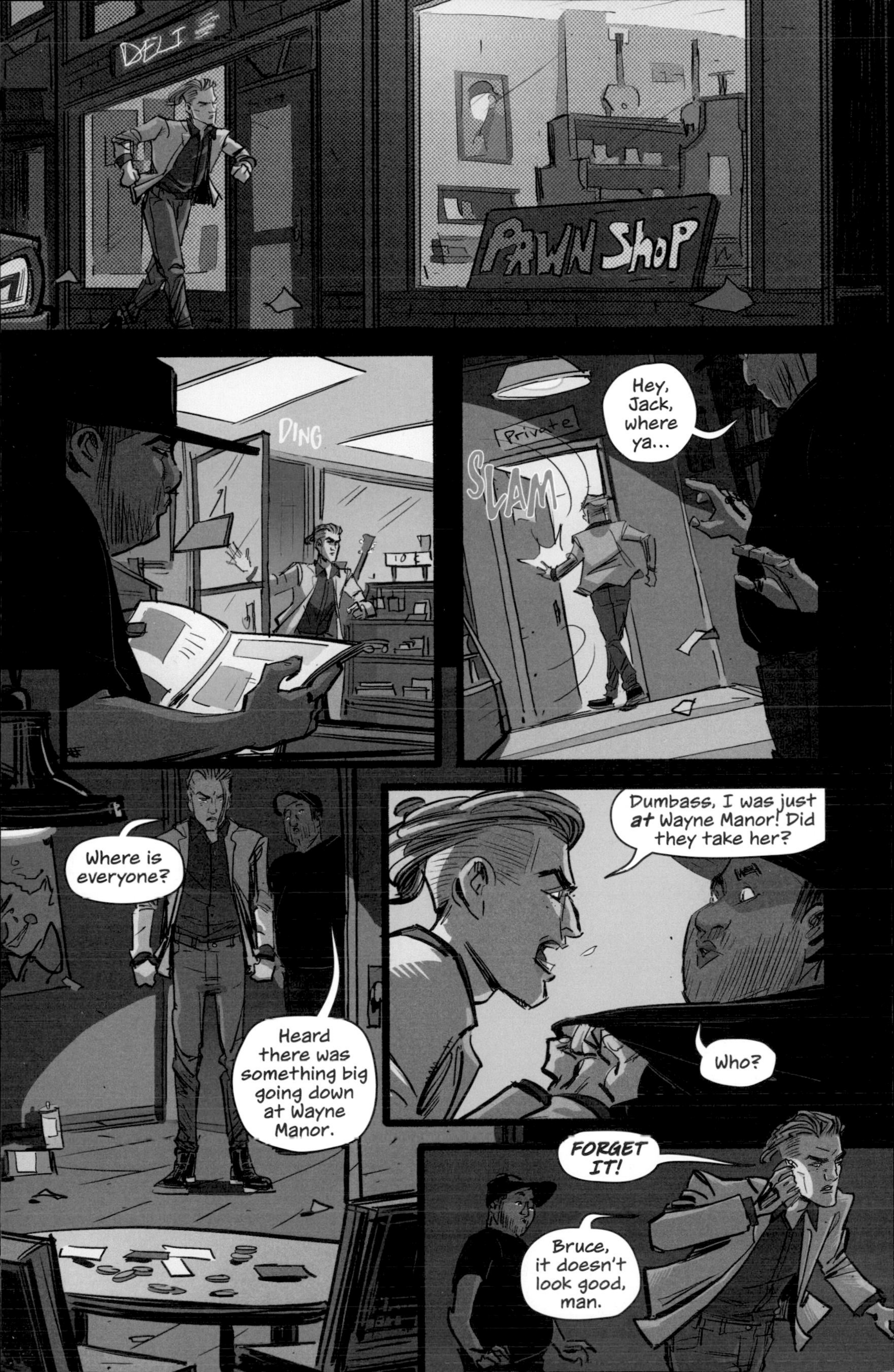
DELI
PAWN SHOP
DING
Hey, Jack, where ya...
Private
SLAM
Where is everyone?
Heard there was something big going down at Wayne Manor.
Dumbass, I was just at Wayne Manor! Did they take her?
Who?
FORGET IT!
Bruce, it doesn't look good, man.

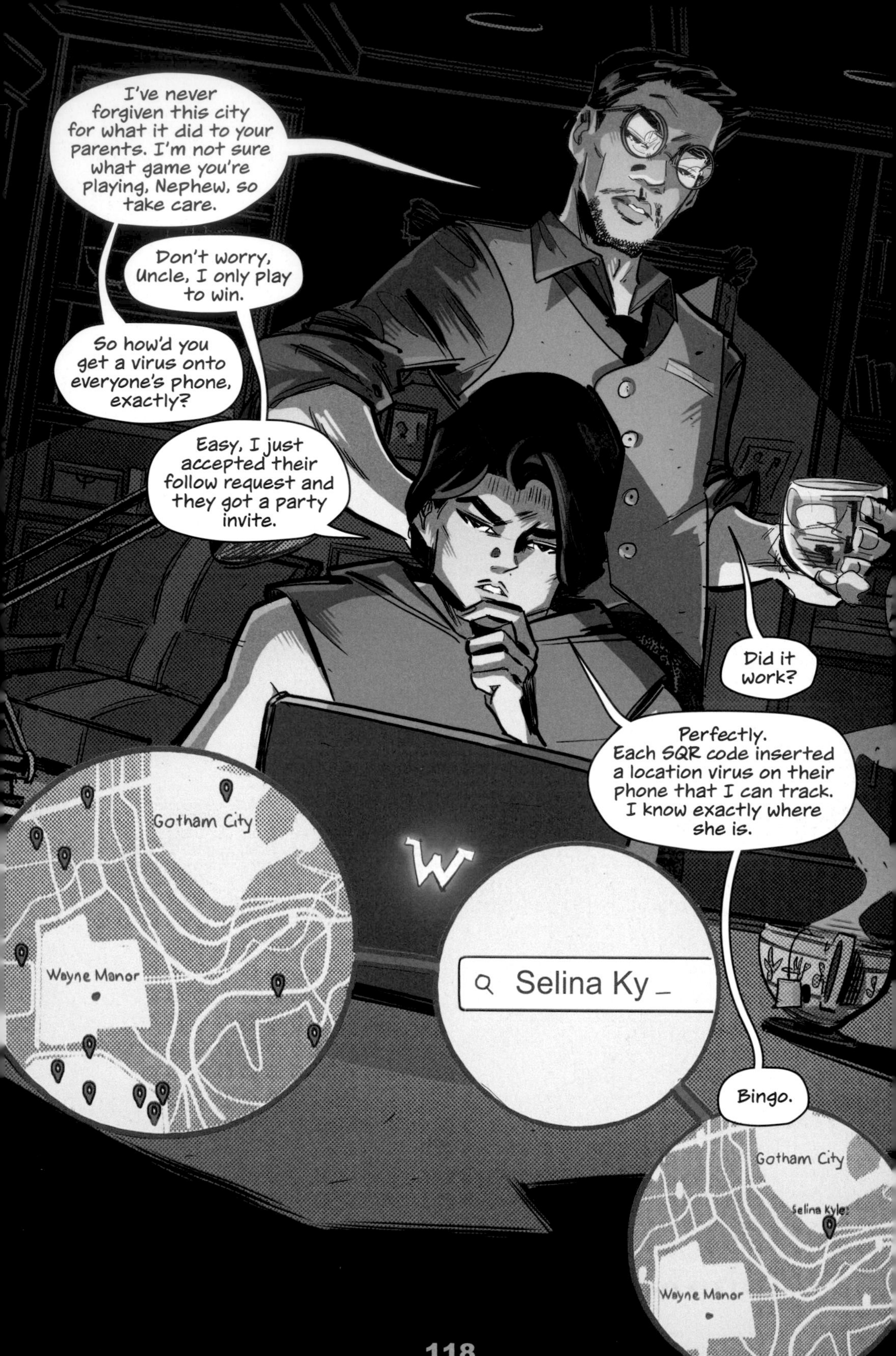
I've never forgiven this city for what it did to your parents. I'm not sure what game you're playing, Nephew, so take care.
Don't worry, Uncle, I only play to win.
So how'd you get a virus onto everyone's phone, exactly?
Easy, I just accepted their follow request and they got a party invite.
Did it work?
Perfectly. Each SQR code inserted a location virus on their phone that I can track. I know exactly where she is.
Gotham City
Wayne Manor
Selina Ky_
Bingo.
Gotham City
Selina Kyle
Wayne Manor

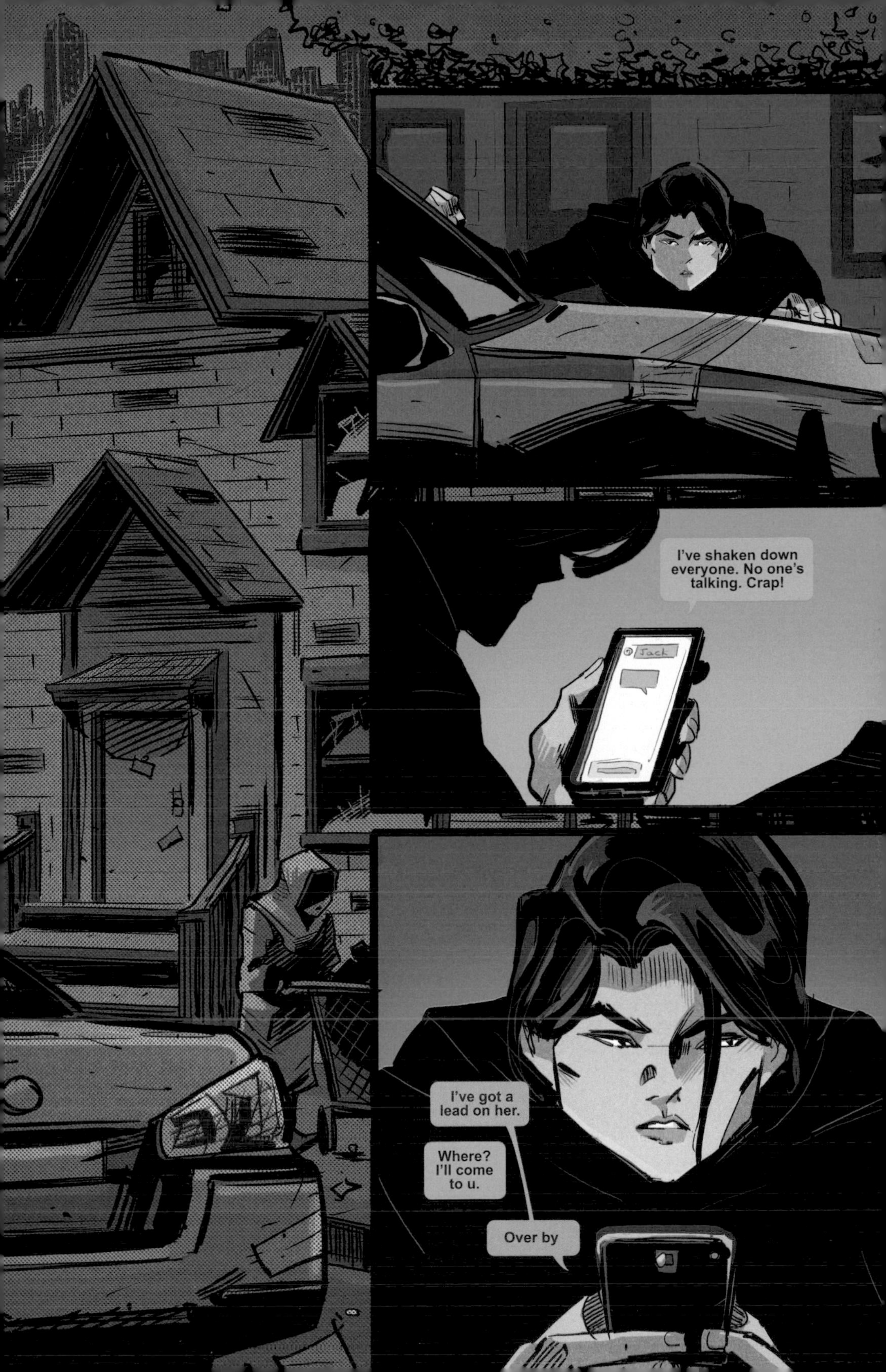
I've shaken down everyone. No one's talking. Crap!
Jack
I've got a lead on her.
Where? I'll come to u.
Over by

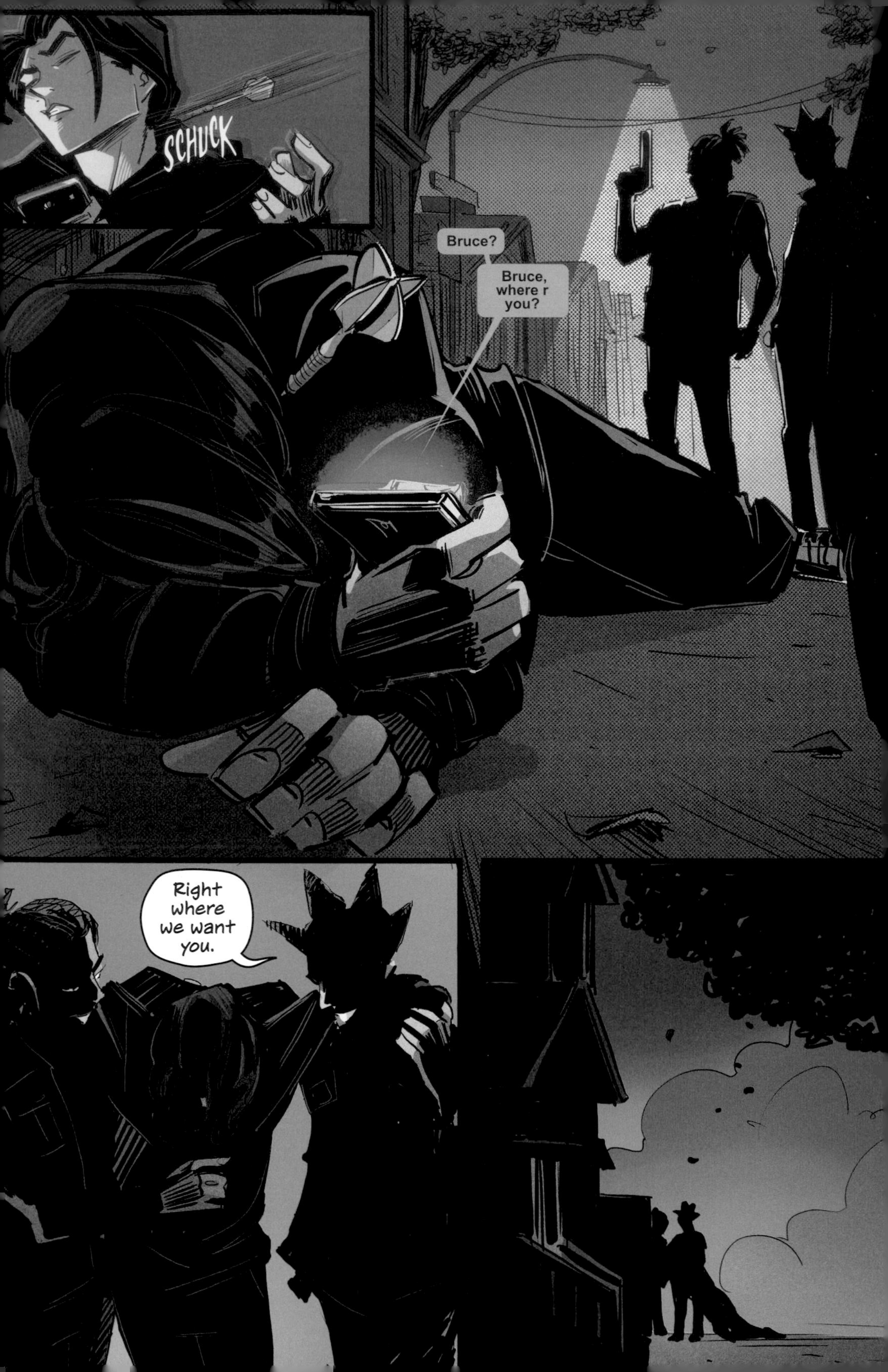
SCHUCK
Bruce?
Bruce, where r you?
Right where we want you.

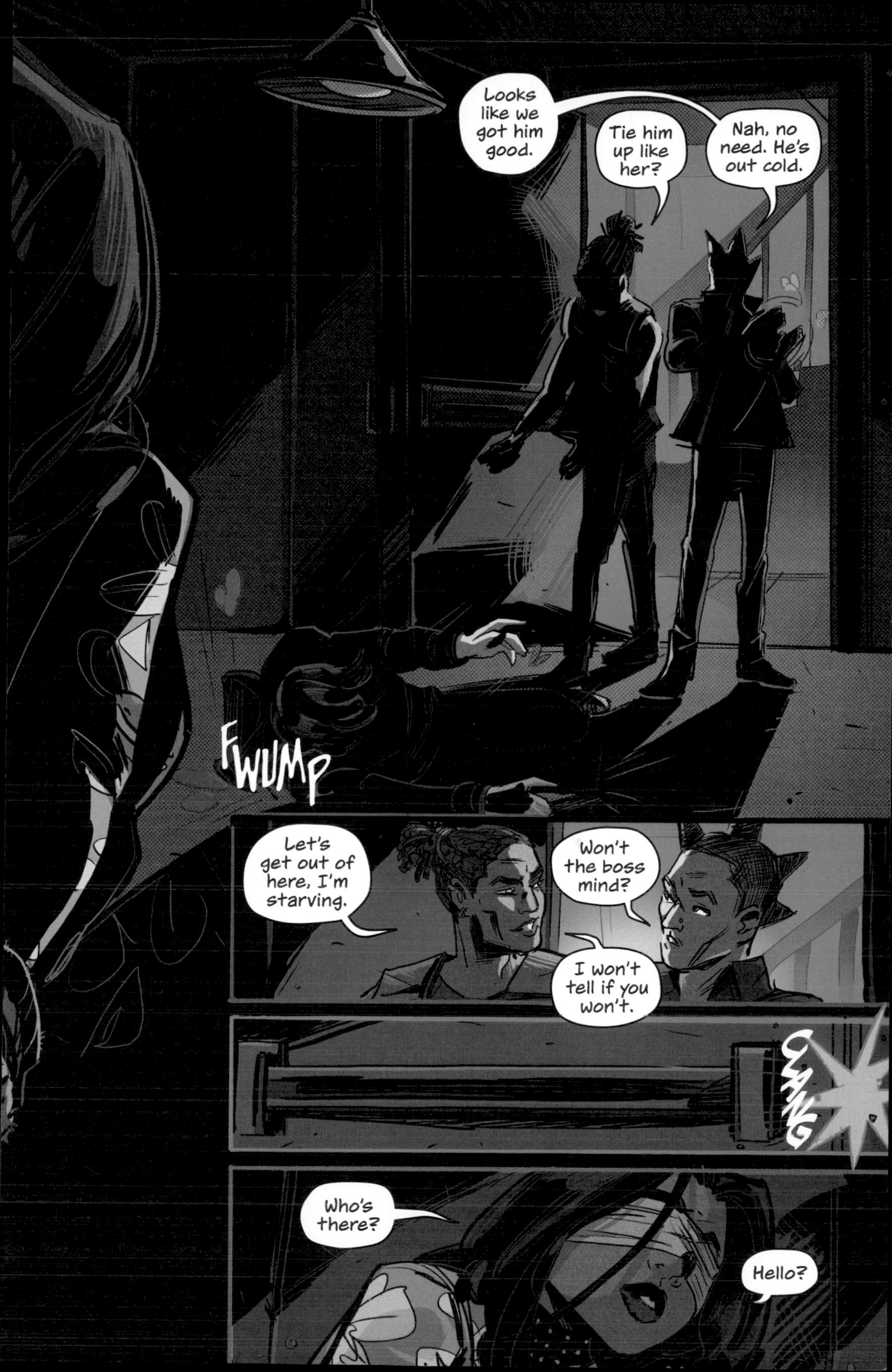
Looks like we got him good.
Tie him up like her?
Nah, no need. He's out cold.
FWUMP
Let's get out of here, I'm starving.
Won't the boss mind?
I won't tell if you won't.
CLANG
Who's there?
Hello?

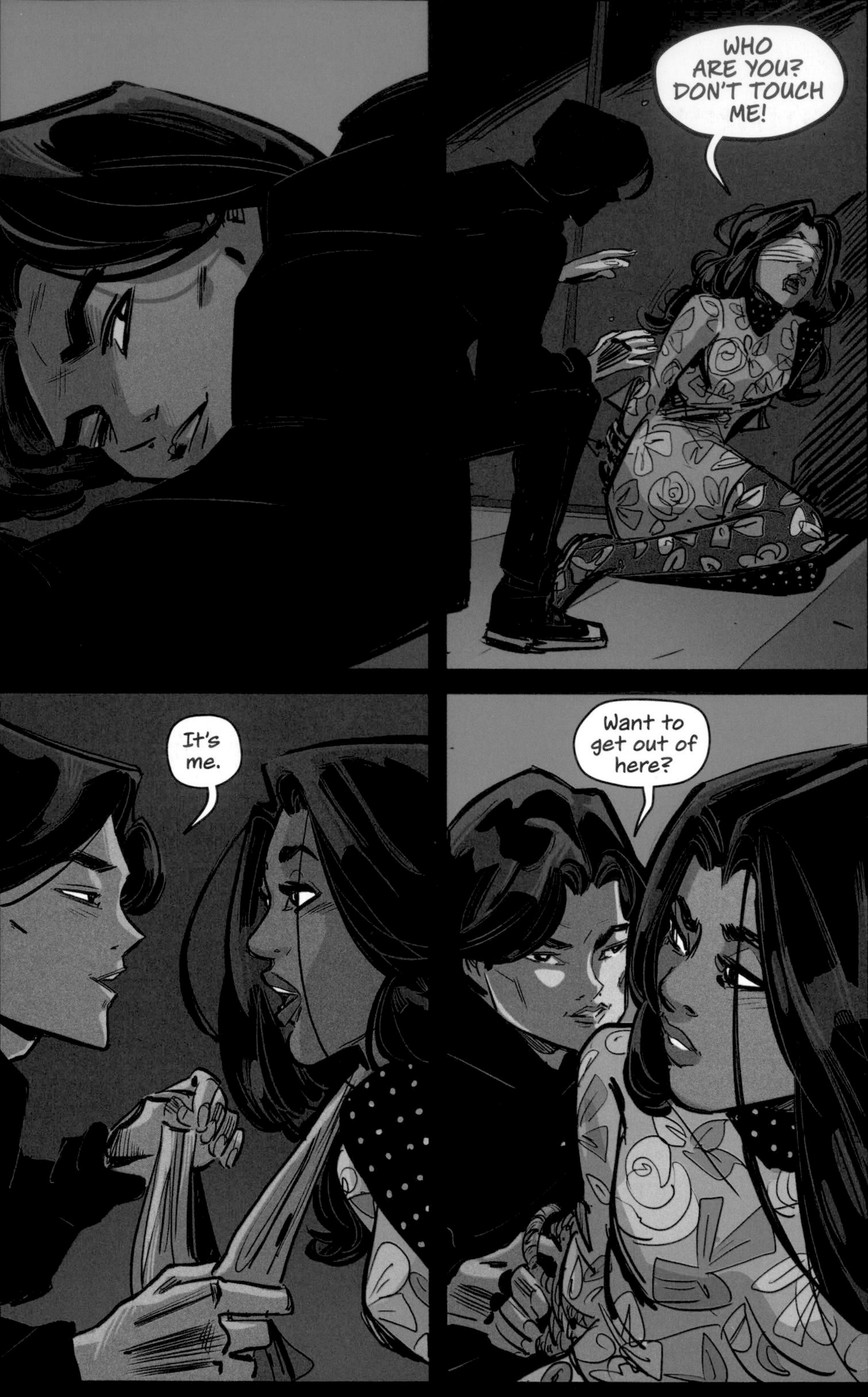
WHO ARE YOU? DON'T TOUCH ME!
It's me.
Want to get out of here?

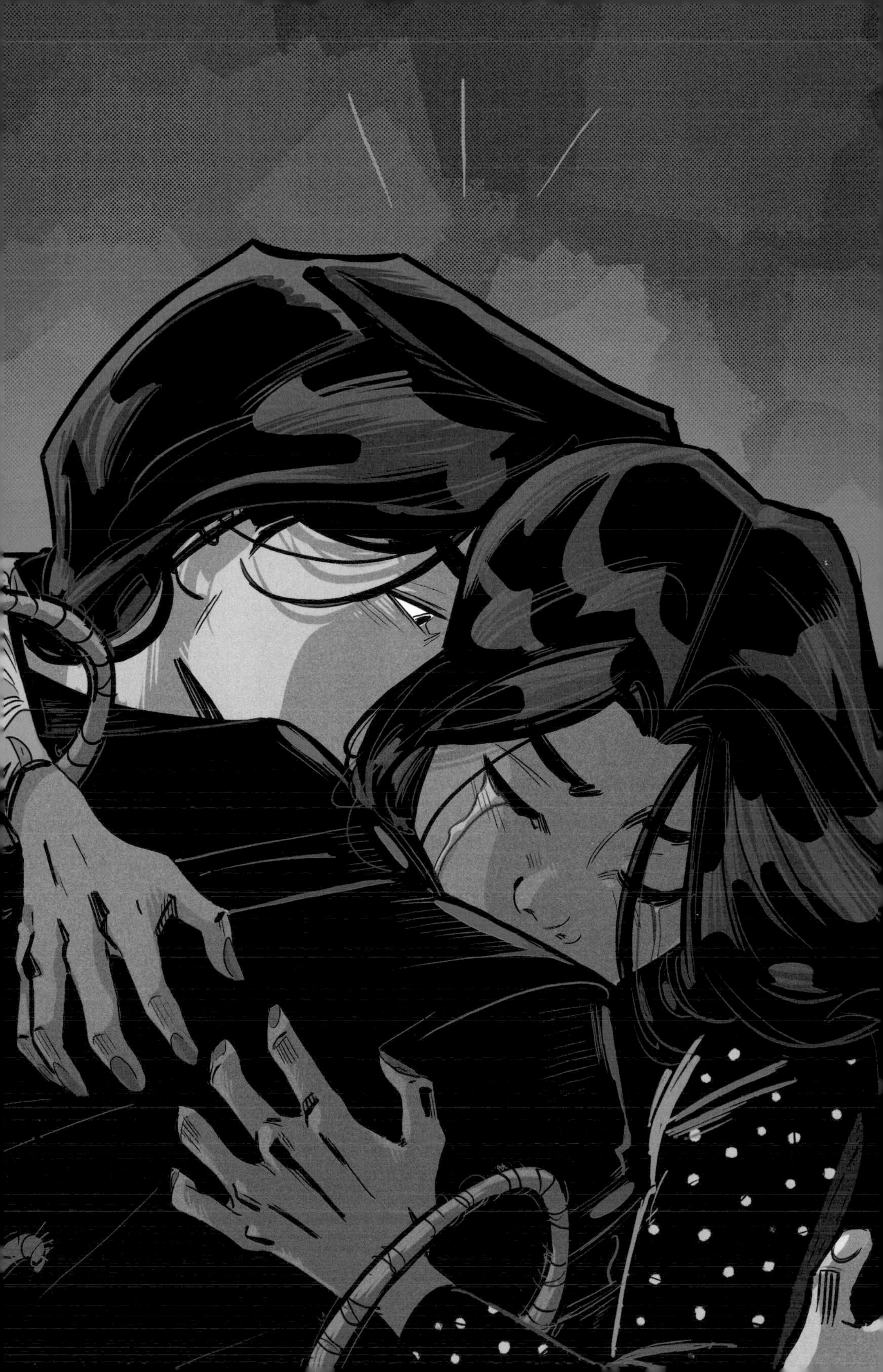

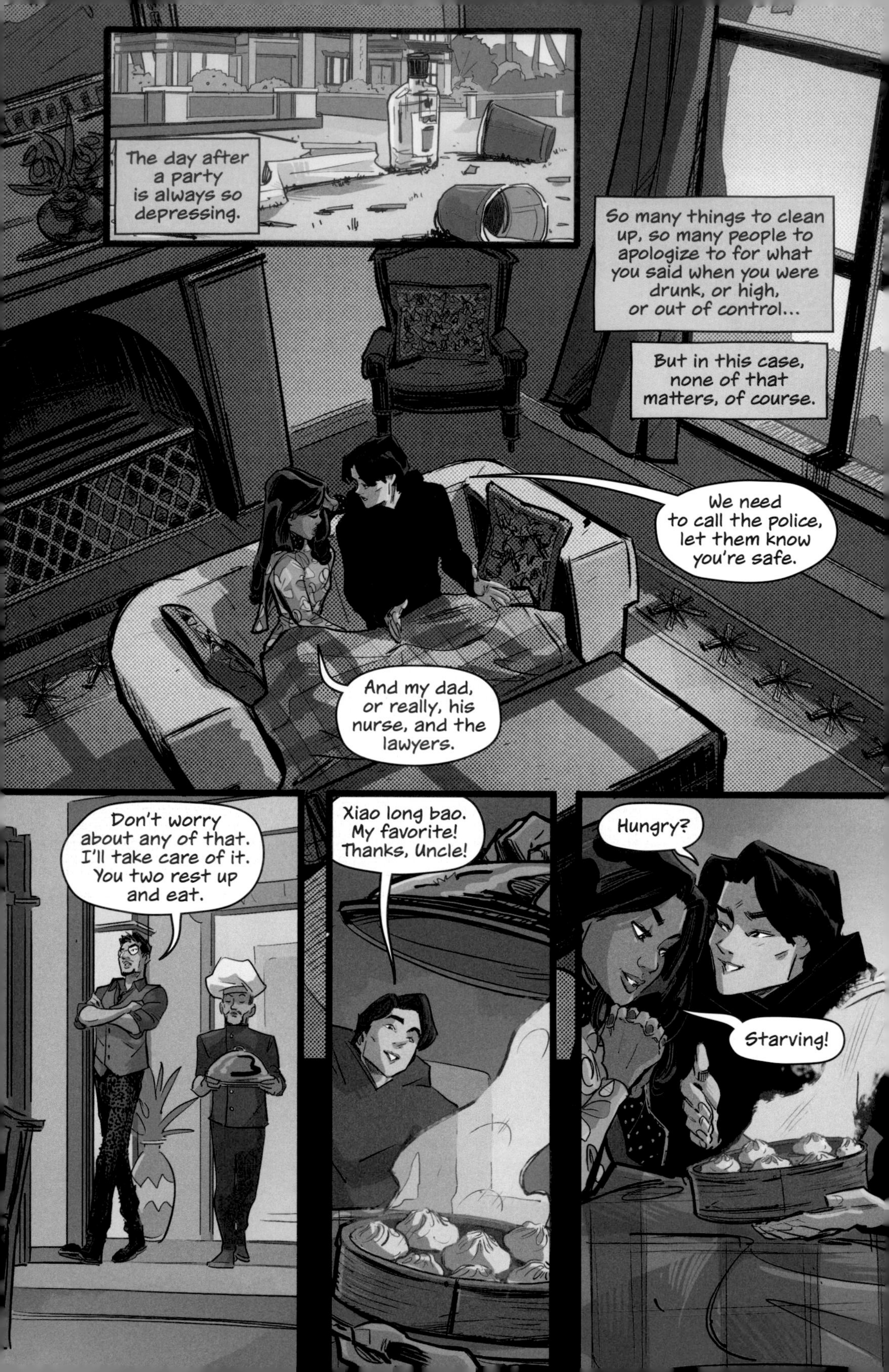
The day after a party is always so depressing.
So many things to clean up, so many people to apologize to for what you said when you were drunk, or high, or out of control...
But in this case, none of that matters, of course.
We need to call the police, let them know you're safe.
And my dad, or really, his nurse, and the lawyers.
Don't worry about any of that. I'll take care of it. You two rest up and eat.
Xiao long bao. My favorite! Thanks, Uncle!
Hungry?
Starving!

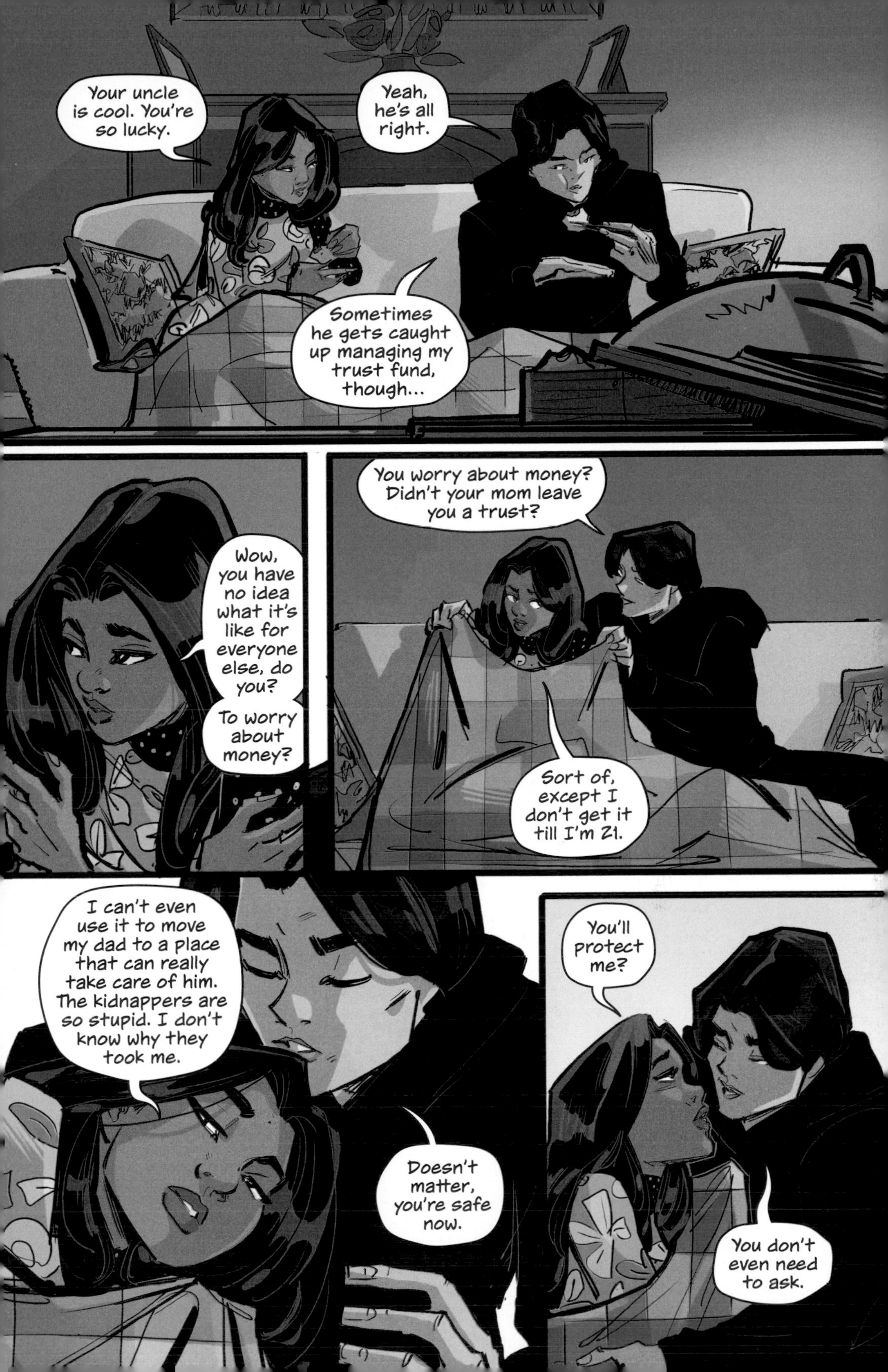
Your uncle is cool. You're so lucky.
Yeah, he's all right.
Sometimes he gets caught up managing my trust fund, though...
Wow, you have no idea what it's like for everyone else, do you?
To worry about money?
You worry about money? Didn't your mom leave you a trust?
Sort of, except I don't get it till I'm 21.
I can't even use it to move my dad to a place that can really take care of him. The kidnappers are so stupid. I don't know why they took me.
Doesn't matter, you're safe now.
You'll protect me?
You don't even need to ask.

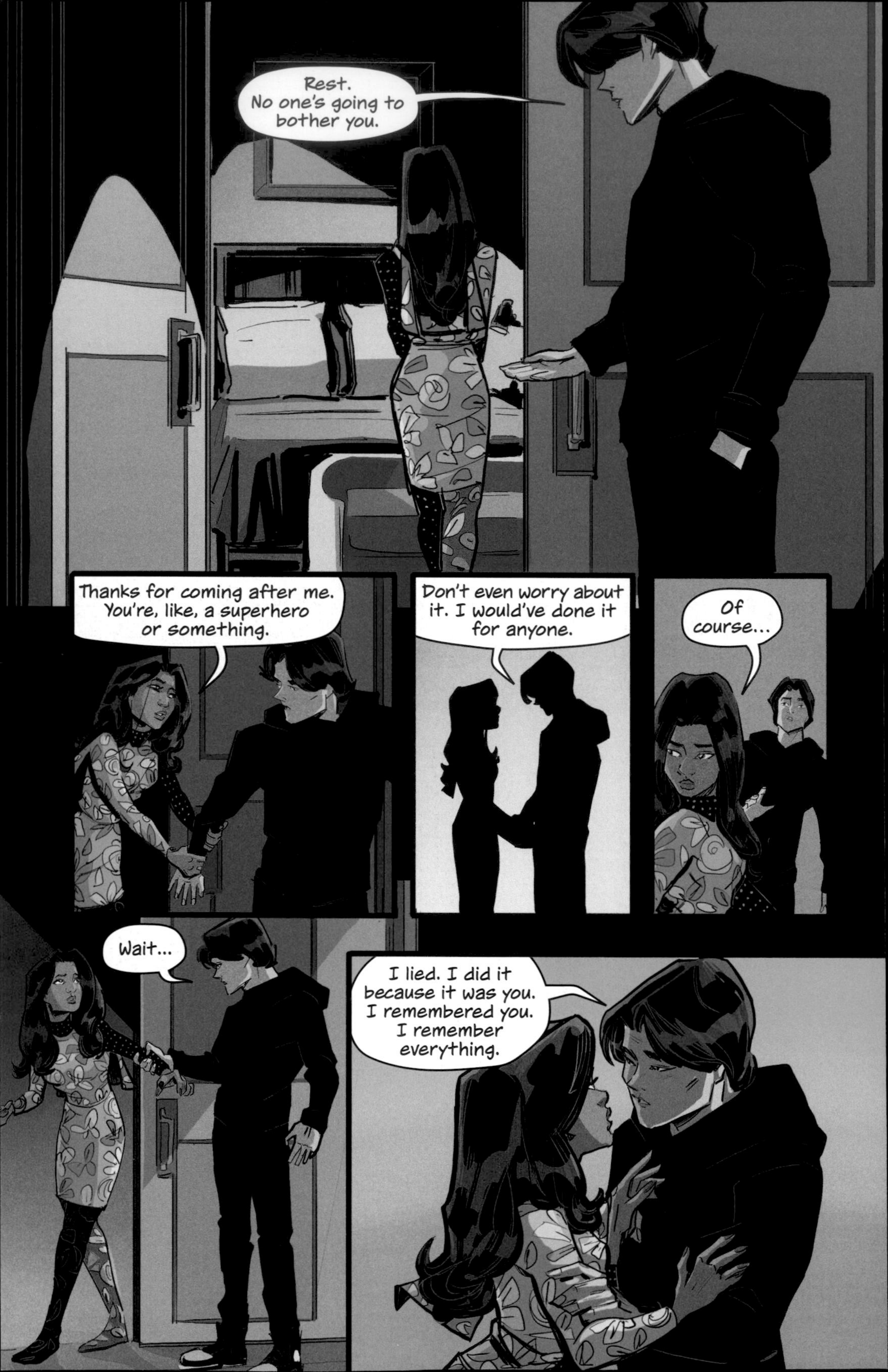
Rest. No one's going to bother you.
Thanks for coming after me. You're, like, a superhero or something.
Don't even worry about it. I would've done it for anyone.
Of course...
Wait...
I lied. I did it because it was you. I remembered you. I remember everything.

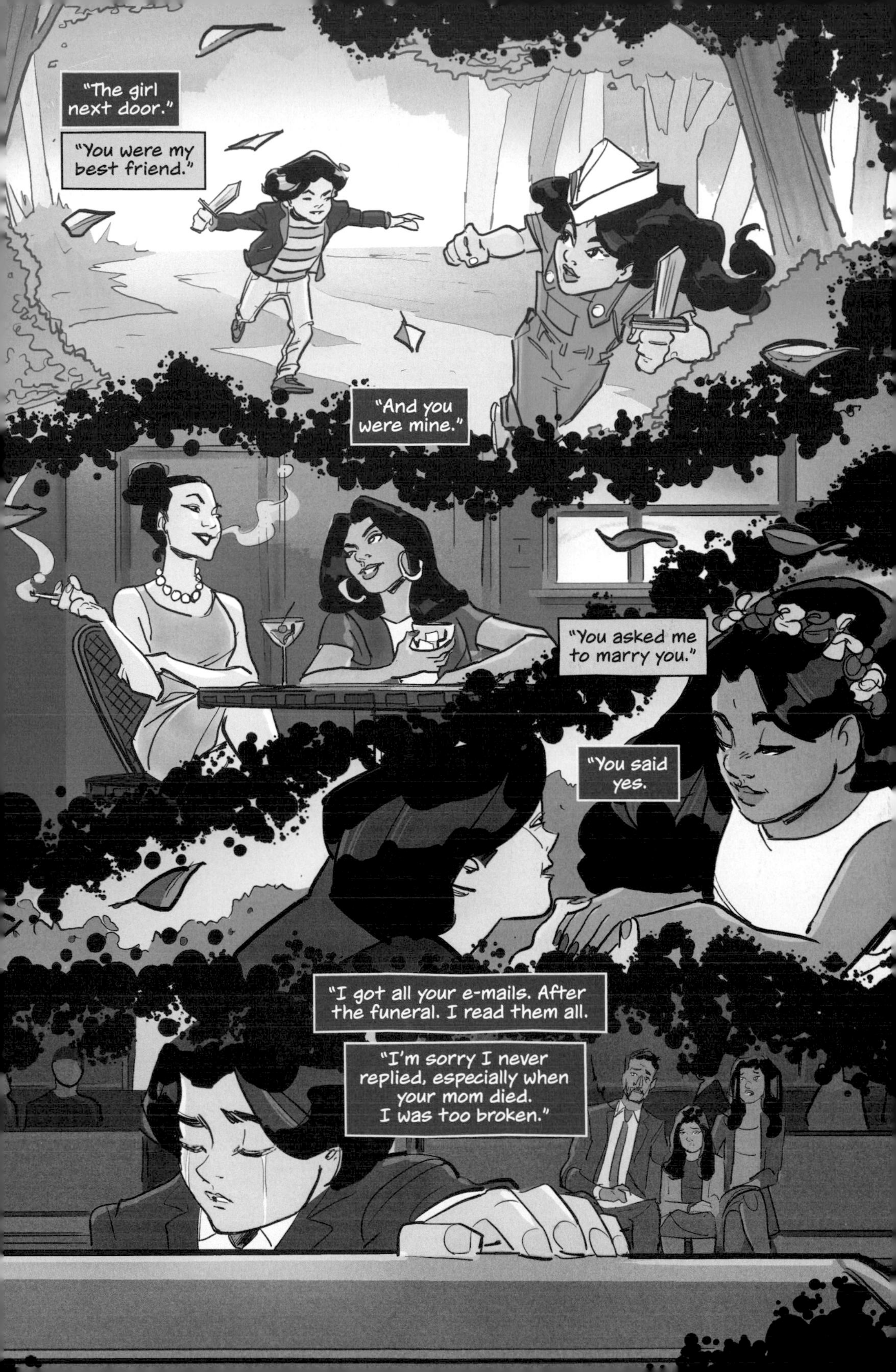
"The girl next door."
"You were my best friend."
"And you were mine."
"You asked me to marry you."
"You said yes.
"I got all your e-mails. After the funeral. I read them all.
"I'm sorry I never replied, especially when your mom died. I was too broken."

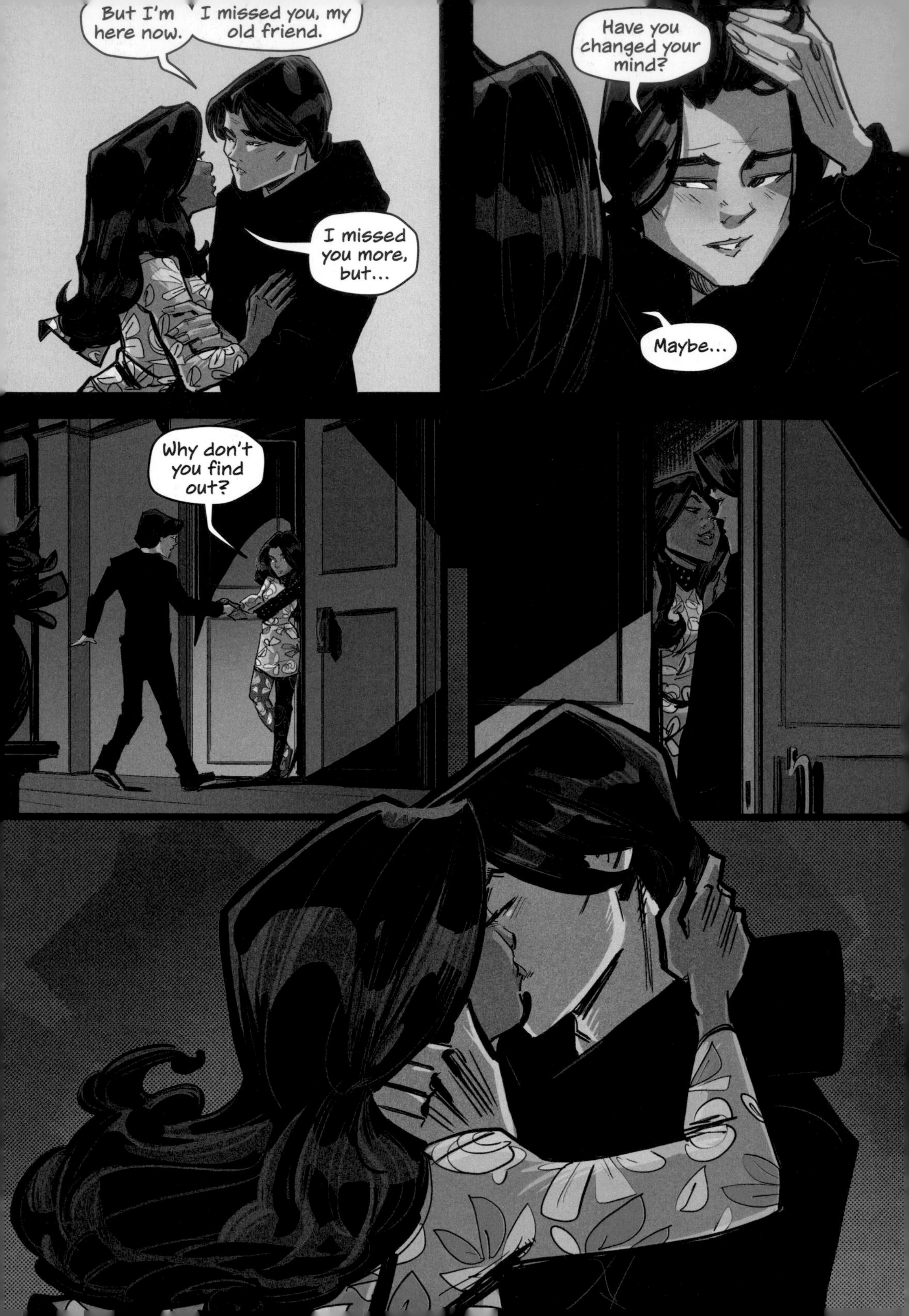
But I'm here now.
I missed you, my old friend.
I missed you more, but...
Have you changed your mind?
Maybe...
Why don't you find out?

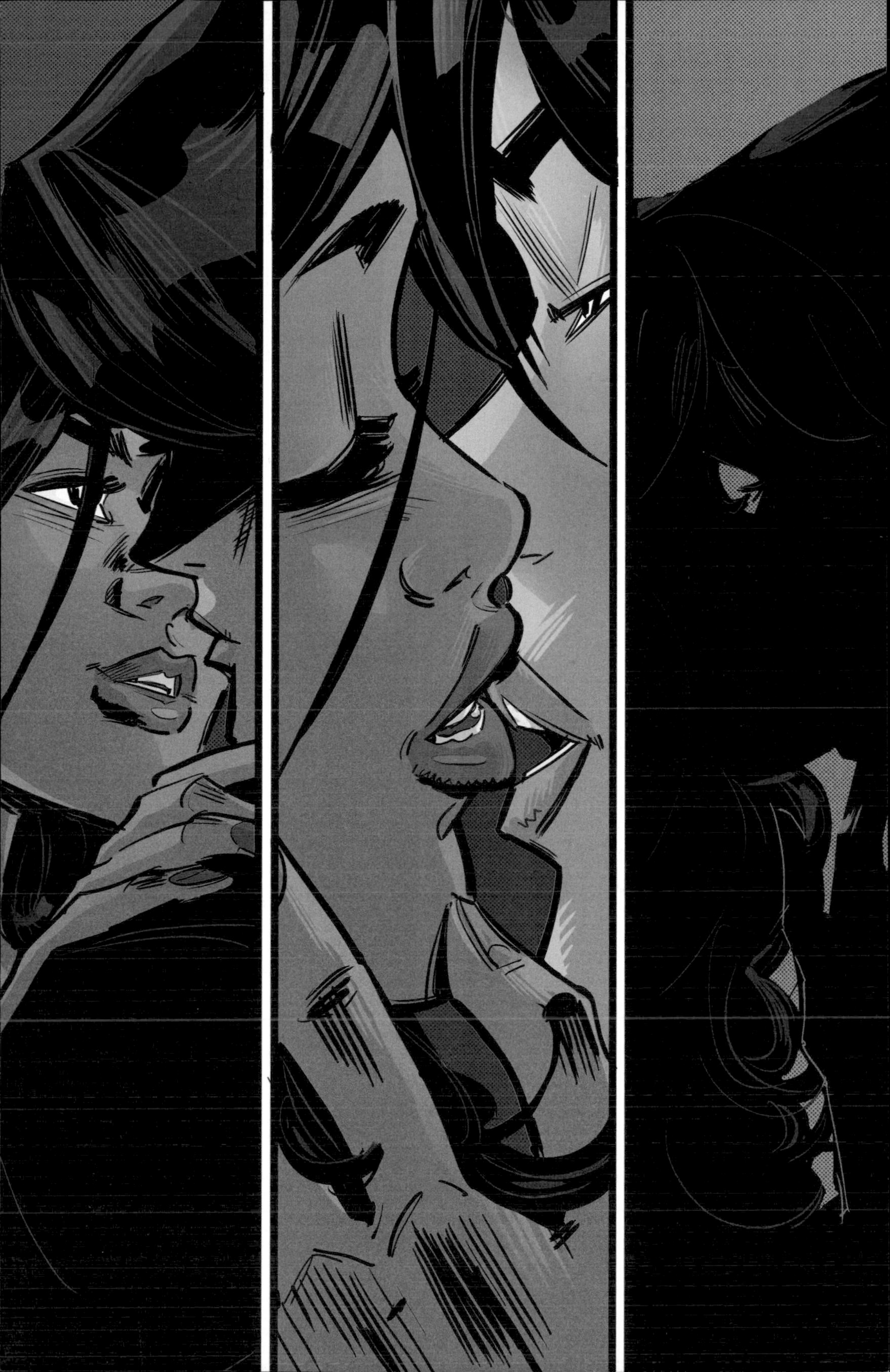

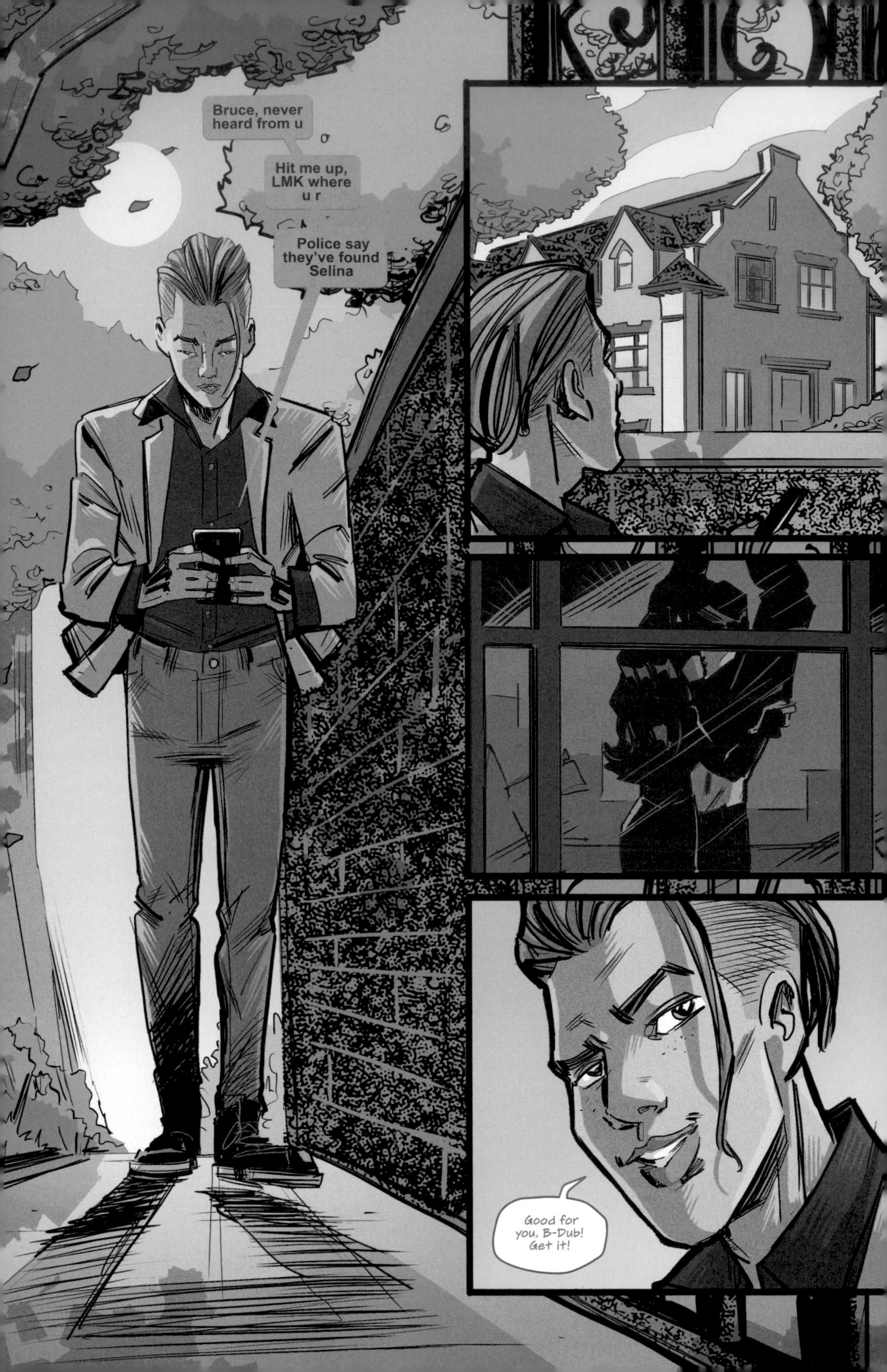
Bruce, never heard from u
Hit me up, LMK where u r
Police say they've found Selina
Good for you, B-Dub! Get it!

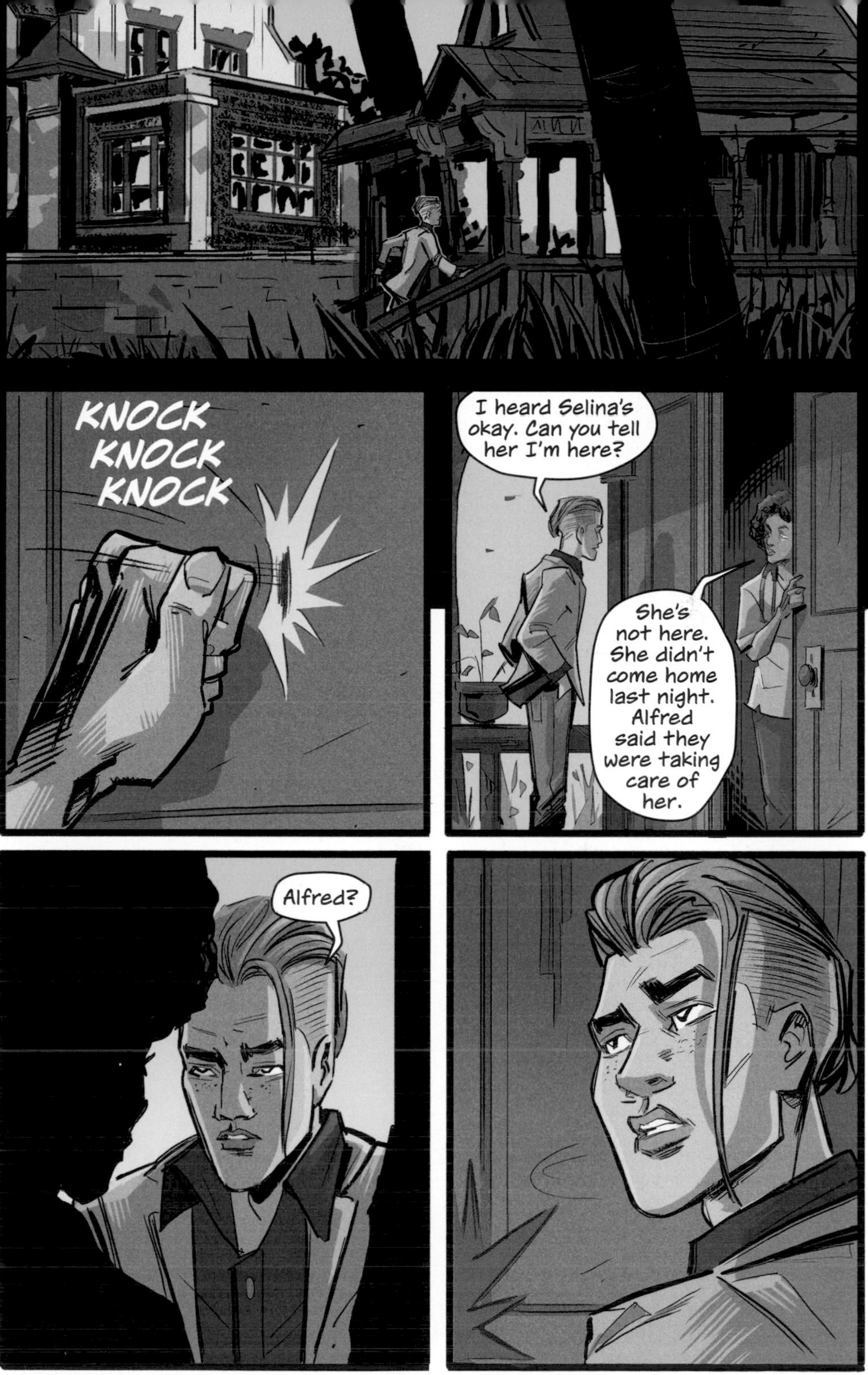

KNOCK
KNOCK
KNOCK
I heard Selina's okay. Can you tell her I'm here?
She's not here. She didn't come home last night. Alfred said they were taking care of her.
Alfred?

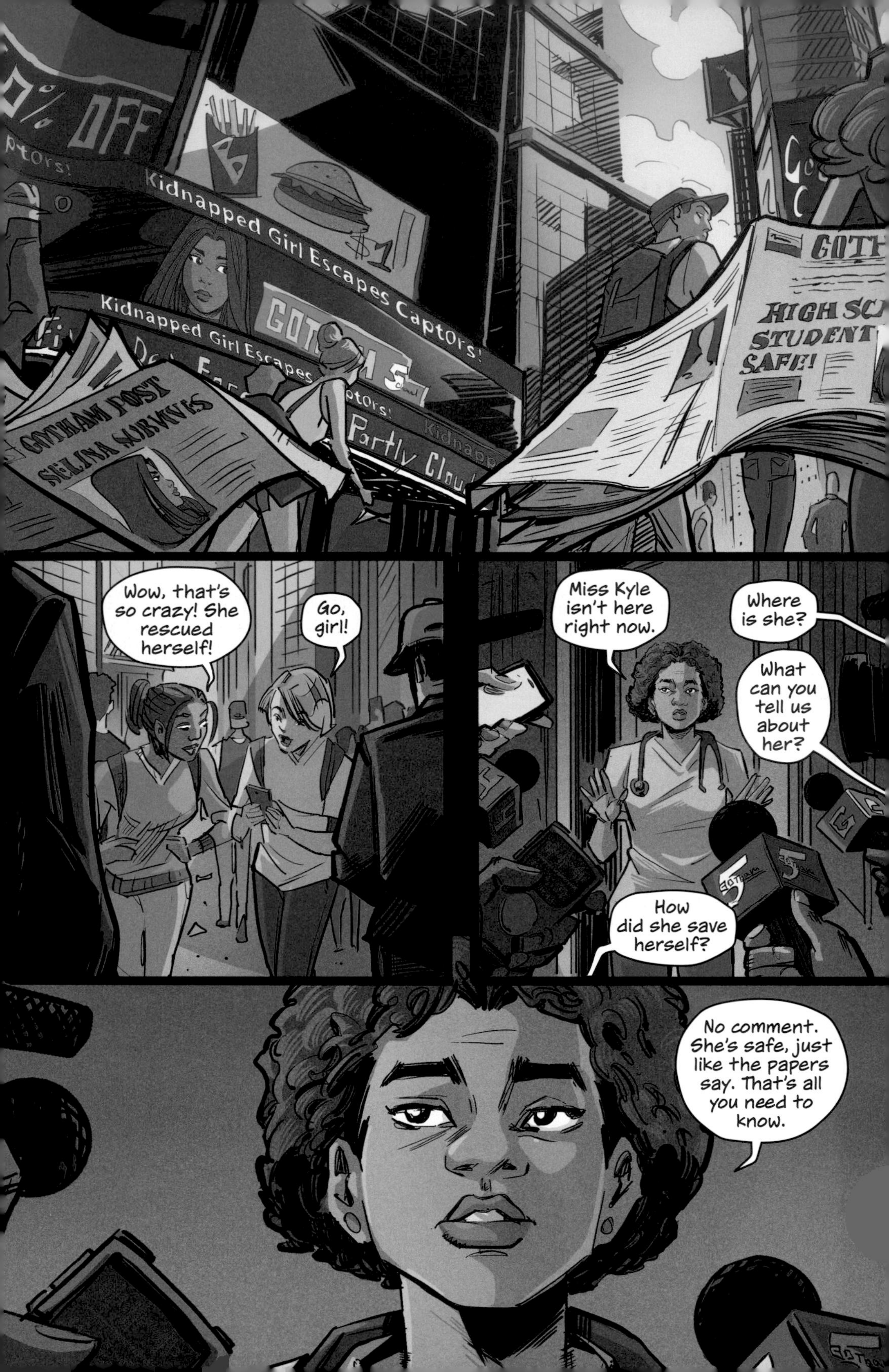
OFF
Kidnapped Girl Escapes Captors!
$1
Kidnapped Girl Escapes Captors!
GOTHAM POST
SELINA SURVIVES
SAFE!
Wow, that's so crazy! She rescued herself!
Go, girl!
Miss Kyle isn't here right now.
Where is she?
What can you tell us about her?
How did she save herself?
No comment. She's safe, just like the papers say. That's all you need to know.

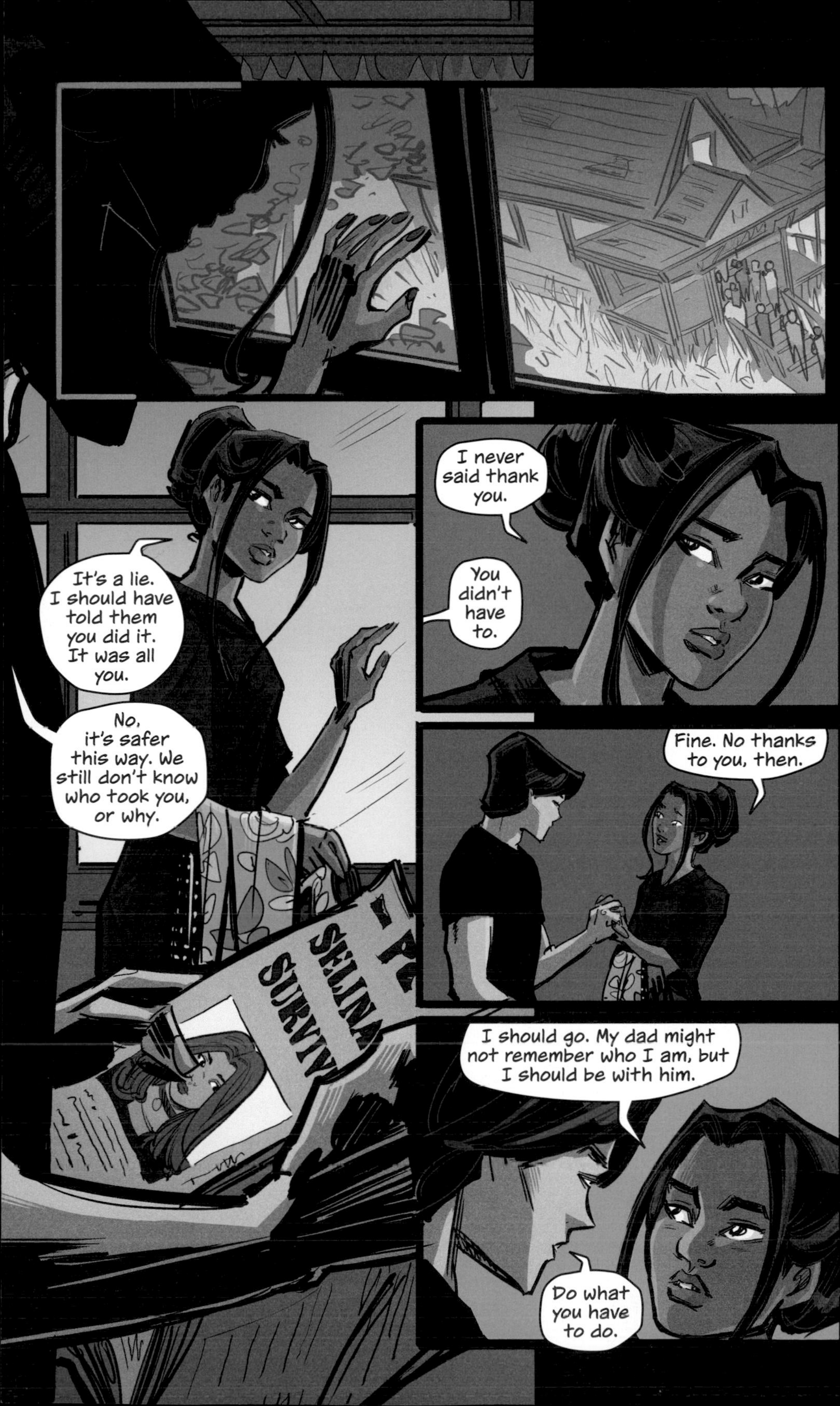
It's a lie. I should have told them you did it. It was all you.
No, it's safer this way. We still don't know who took you, or why.
SELINA
I never said thank you.
You didn't have to.
Fine. No thanks to you, then.
I should go. My dad might not remember who I am, but I should be with him.
Do what you have to do.

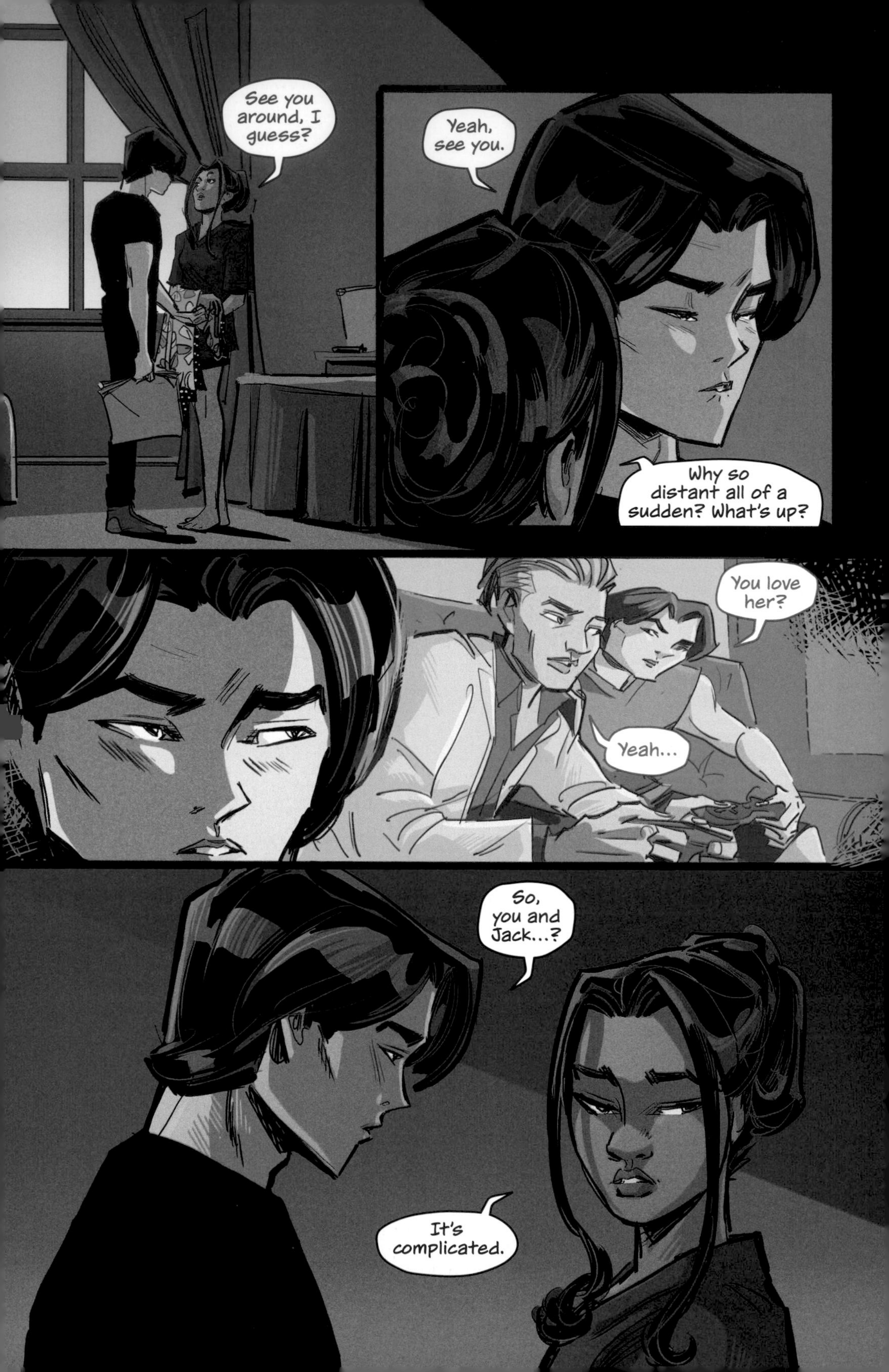
See you around, I guess?
Yeah, see you.
Why so distant all of a sudden? What's up?
You love her?
Yeah...
So, you and Jack...?
It's complicated.

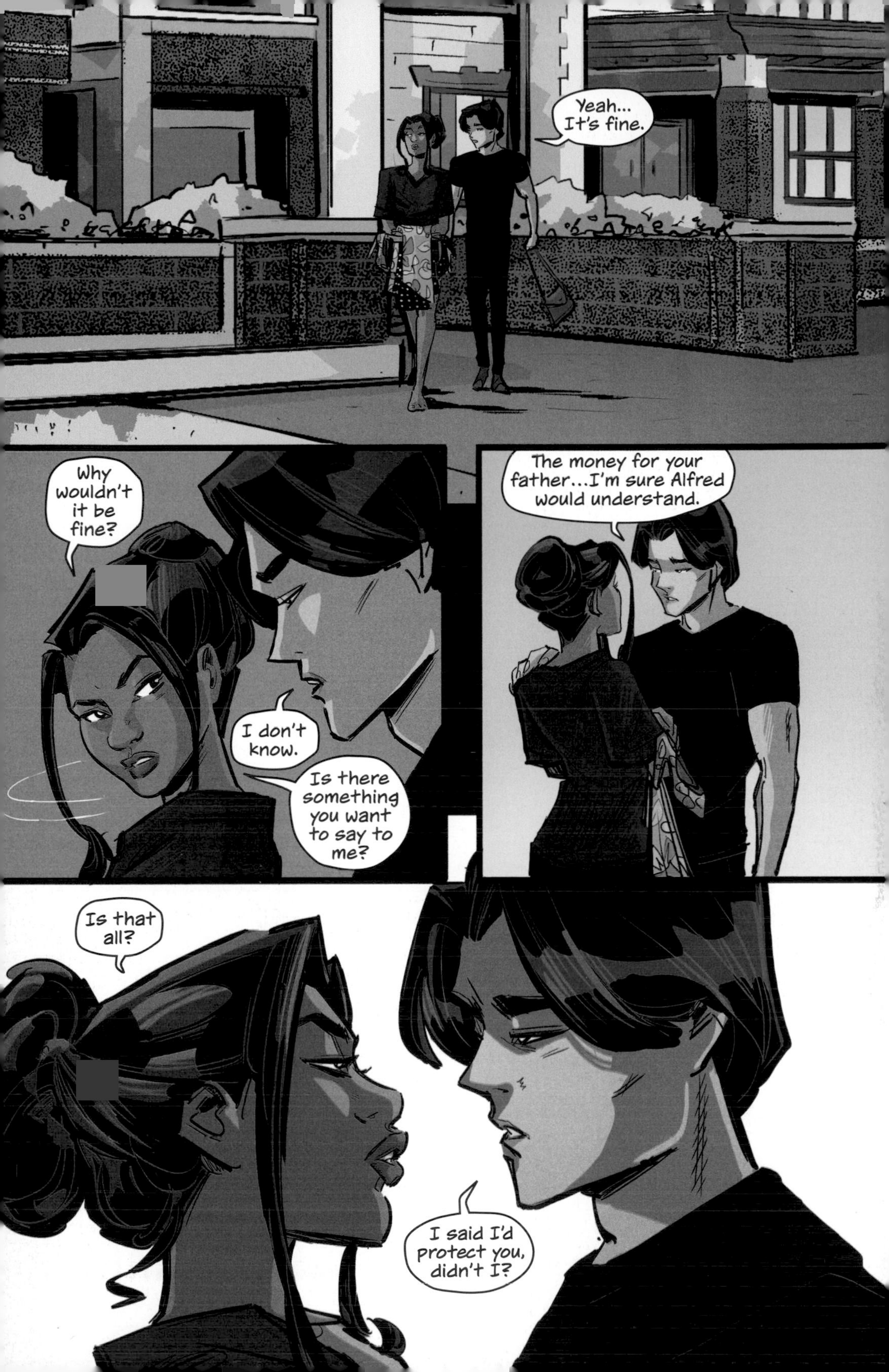
Yeah... It's fine.
Why wouldn't it be fine?
I don't know.
Is there something you want to say to me?
The money for your father...I'm sure Alfred would understand.
Is that all?
I said I'd protect you, didn't I?

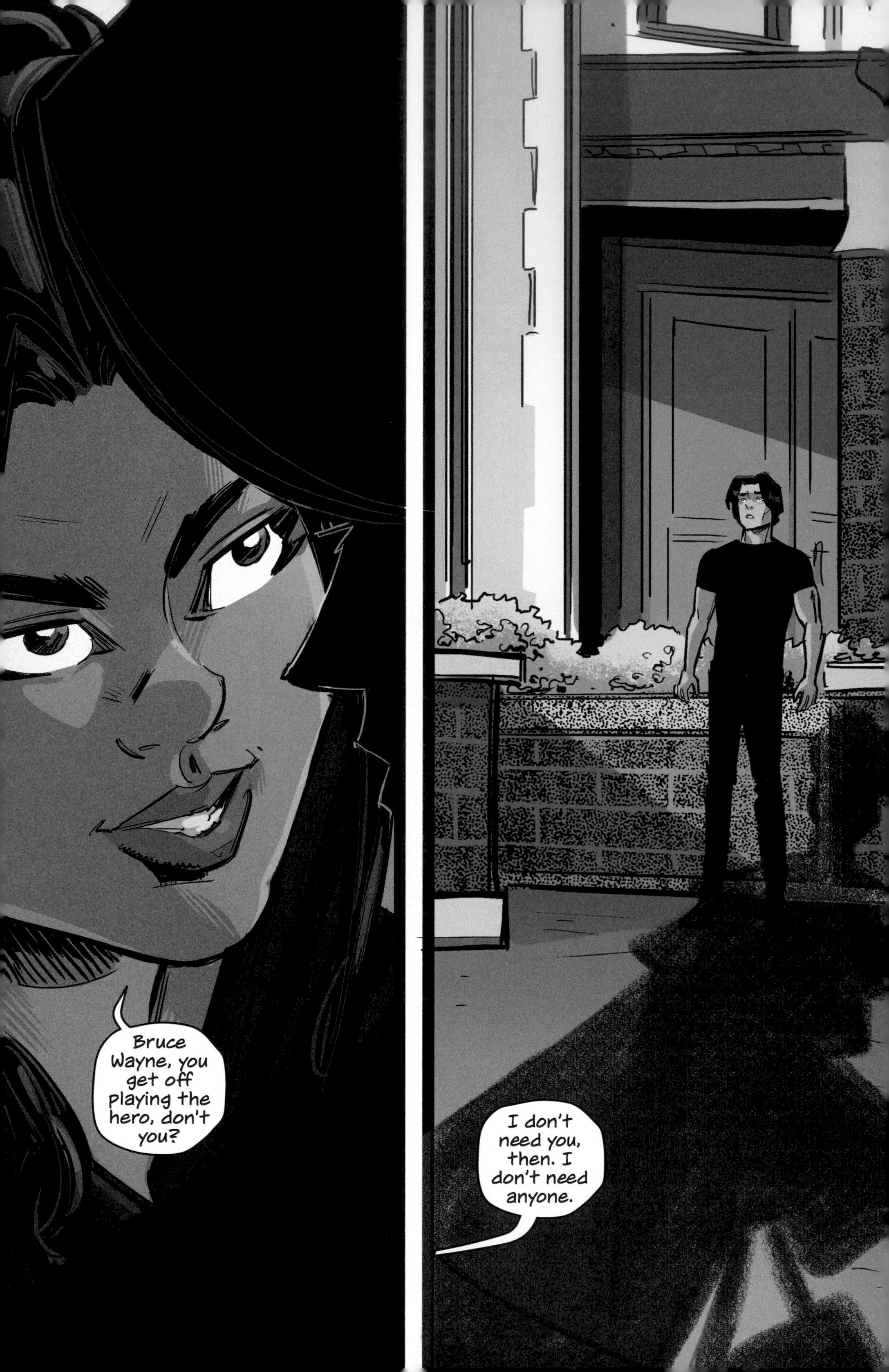
Bruce Wayne, you get off playing the hero, don't you?
I don't need you, then. I don't need anyone.

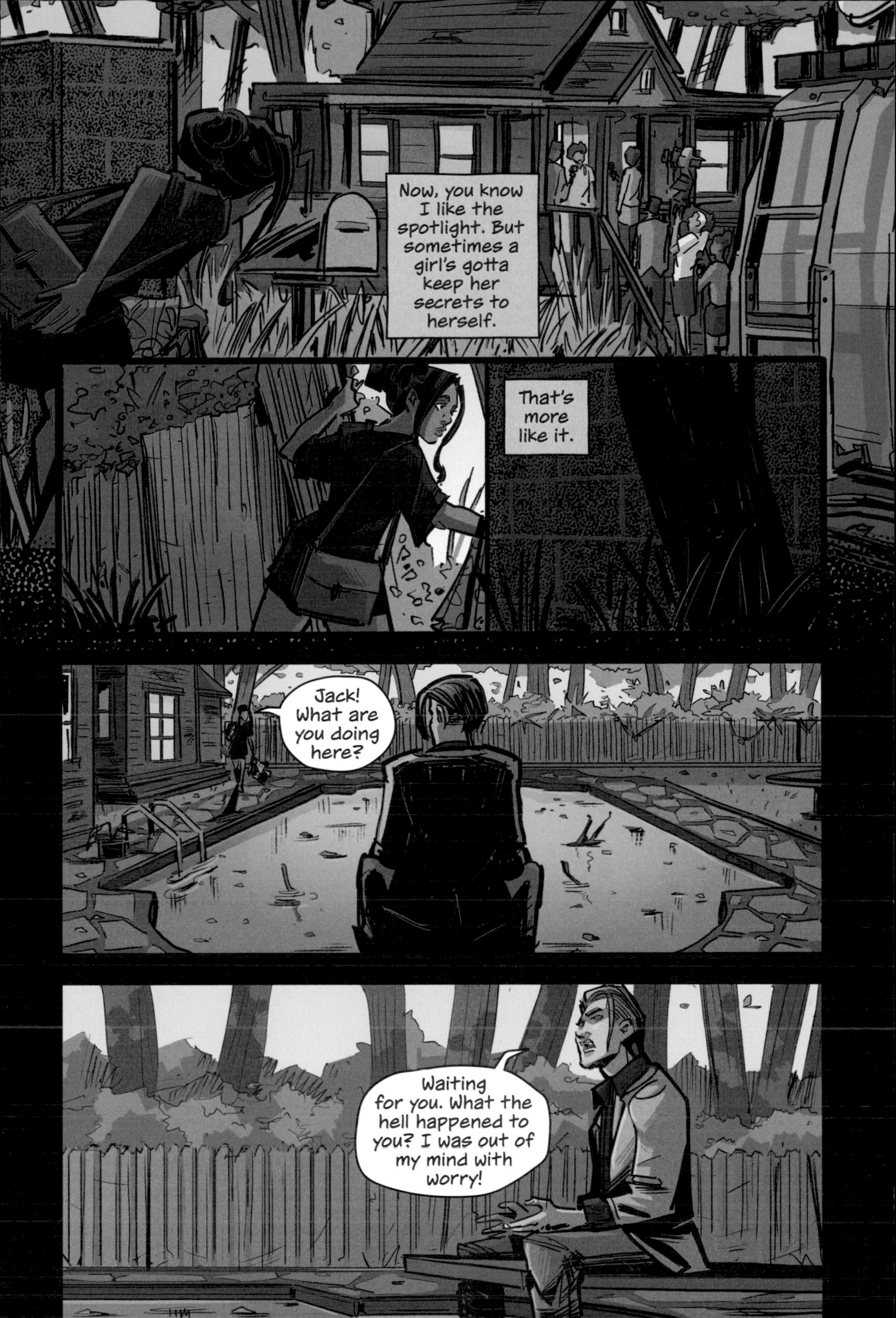
Now, you know I like the spotlight. But sometimes a girl's gotta keep her secrets to herself.
That's more like it.
Jack! What are you doing here?
Waiting for you. What the hell happened to you? I was out of my mind with worry!

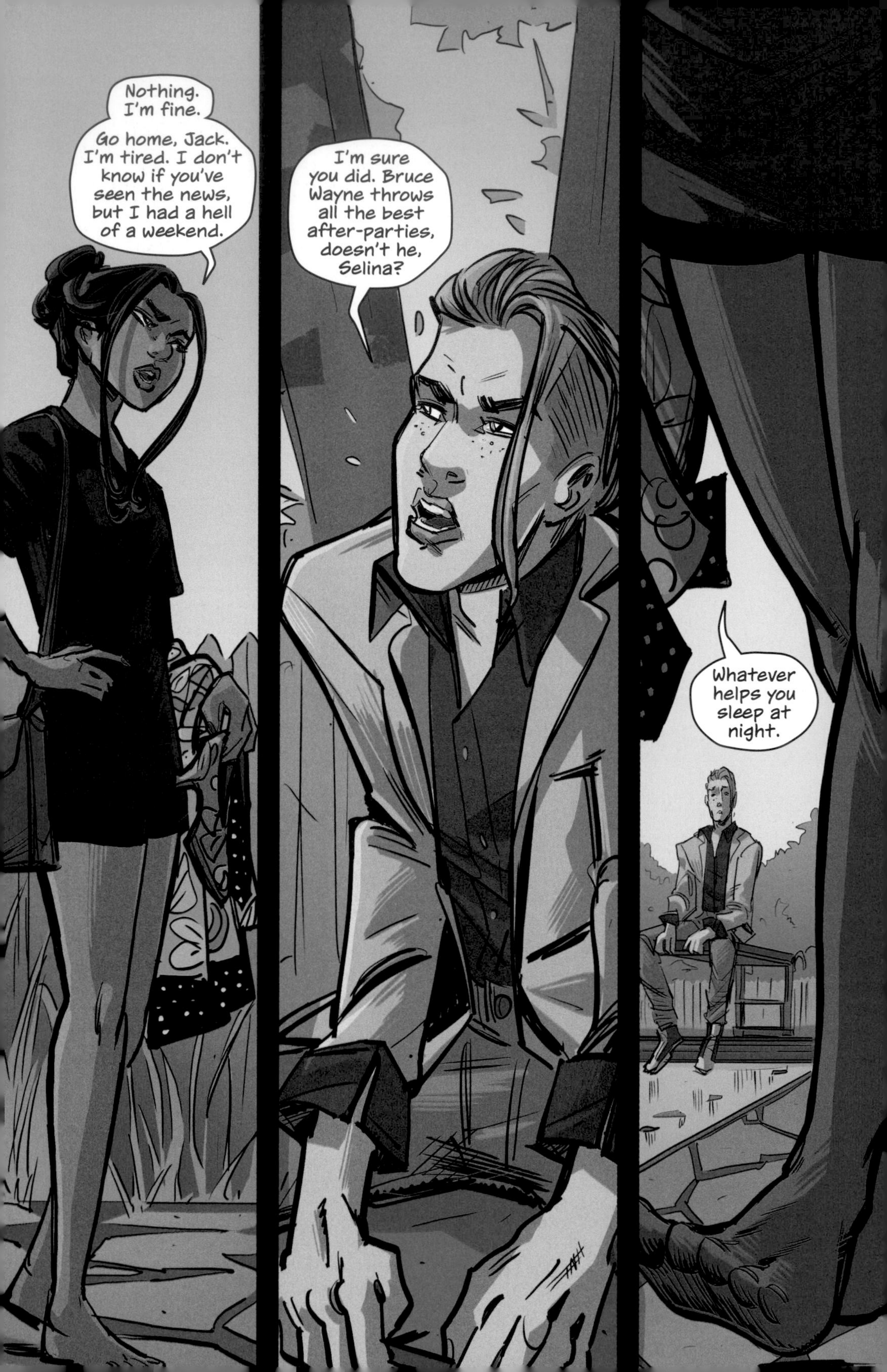
Nothing.
I'm fine.
Go home, Jack. I'm tired. I don't know if you've seen the news, but I had a hell of a weekend.
I'm sure you did. Bruce Wayne throws all the best after-parties, doesn't he, Selina?
Whatever helps you sleep at night.

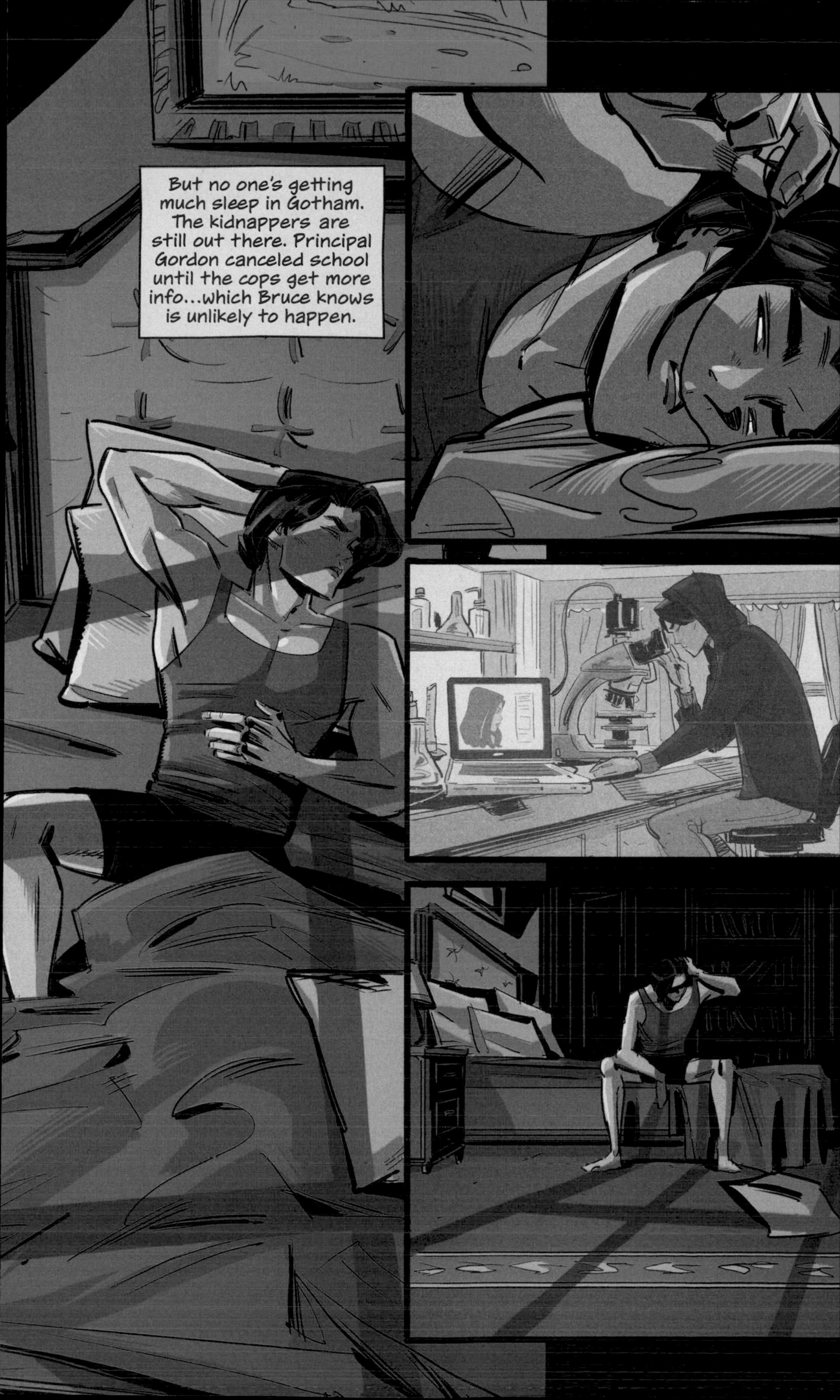
But no one's getting much sleep in Gotham. The kidnappers are still out there. Principal Gordon canceled school until the cops get more info...which Bruce knows is unlikely to happen.

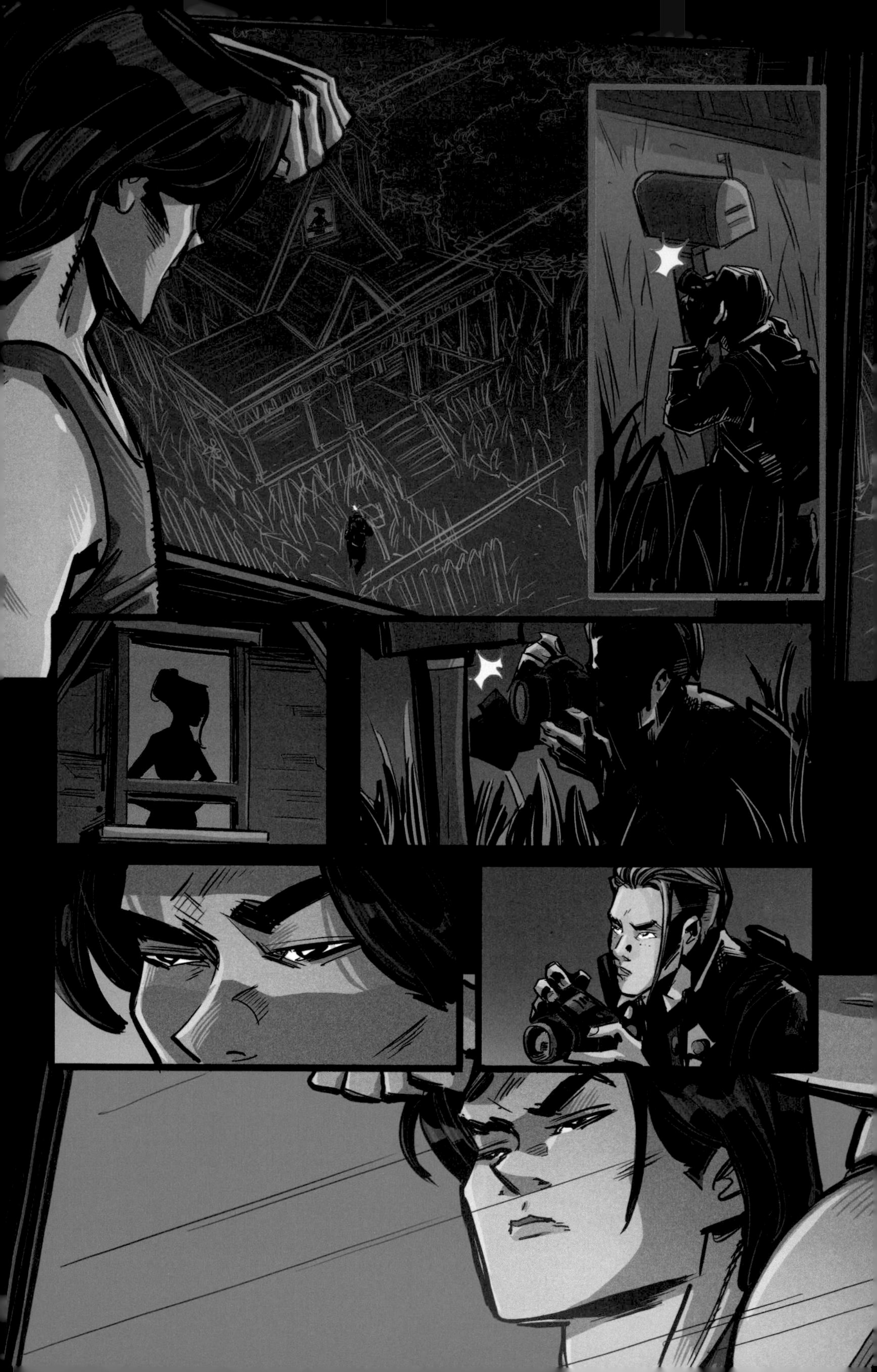

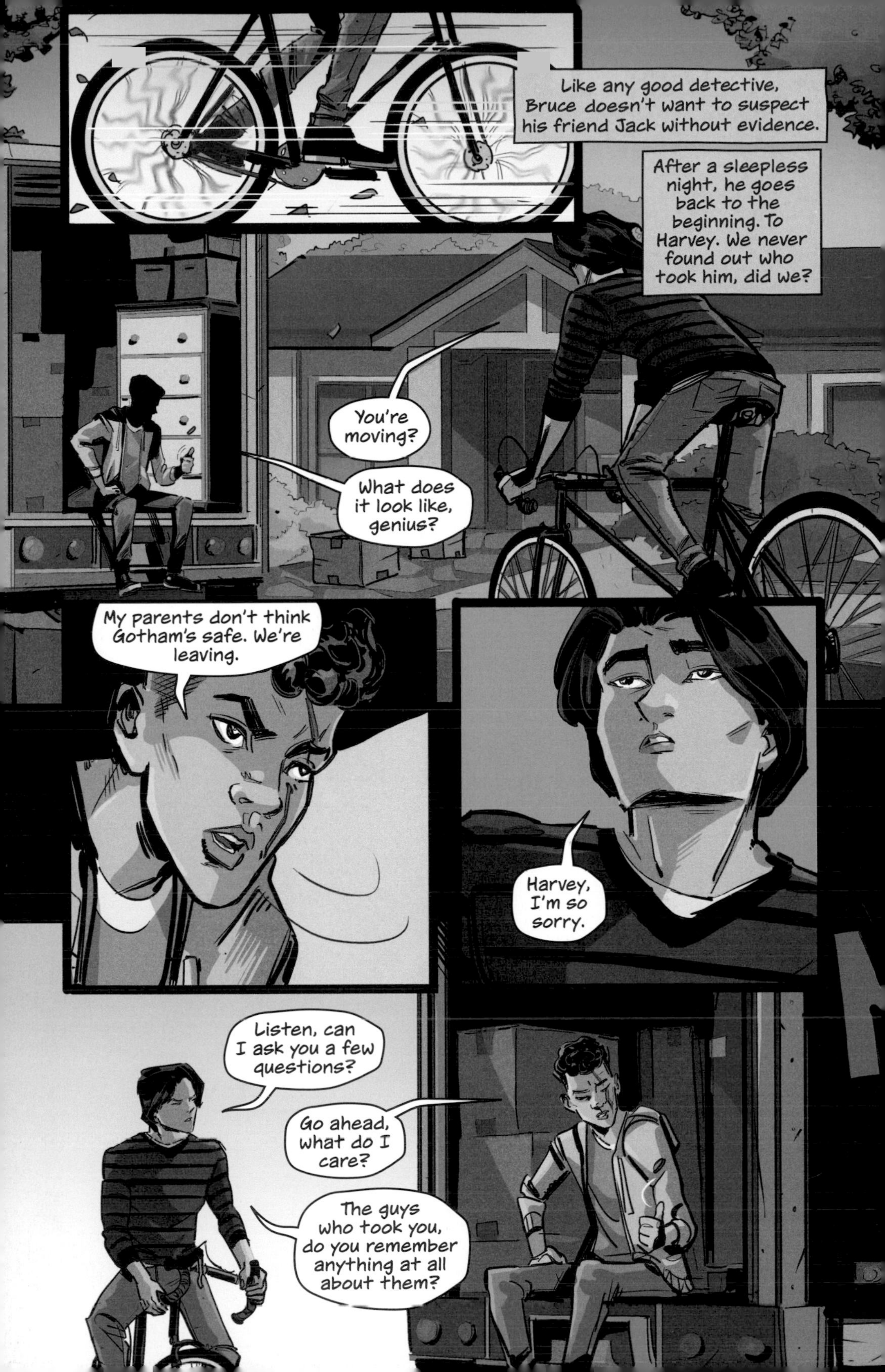
Like any good detective, Bruce doesn't want to suspect his friend Jack without evidence.
After a sleepless night, he goes back to the beginning. To Harvey. We never found out who took him, did we?
You're moving?
What does it look like, genius?
My parents don't think Gotham's safe. We're leaving.
Harvey, I'm so sorry.
Listen, can I ask you a few questions?
Go ahead, what do I care?
The guys who took you, do you remember anything at all about them?

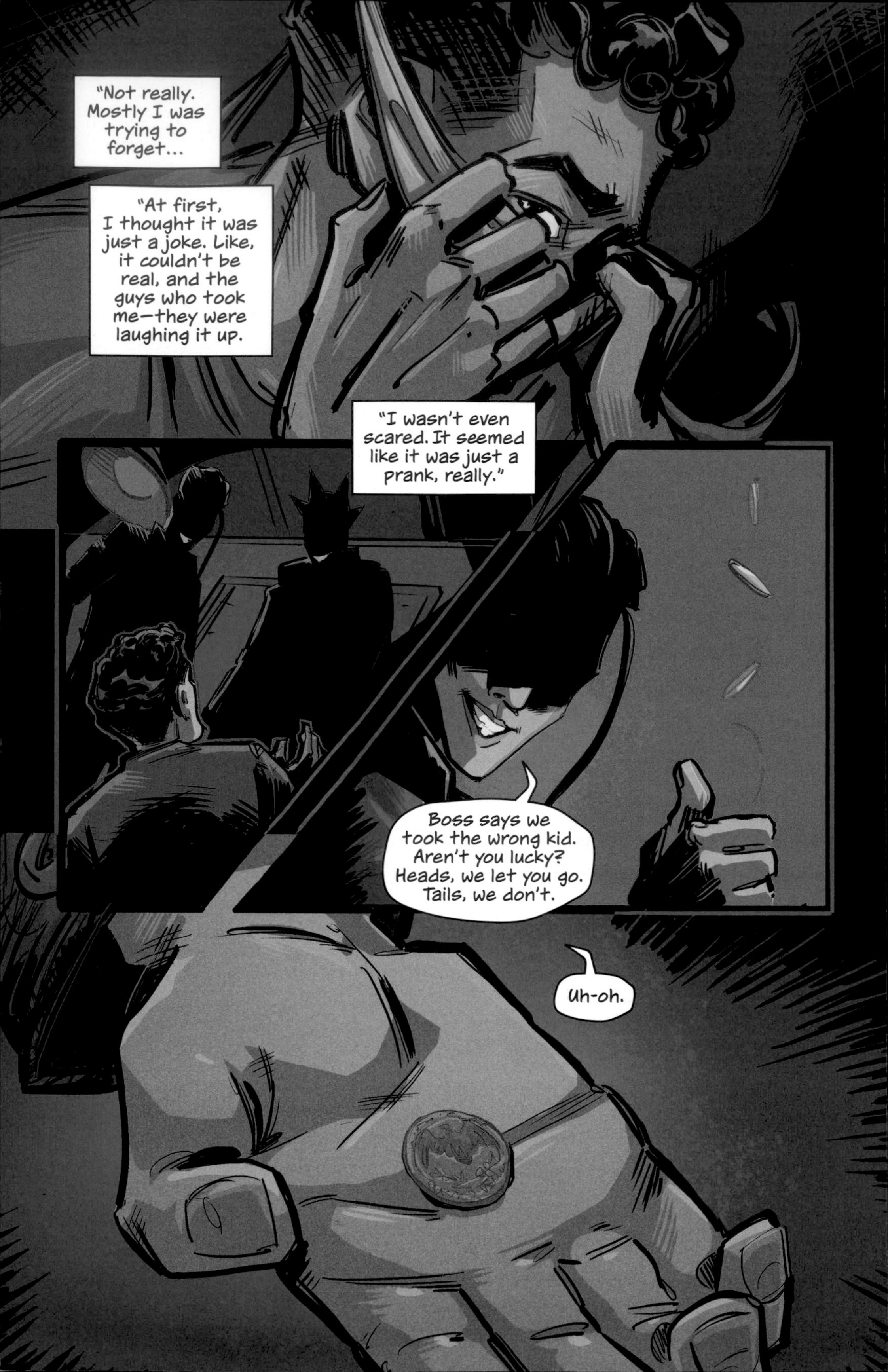
"Not really. Mostly I was trying to forget...
"At first, I thought it was just a joke. Like, it couldn't be real, and the guys who took me—they were laughing it up.
"I wasn't even scared. It seemed like it was just a prank, really."
Boss says we took the wrong kid. Aren't you lucky? Heads, we let you go. Tails, we don't.
Uh-oh.

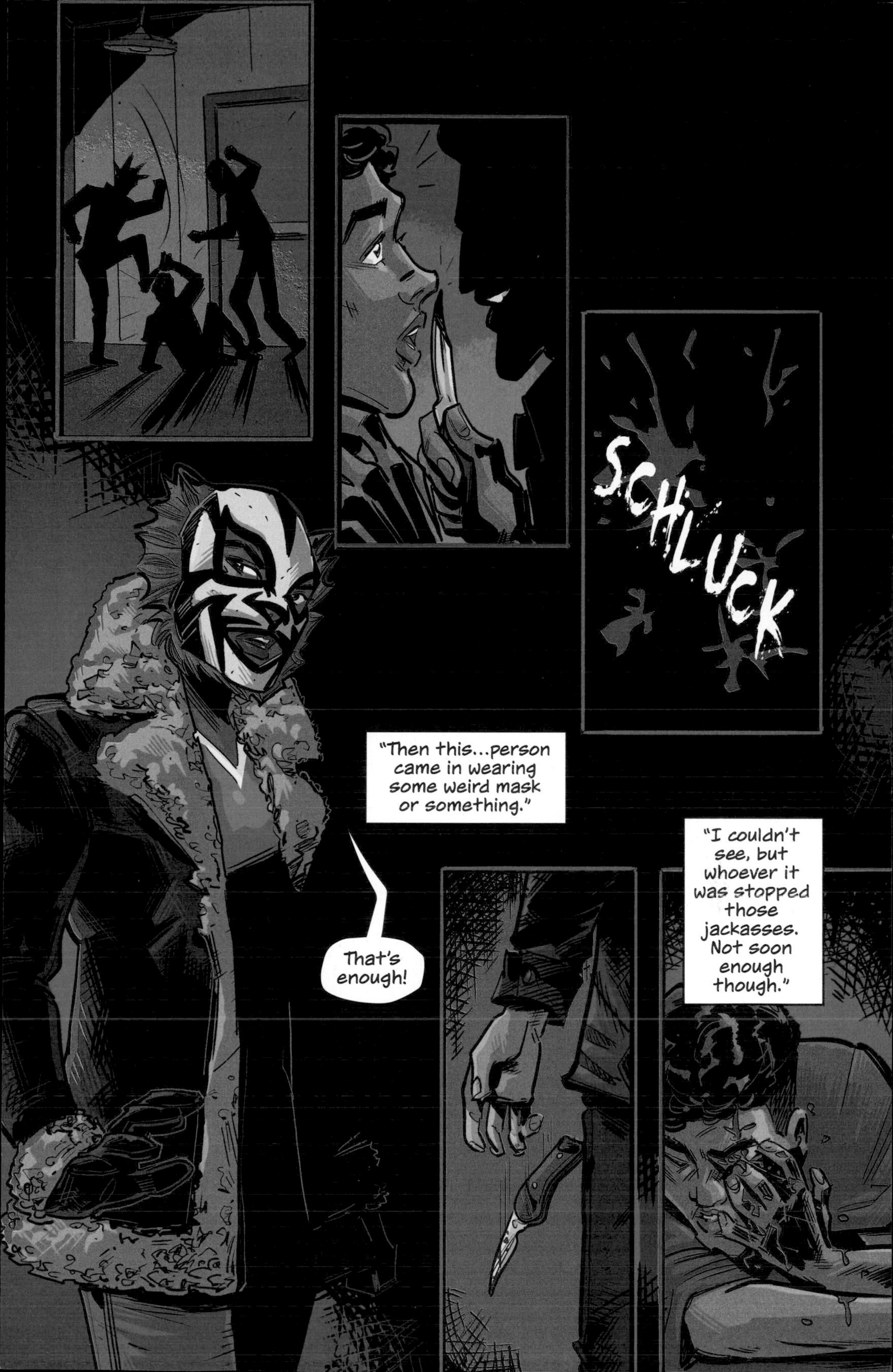
SCHLUCK
"Then this...person came in wearing some weird mask or something."
That's enough!
"I couldn't see, but whoever it was stopped those jackasses. Not soon enough though."

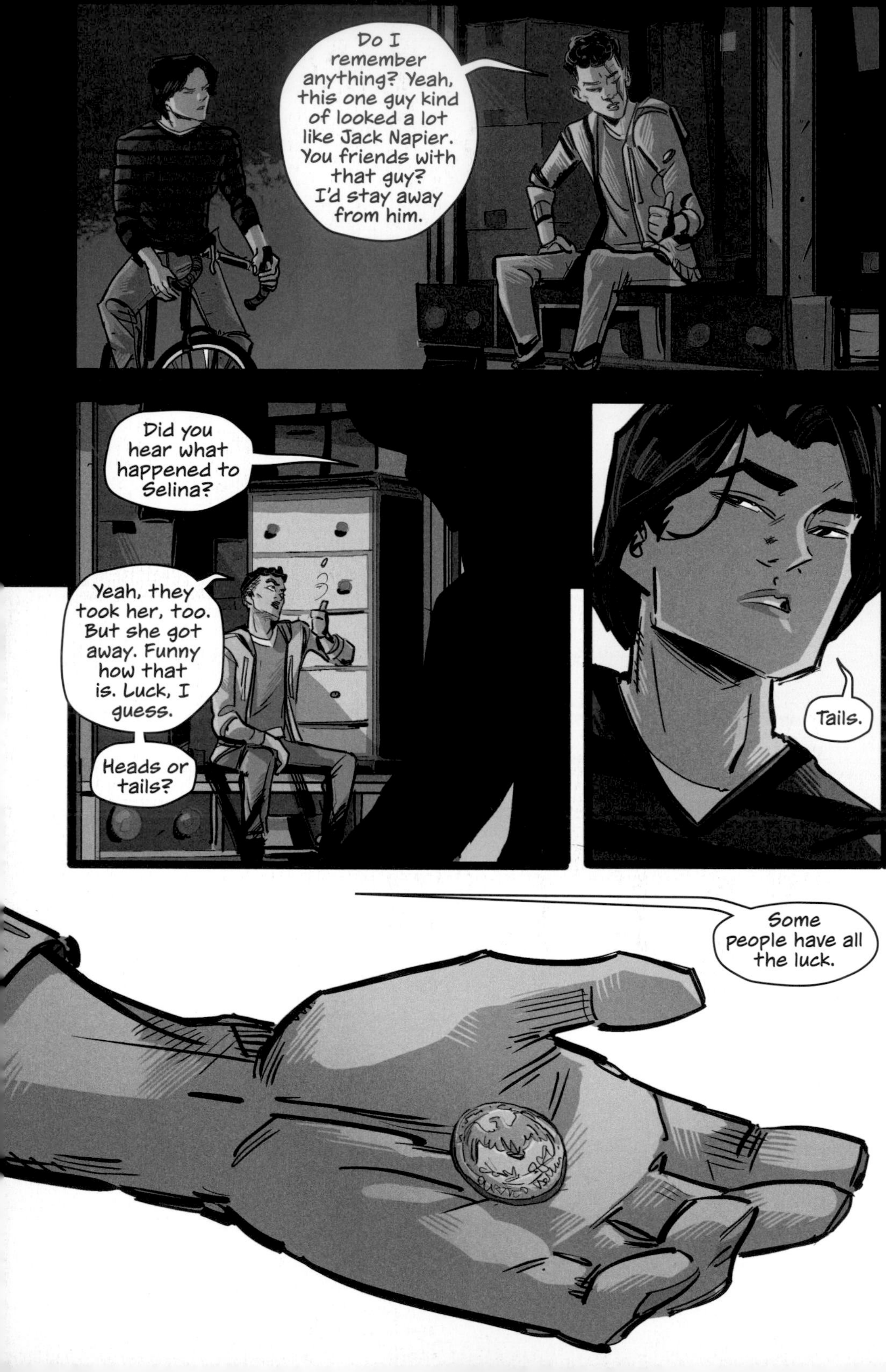
Do I remember anything? Yeah, this one guy kind of looked a lot like Jack Napier. You friends with that guy? I'd stay away from him.
Did you hear what happened to Selina?
Yeah, they took her, too. But she got away. Funny how that is. Luck, I guess.
Heads or tails?
Tails.
Some people have all the luck.

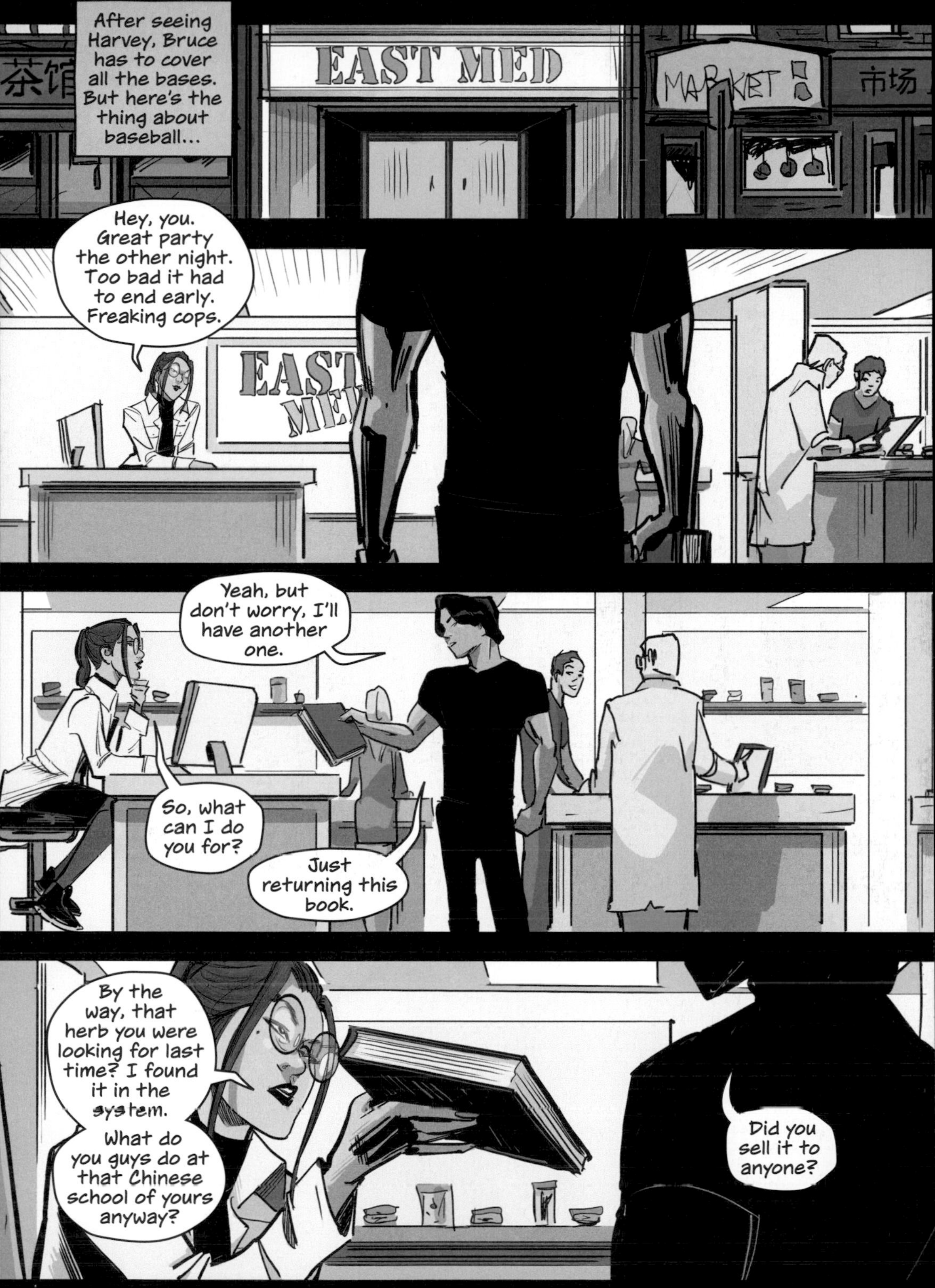
After seeing Harvey, Bruce has to cover all the bases. But here's the thing about baseball...
EAST MED
茶馆
MARKET
市场
Hey, you. Great party the other night. Too bad it had to end early. Freaking cops.
EAST MED
Yeah, but don't worry, I'll have another one.
So, what can I do you for?
Just returning this book.
By the way, that herb you were looking for last time? I found it in the system.
What do you guys do at that Chinese school of yours anyway?
Did you sell it to anyone?

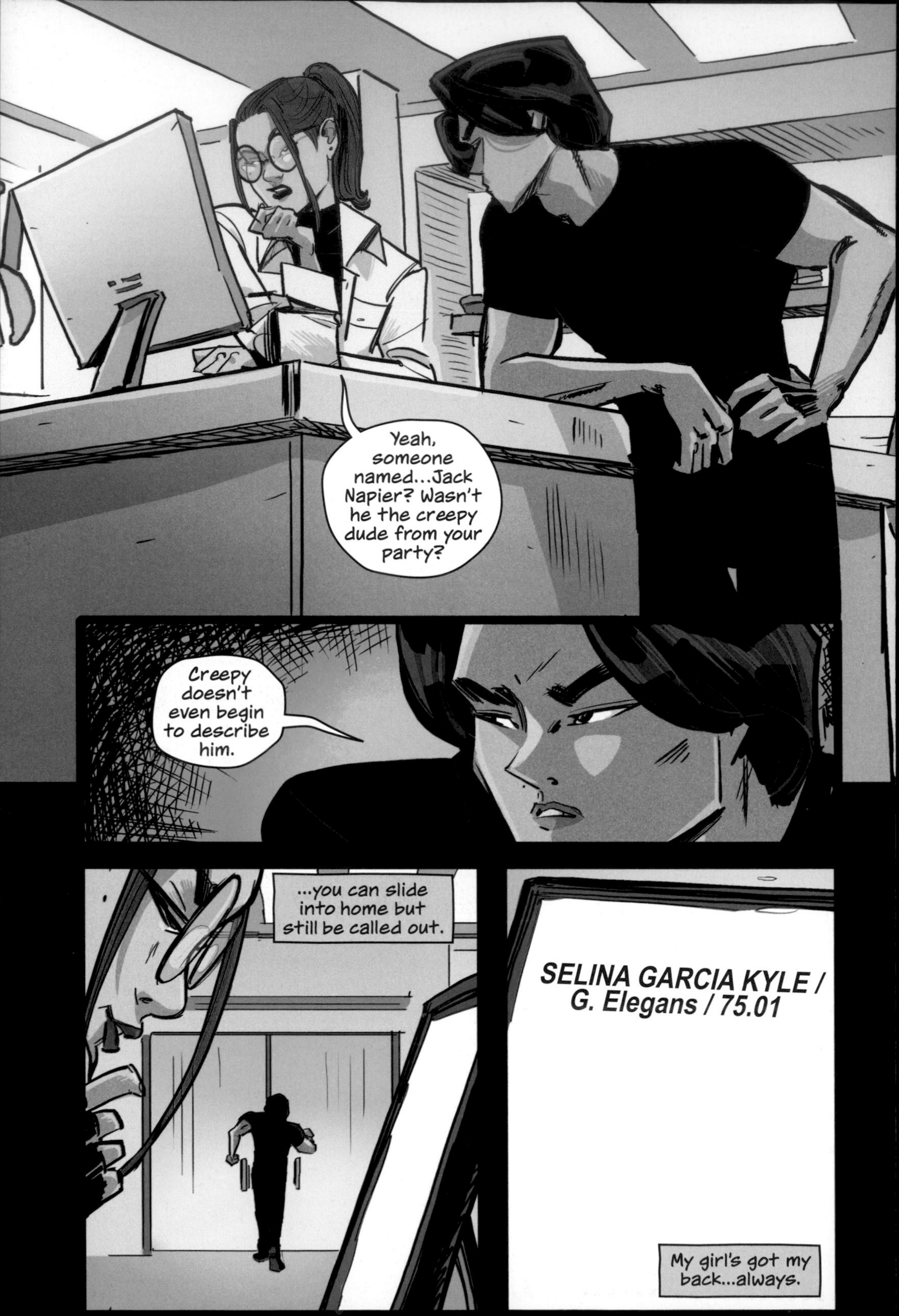
Yeah, someone named...Jack Napier? Wasn't he the creepy dude from your party?
Creepy doesn't even begin to describe him.
...you can slide into home but still be called out.
SELINA GARCIA KYLE / G. Elegans / 75.01
My girl's got my back...always.

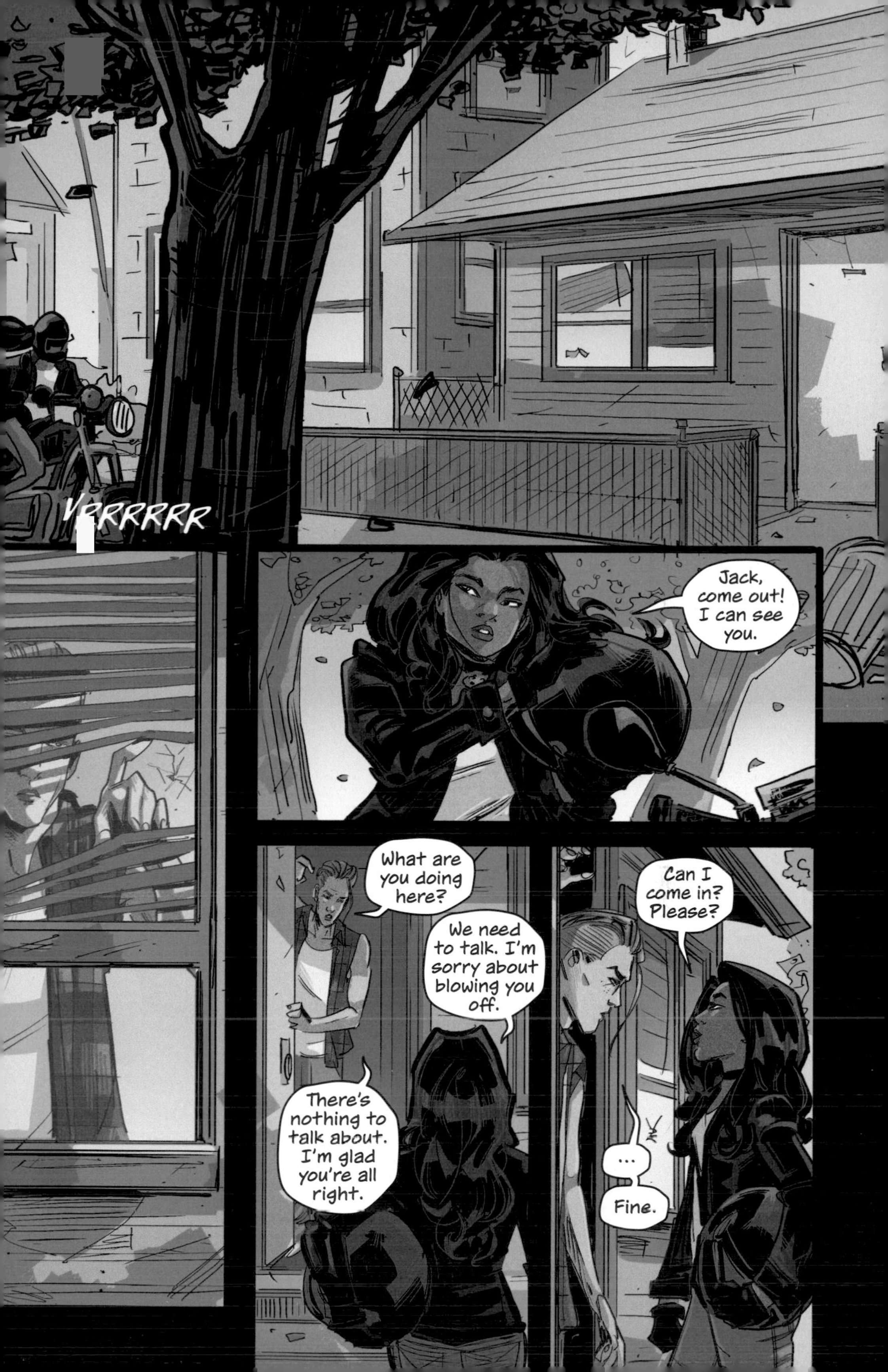
VRRRRRR
Jack, come out! I can see you.
What are you doing here?
We need to talk. I'm sorry about blowing you off.
There's nothing to talk about. I'm glad you're all right.
Can I come in? Please?
...
Fine.

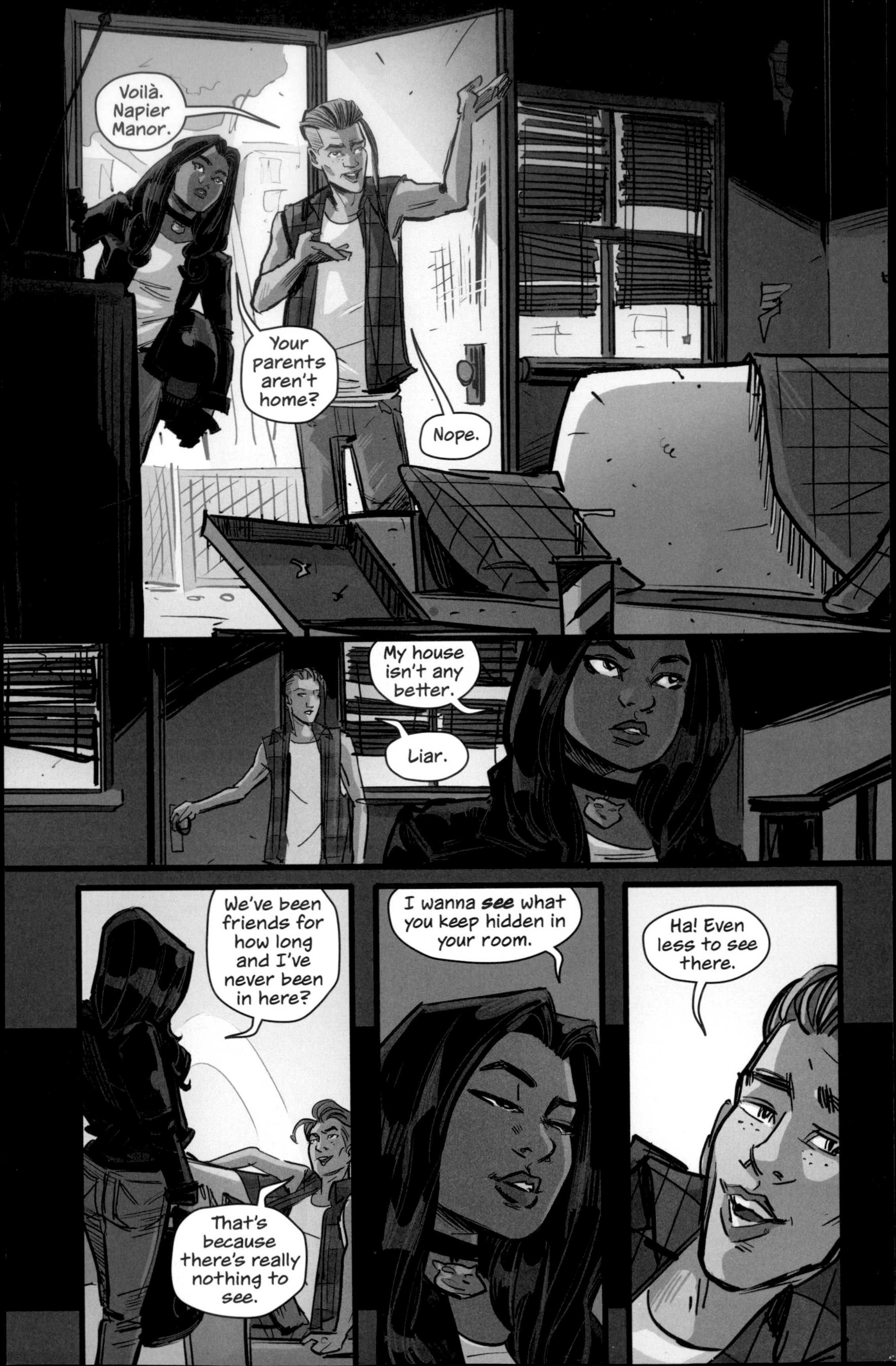
Voilà. Napier Manor.
Your parents aren't home?
Nope.
My house isn't any better.
Liar.
We've been friends for how long and I've never been in here?
That's because there's really nothing to see.
I wanna ***see*** what you keep hidden in your room.
Ha! Even less to see there.

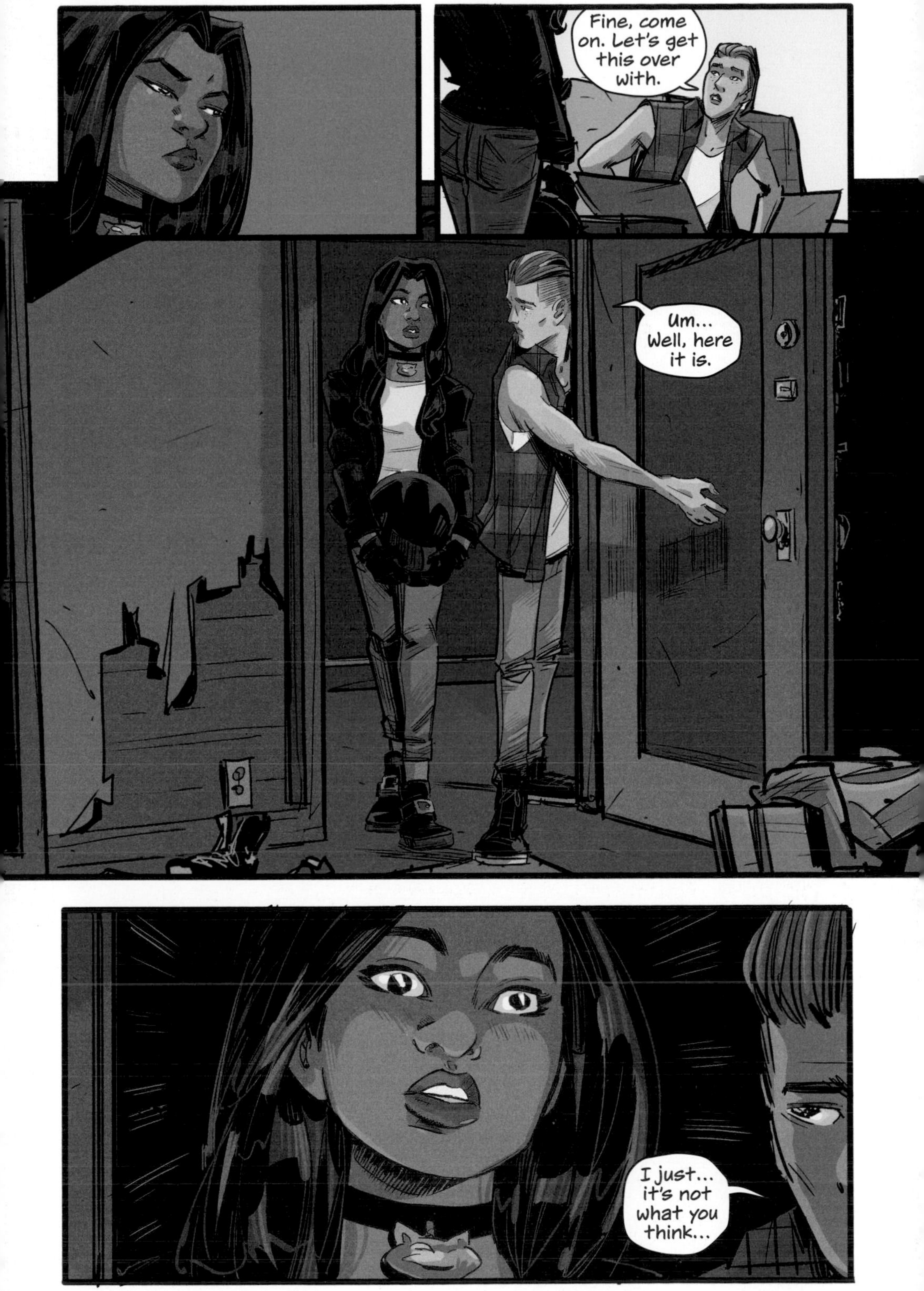
Fine, come on. Let's get this over with.
Um... Well, here it is.
I just... it's not what you think...

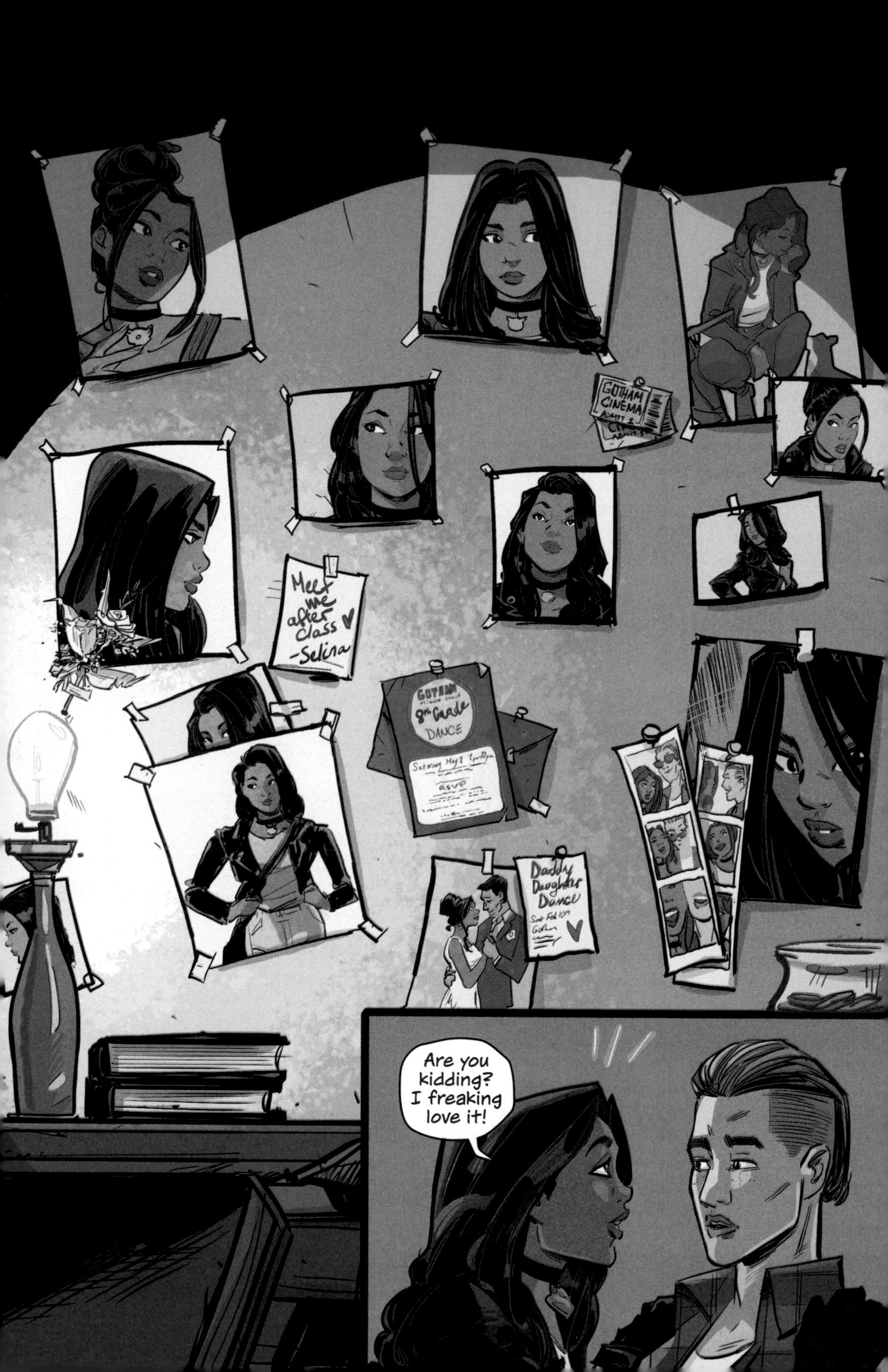

GOTHAM CINEMA ADMIT 2
Meet me after class ♥ -Selina
GOTHAM 8th Grade DANCE
RSVP
Daddy Daughter Dance
Are you kidding? I freaking love it!

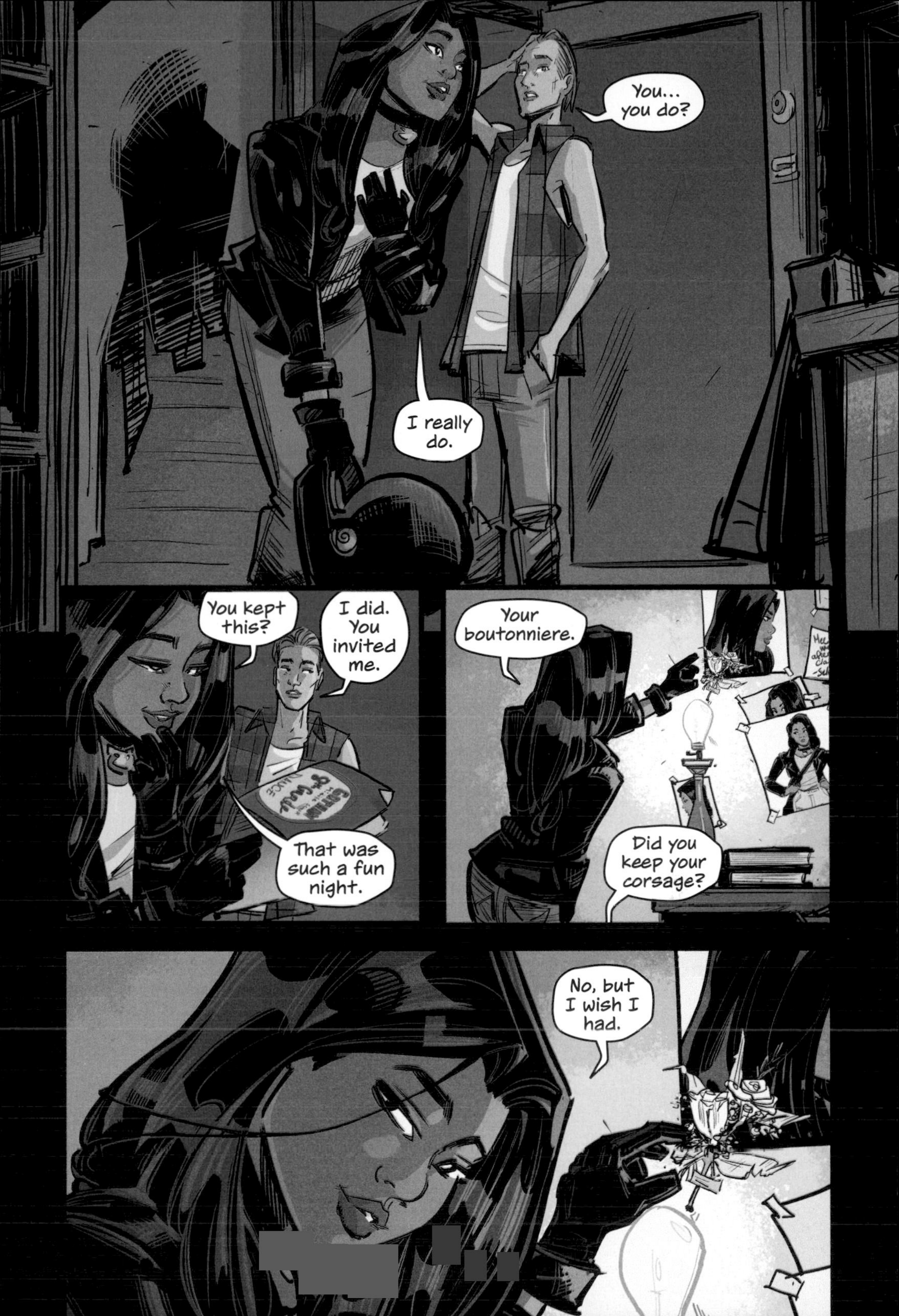

You... you do?
I really do.
You kept this?
I did. You invited me.
That was such a fun night.
Your boutonniere.
Did you keep your corsage?
No, but I wish I had.

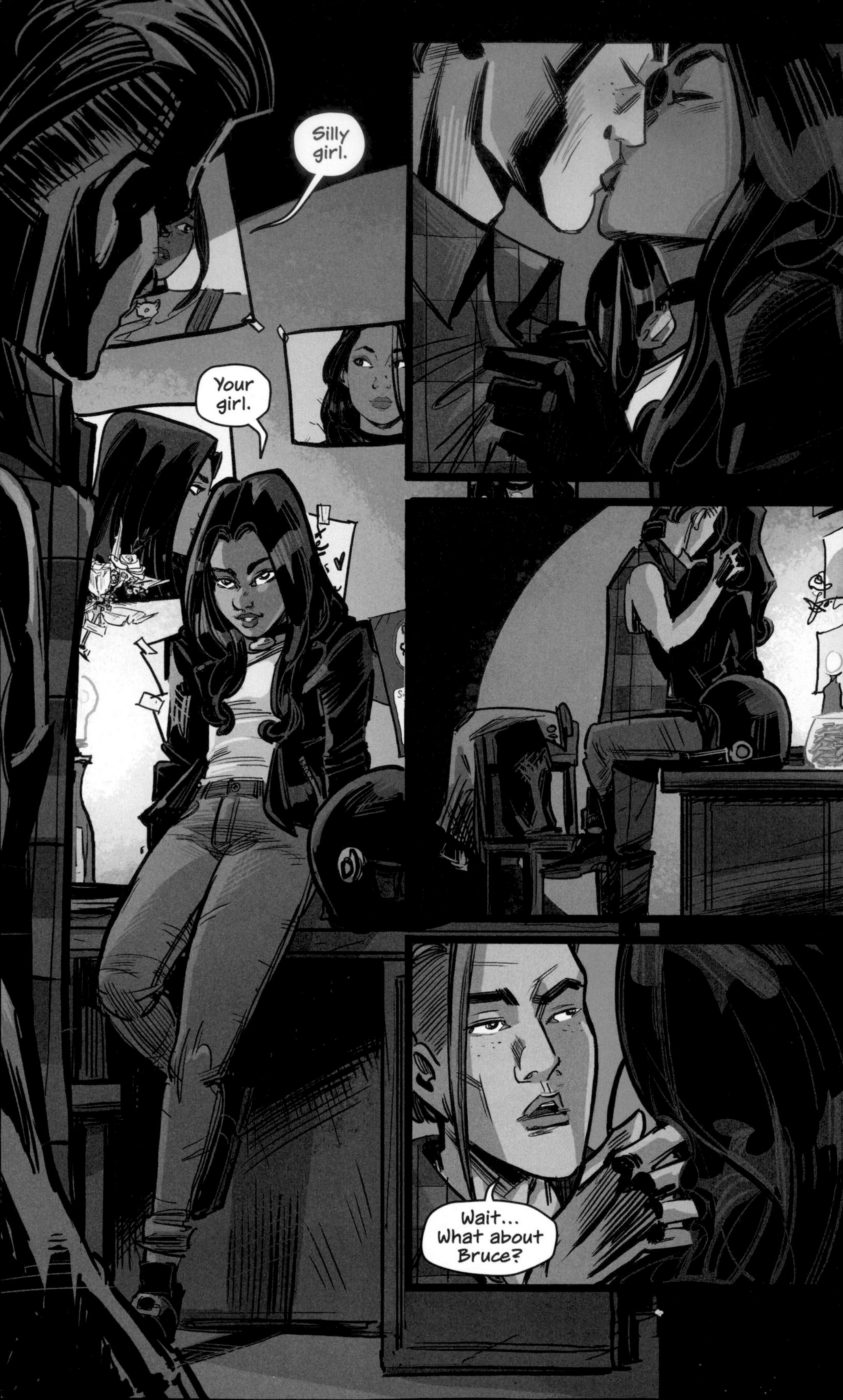
Silly girl.
Your girl.
Wait... What about Bruce?

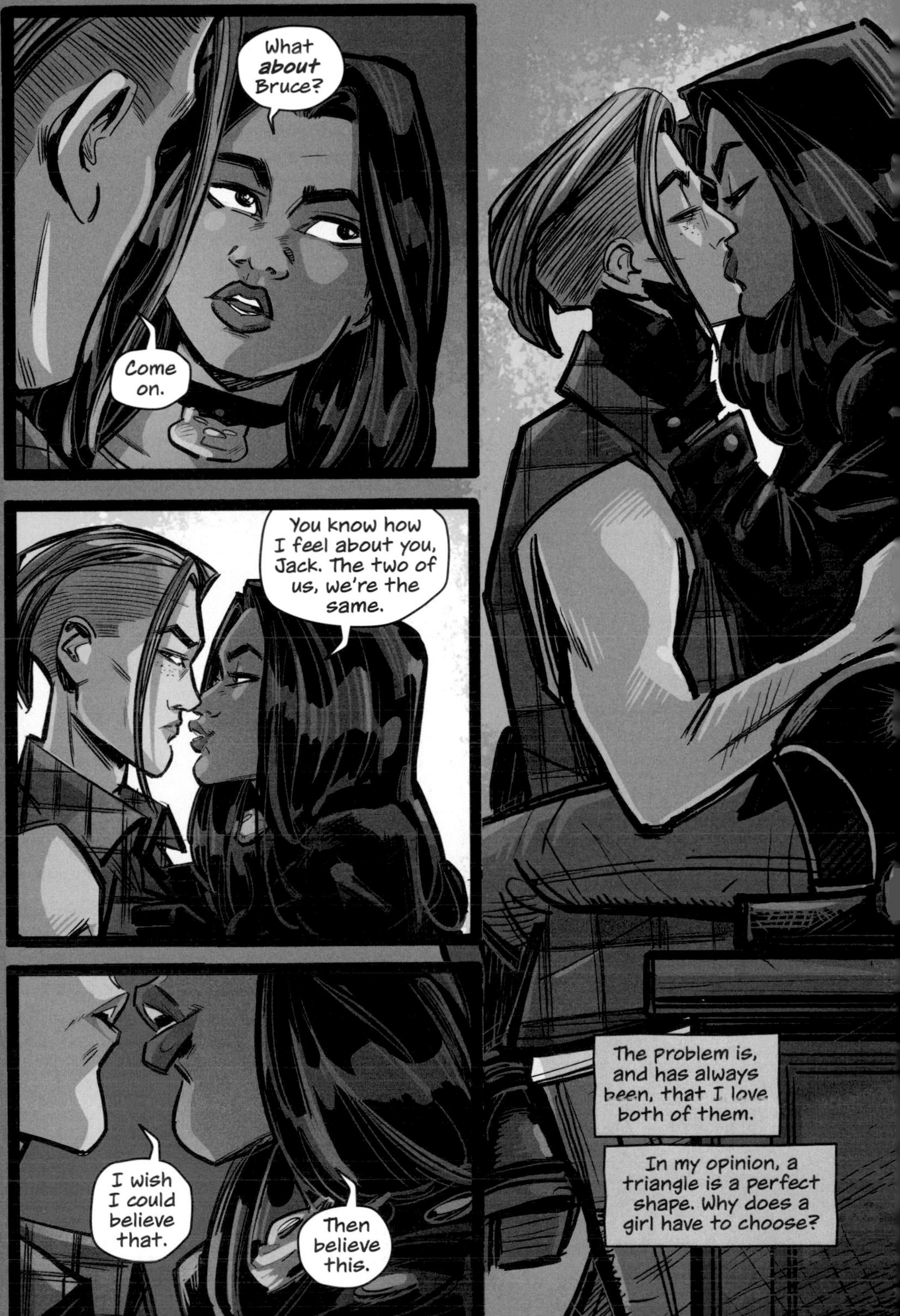
What about Bruce?
Come on.
You know how I feel about you, Jack. The two of us, we're the same.
I wish I could believe that.
Then believe this.
The problem is, and has always been, that I love both of them.
In my opinion, a triangle is a perfect shape. Why does a girl have to choose?

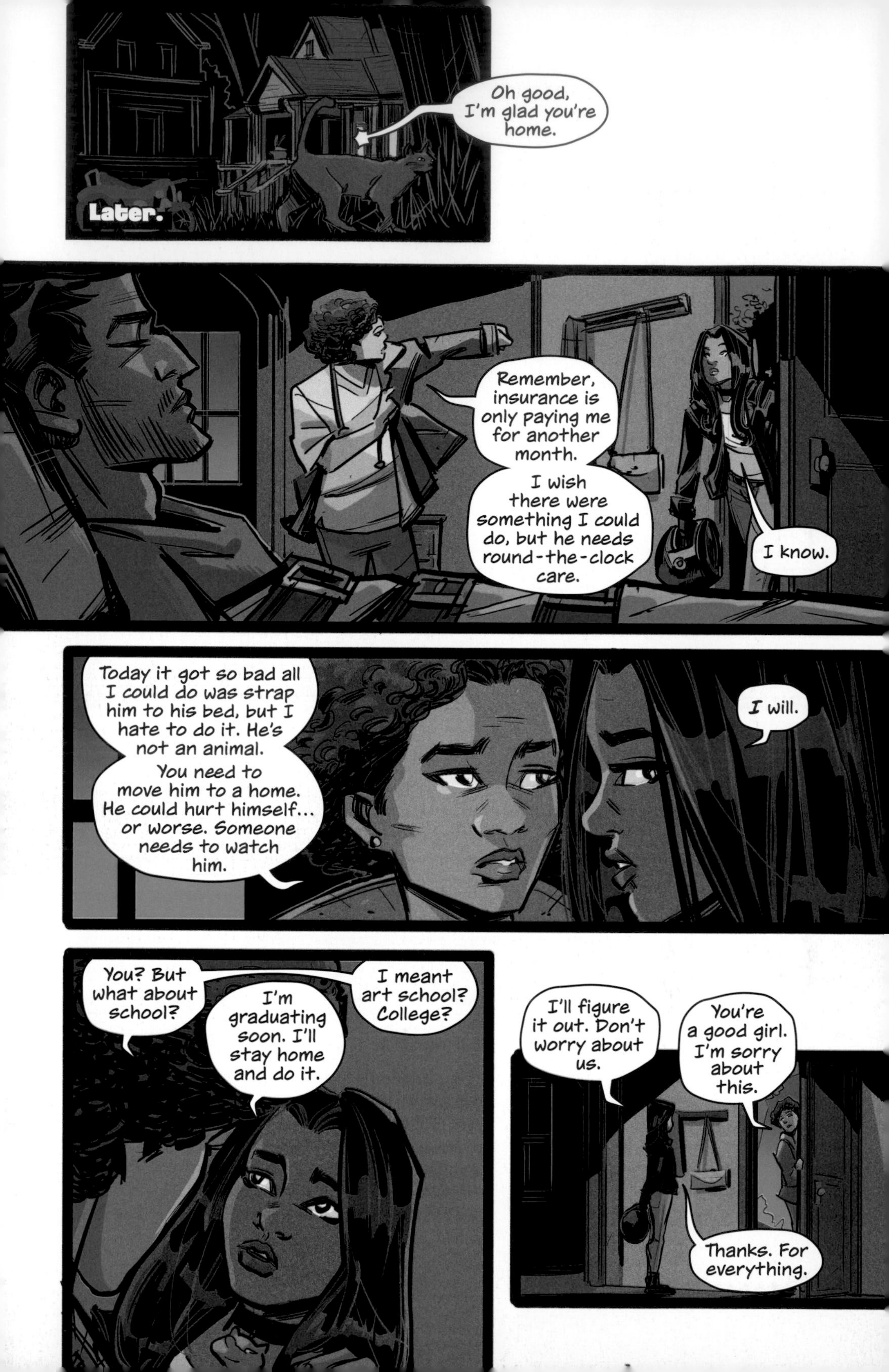
Oh good, I'm glad you're home.
Later.
Remember, insurance is only paying me for another month.
I wish there were something I could do, but he needs round-the-clock care.
I know.
Today it got so bad all I could do was strap him to his bed, but I hate to do it. He's not an animal.
You need to move him to a home. He could hurt himself... or worse. Someone needs to watch him.
I will.
You? But what about school?
I'm graduating soon. I'll stay home and do it.
I meant art school? College?
I'll figure it out. Don't worry about us.
You're a good girl. I'm sorry about this.
Thanks. For everything.

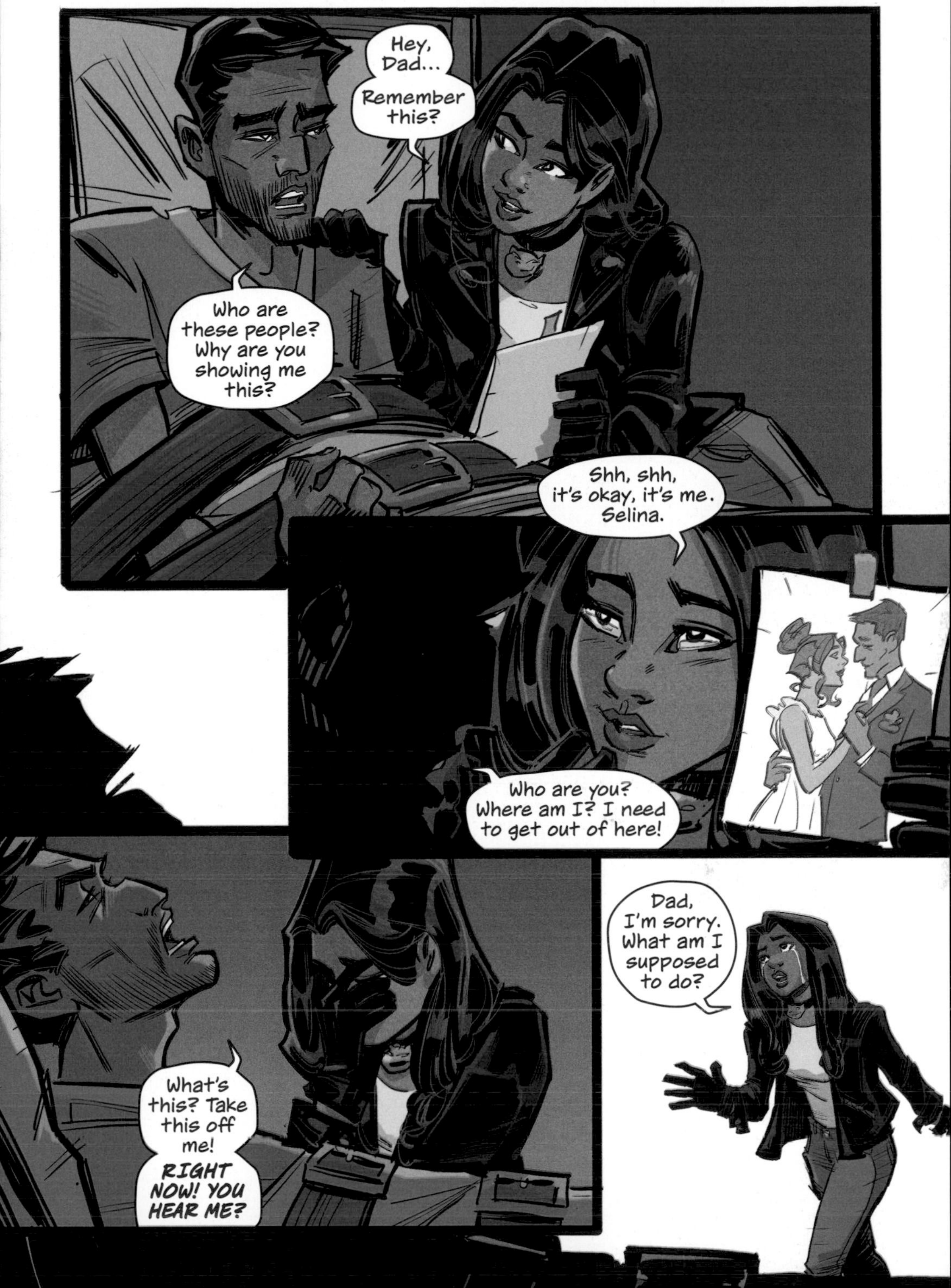
Hey, Dad...
Remember this?
Who are these people? Why are you showing me this?
Shh, shh, it's okay, it's me. Selina.
Who are you? Where am I? I need to get out of here!
What's this? Take this off me!
RIGHT NOW! YOU HEAR ME?
Dad, I'm sorry. What am I supposed to do?

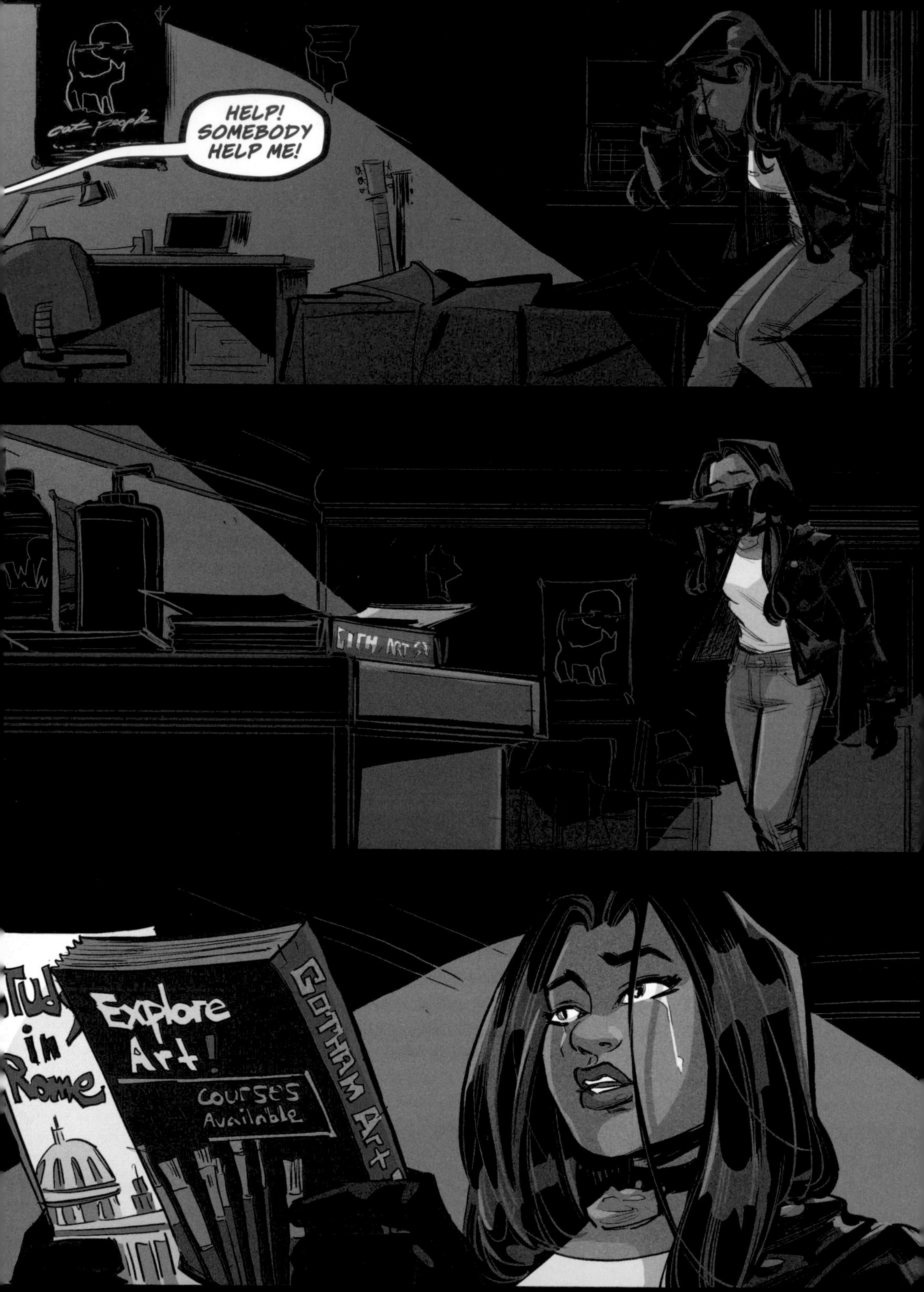
cat people
HELP! SOMEBODY HELP ME!
in Rome
Explore Art!
Courses Available
GOTHAM ART

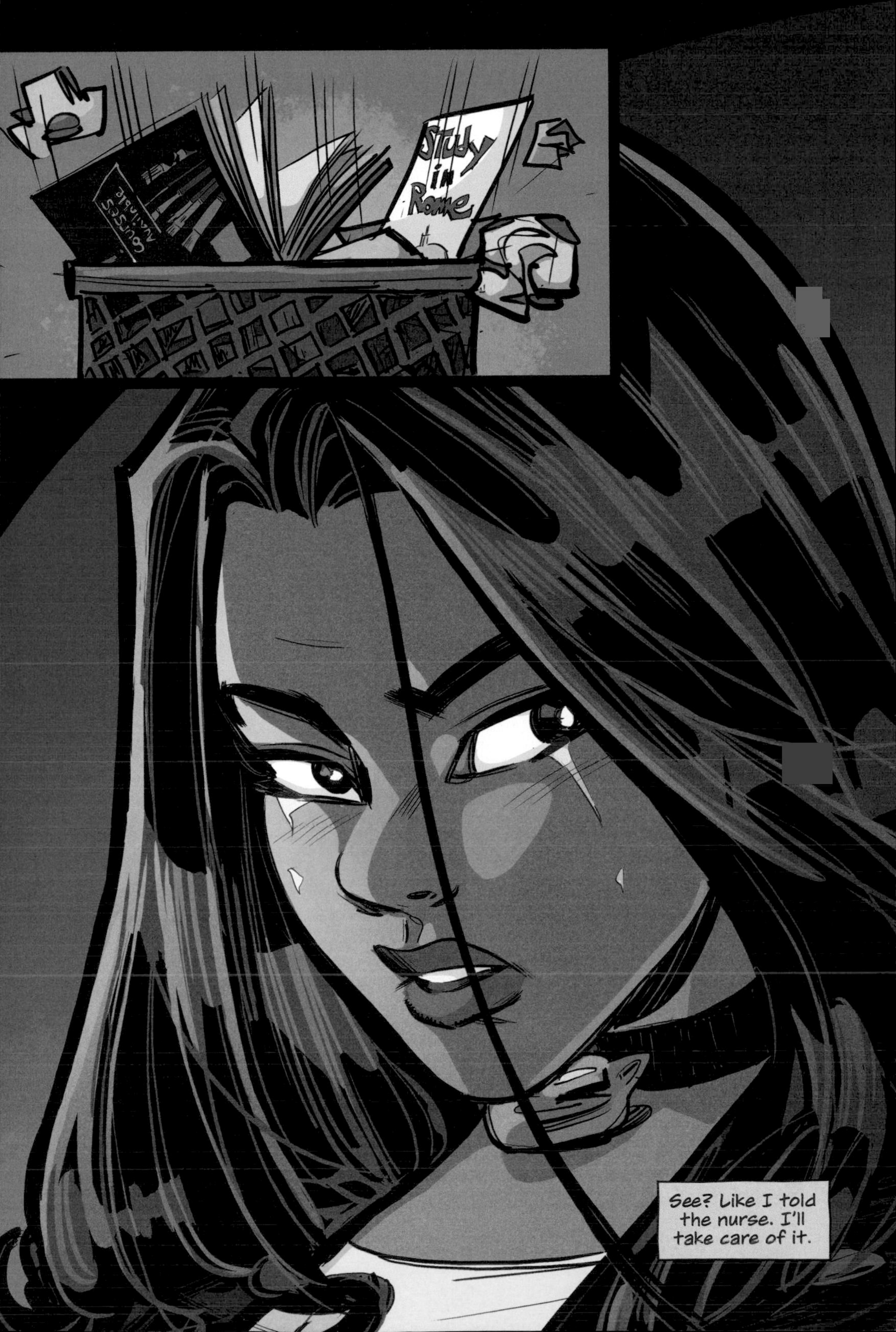
Courses Available
Study in Rome
See? Like I told the nurse. I'll take care of it.

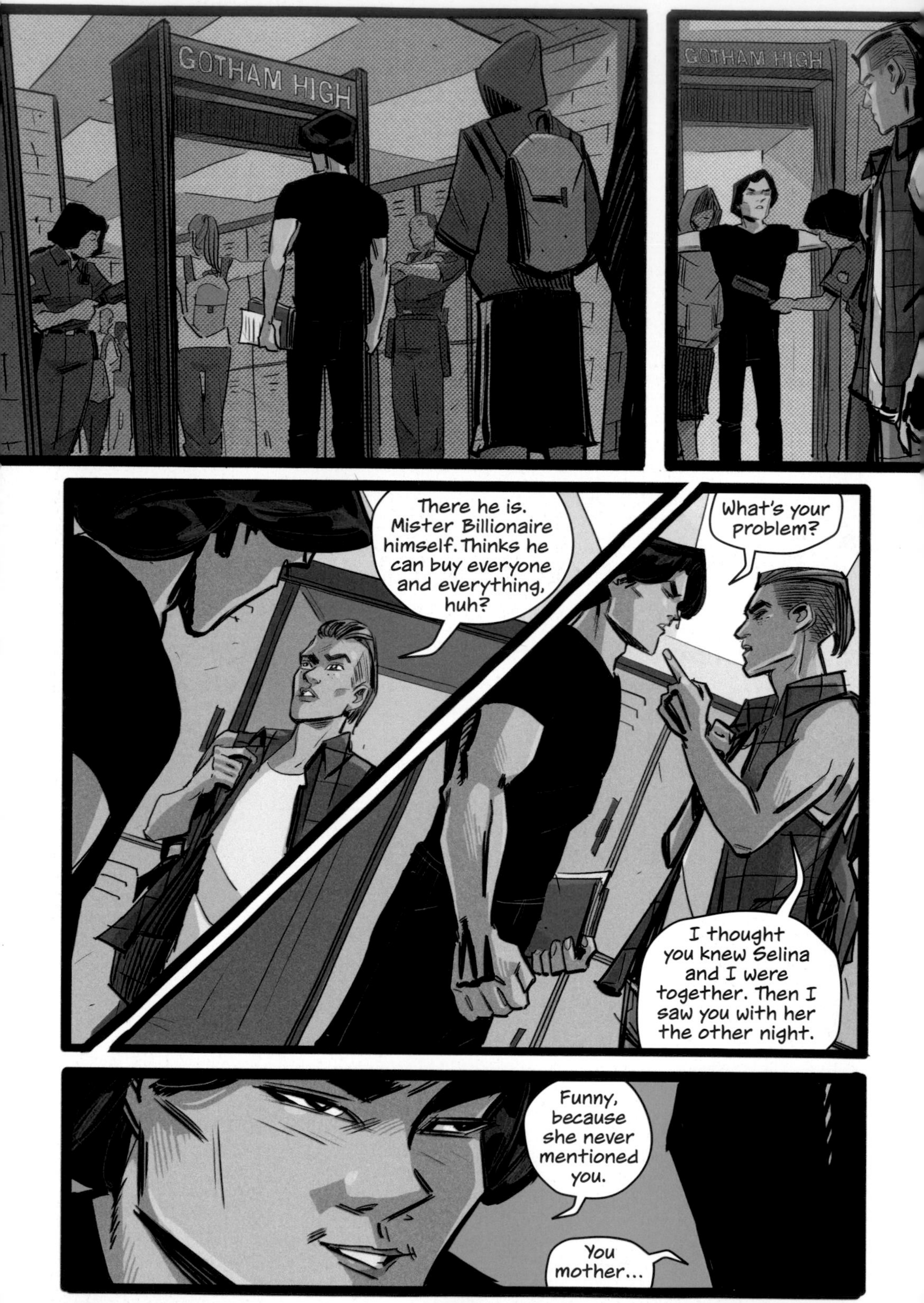
GOTHAM HIGH
GOTHAM HIGH
There he is. Mister Billionaire himself. Thinks he can buy everyone and everything, huh?
What's your problem?
I thought you knew Selina and I were together. Then I saw you with her the other night.
Funny, because she never mentioned you.
You mother...

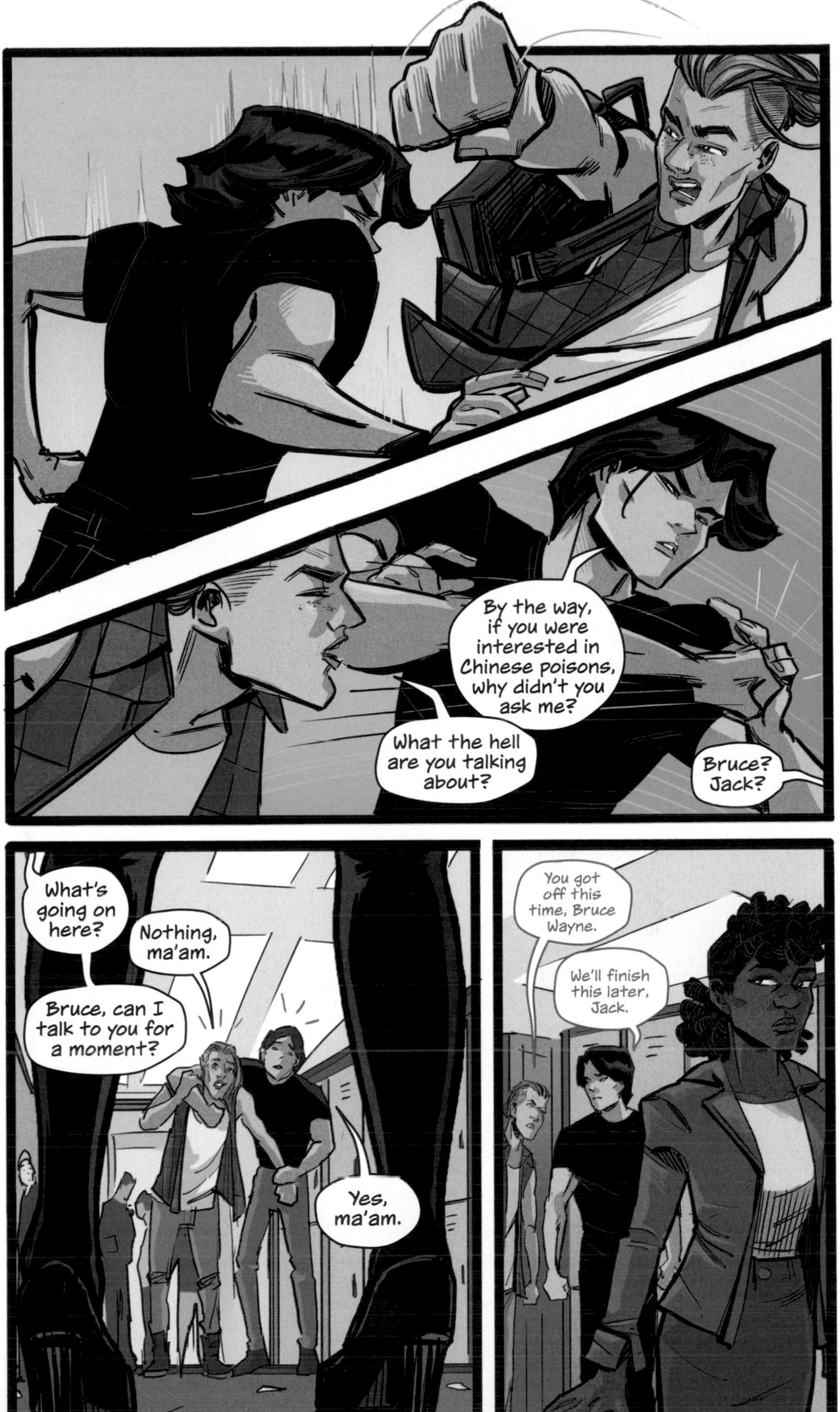

By the way, if you were interested in Chinese poisons, why didn't you ask me?
What the hell are you talking about?
Bruce? Jack?
What's going on here?
Nothing, ma'am.
Bruce, can I talk to you for a moment?
Yes, ma'am.
You got off this time, Bruce Wayne.
We'll finish this later, Jack.

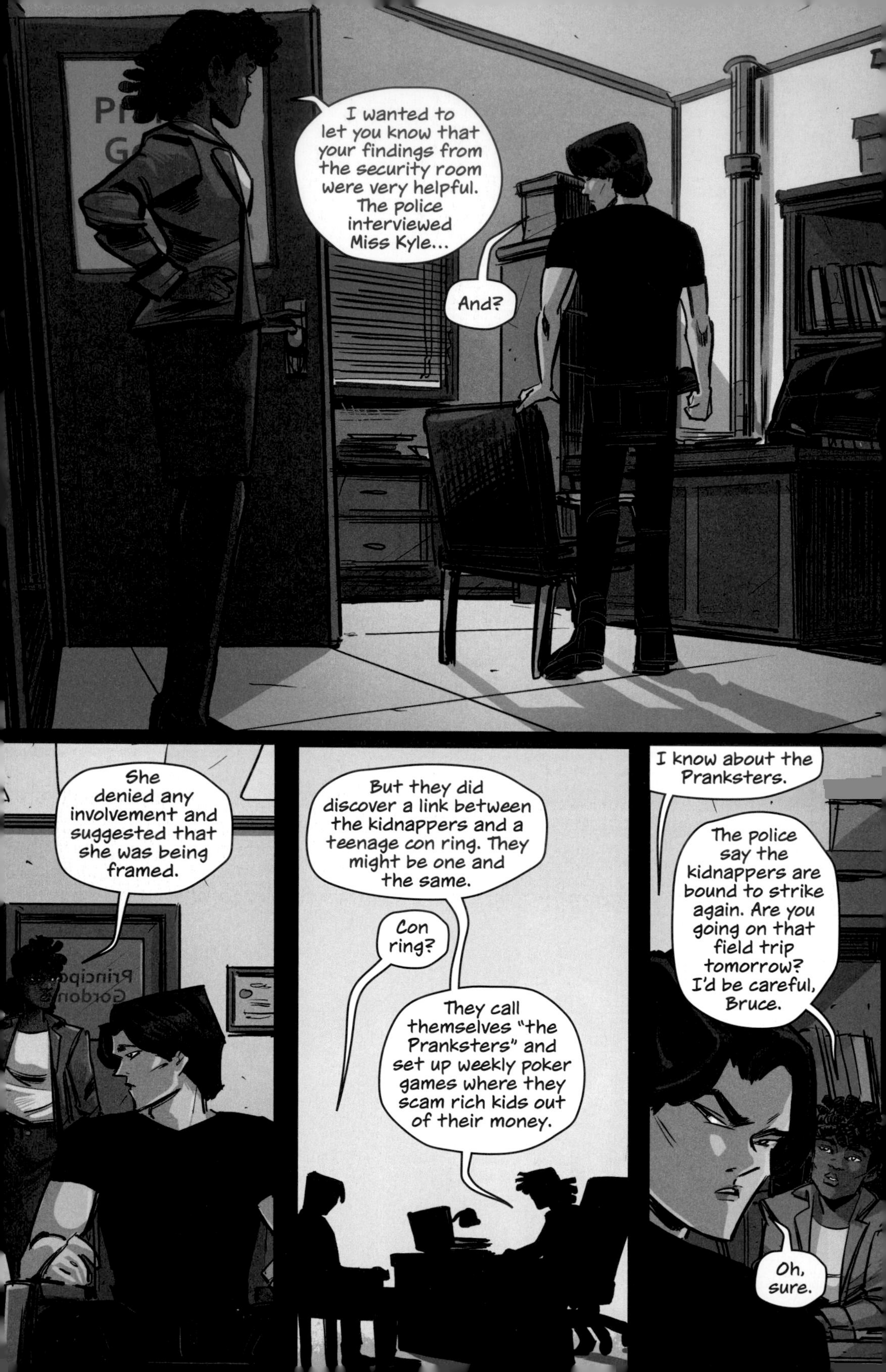
I wanted to let you know that your findings from the security room were very helpful. The police interviewed Miss Kyle...
And?
She denied any involvement and suggested that she was being framed.
Principal Gordon
But they did discover a link between the kidnappers and a teenage con ring. They might be one and the same.
Con ring?
They call themselves "the Pranksters" and set up weekly poker games where they scam rich kids out of their money.
I know about the Pranksters.
The police say the kidnappers are bound to strike again. Are you going on that field trip tomorrow? I'd be careful, Bruce.
Oh, sure.

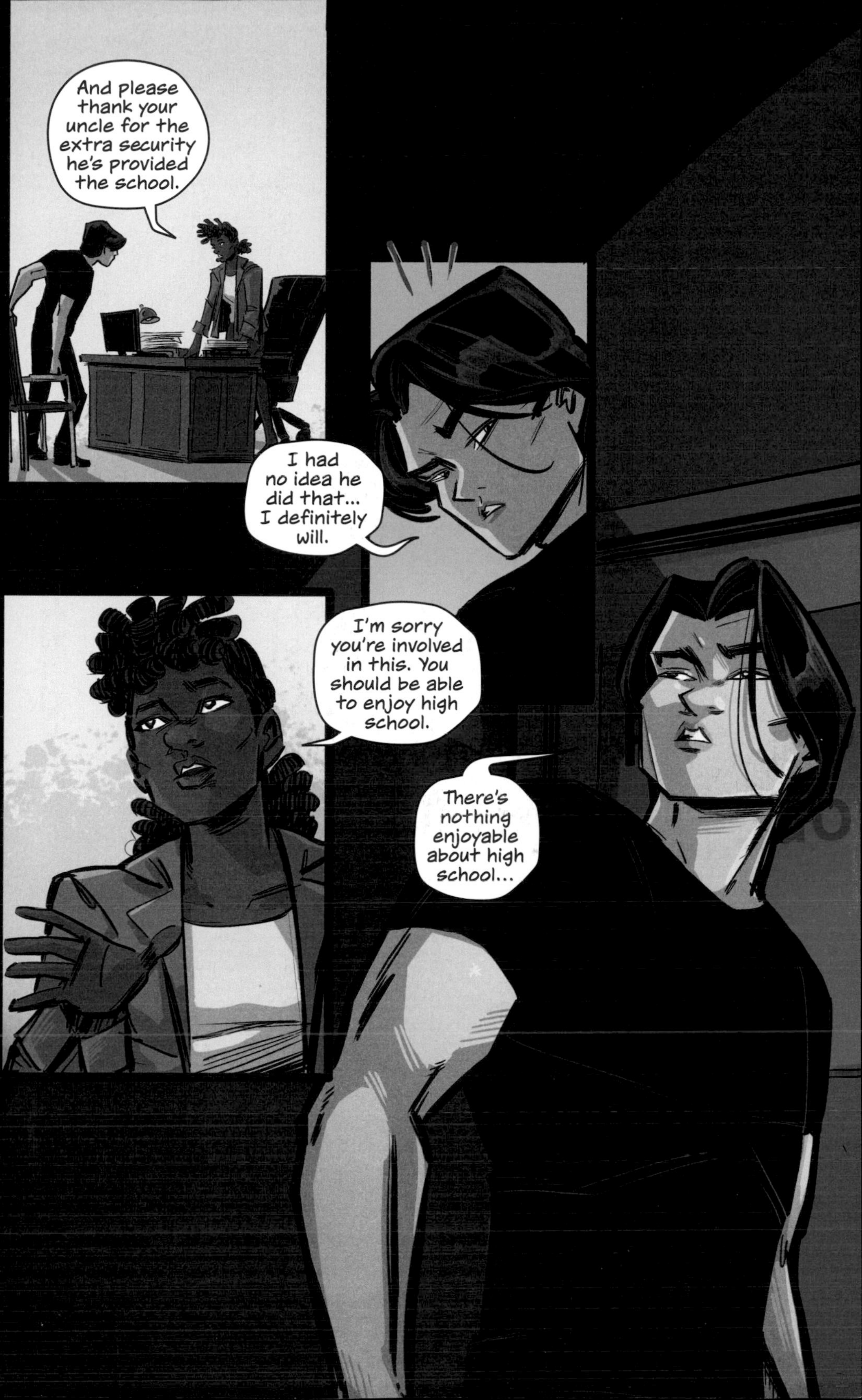
And please thank your uncle for the extra security he's provided the school.
I had no idea he did that... I definitely will.
I'm sorry you're involved in this. You should be able to enjoy high school.
There's nothing enjoyable about high school...

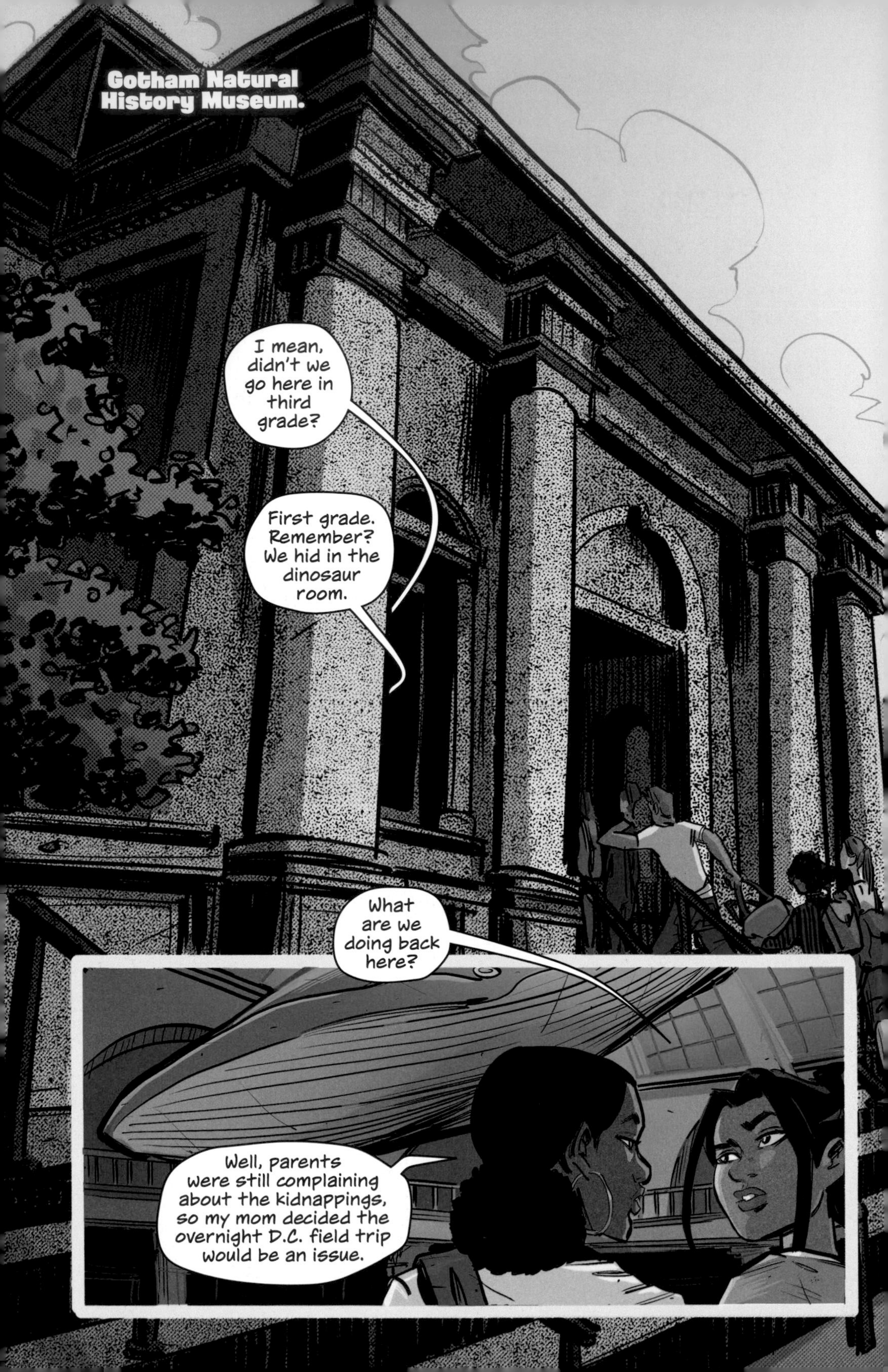
Gotham Natural History Museum.
I mean, didn't we go here in third grade?
First grade. Remember? We hid in the dinosaur room.
What are we doing back here?
Well, parents were still complaining about the kidnappings, so my mom decided the overnight D.C. field trip would be an issue.

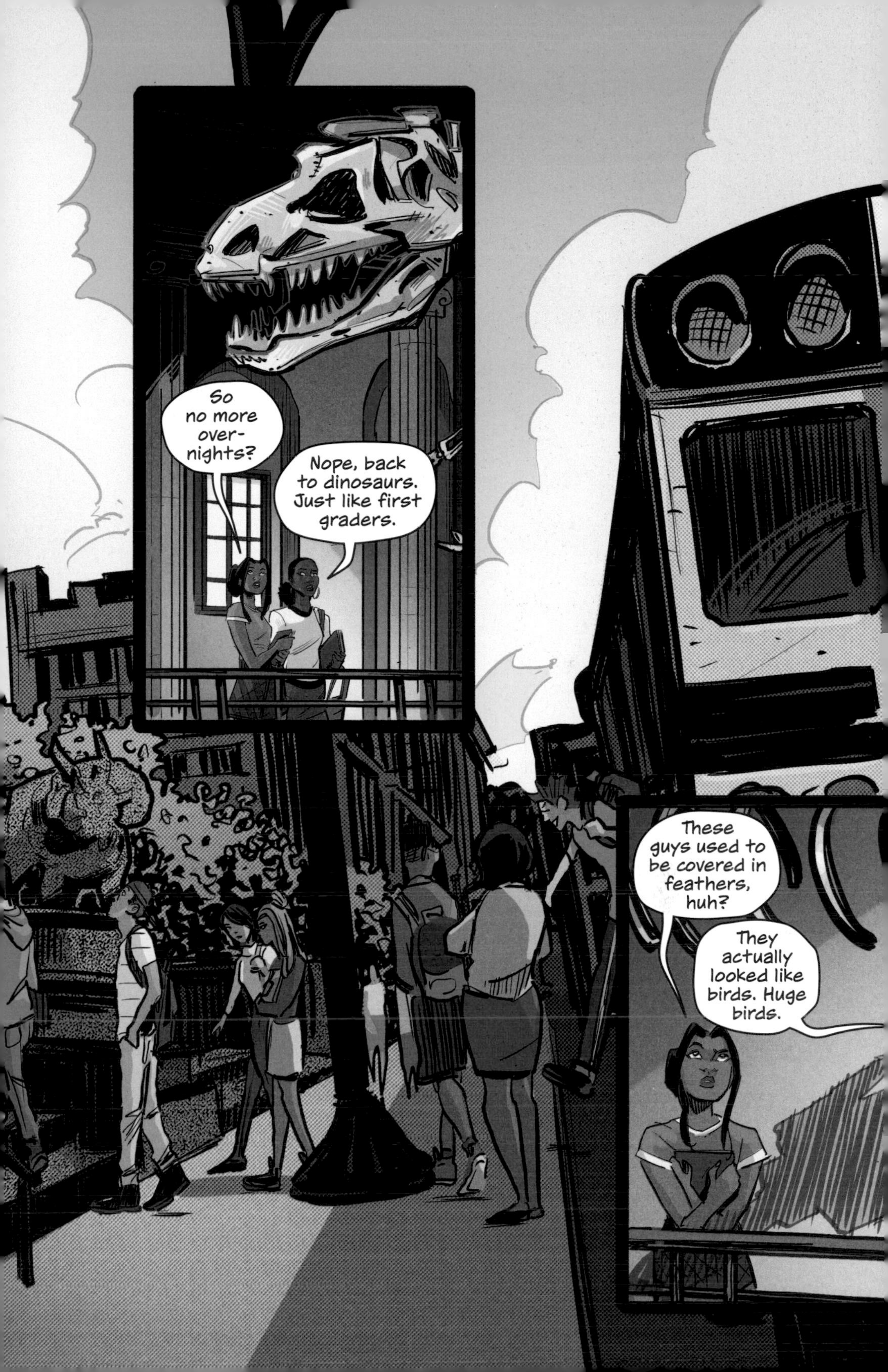
So no more over-nights?
Nope, back to dinosaurs. Just like first graders.
These guys used to be covered in feathers, huh?
They actually looked like birds. Huge birds.

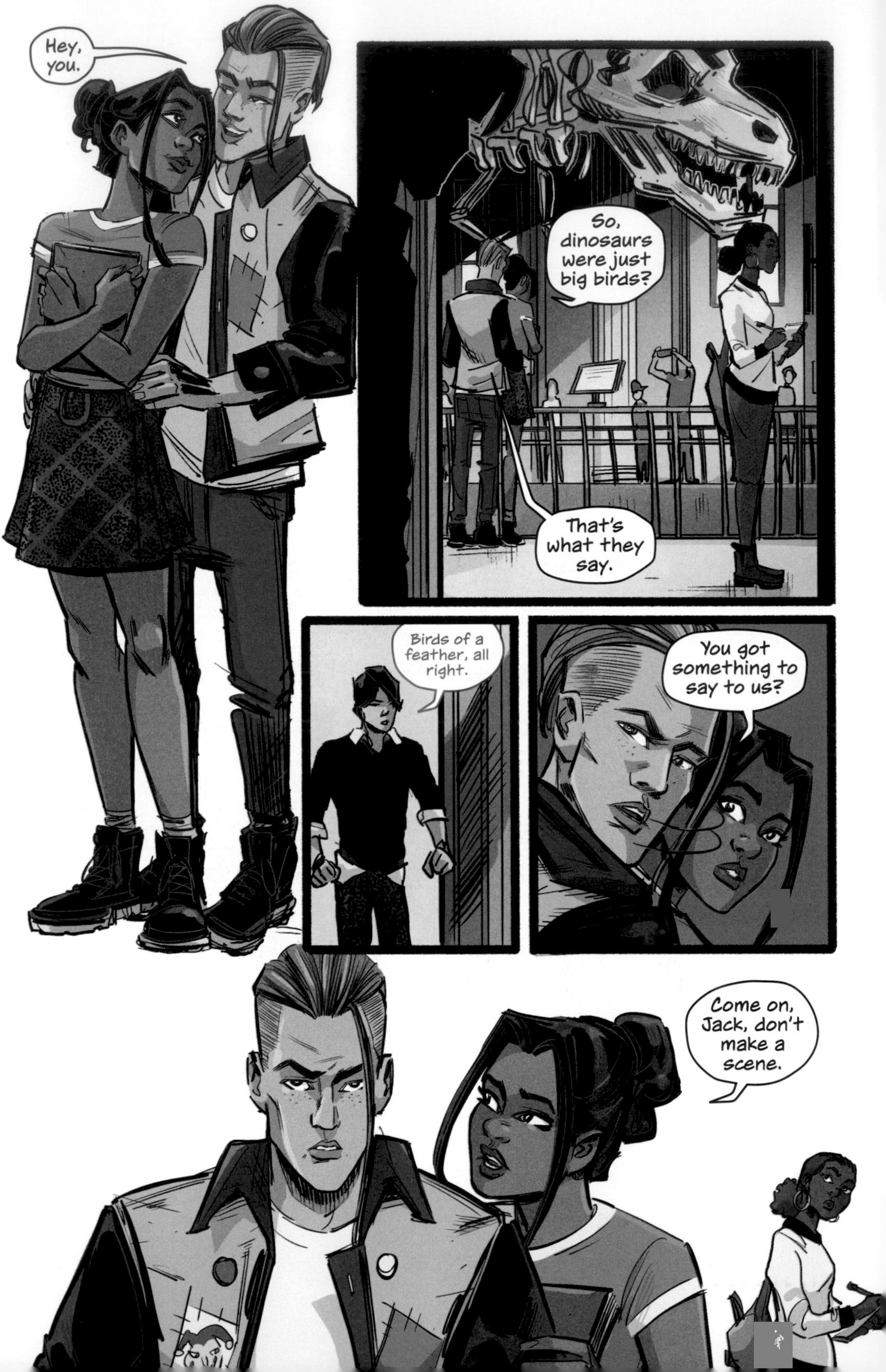
Hey, you.
So, dinosaurs were just big birds?
That's what they say.
Birds of a feather, all right.
You got something to say to us?
Come on, Jack, don't make a scene.

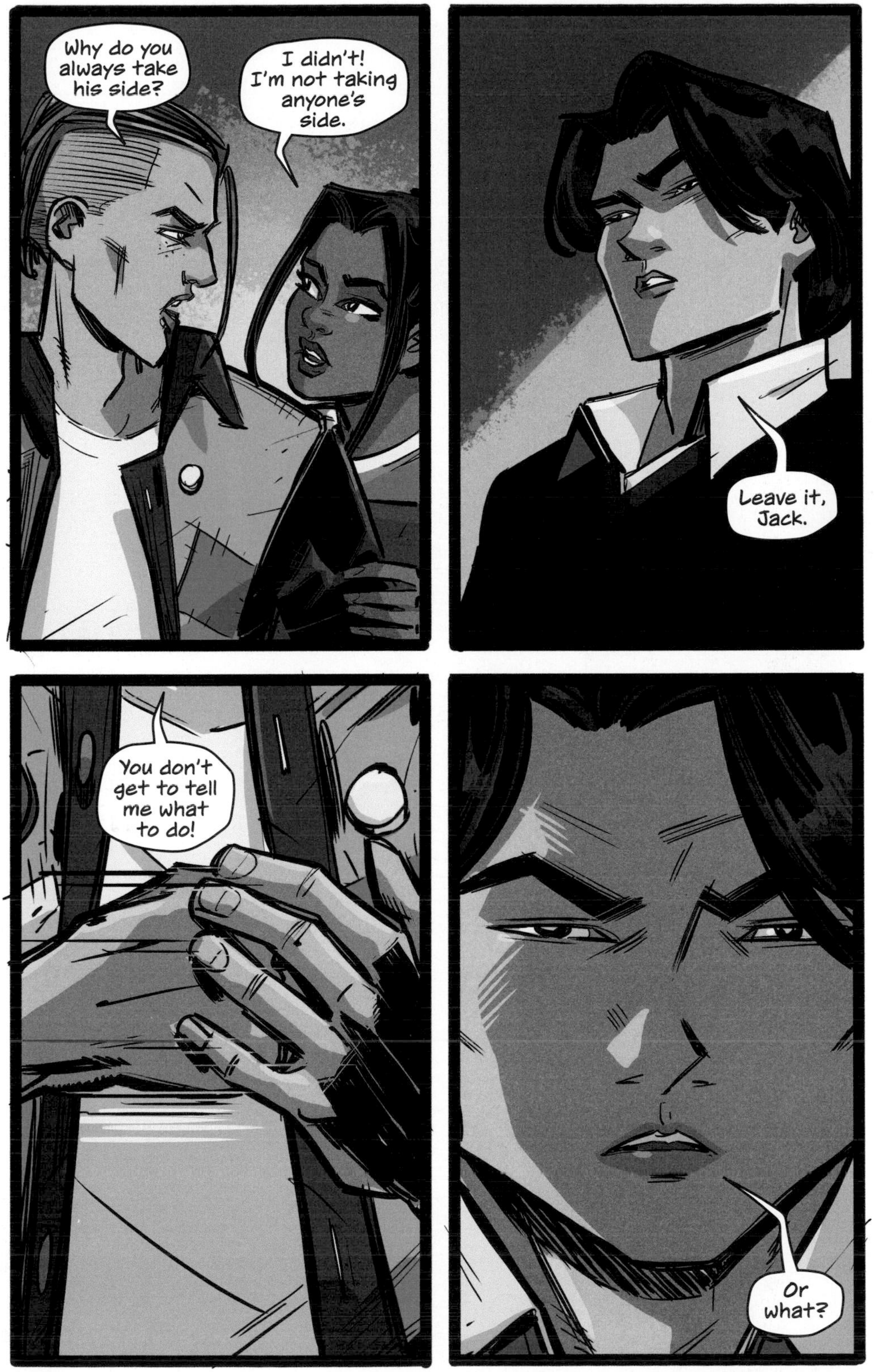
Why do you always take his side?
I didn't! I'm not taking anyone's side.
Leave it, Jack.
You don't get to tell me what to do!
Or what?

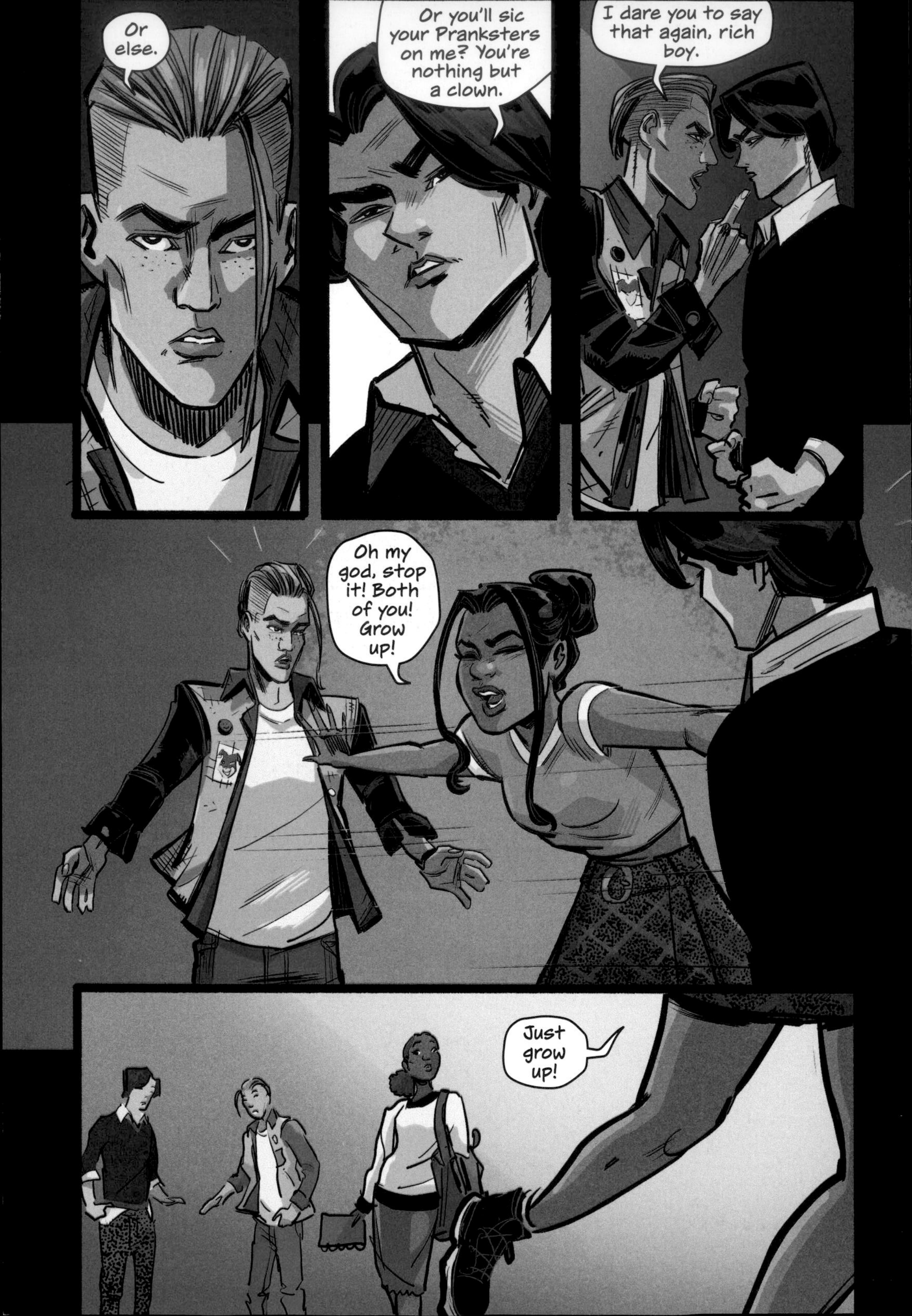
Or else.
Or you'll sic your Pranksters on me? You're nothing but a clown.
I dare you to say that again, rich boy.
Oh my god, stop it! Both of you! Grow up!
Just grow up!

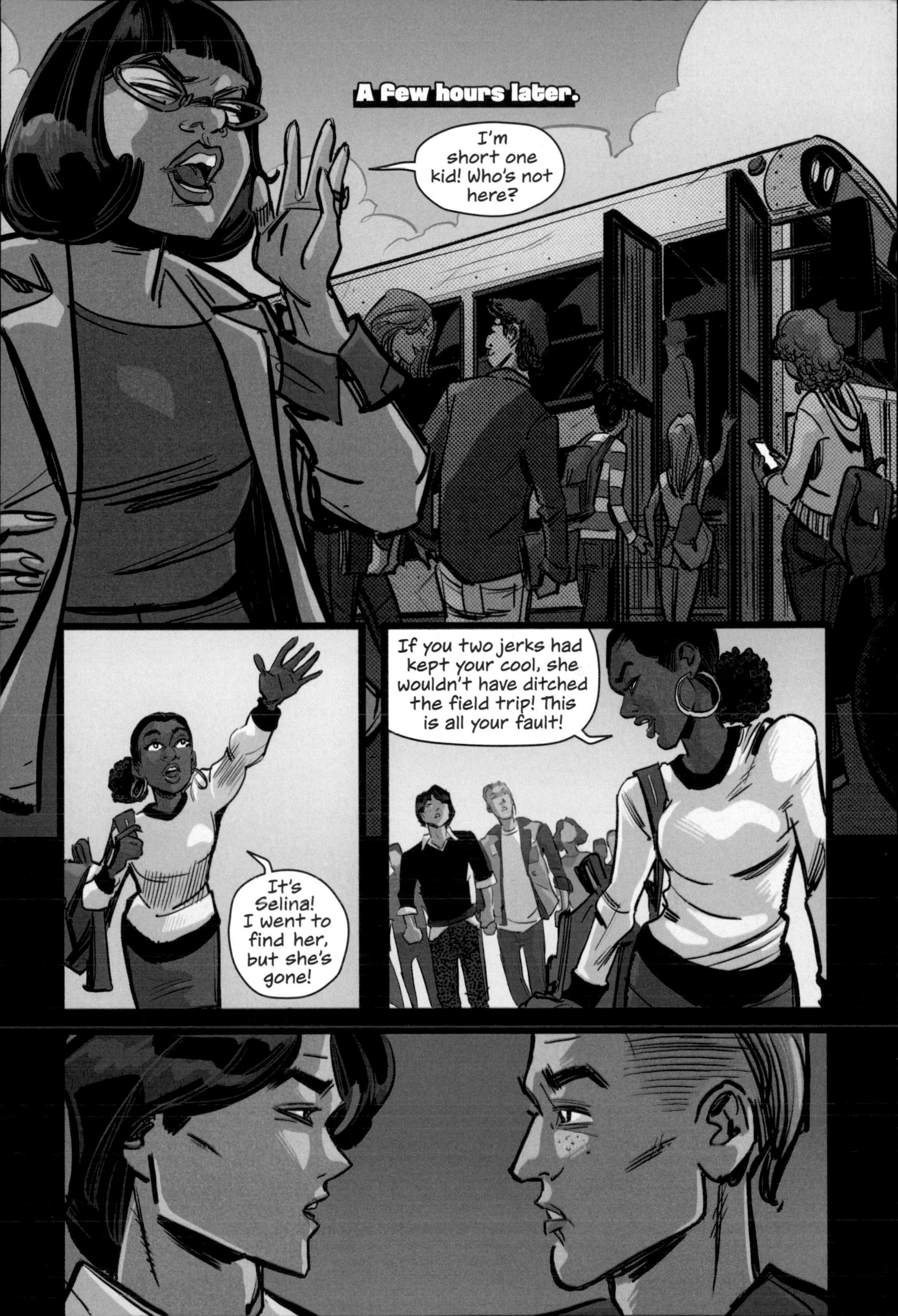
A few hours later.
I'm short one kid! Who's not here?
It's Selina! I went to find her, but she's gone!
If you two jerks had kept your cool, she wouldn't have ditched the field trip! This is all your fault!

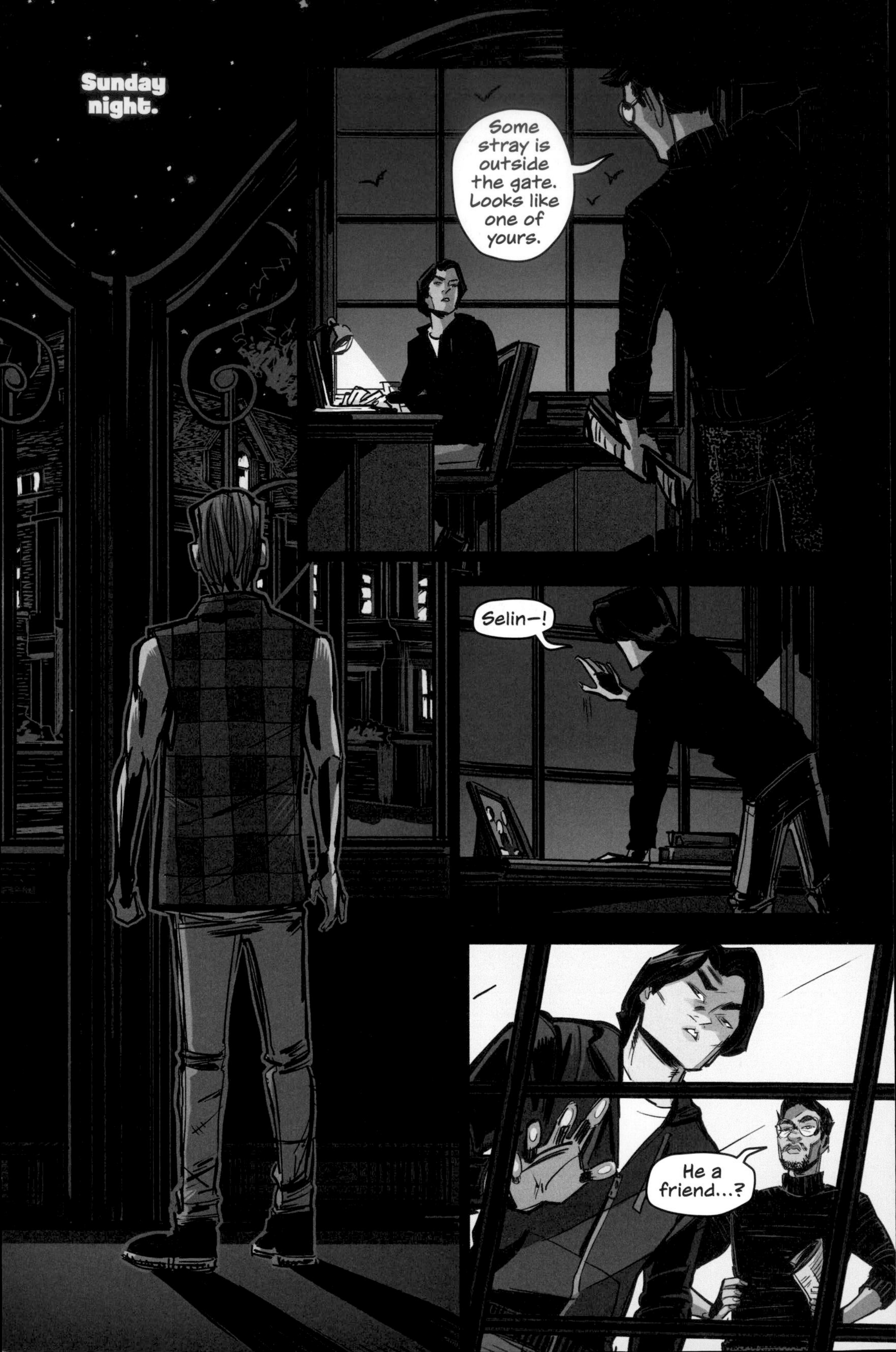
Sunday night.
Some stray is outside the gate. Looks like one of yours.
Selin—!
He a friend...?

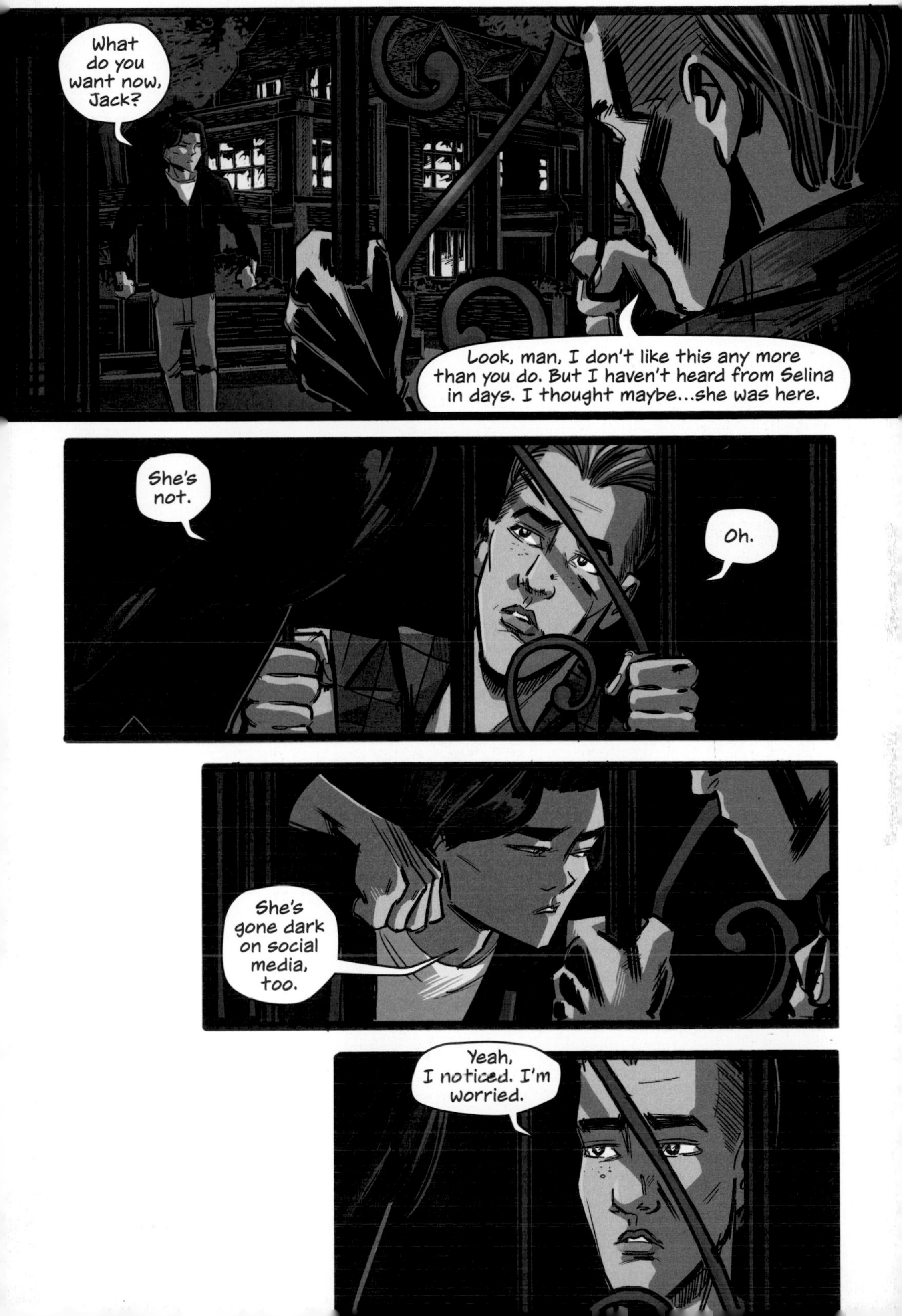
What do you want now, Jack?
Look, man, I don't like this any more than you do. But I haven't heard from Selina in days. I thought maybe...she was here.
She's not.
Oh.
She's gone dark on social media, too.
Yeah, I noticed. I'm worried.

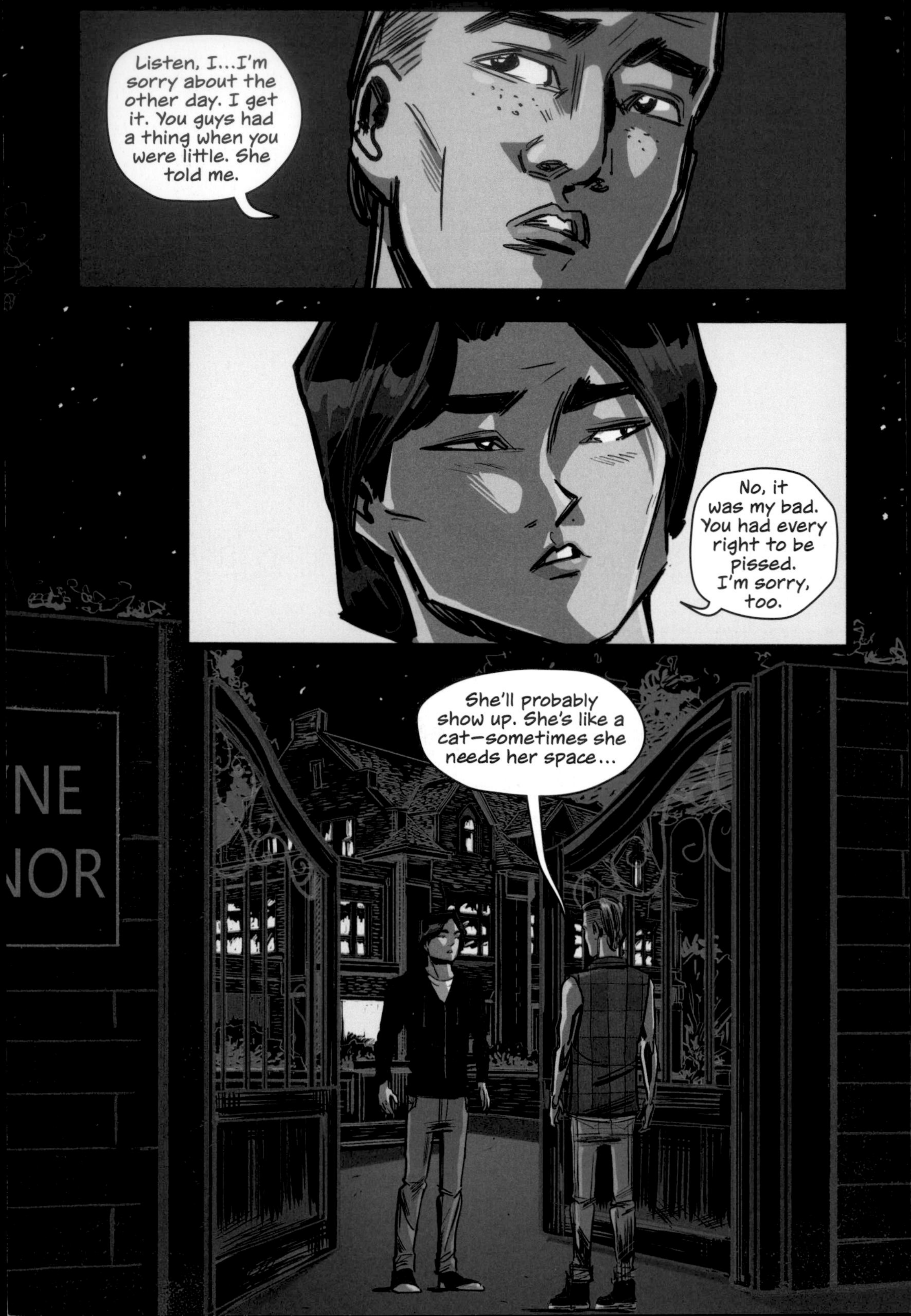
Listen, I...I'm sorry about the other day. I get it. You guys had a thing when you were little. She told me.
No, it was my bad. You had every right to be pissed. I'm sorry, too.
She'll probably show up. She's like a cat—sometimes she needs her space...
NE
NOR

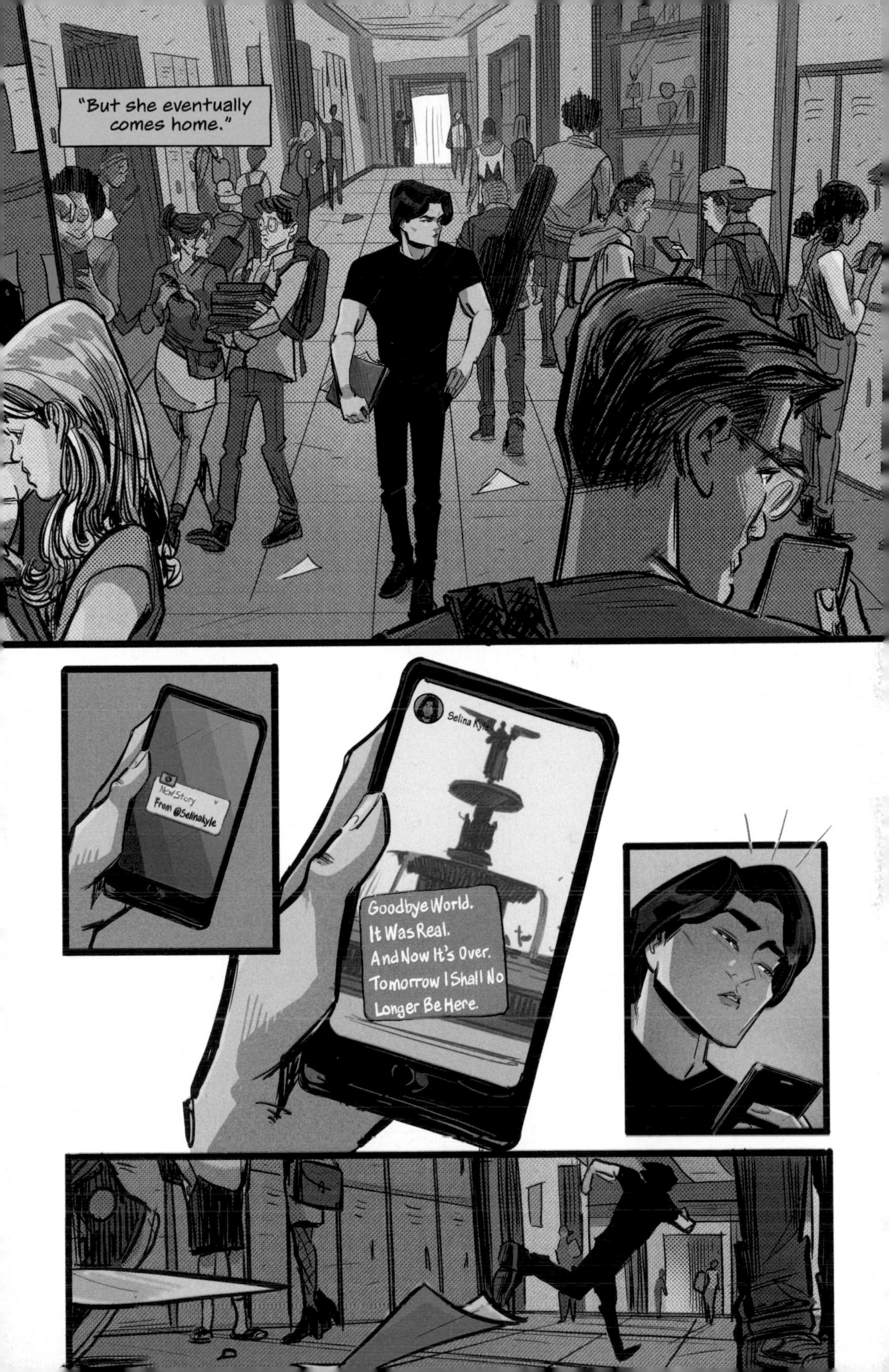
"But she eventually comes home."
New Story
From @Selinakyle
Selina Kyle
Goodbye World.
It Was Real.
And Now It's Over.
Tomorrow I Shall No
Longer Be Here.

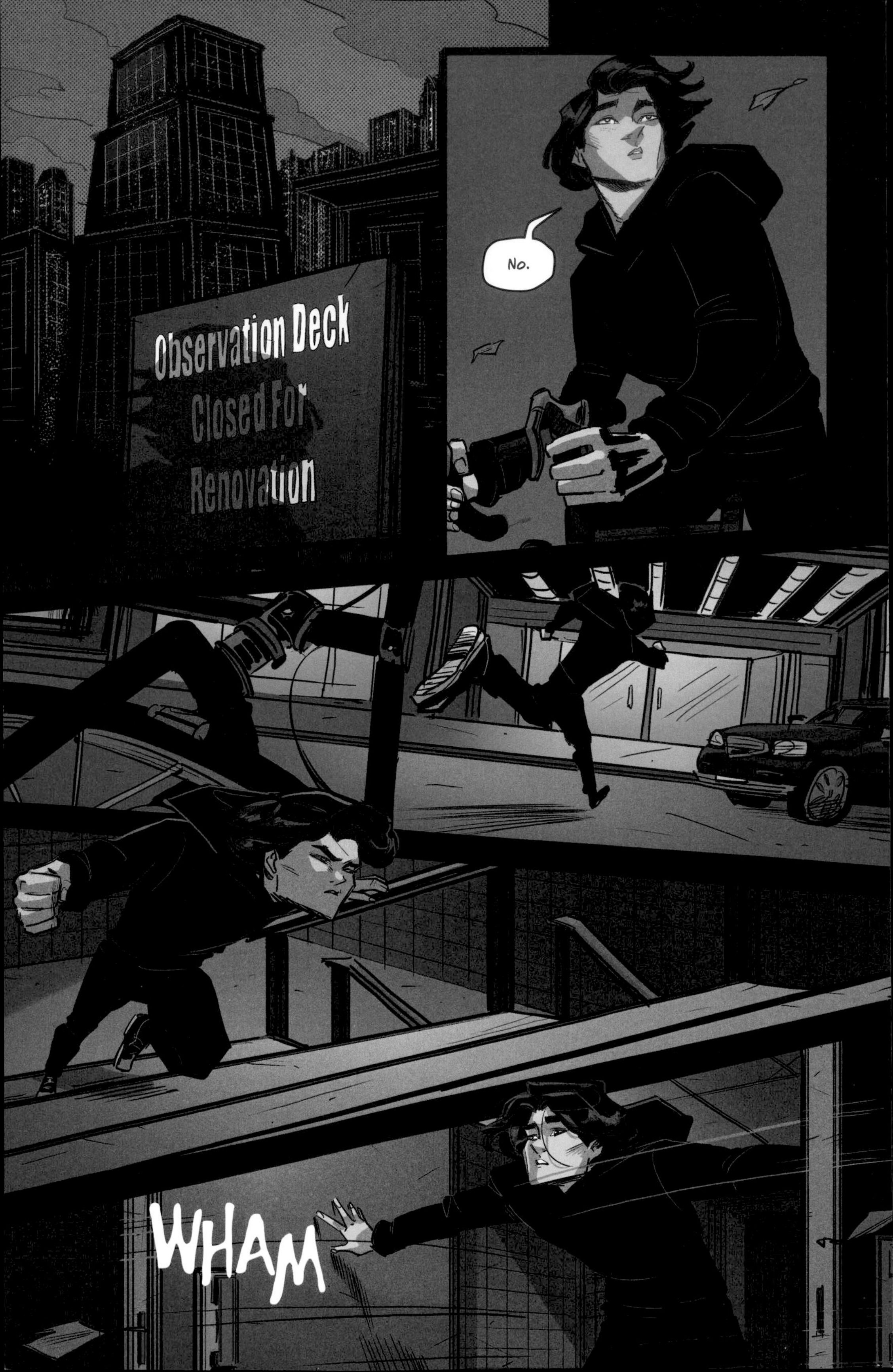
Observation Deck
Closed For
Renovation
No.
WHAM

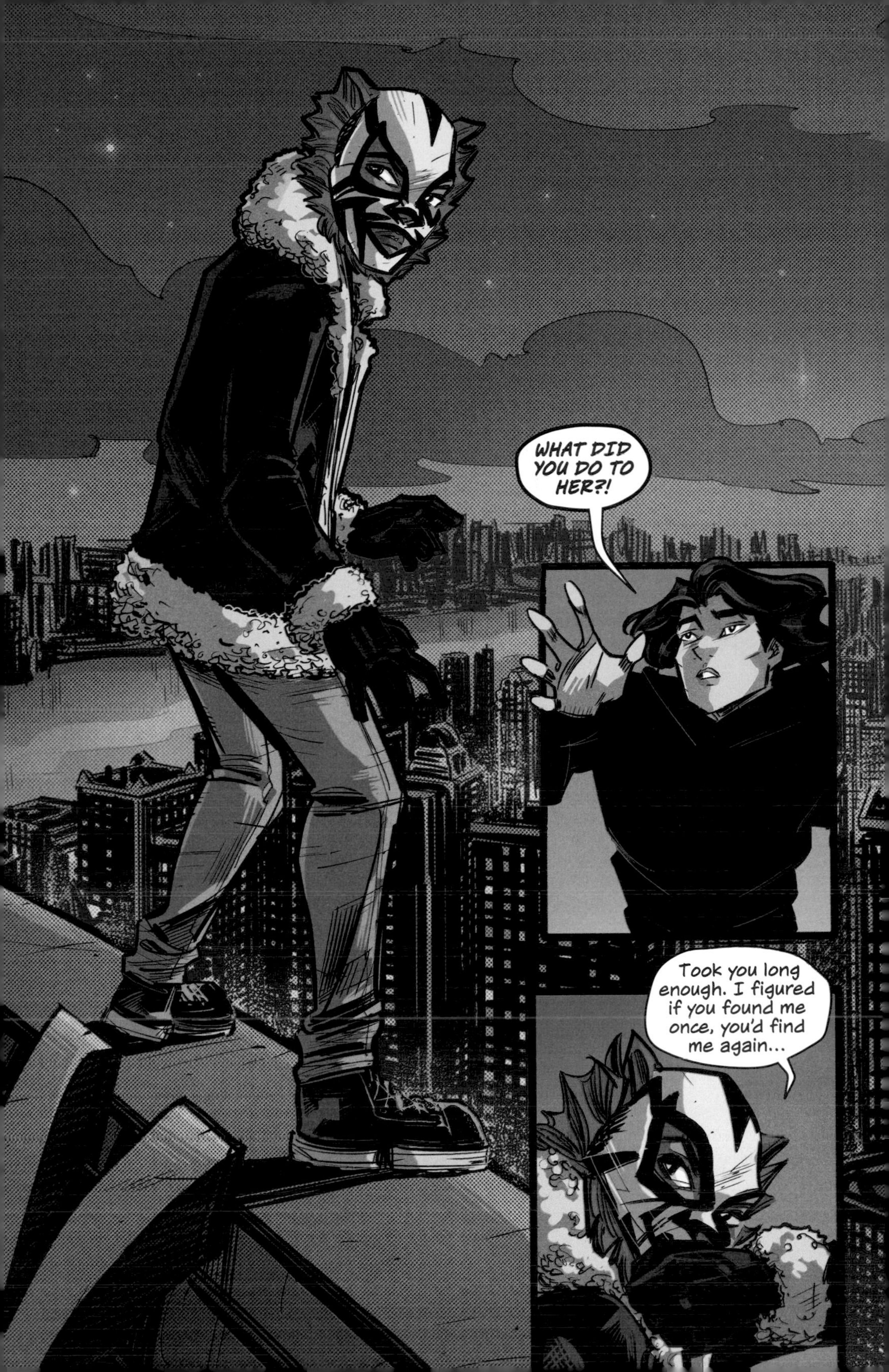
WHAT DID YOU DO TO HER?!
Took you long enough. I figured if you found me once, you'd find me again...

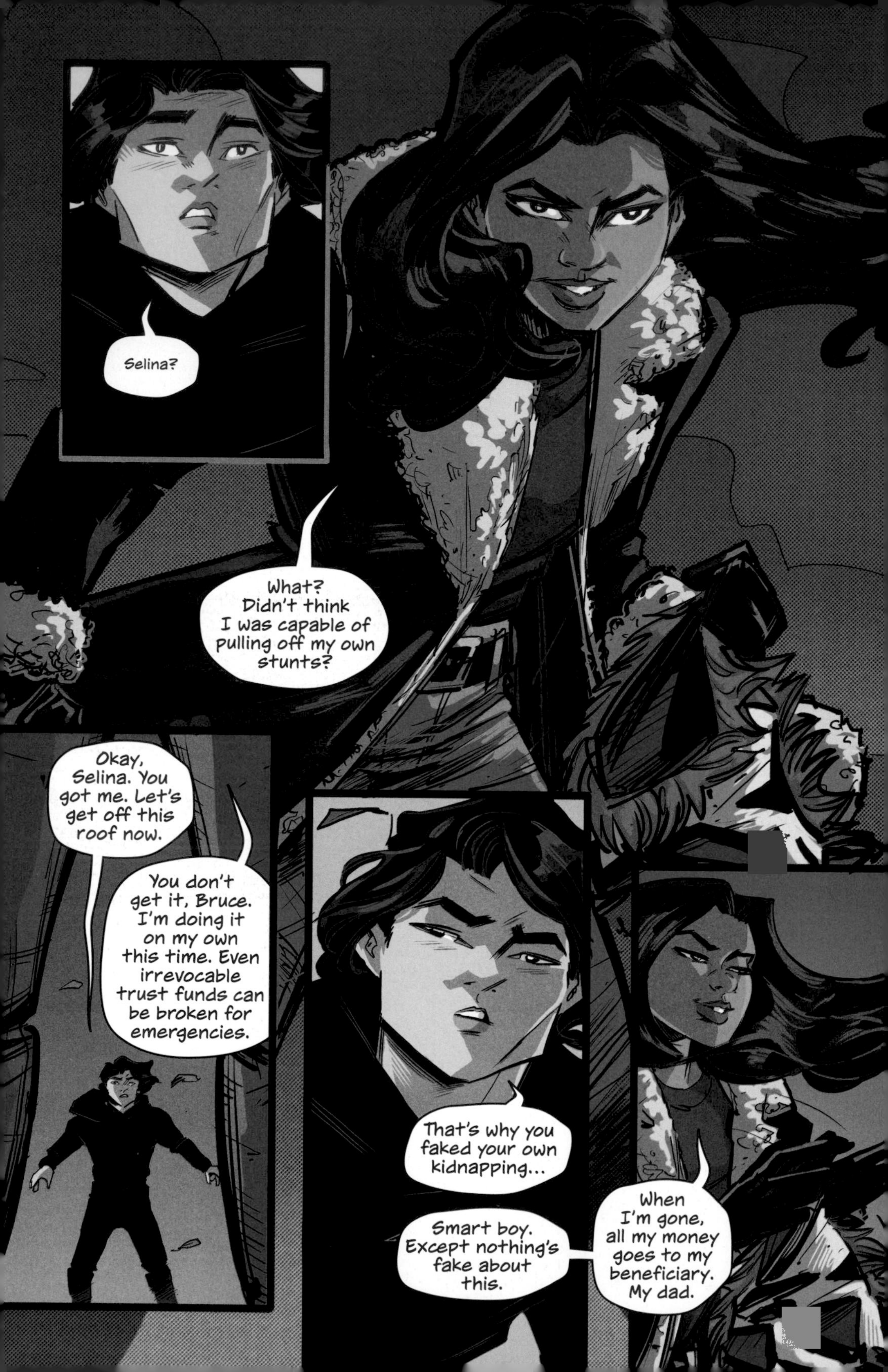
Selina?
What? Didn't think I was capable of pulling off my own stunts?
Okay, Selina. You got me. Let's get off this roof now.
You don't get it, Bruce. I'm doing it on my own this time. Even irrevocable trust funds can be broken for emergencies.
That's why you faked your own kidnapping...
Smart boy. Except nothing's fake about this.
When I'm gone, all my money goes to my beneficiary. My dad.

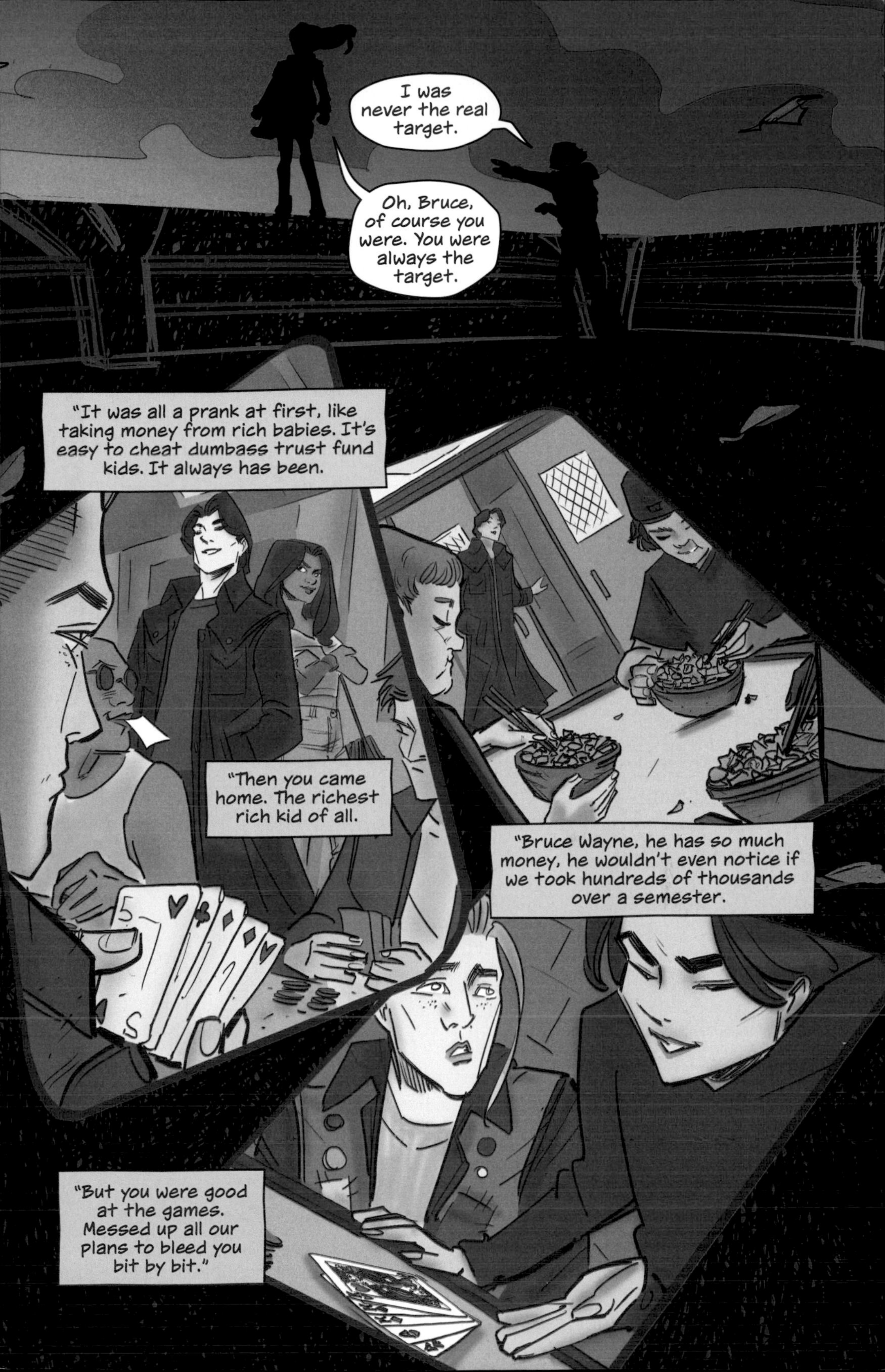
I was never the real target.
Oh, Bruce, of course you were. You were always the target.
"It was all a prank at first, like taking money from rich babies. It's easy to cheat dumbass trust fund kids. It always has been.
"Then you came home. The richest rich kid of all.
"Bruce Wayne, he has so much money, he wouldn't even notice if we took hundreds of thousands over a semester.
"But you were good at the games. Messed up all our plans to bleed you bit by bit."

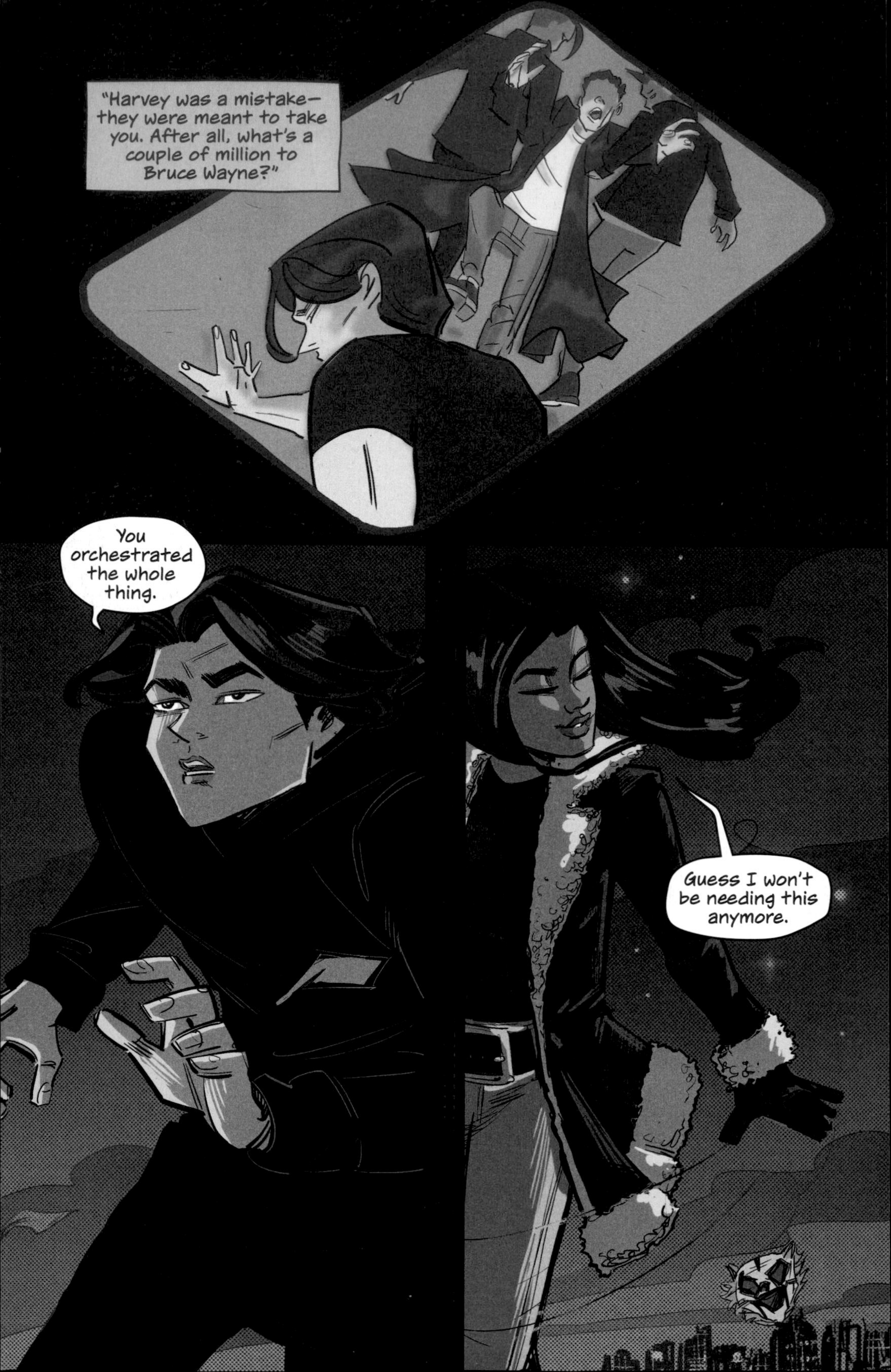
"Harvey was a mistake— they were meant to take you. After all, what's a couple of million to Bruce Wayne?"
You orchestrated the whole thing.
Guess I won't be needing this anymore.

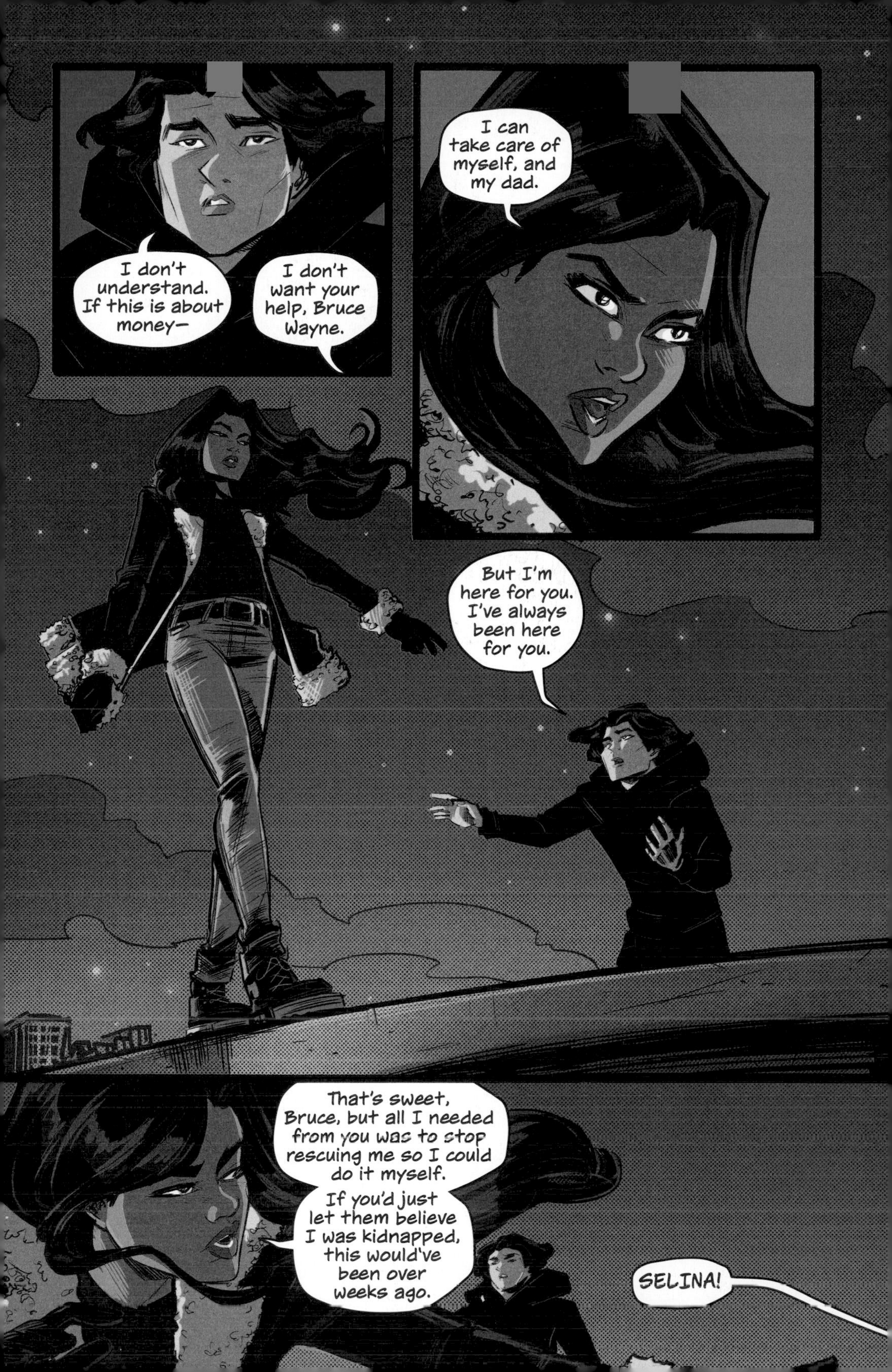
I don't understand. If this is about money—
I don't want your help, Bruce Wayne.
I can take care of myself, and my dad.
But I'm here for you. I've always been here for you.
That's sweet, Bruce, but all I needed from you was to stop rescuing me so I could do it myself.
If you'd just let them believe I was kidnapped, this would've been over weeks ago.
SELINA!

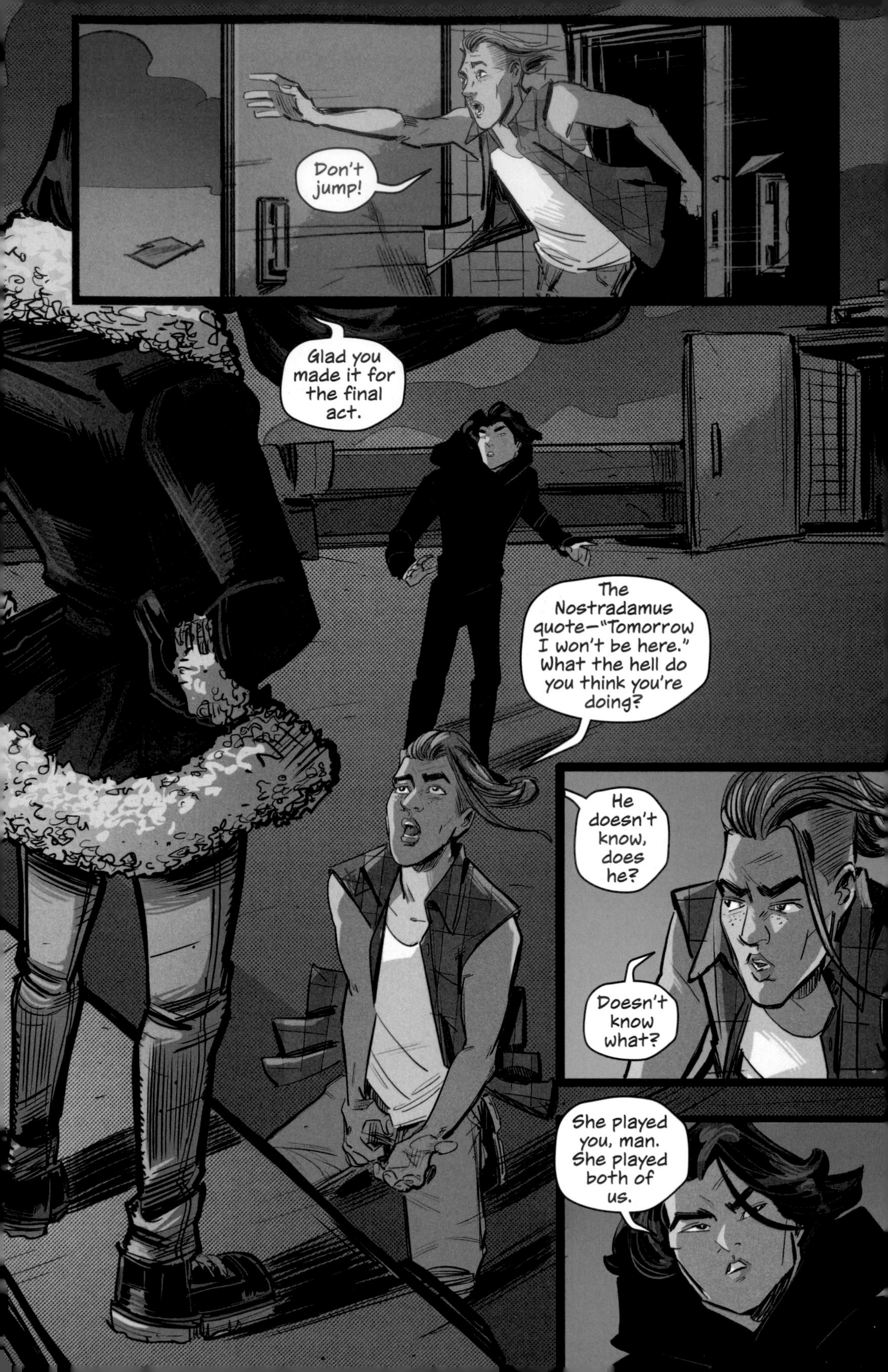
Don't jump!
Glad you made it for the final act.
The Nostradamus quote—"Tomorrow I won't be here." What the hell do you think you're doing?
He doesn't know, does he?
Doesn't know what?
She played you, man. She played both of us.

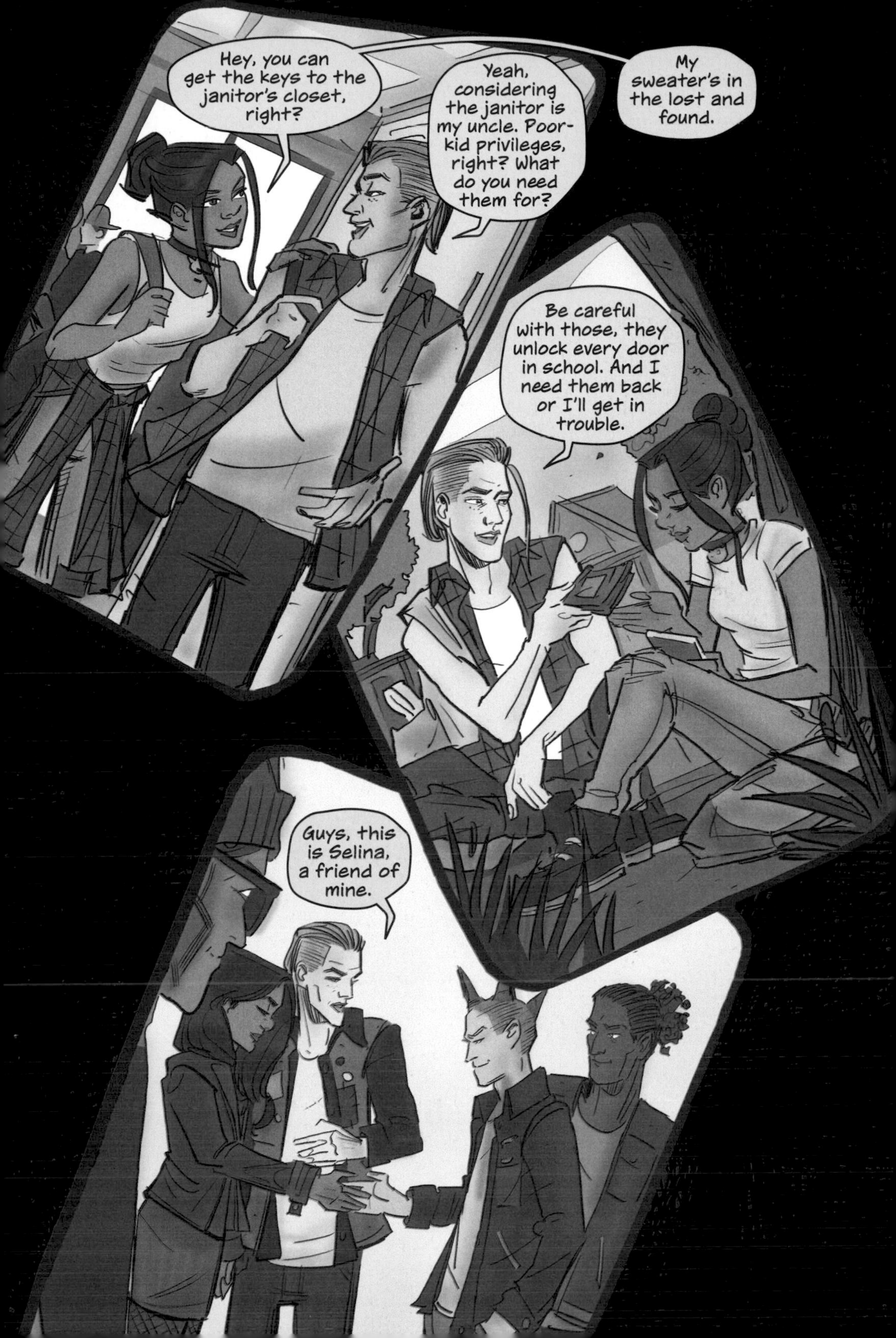
Hey, you can get the keys to the janitor's closet, right?
Yeah, considering the janitor is my uncle. Poor-kid privileges, right? What do you need them for?
My sweater's in the lost and found.
Be careful with those, they unlock every door in school. And I need them back or I'll get in trouble.
Guys, this is Selina, a friend of mine.

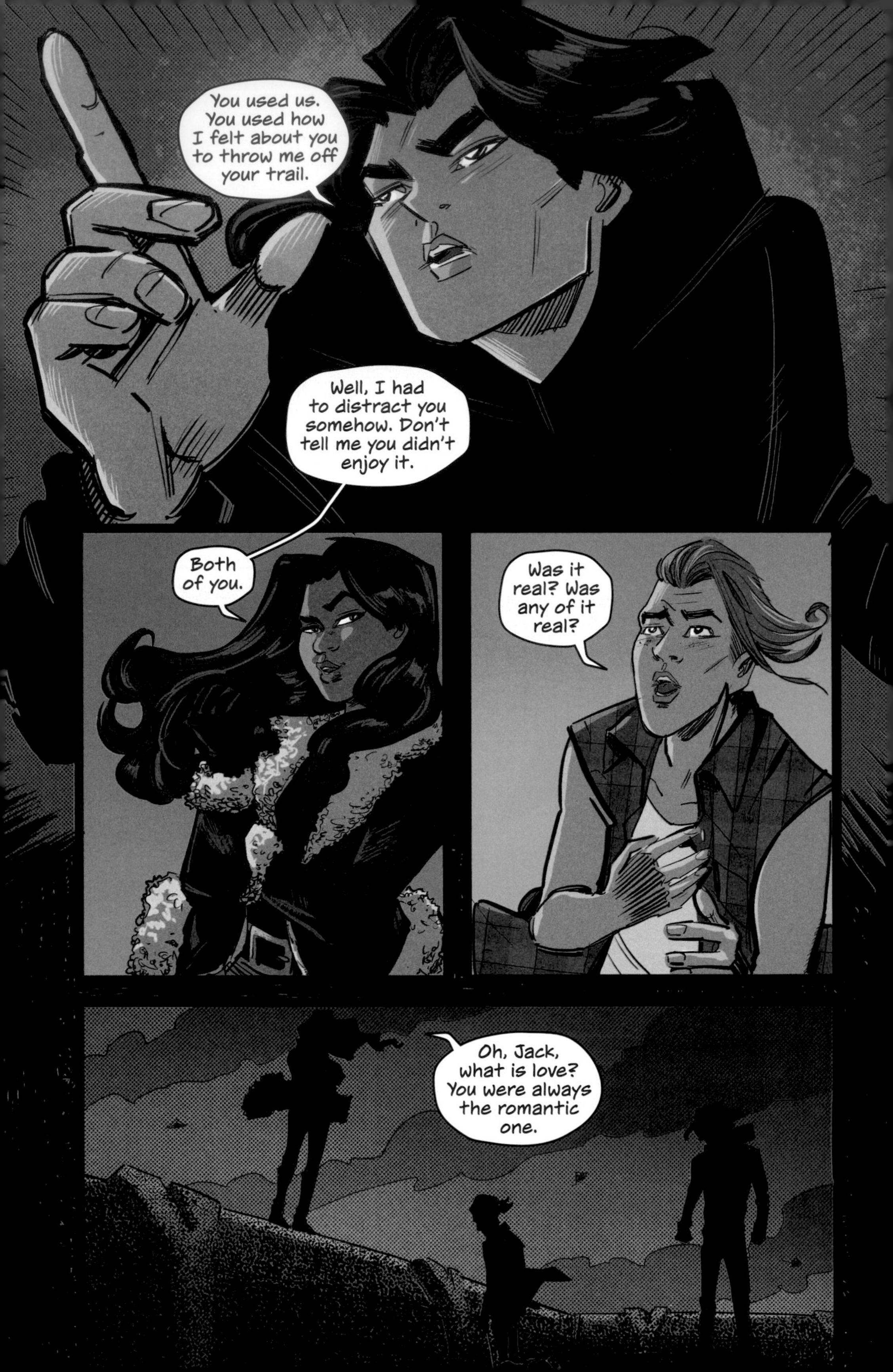

You used us. You used how I felt about you to throw me off your trail.
Well, I had to distract you somehow. Don't tell me you didn't enjoy it.
Both of you.
Was it real? Was any of it real?
Oh, Jack, what is love? You were always the romantic one.

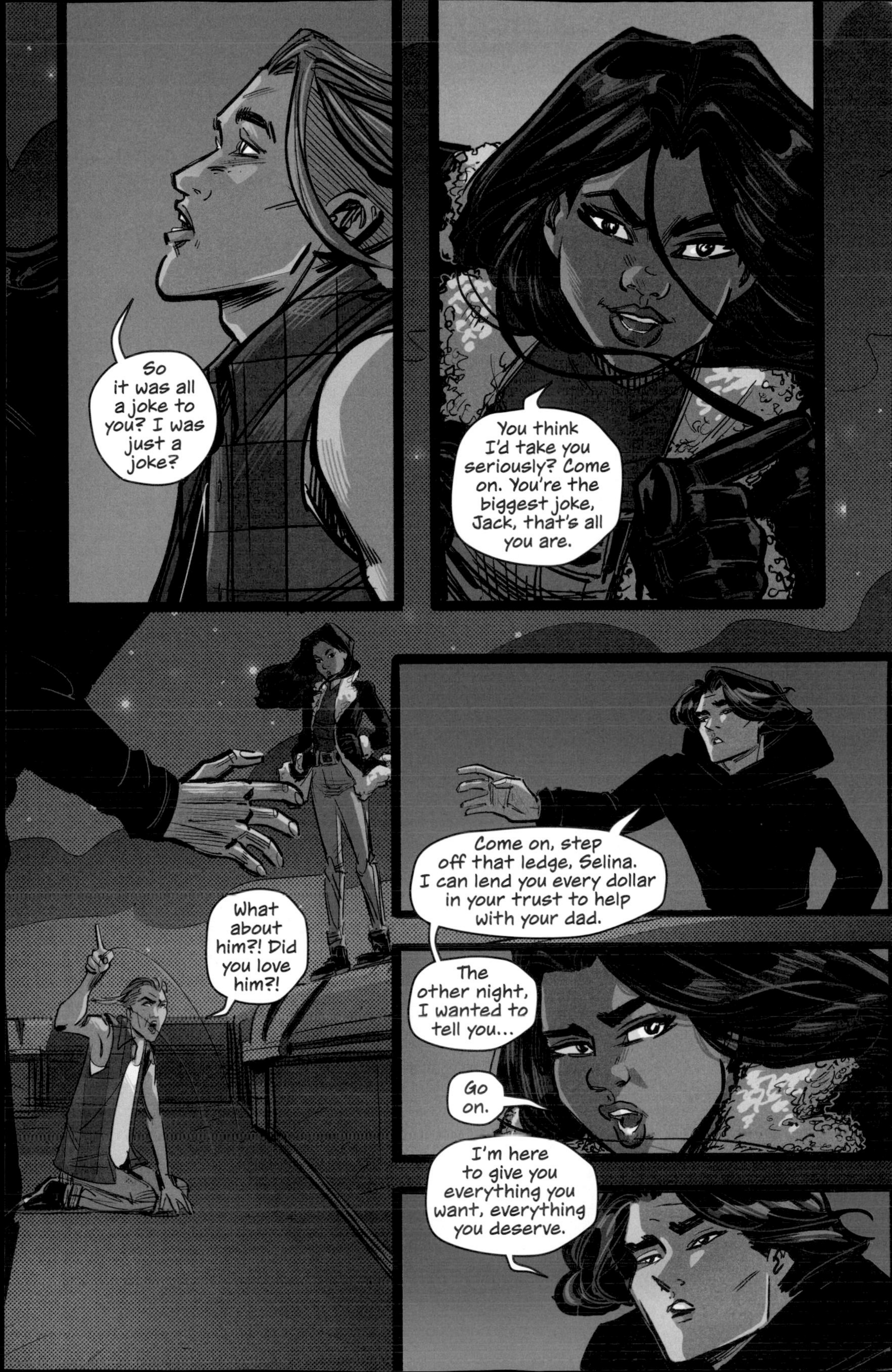
So it was all a joke to you? I was just a joke?
You think I'd take you seriously? Come on. You're the biggest joke, Jack, that's all you are.
Come on, step off that ledge, Selina. I can lend you every dollar in your trust to help with your dad.
What about him?! Did you love him?!
The other night, I wanted to tell you...
Go on.
I'm here to give you everything you want, everything you deserve.

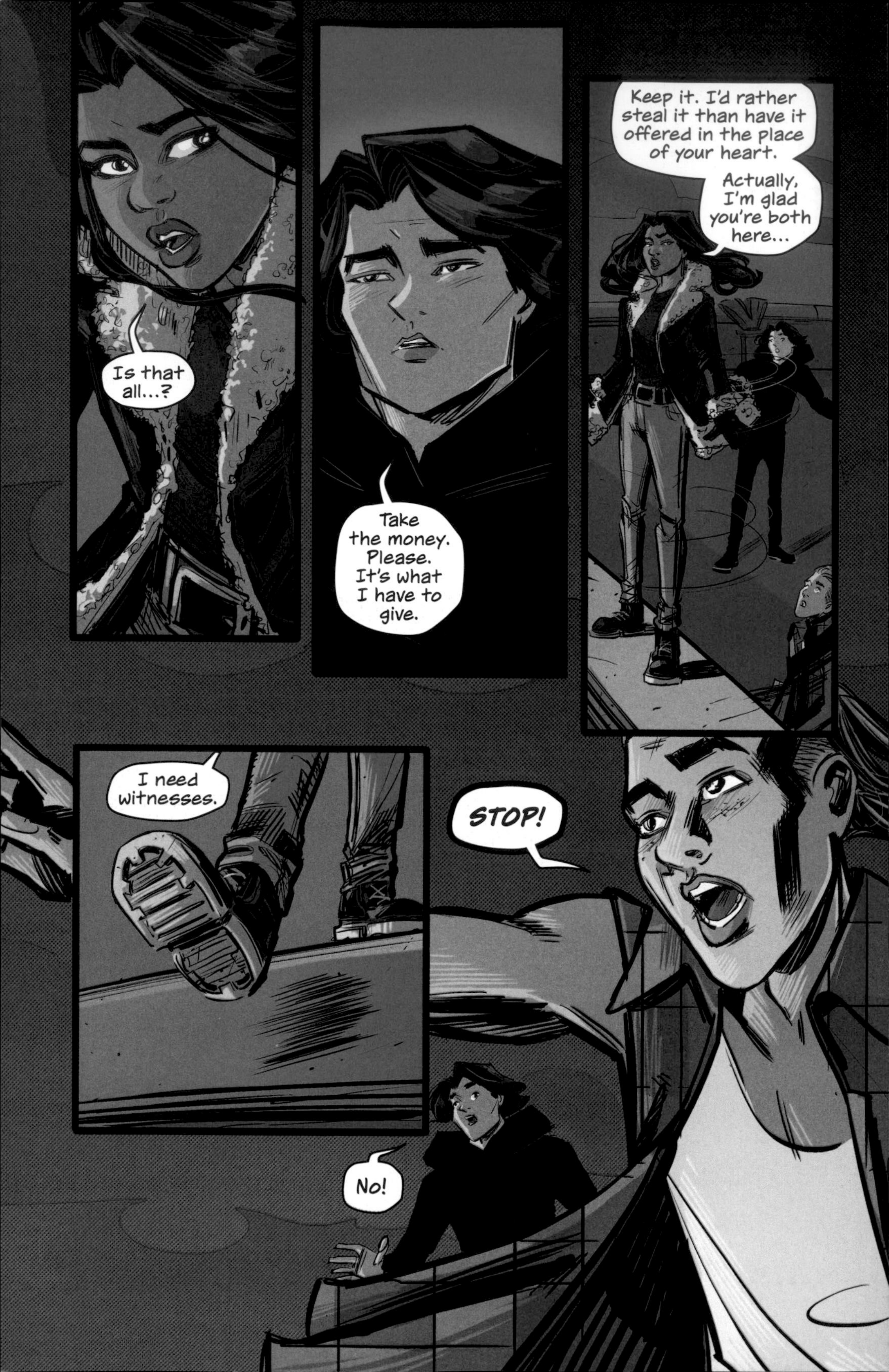
Is that all...?
Take the money. Please. It's what I have to give.
Keep it. I'd rather steal it than have it offered in the place of your heart.
Actually, I'm glad you're both here...
I need witnesses.
STOP!
No!

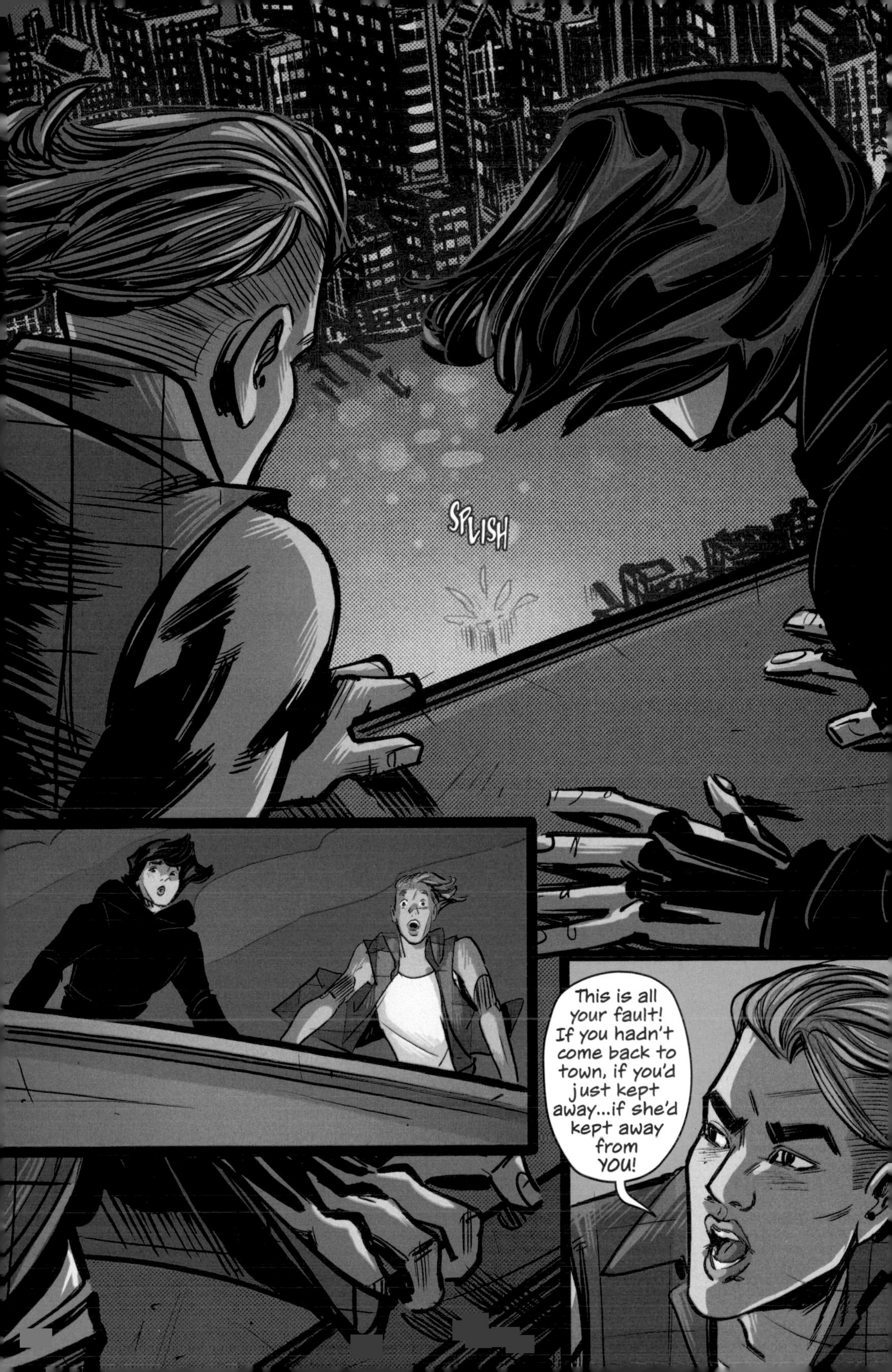
SPLISH
This is all your fault! If you hadn't come back to town, if you'd just kept away...if she'd kept away from YOU!

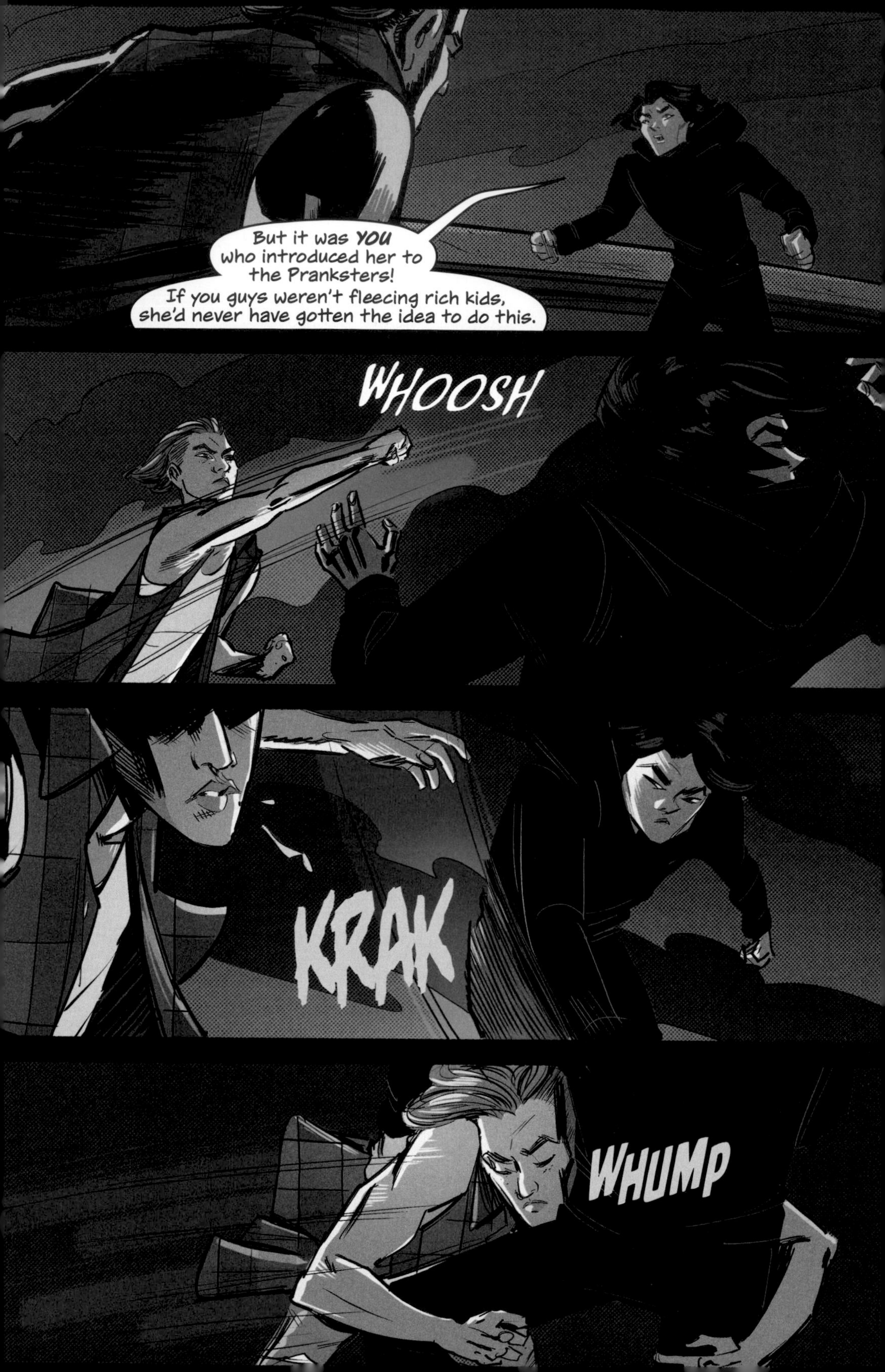
But it was YOU who introduced her to the Pranksters! If you guys weren't fleecing rich kids, she'd never have gotten the idea to do this.
WHOOSH
KRAK
WHUMP

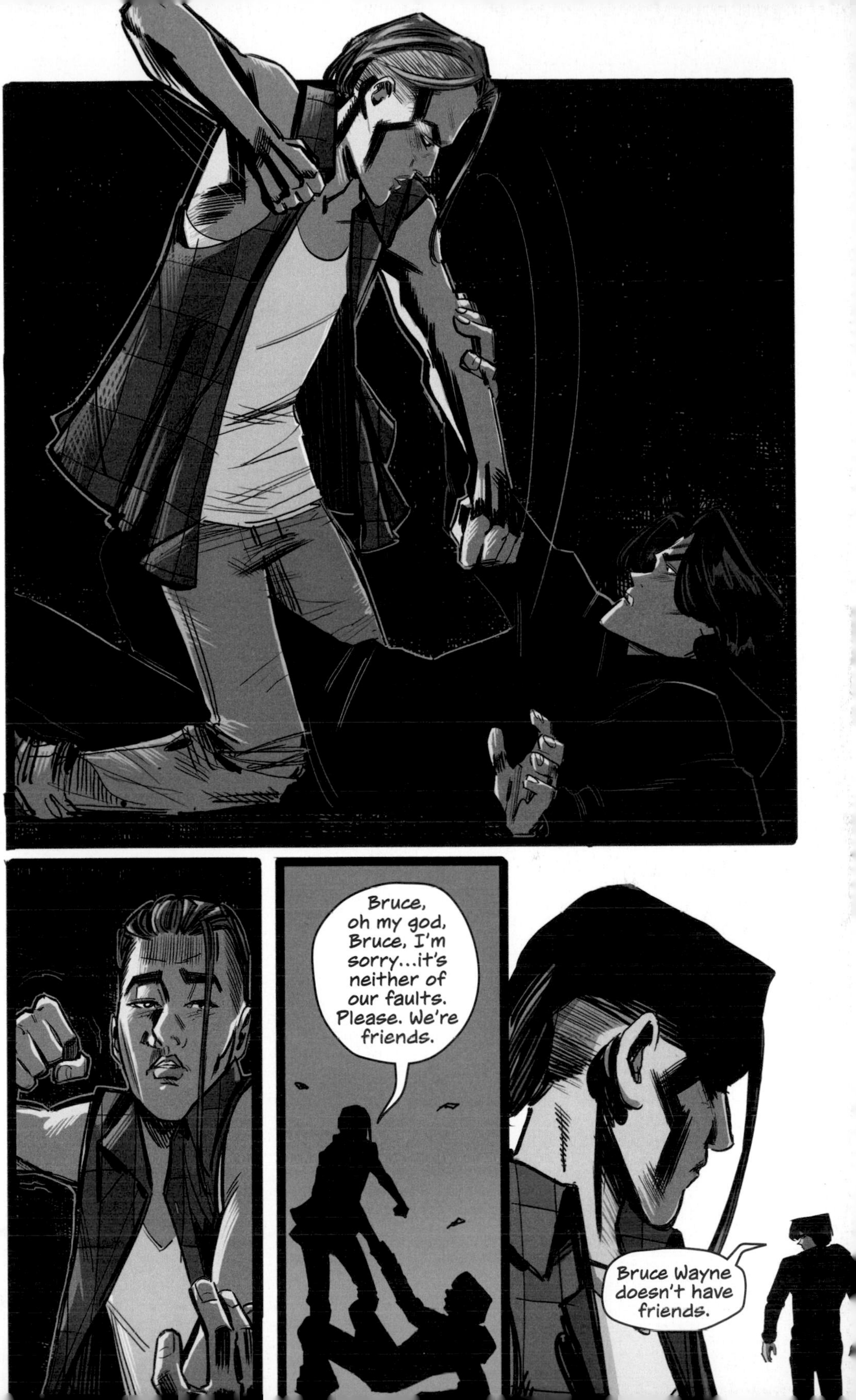
Bruce, oh my god, Bruce, I'm sorry...it's neither of our faults. Please. We're friends.
Bruce Wayne doesn't have friends.

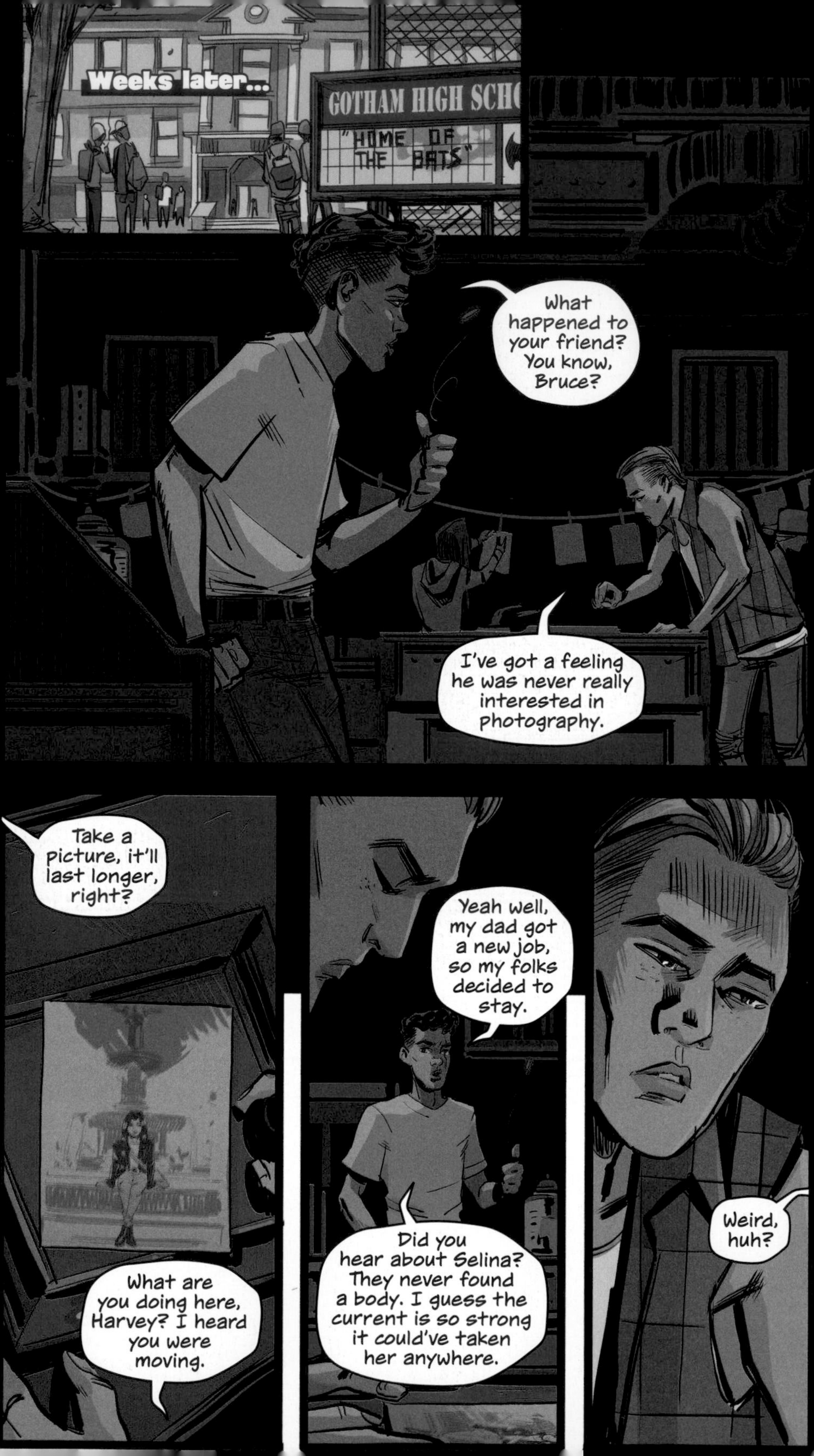
Weeks later...
GOTHAM HIGH SCHO
"HOME OF THE BATS"
What happened to your friend? You know, Bruce?
I've got a feeling he was never really interested in photography.
Take a picture, it'll last longer, right?
What are you doing here, Harvey? I heard you were moving.
Yeah well, my dad got a new job, so my folks decided to stay.
Did you hear about Selina? They never found a body. I guess the current is so strong it could've taken her anywhere.
Weird, huh?

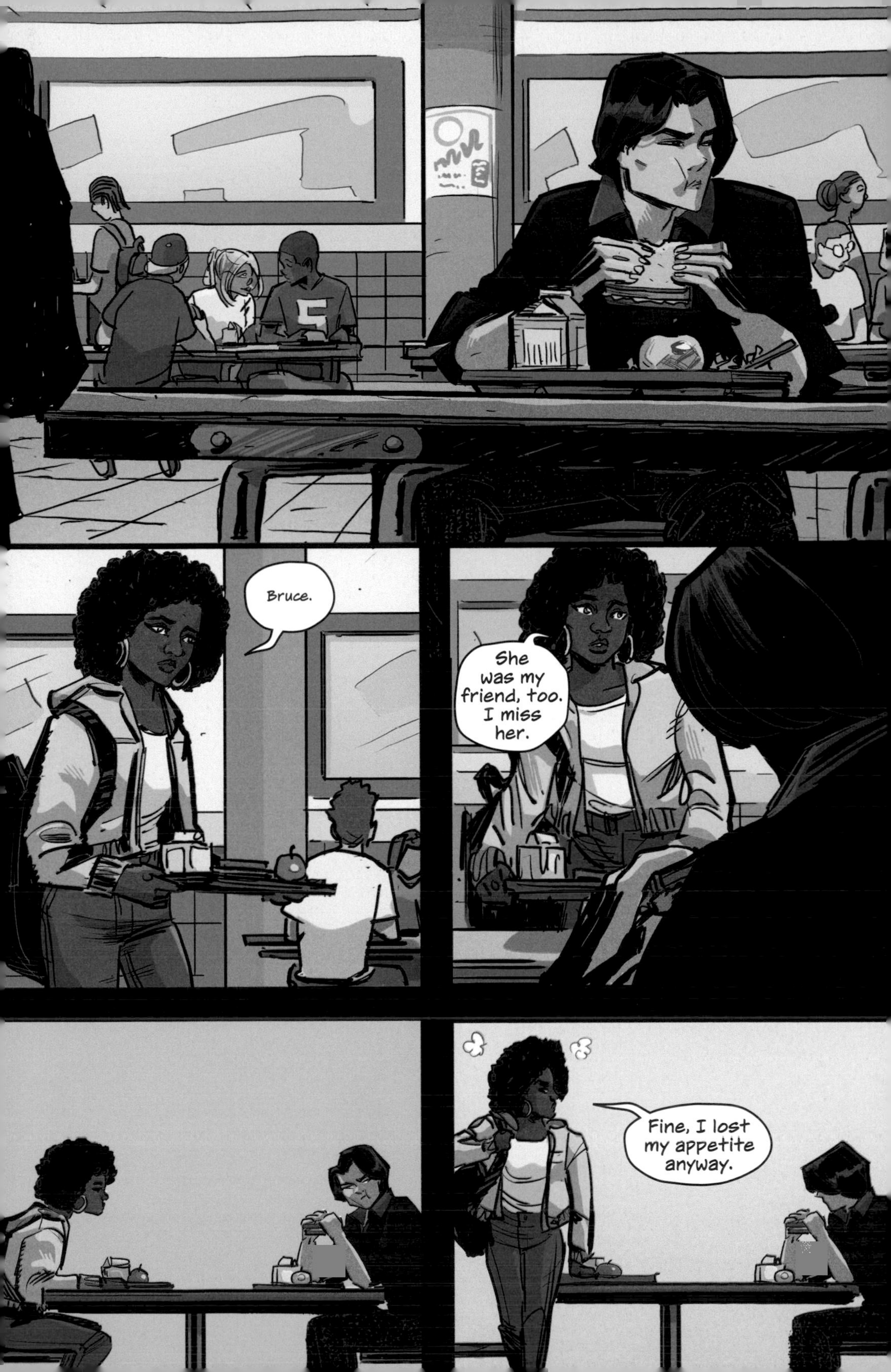
Bruce.
She was my friend, too. I miss her.
Fine, I lost my appetite anyway.

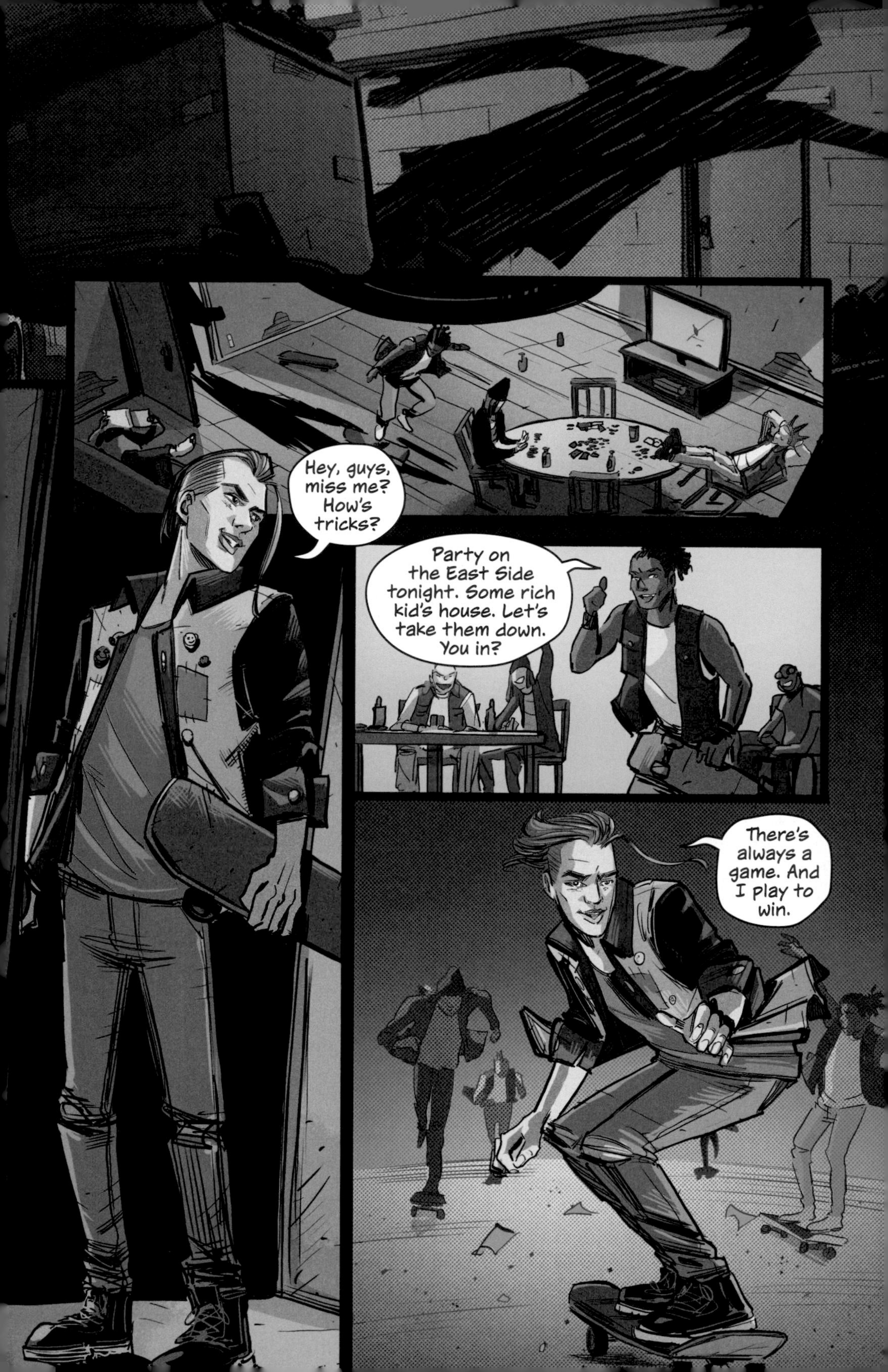
Hey, guys, miss me? How's tricks?
Party on the East Side tonight. Some rich kid's house. Let's take them down. You in?
There's always a game. And I play to win.

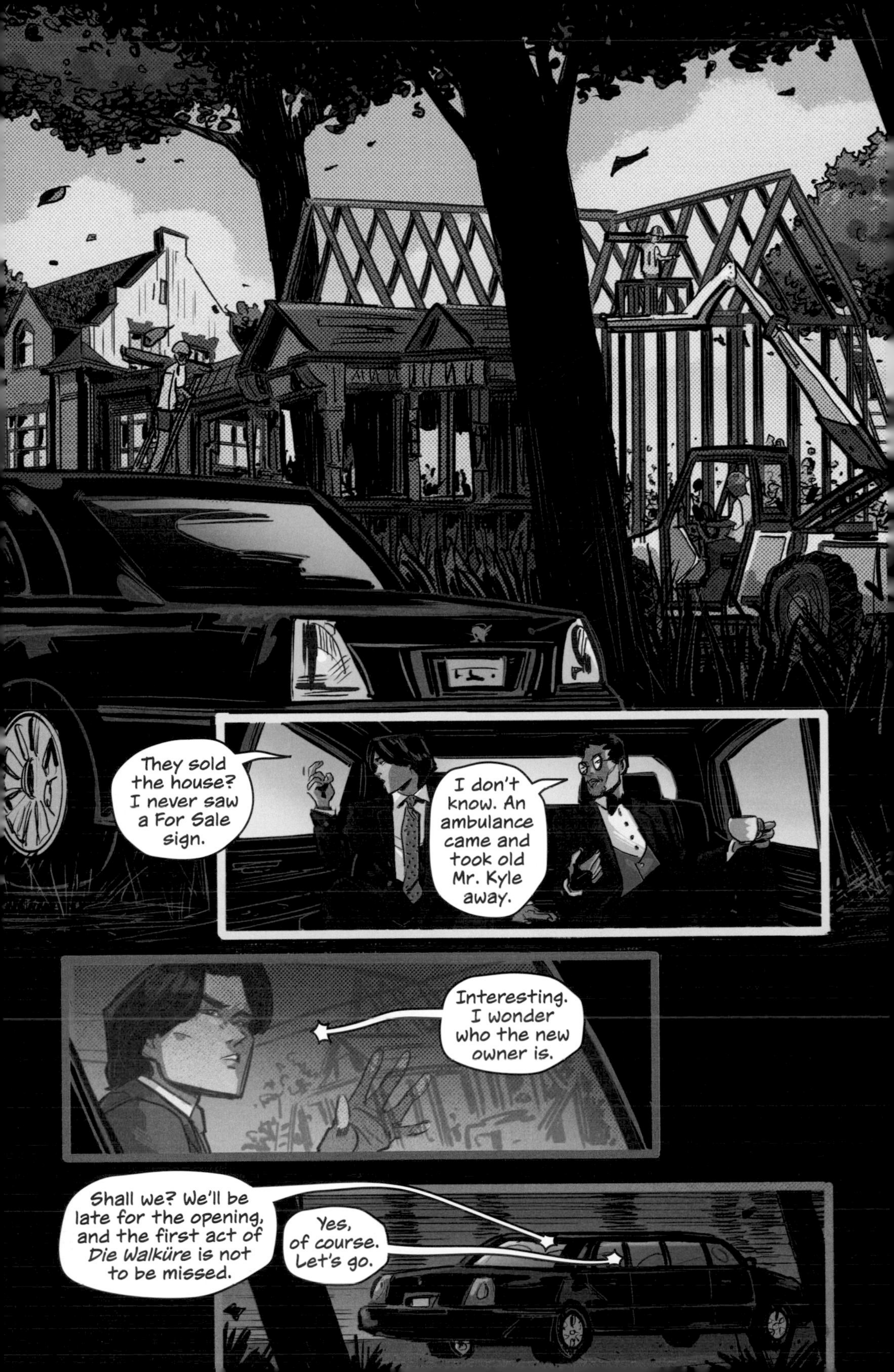
They sold the house? I never saw a For Sale sign.
I don't know. An ambulance came and took old Mr. Kyle away.
Interesting. I wonder who the new owner is.
Shall we? We'll be late for the opening, and the first act of *Die Walküre* is not to be missed.
Yes, of course. Let's go.

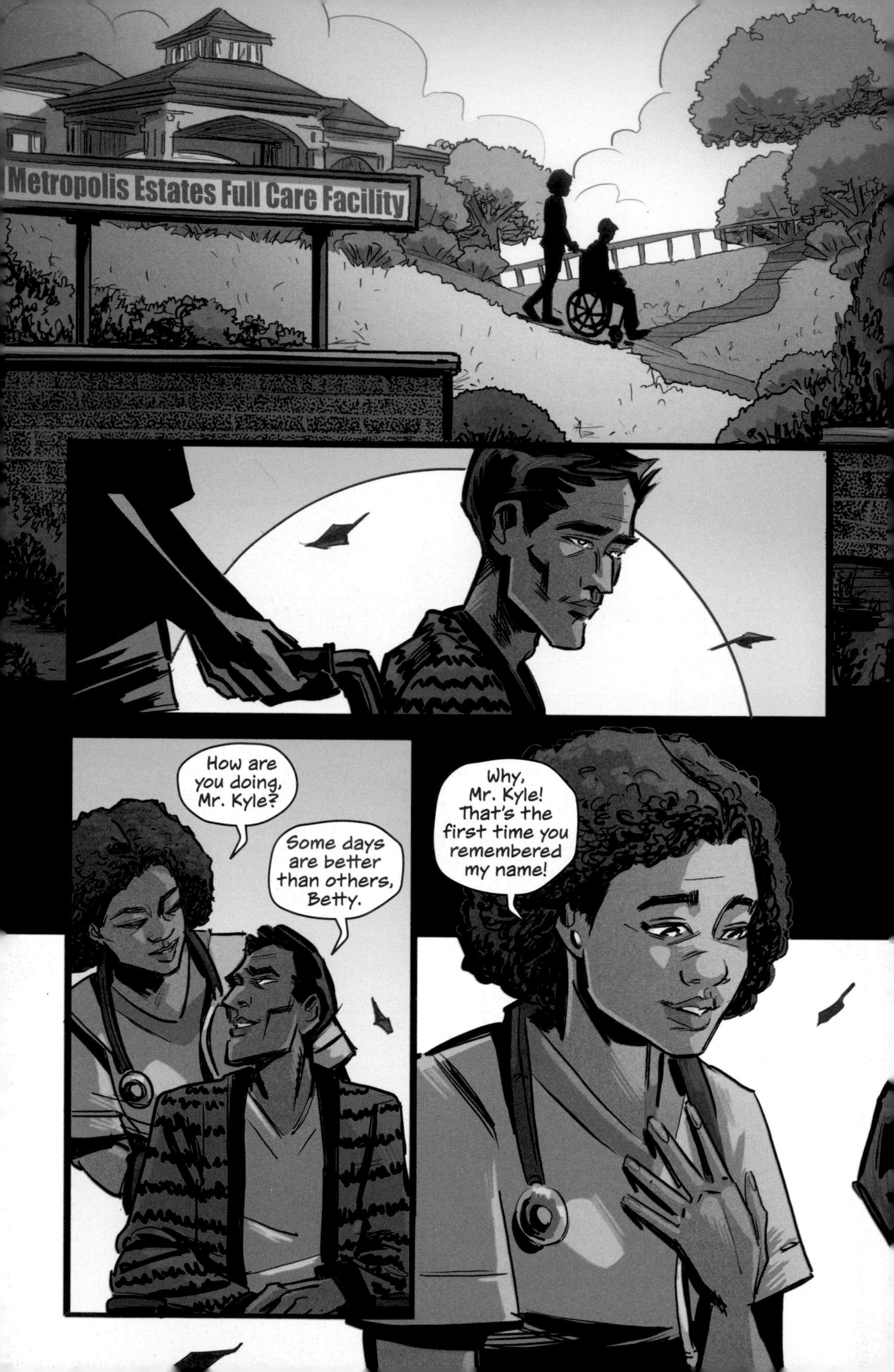
Metropolis Estates Full Care Facility
How are you doing, Mr. Kyle?
Some days are better than others, Betty.
Why, Mr. Kyle! That's the first time you remembered my name!

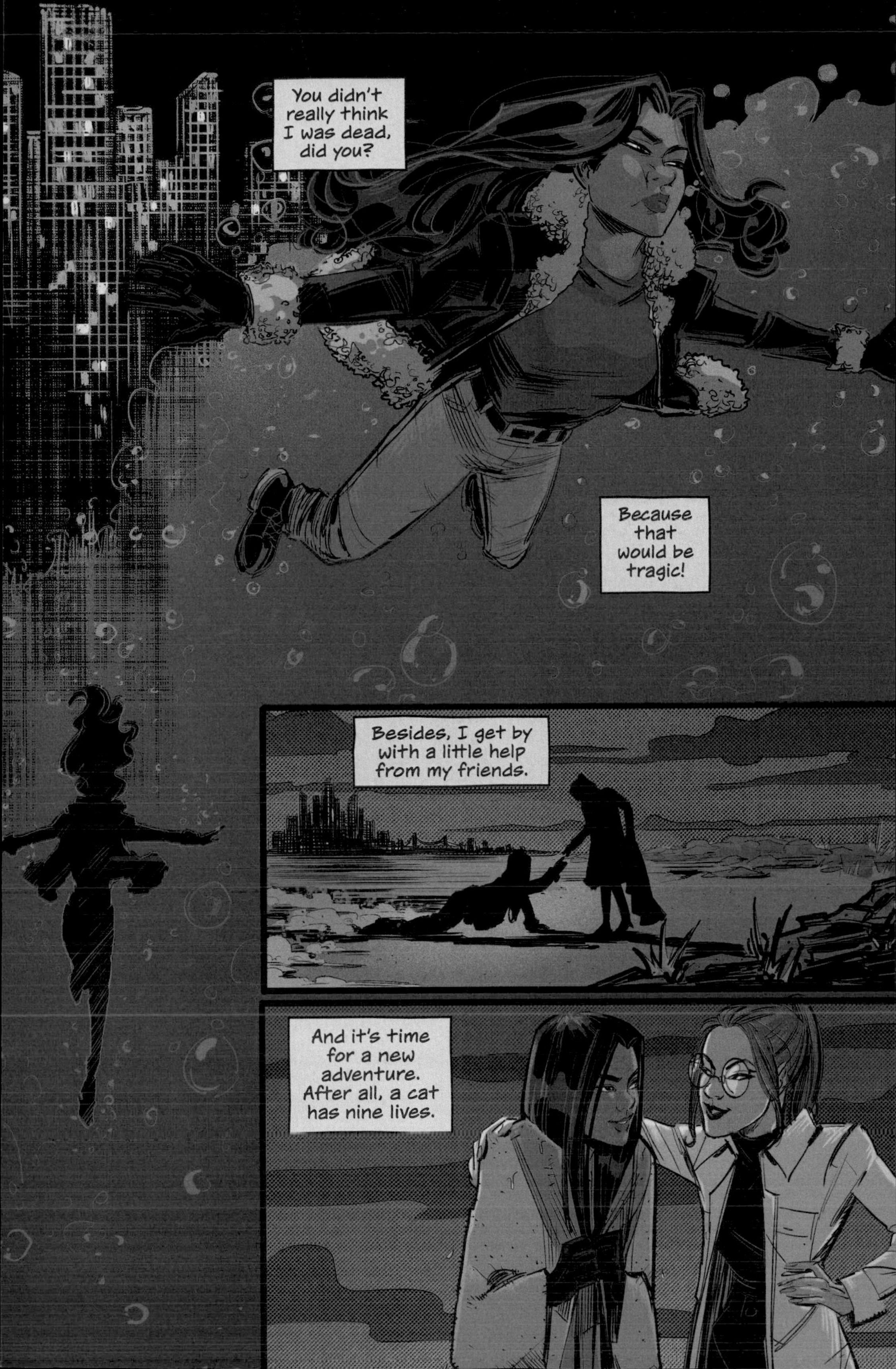
You didn't really think I was dead, did you?
Because that would be tragic!
Besides, I get by with a little help from my friends.
And it's time for a new adventure. After all, a cat has nine lives.

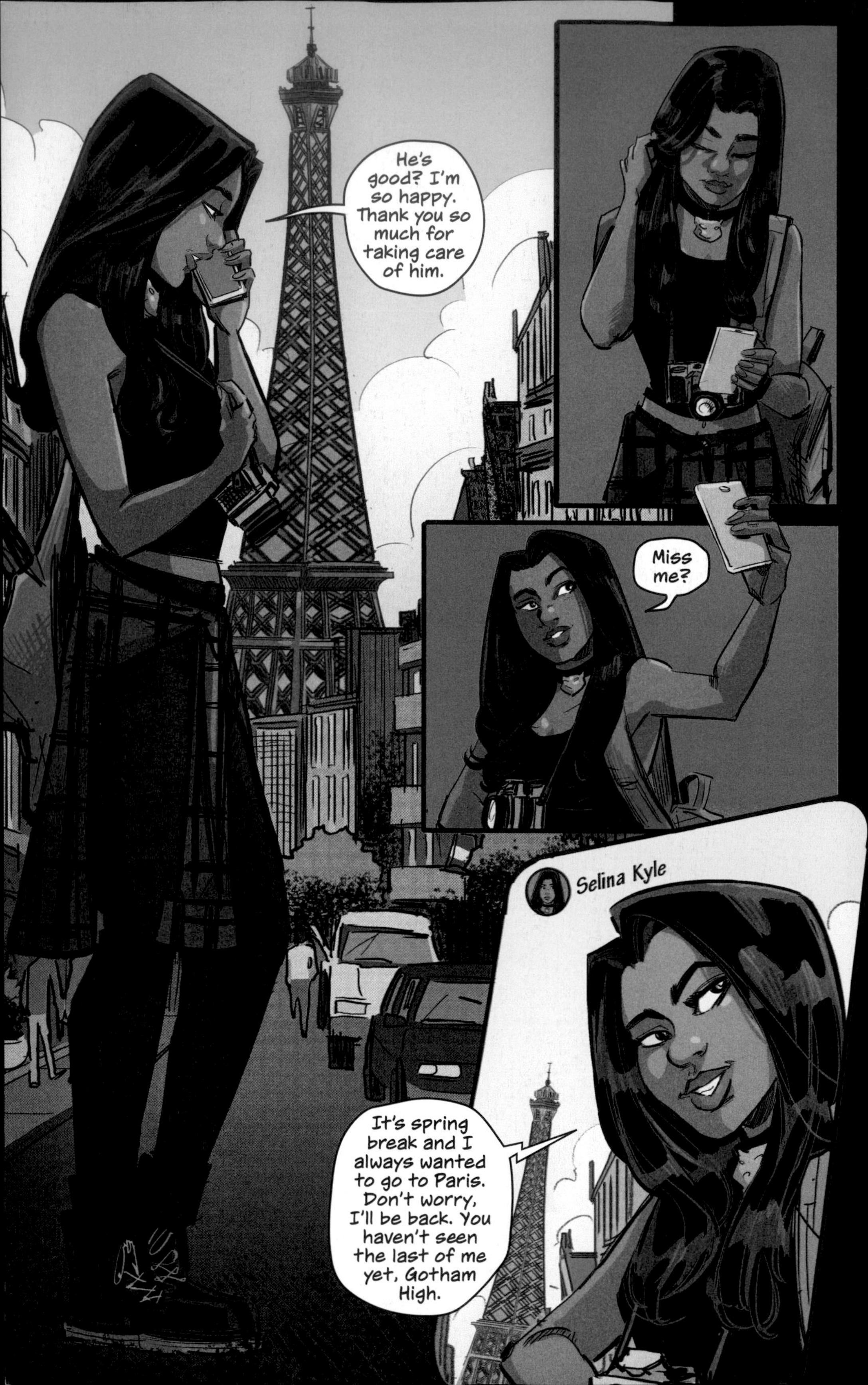
He's good? I'm so happy. Thank you so much for taking care of him.
Miss me?
Selina Kyle
It's spring break and I always wanted to go to Paris. Don't worry, I'll be back. You haven't seen the last of me yet, Gotham High.

Melissa de la Cruz

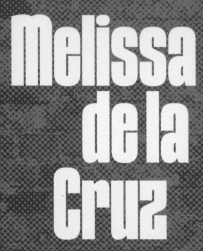

Melissa de la Cruz is the #1 *New York Times*, #1 *Publishers Weekly*, and #1 IndieBound bestselling author of many critically acclaimed and award-winning novels for readers of all ages, including *Alex and Eliza*, *Descendants*, *The Witches of East End*, and *Blue Bloods*. Her more than 30 books have also topped the *USA Today*, *Wall Street Journal*, and *Los Angeles Times* bestseller lists and have been published in over 20 countries.

Thomas Pitilli is an illustrator and comic book artist living in his native land of Brooklyn, New York. His work can be found in the series *Riverdale* from Archie Comics. His illustrations have appeared in publications such as the *New York Times*, *Wall Street Journal*, and *Washington Post*, as well as many others. When not making art, Thomas enjoys music, museums, and summertime in NYC.

RESOURCES

If you, or a loved one, need help in any way, you do not need to act alone.
Below is a list of resources that may be helpful to you.
If you are in immediate danger, please call emergency services in your area
(9-1-1 in the U.S.) or go to your nearest hospital emergency room.

National Suicide Prevention Lifeline
Available 24 hours a day, 7 days a week.
Phone: 1-800-273-8255
Website: https://suicidepreventionlifeline.org
Online chat: chat.suicidepreventionlifeline.org/gethelp/lifelinechat.aspx

The Jed Foundation
A nonprofit that exists to protect emotional health and prevent suicide
for our nation's teens and young adults.
Text "START" to 741-741 or call 1-800-273-TALK (8255)
Website: jedfoundation.org

International Hotlines
The above hotlines are based in the U.S. and Canada.
A list of international suicide hotlines is listed at
http://www.suicide.org/international-suicide-hotlines.html, compiled by
suicide.org. Another list can be found at https://www.iasp.info/index.php,
compiled by the International Association for Suicide Prevention.

Shatter Proof
A national nonprofit organization dedicated to ending the devastation
addiction causes families. Visit shatterproof.org for more information.

Safe Horizon
The largest provider of comprehensive services for domestic
violence survivors and victims of all crime and abuse including rape
and sexual assault, human trafficking, stalking, youth homelessness,
and violent crimes committed against a family member or within
communities. If you need help, call their 24-hour hotline at
1-800-621-HOPE (4673) or visit safehorizon.org.

Writer Michael Moreci and artist Sas Milledge redefine Dick Grayson in *The Lost Carnival*, a young adult graphic novel exploring the power and magic of young love.

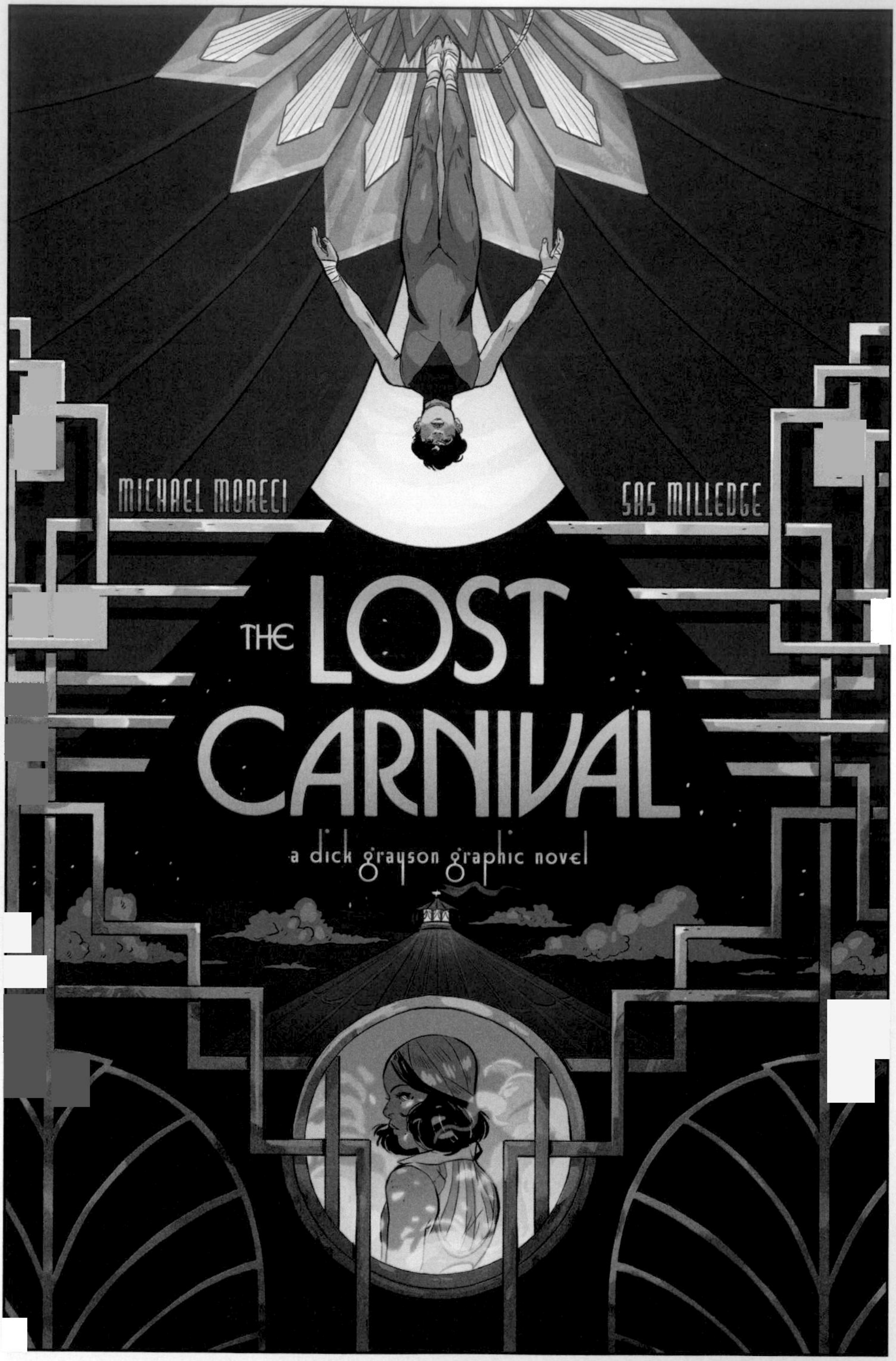

MICHAEL MORECI
SAS MILLEDGE
THE LOST CARNIVAL
a dick grayson graphic novel

On sale March 5, 2020.
Read on for an exclusive sneak preview!

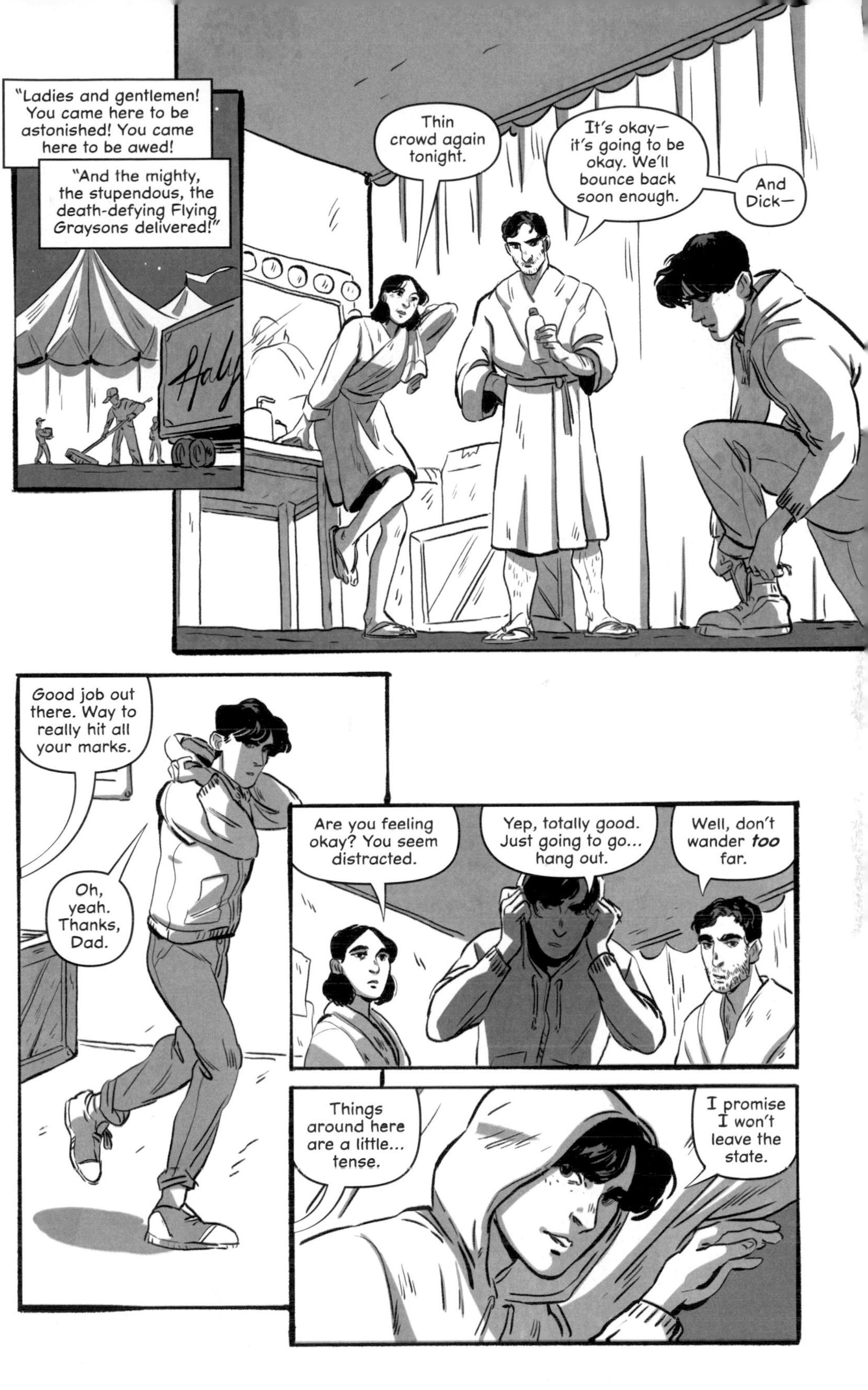
"Ladies and gentlemen! You came here to be astonished! You came here to be awed!
"And the mighty, the stupendous, the death-defying Flying Graysons delivered!"
Haly
Thin crowd again tonight.
It's okay— it's going to be okay. We'll bounce back soon enough.
And Dick—
Good job out there. Way to really hit all your marks.
Oh, yeah. Thanks, Dad.
Are you feeling okay? You seem distracted.
Yep, totally good. Just going to go... hang out.
Well, don't wander ***too*** far.
Things around here are a little... tense.
I promise I won't leave the state.

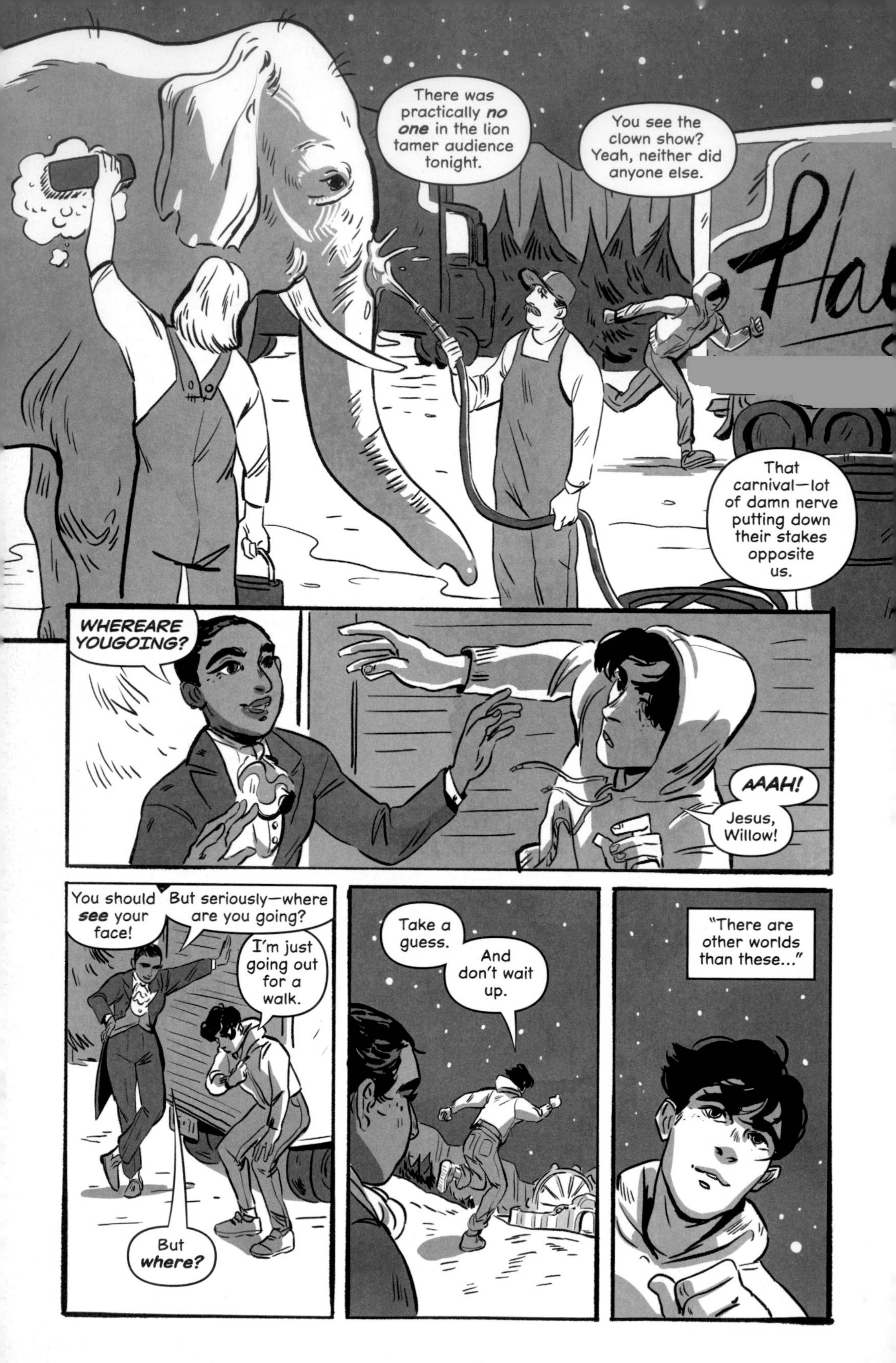
There was practically **no one** in the lion tamer audience tonight.
You see the clown show? Yeah, neither did anyone else.
That carnival—lot of damn nerve putting down their stakes opposite us.
WHEREARE YOUGOING?
AAAH!
Jesus, Willow!
You should **see** your face!
But seriously—where are you going?
I'm just going out for a walk.
But **where?**
Take a guess.
And don't wait up.
"There are other worlds than these..."

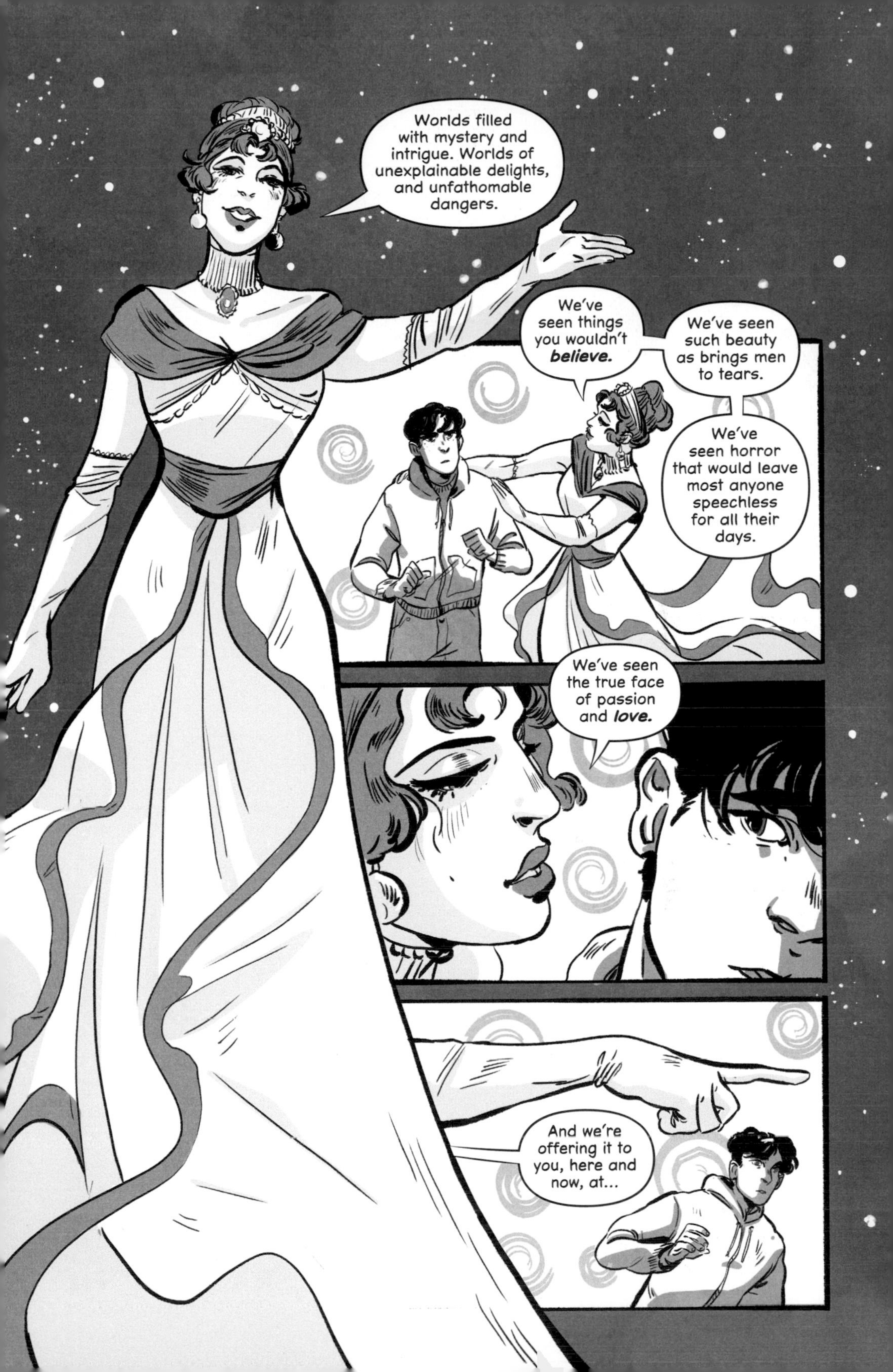

Worlds filled with mystery and intrigue. Worlds of unexplainable delights, and unfathomable dangers.
We've seen things you wouldn't ***believe.***
We've seen such beauty as brings men to tears.
We've seen horror that would leave most anyone speechless for all their days.
We've seen the true face of passion and ***love.***
And we're offering it to you, here and now, at...

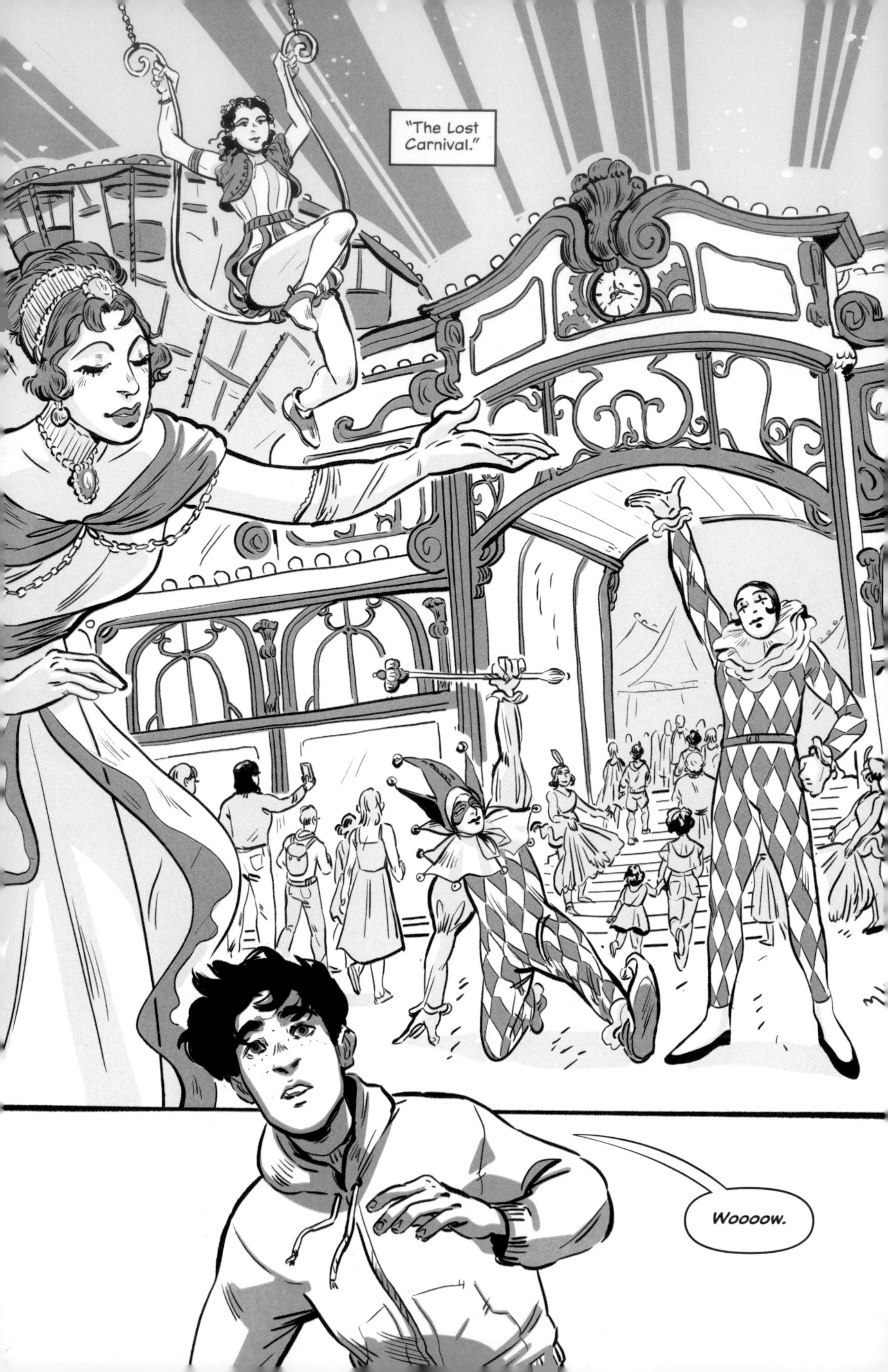
"The Lost Carnival."
Woooow.

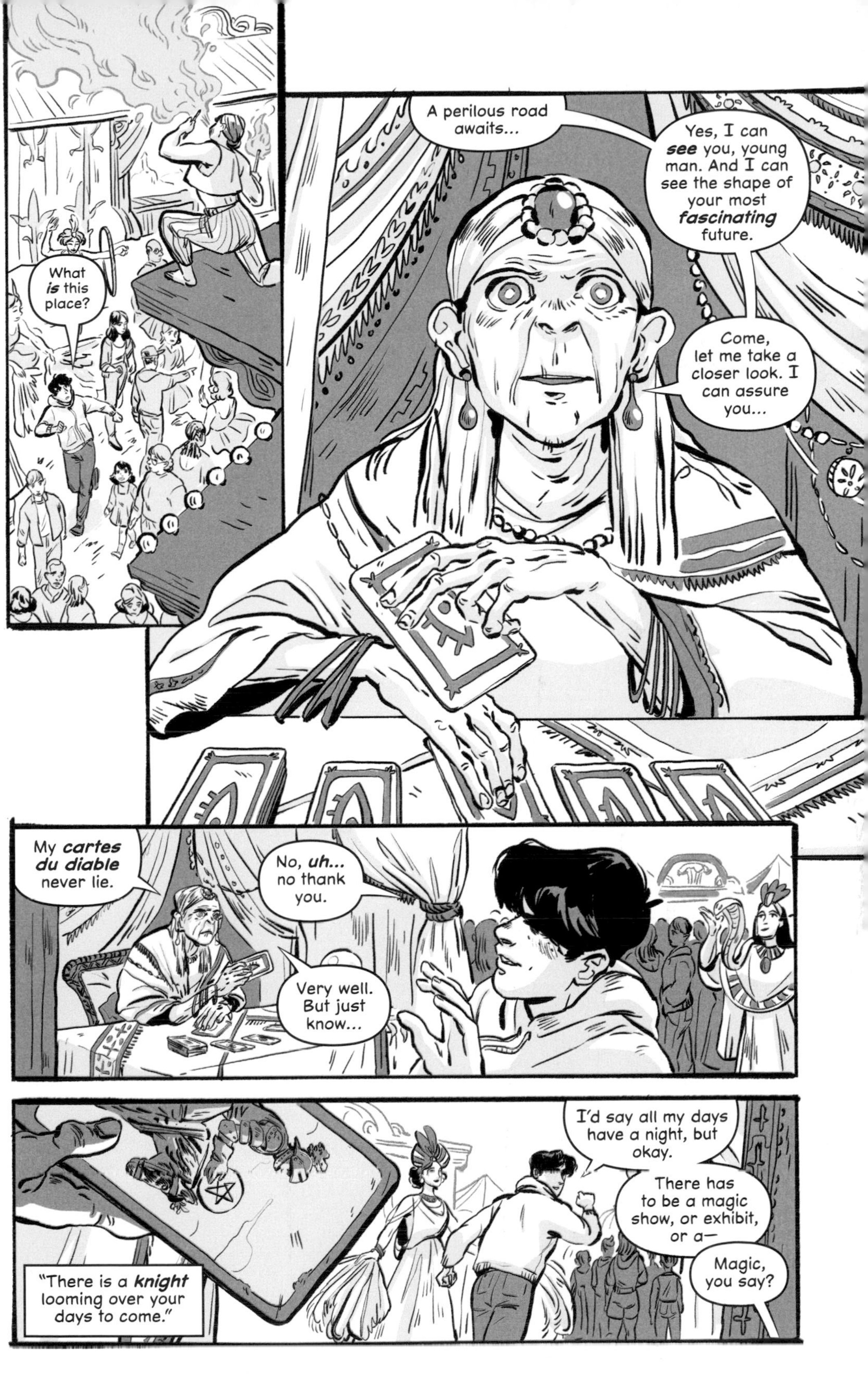
What *is* this place?
A perilous road awaits...
Yes, I can ***see*** you, young man. And I can see the shape of your most ***fascinating*** future.
Come, let me take a closer look. I can assure you...
My ***cartes du diable*** never lie.
No, ***uh...*** no thank you.
Very well. But just know...
"There is a ***knight*** looming over your days to come."
I'd say all my days have a night, but okay.
There has to be a magic show, or exhibit, or a—
Magic, you say?

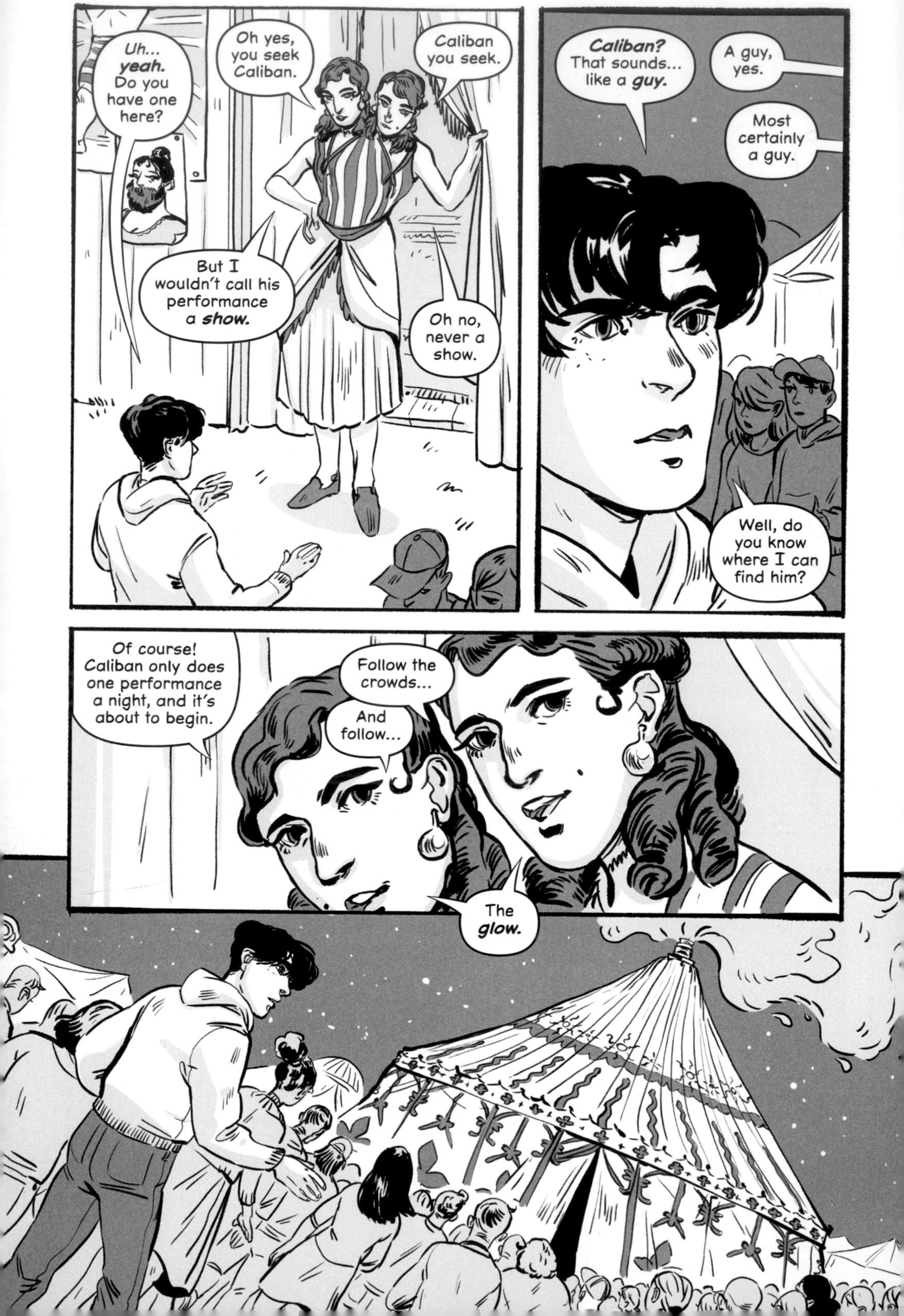
Uh... **yeah.** Do you have one here?
Oh yes, you seek Caliban.
Caliban you seek.
But I wouldn't call his performance a **show.**
Oh no, never a show.
Caliban? That sounds... like a **guy.**
A guy, yes.
Most certainly a guy.
Well, do you know where I can find him?
Of course! Caliban only does one performance a night, and it's about to begin.
Follow the crowds...
And follow...
The **glow.**

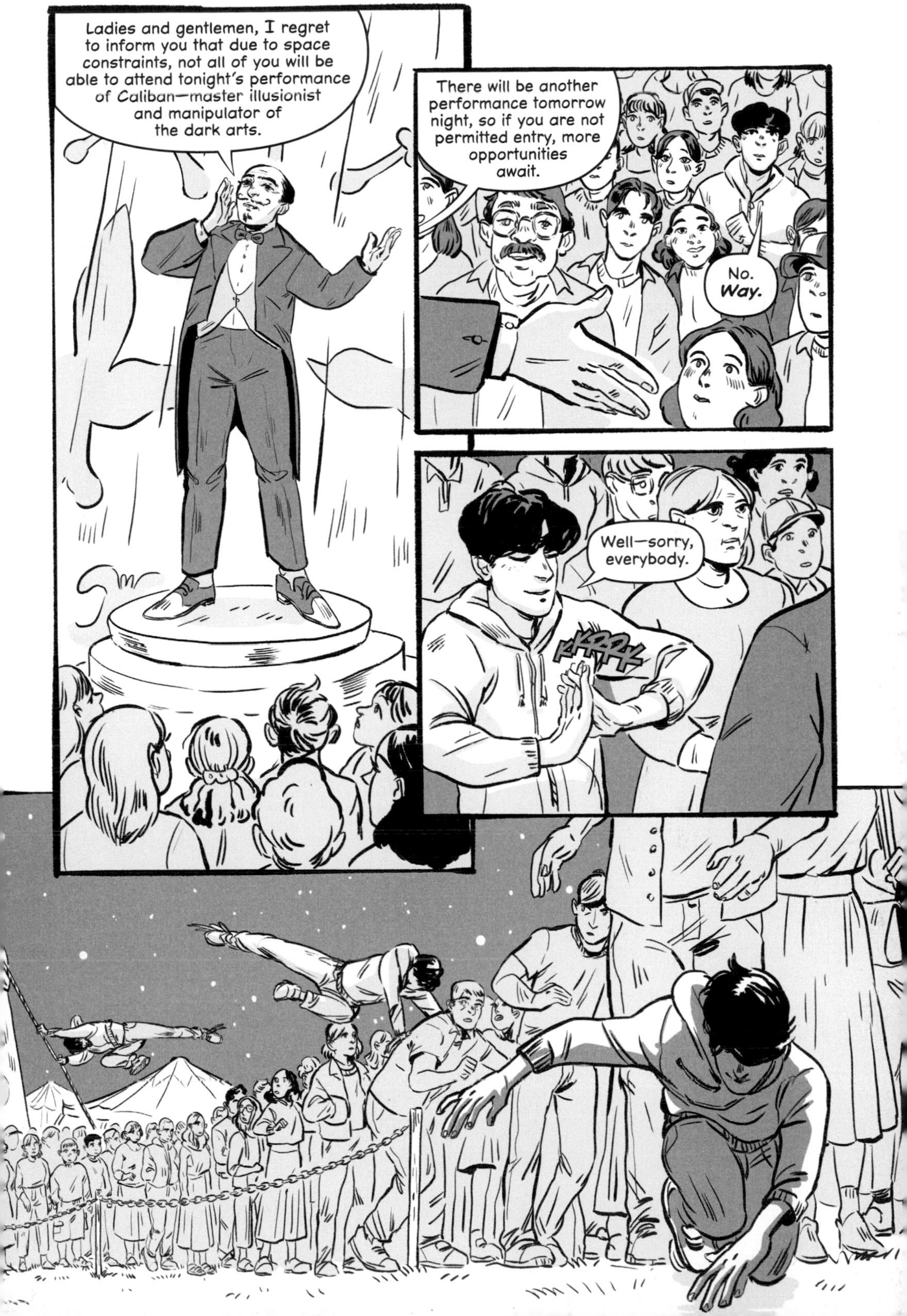
Ladies and gentlemen, I regret to inform you that due to space constraints, not all of you will be able to attend tonight's performance of Caliban—master illusionist and manipulator of the dark arts.
There will be another performance tomorrow night, so if you are not permitted entry, more opportunities await.
No. *Way.*
Well—sorry, everybody.
KRRK

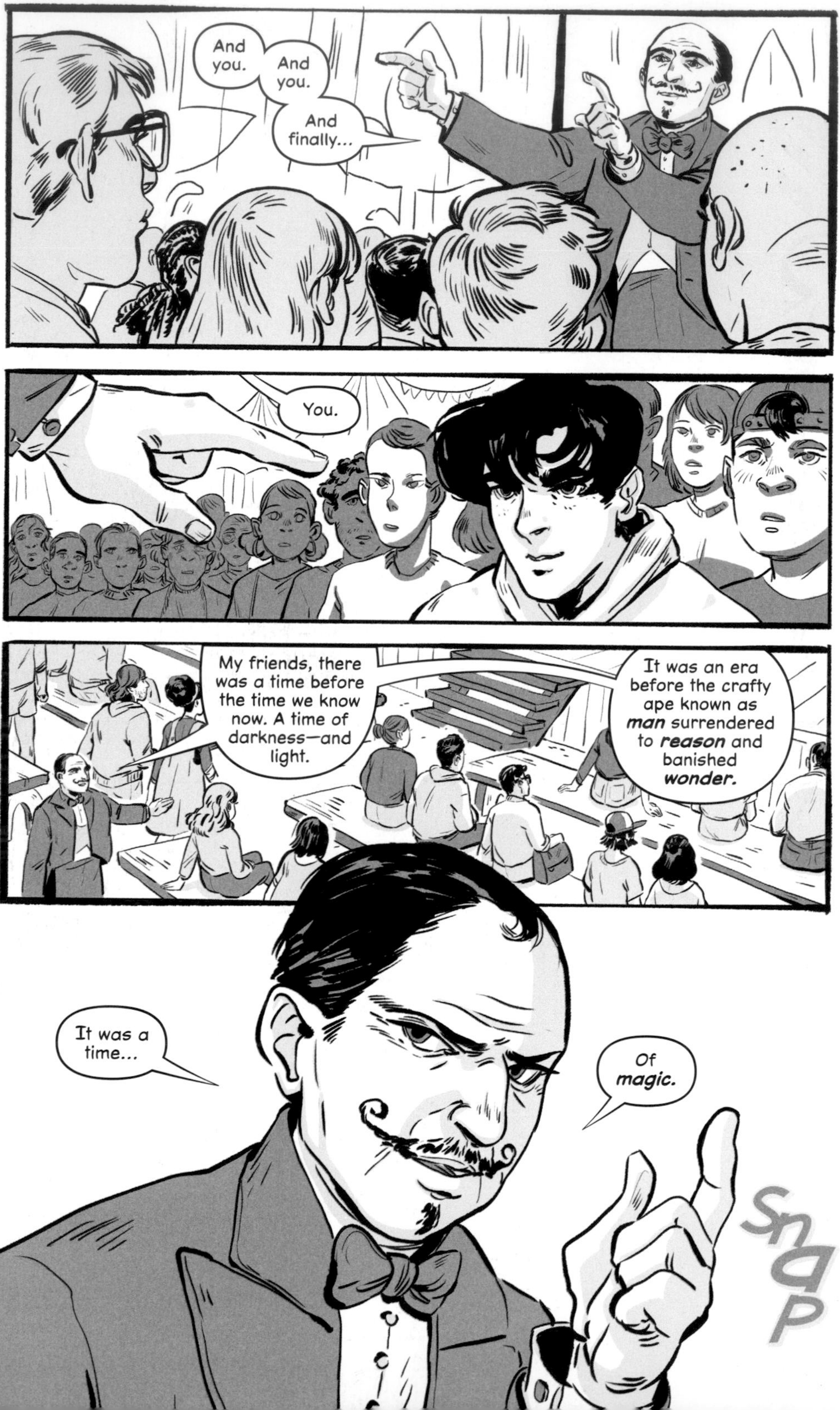
And you.
And you.
And finally...
You.
My friends, there was a time before the time we know now. A time of darkness—and light.
It was an era before the crafty ape known as *man* surrendered to *reason* and banished *wonder.*
It was a time...
Of *magic.*
Snap

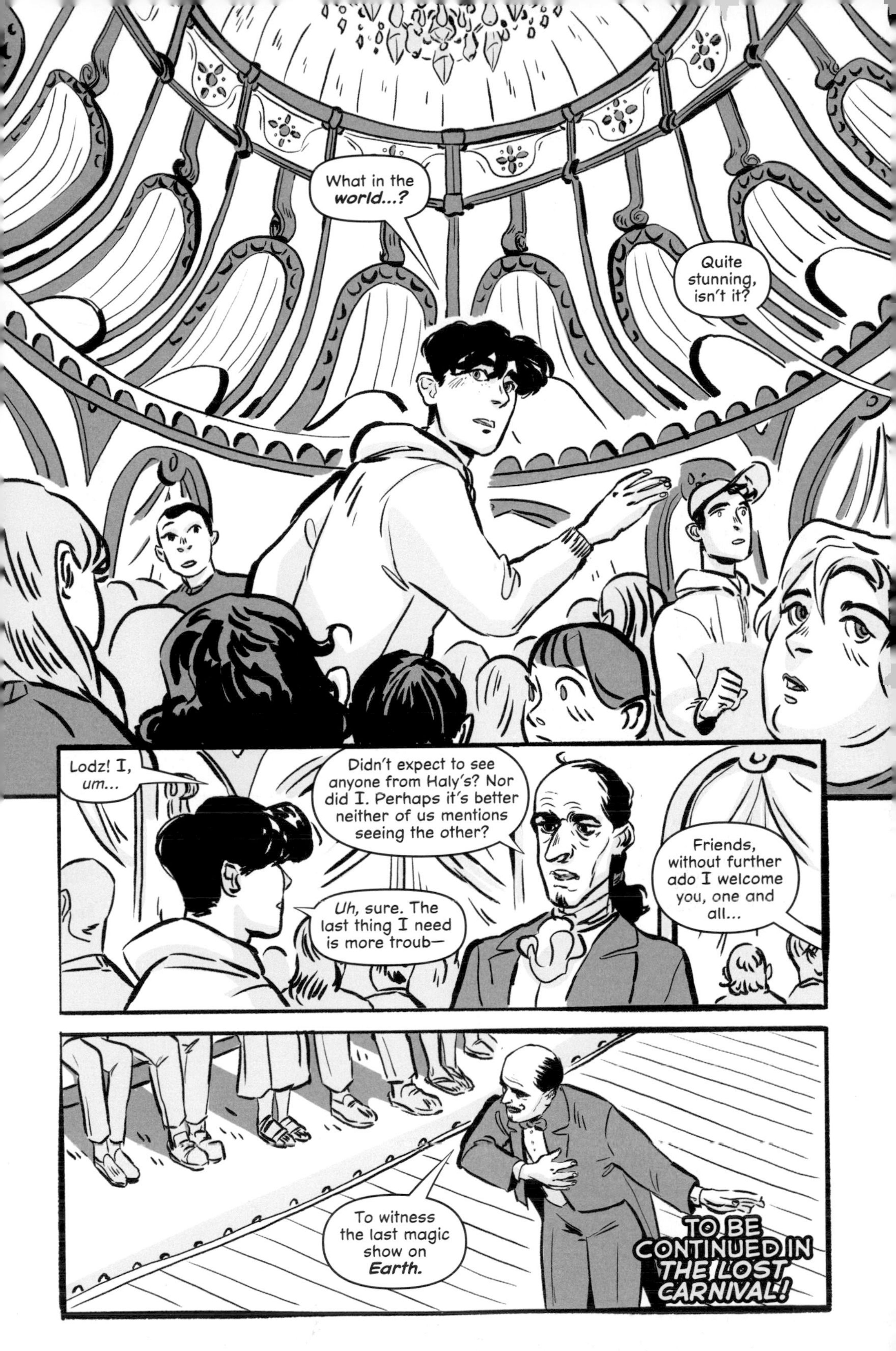
What in the *world...?*
Quite stunning, isn't it?
Lodz! I, um...
Didn't expect to see anyone from Haly's? Nor did I. Perhaps it's better neither of us mentions seeing the other?
Uh, sure. The last thing I need is more troub—
Friends, without further ado I welcome you, one and all...
To witness the last magic show on *Earth.*
TO BE CONTINUED IN *THE LOST CARNIVAL!*

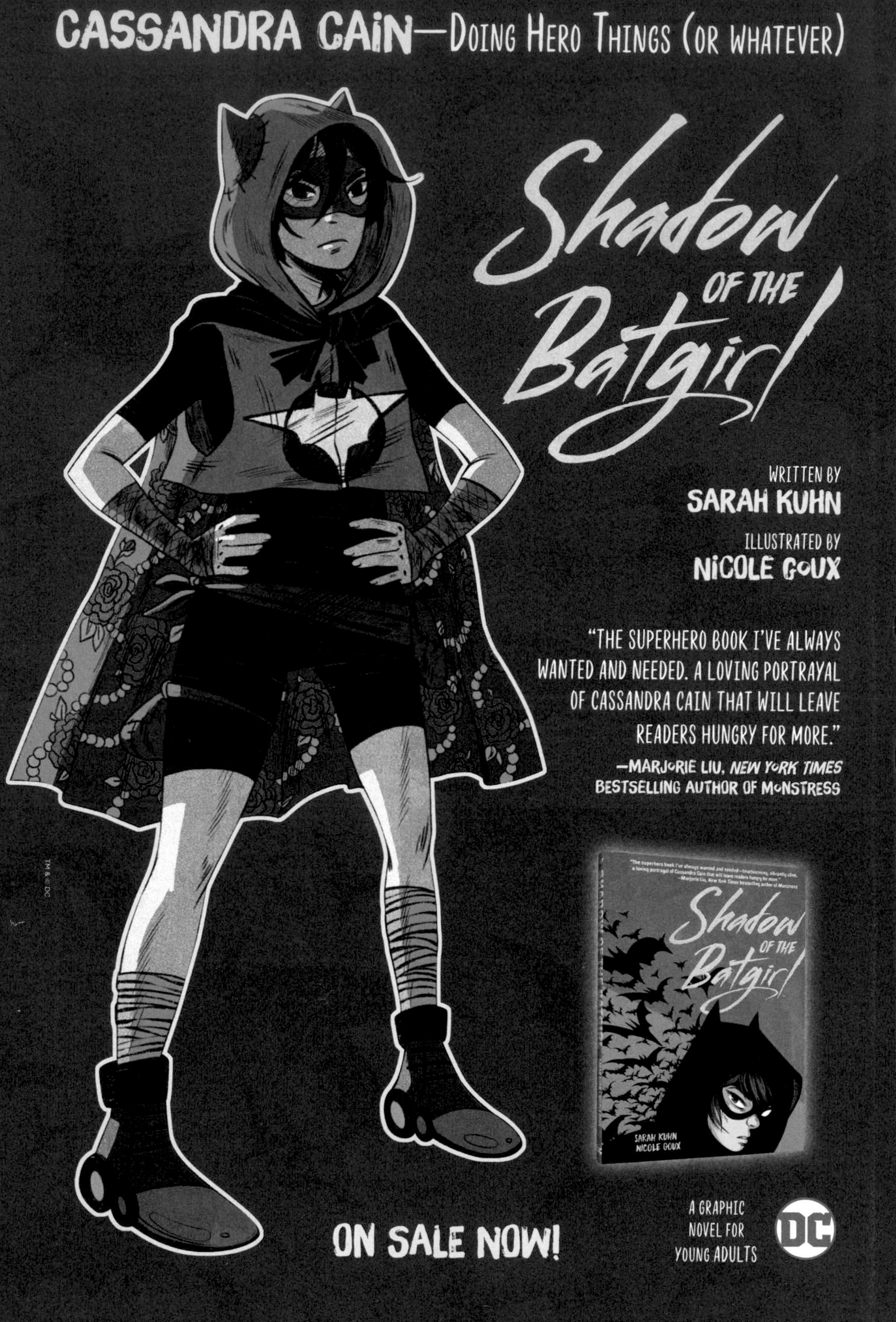

CASSANDRA CAIN—DOING HERO THINGS (OR WHATEVER)
Shadow OF THE Batgirl
WRITTEN BY
SARAH KUHN
ILLUSTRATED BY
NICOLE GOUX
"THE SUPERHERO BOOK I'VE ALWAYS WANTED AND NEEDED. A LOVING PORTRAYAL OF CASSANDRA CAIN THAT WILL LEAVE READERS HUNGRY FOR MORE."
—MARJORIE LIU, NEW YORK TIMES BESTSELLING AUTHOR OF MONSTRESS
Shadow OF THE Batgirl
SARAH KUHN
NICOLE GOUX
ON SALE NOW!
A GRAPHIC NOVEL FOR YOUNG ADULTS
TM & © DC